The Winter Dance Party Murders

a novel

by Greg Herriges

Wordcraft of Oregon

The Winter Dance Party Murders

a novel

by Greg Herriges

The author gratefully acknowledges the contributions of the following individuals:

Thomas E. Kennedy, for encouragement and guidance.

Mark Breyer, for beer and Skooshny rock 'n' roll.

Randy Franklyn, for motion picture representation.

Rick Vittenson, for Yiddish and laughs.

John Patton, for extraordinary computer wizardry.

And most of all, David Memmott, for believing in me.

#18 in Wordcraft Speculative Writers Series
Cover Designed by Brian C. Clark

Wordcraft of Oregon
P.O. Box 3235
La Grande, OR 97850
wordcraft@oregontrail.net

ISBN: 1-877655-26-0
First Edition: 1998

Printed in the USA by Complete Reproduction Service, Santa Ana, California

For my son, Jeremy

"Do you believe in rock 'n' roll?
Can music save your mortal soul?
And can you teach me how to dance real slow?"

— From "American Pie,"
Don McLean

1   'Bop-Sha-Bop'

You should see what the critics are already writing about this book. "Shocking," says one reviewer. "Feculent, raunchy," says another. *"The Winter Dance Party Murders* is without a doubt the most far-fetched and embarrassingly crude display of immature scatology..." – wait. Skip that one. To hell with that bastard. What does he know about rock and roll history, anyway? *I* was in the delivery room when rock was born. I was like its midwife, the guy who pulled out its placenta. I knew the big acts, the giants – guys like Buddy Holly, Ritchie Valens, Eddie Cochran, Gene Vincent. I'm talking big, BIG stars – Bobby Darin, Sam Cooke, Brian Jones, John Lennon – and I know what happened to them. I mean what *really* happened to them.

What – you believed that crap about overdoses and airplane crashes? Give me a reality burger. What are the chances – infinity to one? I'm willing to bet you don't personally know *anyone* who ever died like that. No, you don't. No, you don't. QUIT LYING! Do you see 727s falling out of the sky every ten minutes, or overdose victims piling up on the sidewalk? If you answered "Yes," then it's time for your Thorazine.

And so you say, "Who would make up lies about how those stars died?" Jesus, what a stupid question. You ought to *think* before you ask something like that. It was *them.*

And so you ask, "Them *who?"*

What's the matter with you – don't you ever shut up? I'm going to *tell* you who. But first we're going back, way *back,* to 1958. I'd just graduated from Abraham Lincoln High School in Brooklyn. My mother, she wanted me to be a butcher like my Uncle Myshkin. Give me a king-size break. I could just see me making sausage all day while Uncle Myshkin swore at me in German and Yiddish. No thanks. You'd walk into his butcher shop and see chickens all plucked with their heads still on, hanging upside-down in the window like executed guys. Old lady Schulstein would walk in, making the little bell on the door ring, and she'd say, "The Chee-ken – iz fresh?" And Uncle Myshkin's face would get all red, his whole bald head and everything, with these crooked blue veins that looked like they wanted to pop right out of his skin, and he'd say, "Iz fresh? Ya! Iz fresh-*est*!" And then he'd bang his hand down on the stainless steel counter so hard he'd almost break the glass display window. Mrs. Schulstein would poke the chicken two, three times, and look under its wings. "Vich vun? Vich iz de fresh-est?" And Uncle Myshkin would run from behind the counter, grab each dead plucked chicken one at a time, slap its naked bumpy skin with the palm of his hand, and say, "All! Ev-ree fuggin' vun iz de fresh-est goddamn chee-ken you ev-ah zeen!" They'd scream and yell at each other like that for fifteen minutes. It happened every time. Mrs. Schulstein would end up buying the first chicken she looked at, folded in white paper so she could carry it home under her arm. The minute the door slammed and that little bell jingled again, Uncle Myshkin would push a button on the cash register, toss in the buck and a half, and say under his breath, "She should choke on de goddamn ting."

His customers treated him like an idiot, but he was a prince, Uncle Myshkin. All that for a dollar fifty. You think I could've watched that happen every day for the rest of my life, up to my elbows in *schmaltz*? Give me a reality sandwich. Pumpernickel. Mayo. Hellman's, not Miracle Whip.

So my mother, she wanted to know what Mr. Big Shot thought he was going to do with his future. (That's me. I was Mr. Big Shot.) And I told her, "Ma, I'm gonna be a star."

And she told me, "Rudolph, vot kinda stah you gonna be vit a name like Rudolph Kearns and a *punim* like yours?"

She might just as well have said, "Look, kid. You've got a funny name and you're ugly." Okay – so I was five-five and my ears stuck out. So sue me. You take care of one thing at a time. First – I grew my hair a little longer on the sides so it covered the tops of my ears. A touch of Alberto VO-5, and *boom*. Instant pompadour. I wanted to be a rebel, a rocker, just like Buddy Holly. Buddy was cool, a rock-and-roll *mavin*. I liked a lot of other performers – the Everlys, Chuck Berry – but Buddy was the top of the heap. He had heart, and his songs were the best in the business. *Oy*. Ma would've had one of those apocalypse fits she always said she'd have if she would've known I wanted to go into rock and roll. You know what she would've said? She would've said, "That's vy your faddah sold insurance and bought you expensive violin lessons? Zo you could be shakin' yer heeps and singin' like a *goyim* greaseball?"

Hey – it was 1958. There was no political correctness. Ma's formal education about America had come from her first and only vacation – to Ellis Island, twenty-four years earlier, where the immigration officials took the little money she had and then robbed her of her name. She used to watch me run home from my music lesson, my violin tucked under my arm like one of Mrs. Schulstein's chickens, because I was being chased by the Fordham Baldies. They'd yell, "Hey, Jew-boy," and you'd yell back, "Hey *this*, guinea *schmuck*." Nobody knew about prejudice. We were too busy insulting each other equally.

That summer I'd leave home every morning at eight o'clock, wearing a white shirt and a tie, carrying my violin case. Ma thought I was auditioning for orchestras. But what I was really doing was stopping by Jimmy Salvo's apartment, where I'd change into a pair of jeans and a t-shirt, grab the guitar I was buying on time from Jimmy's father, and then I'd take the D-Train into Manhattan. Jesus, those were exciting times. All the businessmen in their suits, and the ladies in their dresses walked like zombies past you on the street, and there you were, struttin' your stuff like an important guy, holding on to that guitar case like it was made out of gold or something. You could smell the garbage being picked up at the restaurants as you walked past them, and you saw guys hosing down the sidewalk on Seventh Avenue near Forty-fourth Street, and the sun popping up over the East River, where you just knew Gretta Garbo was living in secret in one of those tall apartment buildings, probably reading a paper and thinking, "Okay, so I'm alone. Now what?"

Yeah, boy. But I digress.

The Brill Building – that was my destination. Tin-Pan-Alley. I was a songwriter – in my imagination, I guess. But every great star was a nobody at first. All they had was an imaginary picture in their heads of the way they wanted to be in the future. The hard part was getting other people to see that imaginary picture, too. So me and my imaginary picture made the same walk all the other great songwriters had made. I'd stop by every music publishing office in the whole building, wait in line, and listen to some *shnorrer* in the next room audition on the piano. Then the door would open and the line would go down by one, and my hands would sweat and my heart would pound, and I'd take out that lyric sheet from the pocket of my jeans and unfold it, thinking, *This could be it. This could be my big break.*

Finally the door would open for me. Some guy with a cigar would blow out a cloud of stinking smoke and say, "What've ya got, kid?"

And I'd say, "Would you like to hear it on the piano, or the guitar?"

And he'd say, "Play it on the skin flute, for all I care, but let's *hear* it."

The song I was trying to sell was my best effort to date – I called it, "Radda-Radda-Ready." It jumped. It had that rock and roll rhythm. Now, on this one day that comes to mind, I sat down at the piano and handed the guy the lyric sheet, and before I got two bars into the damn song, he stopped me and said, "We don't do novelty songs here."

My hands were slippery from sweat. I could feel them on the piano keys, just dripping. "Look," I said, "this isn't a novelty song. It's called rock and roll."

"It's called 'Radda-Radda-Ready.' What the fuck is that? That's got meaning? That's got sentiment?"

I said, "Yeah. If you'd let me finish the thing. It's got tons of meaning and sentiment."

"Next!" he said, shoving the lyric sheet back at me.

I felt about two inches tall as I slumped out of that office. I was so down I couldn't stand to face anyone in the elevator, so I took the stairs. Fifteen flights – all the way with the hollow sound of my shoes clicking on the steps. Nice shoes, though. I bought them at Thom McAn. Black high-heeled boots.

Now let's get some historical perspective on this. Just because a song is called "Radda-Radda-Ready," that makes it a novelty? That means it won't sell? Can I just remind someone about "Da Doo Ron Ron"? Does anyone remember "Oobie Doobie" by Roy Orbison? Or how about "Ting-A-Ling" by Buddy Holly – ring any bells? That publisher guy turned down a fortune just waiting to happen. And to set the record straight – read the lyrics for yourself:

> *Radda-radda-ready,*
> *Gonna pick up Betty.*
> *Take her for a ride,*

So she'll be my steady.
Radda-radda-dum,
Radda-radda-dee,
Radda-radda-Betty,
Is the girl for me.

Can you miss the meaning of *that?* Are you going to tell me there's no sentiment in those lyrics? Please. Open me a window and let some reality blow in.

It was one of those hot New York days where you could see the air. That's how thick and heavy it was – you could see the goddamn air. I bought a pretzel from a vendor and leaned up against a shop window, my guitar case on the ground next to me, and wondered if I should give up. Success seemed out of reach. The pretzel sat in my stomach like a bowling ball – and that's when it came to me. Inspiration.

I took my guitar out of its case and played heavy on the bass strings, the way you would on the low keys of a piano. Yeah, it had that rock and roll feel. I liked it. It hit me like a brick thrown at a subway train – Rudolph Kearns was dead. From then on I'd call myself Rudy Keen. And the lyrics jumped out the first time I played it, right there on the corner next to the vendor, in that white, laundry-smelling New York air –

Bop-sha-bop,
Wop, wop, wop.
You make me wanna pop.
Please don't stop.
Bop-sha-bop.

When I finished, a few people applauded and threw some change in my guitar case. I had a hit. I just knew I did. Move over, Little Richard. Slide down the glide, Fleetwoods. Rudy Keen is here.

I went back into the Brill Building with the salty taste of pretzel in my mouth and a new confidence, an attitude. I took the elevator to the seventh floor – K.0. Publishing. The place was crawling with hopefuls waiting for the bosses to get back from lunch. The secretary looked like she was losing her mind. The phone kept ringing and this one blond curl fell down over her eyes while she wrote messages and slammed the receiver back in its cradle. She sort of glanced up at me as if she was going to cry.

"They're not back from lunch yet," she told me.

"That's okay," I said. "Tell them Rudy Keen wants to see them. I've got their next hit."

You could tell what she was thinking – *Sure, you and every other nobody in the office.* But she wrote down my name. I took a chair and started pounding out drum riffs on my case. Music history was about to be made.

"Rudolph? Rudolph Kearns?"

My head spun so fast I felt my brain hit the inside of my skull. Gave myself a brain-sprain. Ouch. It was Davey Corelli, a kid I knew from the neighborhood. He'd gotten lucky and become a go-fer for Alan Freed, the disc jockey. He wasn't exactly my best friend, but it paid off staying on good terms with people in the business.

"I'm Rudy Keen, now," I said.

"Good name," he said. "What're you doin' here?"

"Got a new song."

"Yeah? You performing, or writing?"

"Both," I said.

"I thought you played the violin."

Jesus. I wished he'd shut up. He was ruining my new image. I stuck my leg out in front of me so he could check out my high-heeled boots, and said, "I was classically trained. I'm versatile."

"Yeah? That's great. Hey – I'd like you to meet a friend of mine," he said, turning to this guy with acne and greasy hair. "Charles Westover, this is Rudolph – "

"Rudy," I said, standing up.

"Oh, yeah. Rudy Keen. Rudy, this is Charles – "

I shook his hand. "Yeah, yeah, yeah. Nice to meet'cha."

They were ruining my concentration. I still needed to come up with a bridge for my new song, but they wouldn't leave me alone. That Charles guy sort of leaned over and rapped a few times on my guitar case, and in a real flat Midwestern accent said, "Can you play that thing?"

What a goof. I gave him a hard-assed look and said, "No. I just carry it around for exercise."

I was hoping the publishers would get back from lunch, because with these two guys yapping at me, I was starting to forget how the song went.

12

"The reason I ask is," Charles said, "I've got recording time booked next week and I'm short a session man."

Big shot. "I'd really like to, Charles, but I'm very busy. Tell you what, though. Maybe you could be a session man for *me* sometime – if you can play *that* thing." I rapped on *his* guitar case then. Gave it right back to him.

"Oh. he can play, Rudolph," Davey said.

"*Rudy*," I corrected him.

"Right. Rudy. Listen, Charles is gonna be the next Elvis."

I couldn't help it. I broke out laughing. "Sure. Sure he is. Elvis Charles," I said.

Davey looked at me kind of blank-like, like he didn't get it. "Really, Rudy. I mean it. We've got a new name for him."

"Maybe you could call him *Chelvis*," I said.

"No. We're goin' with Del Shannon."

I said, "Very original. Dell Vikings, Del-Satins. How about Del Pickle?"

Oy! All right, all right! I was *stupid*. How was I to know the guy would be a star someday? When I met him he was just some jamoke with more potholes in his face than ten blocks of West Side Highway. They got irritated with me and walked away after I made that crack about his name. What kind of rock and roll *putz* was I?

Then two guys walked into the office – one in a short sleeve shirt, and the other in a suit. They cut right through the crowd of sideburns and slammed the office door. In a little while the receptionist started calling out names, and someone would go in, and in a few minutes come right back out looking like he'd just had his heart speared.

"Simon – "

This short guy went in and walked out even shorter.

"Valli – "

In-And-Out Burger, man.

"Keen – "

I looked around to see who that was, and then remembered it was me. I scrambled up and grabbed my guitar case. I stood in the doorway like a statue, wondering if I should wait for the two guys to invite me in. They didn't even notice me. One of them was on the phone, covering the mouthpiece, saying to the business-looking guy, "Did you get the BMI listings from the last quarter yet?"

The business guy was going through a bunch of papers. "Had

'em a minute ago."

"And where's the next act?"

I rapped on the open door. They both looked up at me and I just looked at them. I was getting a case of stage fright. Make that stage terror.

"What – " the guy on the phone said, "you're gonna perform in the goddamn doorway? Get in here."

I closed the door behind me.

"What do you have, son?" the business guy said.

I opened my guitar case and put the strap around my shoulders. "It's a song," I said.

The guy on the phone said to whoever he was talking to, "It'll be about two grand, but I can't pay you till they pay us. All right. All right. Keep it hanging," and he hung up. He looked at me like he'd forgot already who I was. "Are you Keen?"

"I sure am."

"Got a lead sheet?"

"No – I just wrote it. Just a few minutes ago."

"What am I supposed to do without a lead sheet?"

"I thought I'd just play it and sing it for you."

"All right. Let's hear what you got."

I'd only played the song once before. I was pretty nervous. I went into the bass string riff, you know, chucka-chucka-boom. Then the phone rang.

"Hello? Yeah. I got it right here. No problem. I'll send it right over. He's gonna get two plays a day, right?"

I stopped playing and let my arms hang down at my sides. I had no circulation in my hands. The business guy scratched his head with the eraser of his pencil.

"Right. Okay – see ya." The short-sleeved guy looked back at me. "Well? I thought you were gonna play the song?"

So I started picking the bass strings again and got as far as, "Bop-sha-bop, wop-wop-wop – " when the phone rang again.

"Hello? Oh, hi baby. What? What're you talkin' about? That's not true. I don't care who you heard it from. No. I wasn't with any brunette. I was in the studio with a new act. I've been trying to break this act for a month now. Yes, I *did* tell you about him. His name?" He covered the mouthpiece. "What's your name, kid?"

"Rudy Keen."

"No, really."

"That's it," I said. "Rudy Keen."

He shook his head and took his hand away. "Rudy Keen. No, I'm not kidding. He's gonna be the next Elvis. I don't care – it's the truth. Look, you want to hear it from him? Come on. Don't do that. Listen, angel ..." He held the phone about six inches from his ear, and then slowly hung it up. He just sat still for a minute, and then turned toward me.

"Kid – I like what you got there. How would you like to do a demo session?"

"But you haven't even *heard* it," I said.

"Hey – you hear five seconds of 'Hound Dog,' what else do you need? Wanna do a session?"

The business guy was rubbing his forehead and looking straight down at his desk.

"Who – *me*? Sure!"

"All right. I've got time booked at Allegro next Monday. Be there at about two. And – oh, say. I've got this little problem I was hoping you could help me with."

The little problem was his girlfriend. He jotted down an address of a Schrafft's on a piece of paper and told me to ask for Brenda. She was a waitress. He started to explain what I had to do, but I interrupted him. "I know, I know," I said. "We were together last night in the studio. You've been trying to break my act for a month."

He sort of sized me up. "Don't do it if you don't think you can pull it off."

"I can pull it off."

"And I want you to know something. I really *was* in the studio. It's just that Brenda, she's a little jealous, you know?"

I packed up my guitar and the phone rang again and no one even said good-bye to me. The receptionist yelled out, "Del Shannon – you're next."

And that's how I met Sal DeGrazzia and his partner, Sherman Katz. I didn't have a clue as to how important those two guys were going to be in my life from then on.

♪　♫　♪

I only had enough money to take the D-Train back to Brooklyn, so I had to walk ten lousy blocks to the Schrafft's. There were two waitresses flying around behind the counter like guided missiles, but I knew which one of them was Brenda in a second. She was young – maybe a couple years older than me. She wore a checkered blouse and an apron and she had two of the saddest, sweetest eyes I'd ever seen. I put my guitar case down on the floor next to my stool and ordered a Coke. It looked like I'd be hitching back home. That was my last twenty-five cents.

Brenda was wiping the counter in front of me while I sort of stirred the ice cubes around in my glass with my straw. "I think I know your boyfriend," I said.

She stopped and looked up at me with those goddamn Bambi eyes.

"You know Sal?"

I didn't even know his name till she said it.

"Yeah. As a matter of fact, I was with him last night. We could hardly get any work done. All he did was talk about you."

She narrowed her eyes and twisted her mouth a little – pretty little mouth. "Did he *send* you over here just now?"

That rat didn't deserve her, I'll tell you that much.

"Heck, no. He mentioned you worked here during the session last night. I picked you out in a second from the way he described you."

"Are you Rudy Keen?"

I forgot that he'd told her my name, and I got excited all of a sudden. "Why, yes. Yes, I am. Have you heard of me?"

She threw the dishrag in an aluminum sink and said, "The big lug just mentioned you – for the first time."

"Oh. Well, he's a pretty busy guy, Sal is. I wouldn't hold it against him. He's going to be a heavy hitter someday."

"You really *like* him?"

"Who – Sal? Oh, yeah. What's not to like?"

She shrugged and looked away. "It's just that the way he treats most of his acts – never mind." She bit her thumbnail a few times and then said to herself, "Geez, I guess I owe him an apology."

I sipped my Coke and felt sorry for her. She had on those flat white gym shoes waitresses wear, and looked like she'd been running back and forth all day.

"I wouldn't worry about it, if I were you. He's a pretty understanding guy and everything. You two are very lucky."

Her eyes targeted me. "You think so?"

16

"Hey," I said. "How many people are crazy about each other the way you two are? You can't buy that. It's better than gold."

"It's just that all Sal ever seems to think about is the business and money. Sometimes a girl can't help feeling – " She stopped talking and looked far off, like she was daydreaming or something. Her fingers started playing with this little charm that hung from a chain around her neck. You know how girls do that when they're deep in thought. It was a Cupid, the charm – a little silver Cupid. Sal probably bought it for her, the cheap bastard. "I don't mean to bore you with my problems," she said, like she'd just remembered I was there.

"You're not boring me," I said. She wasn't, either. I could've sat there all day listening to her.

She smiled and said, "You're really very sweet, Rudy. I sure hope your career takes off." She put her hand on top of mine, just for a second. It was soft and warm. Christ, she was a looker. I can still see her in my mind standing there at Schrafft's counter. "That's on the house, by the way." She meant my Coke.

I was about to say thanks, but she got called away by a customer. Some fat guy with his ass sticking out of the back of his pants wanted coffee and ruined the whole moment. It's a good thing he did, too, because I almost asked Brenda out. Wouldn't that have been a smart move – asking out my publisher's girlfriend? And on the same day I snubbed Del Shannon. Ever since then I've tried to keep my idiotic career-ruining mistakes down to one a day. And believe me, sometimes it isn't easy.

I sat around for a while, watching her stack plates and fill orders till I finished my Coke and the straw started making sucking noises on the bottom of the glass. Then I picked up my guitar and walked away kind of slow, turning around once in a while in case Brenda said so long, but she didn't. She was too busy. When I got to the door, all I could see of her was her hair – it was kind of blond, kind of brown. What do you call that – dishwater blond? I think that's what you call it. But her hair was a lot prettier than the way that makes it sound. *Dishwater blond* makes it sound like some girl just stuck her head in a dirty sink. It's a stupid expression.

But I digress.

I should've been happy, sitting on the subway, heading back to Brooklyn. I had a publisher and a recording session booked. But *happy* was about the last thing I felt. I'd just lied to one of the

17

prettiest, nicest girls I'd ever met, for some guy I didn't even know. I was damned sorry I'd done it. Now Brenda would go on believing that Sal was a swell guy, till she found out the truth the hard way. What I could have done, I could've told her, "Your boyfriend's a stinking rat. Stay away from him." But I was in too much of a goddamn hurry to be famous, a sensation. I blame it all on rock and roll. I really do.

The subway car shook, rattled and rolled down the tunnel. It was a long ride home.

2 'Radda-Radda-Ready'

"So – have you got a job yet, Mister I-Vanna-Be-A-Star? Is your name in lights yet, huh? Cuz I dunt vant you should do something foolish, like maybe get a college edju-*ca*-tion."

Every time I was home that's all I heard. I never should've told Ma about my dream, because she was going to club me over the head with it for the rest of my life. It was almost a whole week until the recording session, and it was taking forever for that week to go by. Just to get her off my back, I told her I had an audition with Paul Whiteman's Orchestra.

She said, "Go on."

And I said, "No, really."

And she said, "Go on," again.

And I said, "No, really."

Then she called up every *yenta* friend she had and told them that her Rudolph had an audition with Paul Whiteman's Orchestra. The whole neighborhood was waiting for me to show up on television playing "Stardust" on my violin. I'd go down to the pharmacy and Mr. Rosenstern would say, "Rudolph, *mazeltov*! I heard the good news about the Whiteman deal." I'd stop by Leo's dry cleaners, and Leo and his wife would come out from the back and ask when I was going to have my tuxedo cleaned "... for the big T and V performance."

What tuxedo? I didn't *own* a goddamn tuxedo.

I knew then already what I'd have to do. I'd have to move.

♪　♫　♪

"'Early In The Morning,' take five."

Allegro Sound Studios – 4:00 p.m.. I'd been waiting for three hours for my session, but Sal hadn't said a word to me. He was working with this guy named Walden Cassotto, trying to get a good take of a song he'd brought in. It was an okay song – a little too country for my tastes, but all right. Cassotto himself was a nice guy. Twice he asked me what I thought of the recording, and I gave him the thumbs-up, and he smiled and nodded.

But then after a good take, when I thought it was finally my turn, Sal got into it with Cassotto about what name the song would be released under.

"You *can't* call yourself Walden Cassotto, for Christ's sake!"

"Why not?" Cassotto wanted to know.

"Why not? Why *not*? Because *Walden Fuckin' Cassotto* sounds like a woods in *Sicily*. You might as well call yourself *Sherwood Fungulo*."

I didn't say anything at the time, because they were really pissed at each other, but I thought Sherwood Fungulo had possibilities.

Cassotto said, "There's nothing wrong with my name. It's my *name*, Sal."

"So what, it's your name? You think Dean Martin woulda become a star if he'd called himself Martin Crocetti? Huh? It sounds stupid! That's why you can't call yourself Walden Cassotto! People will get you confused with a kind of salami. Jesus, use your head. We need something like Tony ... Tony something. Tony, uh – "

"Spumone," Cassotto said. "Call me Tony Spumone. Very good, Sal. That doesn't sound stupid at all."

Sal was walking back and forth in alligator shoes, pounding his fist in his hand. I noticed his nails were polished. I'd never seen that on a man before, a manicure. I looked at my own nails, all bitten down and crummy looking. I put my hands in my pockets.

"Look," Sal said. "I got the president of Atlantic Records waiting for a call to find out what we're going to call you. You'd better come up with something fast, or you might just end up being the Rinky-Dinks, or any other goddamn name I decide to give you."

Cassotto threw his music arrangement on the floor. "Fine! That's who I am. I'm the goddamn Rinky-Dinks. Are you happy now?"

He stormed out of the studio. Sal turned to his assistant, the blond receptionist I remembered from the publishing office. "Lisa, call Atlantic. Tell them 'Early In The Morning' should be released under the name The Rinky-Dinks. I'll fix his goddamn wagon."

"Bobby," I said.

Sal turned around and looked at me. "What?"

"Call him Bobby."

He snorted, "Just what the music business needs – another Bobby." Then he took out a cigar, unwrapped it, and said, "Bobby *what*?"

"I don't know. Baron. No – *Darin*. That sounds good. Bobby Darin."

He just kept staring at me with this confused look on his face. "Say, that's not bad. I know you, don't I? What are you doing here?"

When he said that my stomach took an elevator to the ground floor. He didn't even remember me.

"You told me I had a recording session today."

"*I* told you that?"

"Yeah."

He rubbed his chin a few times and looked at the floor. "Look – we're through for the day. Stop by the office sometime and ..."

"You said to meet you here *today*, that we were going to put my song on tape. You said so."

"Look, kid. I don't even know who you are."

"I'm Rudy Keen."

He slapped his head and said, "Rudy *Keen*? Where the hell do you guys come up with names like that? Why don't you just call yourself Walden Cassotto?"

"I played you my song."

"When?"

"When I was in your office."

"I don't remember hearing any song."

Jesus Christ. My big break was going right down the crapper. I stood up and followed him through the control room. "Don't you remember? I only got to play the first couple of bars, and the phone kept ringing, and you said that's all you needed to hear, because you only need to hear five seconds of 'Hound Dog.'"

There was a knock on the control room door. Brenda waved at Sal through the window.

"And I did you a favor with Brenda. I told her you were with me in the studio the night someone saw you with ..."

Sal looked at Brenda and then back at me. "Oh, yeah. Rudy Keen. It's coming back to me now."

Brenda walked in and kissed Sal. She was still wearing her white waitress shoes.

"Hello, Rudy. You boys haven't finished, I hope. I wanted to hear your music."

"Things are running late, baby. I had The Rinky-Dinks in here all day, and – "

"The *who?*" Brenda said.

"The Rinky-Dinks. New group. Hotter than sliced prosciutto. I was just telling Rudy here that we're going to have to cancel his session."

Brenda kind of pouted at me and then turned to Sal. "Cancel? Why? You two have been rehearsing for this for weeks."

"Remember all those nights we rehearsed, Sal?" I said.

Man, that guy shot daggers at me with his eyes. "I know, Rudy, but – "

"Sure would be a shame not to get my song recorded today after *each one of those nights.*"

Sal tried to smile, but he couldn't do it. He didn't know whether to shit or go blind. He rubbed his hand over his hair and tapped his foot a few times and looked at his watch.

"Maybe we can put down a track, if we hurry. Lisa, tell the band not to pack up."

Can you believe that guy? After what I did for him, lying to his girlfriend – who, by the way, had no business being with a slime-ball like him – he was going to stiff me out of his promise. The son of a bitch just used me, that's all. I made up my mind right then and there that if I didn't get a decent tape out of that session, I was going to tell Brenda the truth.

I taught the musicians the song – it didn't take long. They were very good, and the song, well – it wasn't Mozart, you know? It was just a little A-progression with a lead riff ... A, D, E ...

But I'm digressing all over the place again.

The engineer miked my guitar and then went back in the booth. Sal spoke to me through the speakers.

"Which tune are you going to do, Rudy?"

"You know the one. The one we've been rehearsing all week. Every night."

Sal turned those stiletto eyes on me again. "And what are you going to call it, Rudy? It seems to me we had trouble deciding on a title."

"Bop-Sha-Bop," I said.

"I'm sorry. I didn't hear you. It sounded like you said, 'Bop-

Sha-Bop.'"

"That's because that's what I said. It's called 'Bop-Sha-Bop.'"

Sal shook his head and closed his eyes. "No it's not."

And I said, "What do you mean?"

"I mean, 'Bop-Sha-Bop' – that's a noise cows make after they eat. What the hell is that?"

Hey, you can make fun of my ears – I don't mind. Tell me I'm short. It's true; it doesn't bother me. But when someone makes fun of one of my songs, watch out. It's like Elvis and his blue suede shoes. Just lay off of them, get it? So I said, "We shouldn't have taken that one night off last week, Sal. We would've had this straightened out by now. Which night was that – Wednesday? Thursday?"

He turned off the intercom. Brenda was pointing her finger at him and shaking her head, and Sal was crossing his heart like mad.

That's when the drummer said, "This is going to be like a Mickey and Sylvia session."

And the piano player said, "What do you mean?"

"They take *forever*. Days."

"Why's that?" the piano player asked.

"They're the same person. First he comes in as Mickey, and then he has to go home and change and come back as Sylvia."

Sal was back on the intercom. "'Bop-Sha-Bop,' take one."

We tore into the song. Nice steady beat. I got as far as the first chorus when the intercom came on and Sal started yelling, "Cut! Cut!"

What the hell – I didn't know what the problem was. It sounded good to me. Sal came into the studio waving his arms all over the place.

"*Those* are the lyrics? Please tell me you're kidding. Tell me you're just using them until you write the *real* lyrics."

"What's wrong with them?" I asked.

Sal yelled at the engineer to play the song back. He stood there with his arms crossed in front of his big dumb chest while the tape played.

> *Bop-Sha-Bop,*
> *Wop, wop, wop.*
> *You make me wanna pop.*
> *Please don't stop.*
> *Bop-Sha-Bop.*

23

The drummer was snapping his fingers. I was swaying back and forth. "So what's the problem?" I said.

Sal was right in my face, turning red and yelling at me. "What's the problem? Did you say, '*What's the problem?*' I'll tell you what the fuckin' problem is. You got a nice melody and a catchy beat – but you should only write lyrics for Duane Eddy."

"But Duane Eddy only plays instrumentals."

"That's right! That's what I mean. Look, kid, Bop-Sha-Bop, that's just *stupid*. And what's this wop-wop-wop stuff? What're your trying to do – piss off every Italian who hears it? Why don'tcha just say, 'Dago, dago, dago'? And that 'make me wanna pop, please don't stop' – it's dirty, for Chrissake! You're singing about *screwing*! What you've got here is a song that says, 'Those goddamn Italians. Keep touching me like that, baby – I'm gonna make love to your sweater!'"

"I didn't say *any* of that. I wouldn't write a dirty song. They're just *words*, for crying out loud. I didn't say anything about Italians or making love to someone's sweater."

"I like that part," the drummer said. "I think you should put it in."

Sal was turning it all around on purpose. He was just angry because I'd forced him to give me the session he'd promised in the first place. I looked up into the control booth and saw Brenda. Geez, she was pretty. I felt like running up there and telling her to get away from Sal – just run as fast as she could.

"Those are the lyrics," I said. "I'm not changing one damn word. I did you a favor once. Maybe I shouldn't have. Maybe I should just go have a nice little talk with Brenda."

Sal stood there, shaking. His hands were all balled up into tight fists, and I thought for a minute his head was going to explode, just go off like a firecracker. He walked back to the booth and had the engineer rewind the tape and play it again. A few minutes later he was back in the studio.

"Something's missing," he said.

The piano player said, "It sounds hollow. You need background singers."

Sal said, "Tell Lisa to go see if The Silvertones are still in studio A. Tell 'em we got a gig for them, and we'll pay scale."

So there I was, stuck in a studio, waiting. I wondered if Danny And The Juniors had to go through this to make it to the top. It sure didn't help my performance any to have someone yell at me every two seconds.

When the Silvertones got there we ran through the song a few times without taping it, and I showed them what to do on the backgrounds. Then we laid down a track, and when we all sat down afterward to listen to it, Sal was slapping his leg in time with the snare.

"Let's try it once more," he said. "Rudy – this time just play the guitar."

"Huh?"

"Pascuale, [Pascuale was the front man for The Silvertones] you do the lead vocal."

And that's how I got squeezed off my first record. At the end of the session Sal was excited, talking on the phone to different people and making them listen to the playbacks.

"I think we've got something here," he kept saying. "Let's book studio A for Monday and get some violin tracks down."

I said, "Violins? Are you nuts? This is supposed to be rock and roll."

"Maybe some horns – " Sal said.

"No way," I said. "Not one horn."

He listened to the playbacks again. "Maybe you're right," he said. He thought for a second. "Do you hear a place for kettle drums? Maybe just one kettle drum."

I gave up then. I went to sit down in the corner, and a minute later Brenda walked over to me. "I liked the way *you* sang it, Rudy," she said.

That little cupid just hung around her neck and reminded me of the first time we'd met, and how I'd lied to her.

"Thanks," I said.

She touched my shoulder with her hand. I looked at it, and then up at her. I remember thinking, *If she were my girlfriend, I'd take her out to the symphony and dinner, and I'd save up for a little house in White Plains or someplace, and we'd have kids and a swing set in the back yard, and a white picket fence.* But she wasn't my girlfriend. She was the slime-ball's girlfriend.

Sal yelled over to me, "Keen? Can I see you for a minute?"

I thought he was going to give me hell about talking to Brenda, but I should've known better. He wasn't even thinking about Brenda.

He took a wad of bills from his pocket and peeled off a few twenties for me. "I want you to take a cab to the office. Sherm's got

25

the publishing rights papers for you to sign. Consider this an advance. I want you to write for us from now on – exclusive."

"Sixty bucks? You call that an advance?"

He gave me one of his long, slow dagger looks and peeled off two more, and stuck them in my hand.

And I said, "I don't know about this exclusive stuff. I don't much appreciate that bit about the sound cows make after eating, or making love to someone's sweater."

Two, three, four – eight more twenties. I put them in my pocket.

"I just get a little excited once in a while. It's nothing personal, kid," Sal said.

"Sure, Sal."

They were playing the song over and over, and everybody was hyped, and there I was, the guy who wrote the song, leaving the studio all by myself like I wasn't even part of it all. Sal had his hand on Brenda's waist and sort of let it drop down to her ass. When he did that she reached around with her own hand and put it back on her waist. That guy had about as much class as a swine. That's what he should've called himself, *Sal Swine, the ass grabber*.

What did I know about the business? Nothing. When Sherman Katz handed the papers over to me and explained that Sal would be given credit for writing half of "Bop-Sha-Bop" because he'd fronted the session and sold the song to The Silvertones, I just signed. Back then you didn't question the guys in charge. You figured they'd given you your break, and without them you'd be nothing. The bastards. To this day, if you buy a collection of Fifties Oldies, and you look at the credits under "Bop-Sha-Bop," it says, "Keen-DeGrazzia." But from my mouth to God's ears, if He's got any, Sal didn't write a note of the song. I think the swine was tone-deaf.

But hey – I'd gotten my feet wet. I'd been published and my song was released on Daddy-O Records. It showed up on The Hot 100 List at number ninety-seven. I'll never forget that, the first time I saw it listed in the trade papers. I must've stared at those song lists for hours.

"Bop-Sha-Bop," The Silvertones – Daddy-0.

And here's the pisser ... *I couldn't even brag about it.* If my mother would've found out I'd written a rock and roll song, she

26

would've dressed in black and sat *shiva* for the rest of her life. She would've told the neighbors, "Rudolph vas never my child. Ve adopted him. From the *goyim*."

Within two weeks "Bop-Sha-Bop" moved up to number fifty and I started getting calls from agents who wanted to handle my live show. My live show consisted of sneaking out the fire escape and running to Jimmy Salvo's apartment to change into my dungarees and white t-shirt. Some show. So I started rehearsing in the basement of our building. I put together a pretty good set. I threw in a few steps while I sang, nothing flashy, because I danced about as well as a neurological patient.

Sal called me at home, something I told him never to do, on account of my mother. He wanted a new song for some group that was named after a bird. Listen – we might as well be talking about a hundred years ago; I can't remember if it was the Flamingos or the Albatrosses. So while my mother was eavesdropping, I told Sal, "Yes, Mr. Whiteman."

The next day I took the D-Train into Manhattan and showed up at K.O. Publishing bright and early. I'll tell you something, having a hit on the charts certainly changes the way you're treated. Lisa, the receptionist, dropped what she was doing and practically killed herself getting me right into the back office. Pretty cool, man – no less so because Charles Westover was sitting in the waiting room with the other nobody-*schmucks*, and I just glided right past him and said, "How're ya doin', Chelvis?"

What a conceited little shit I was back then! Whenever I remember the way I treated Del Shannon, I want to kick my own ass around the block. ¡uʍop-ǝpᴉsdn ǝʇᴉɹʍ ǝɯ ǝʞɐɯ oʇ ɥƃnouǝ s,ʇI (Knock it off. If anybody saw you turn the book around, they'll think you're a nut.)

When I walked into the back room, Sherm and Sal were yelling and *kvetching* at each other. Sherm was saying, "I don't know who's behind the outfit, but if we were smart, we'd start asking around." And meanwhile Sal spotted me and sort of waved his hand at Sherm to shut him up. He didn't think I saw it, but I saw it. Something was up.

"What's the problem?" I said.

Sherm was swigging back Gelusil straight out of the bottle, for cripes sake. But Sal put on this fake smile, like somebody'd just pointed out a rainbow to him, and he said, "Rude! Look who's here,

Sherm. It's our little songwriting genius!"

I hated when people called me *little*. I was always just Little Rudy to everybody. I don't know how Little Anthony put up with that shit. If I'd been him, I would've made everybody call me *Regular-Sized* Anthony. And what really made me crazy was that I was wearing my high-heeled Tom McAns. Listen, I could've walked in there on fucking *stilts*, and Sal still would've called me ...

Am I digressing again?

So I sat on the piano stool and gave them each the once-over. They just smiled. I'm not exaggerating – the place looked like an enamel contest. And Sal had these real pointy incisors, like a German Shepherd. When he smiled he didn't look happy. He looked like he wanted to take a bite out of you.

"Is there something wrong?" I said.

Sal gave me that I'm-going-to-eat-you grin and said, "Why, no. It's just business, Rudy. Play your new number, babe. Go ahead. Let's hear what you've got."

I got the old piano pumping and sang "Radda-Radda-Ready," and they both flipped. Sal stood up and started walking back and forth, punching his fist into his other hand like he always did when he was excited, saying, "Yes! Yes! Sherm – get RCA on the phone. What's the name of that A and R guy over there?"

"Wendel," Sherman said.

"Wendel *what*?"

"I don't know. Wendel-Shmendel. They'll know who we're talking about when we call. How many Wendels can they have?"

They drew up the papers and had me sign them, one, two, three – just like that. But this time I put up a fight about Sal's name going on the song.

"*I* wrote that song. Sal. Why do *you* have to get half the credit for it?"

He patted my face with his dumb manicured hand. "Rudy, Rudy, Rudy – I'm lookin' *out* for you, baby. You're not established in the business yet. Who's gonna play a record that was written by someone they never heard of? This way, they see *DeGrazzia* on the label, they know me, they respect me – the song takes off. You get rich. What's the matter, you don't wanna be rich?"

"I just don't think it's right for you to say you wrote half of the song. You probably don't even remember the lyrics, even though I just sang them to you."

Then he held both of his hands over his heart, like I'd hurt him real bad. "*Who* doesn't remember? Are you kidding? *I* remember. It goes, 'Radda-Radda-Ready, something about Betty, Gonna pick her up and tra-la-la-la-la, Fuck her with the top down or whatever' – I don't know. The lyrics aren't important anyway. It's the *sound*, man. You've got that sound. Radio stations are gonna wear that record out, once it's a record."

But I told him, "You know, Sal – a lot of agents have been calling me up, and I've decided I'm going to sign with one of them."

Something happened to his face when I said that, like somebody had turned the power off. "Agent?" he said. "Why do you need an agent? So you can give away ten percent of your money?"

"Yeah," I said. "Why would I want to do that, when I can give you fifty percent of it?"

"Okay! Okay! We'll cut a new deal. Forget the agent idea."

But I told him, nothing doing, I needed an agent for my live show. He got this silly-assed grin on his face and said what live show, and I said the one I'd been working on, and he said come on, you're a writer, not a performer, and I said no, I was a performer, too, and he started laughing and said I didn't have the stage presence for an act – that I'd look like I was giving a *bar mitzvah* speech if I ever got behind a microphone.

That's what made me do it – that crack about the *bar mitzvah*. I got up and grabbed the contract and tore it to shreds and threw it on his desk.

"Fine," I said. "I'll just give that song to some cantor who needs a hit."

I started to walk out of the office, when Sal jumped in front of me and plastered himself against the door. I think that was the turning point for me, when I realized how valuable I was to those guys. It was nice to have a hit song on the charts – and more songs would be nice, too. But remember that imaginary picture I talked about before, the one in my head? I still had it, and it was getting bigger all the time. I wanted to be a star – not a name between parentheses under a song title, not (Rudy Keen), but **RUDY KEEN!** I even had my first album cover designed in my imagination. It would be a white background, see? And over to the right, I'd be running with a guitar slung over my shoulder, like I was halfway off the cover, and behind me to the left, about a hundred gorgeous girls would be running after me, their hands out, like they're trying to grab me and rip my clothes off. And I'd call it, KEEN SCENE! And on the back cover it would go to black and white, and I'd be on the ground with my shirt torn and my shoes off, and the girls would have me pinned to the floor, and I'd look real scared. The liner notes would say –

> *No other artist of the decade has changed the course of popular music to the extent that the fabulous Rudy Keen has. Born in Brooklyn and trained in classical music, Rudy Keen has single-handedly forged the most raucous sound to be heard to date – a driving rhythm that supports lyrics of astounding brilliance. Rudy Keen may well be the next Elvis – or perhaps better, the next combination Elvis and William Shakespeare.*

> *Bombarded with marriage proposals from the world's most beautiful women, Rudy Keen has been known to don disguises simply to run down to the local deli for a sandwich in order to avoid the hordes of screaming, wanton, openly lustful females who attempt, on a daily basis, to accost him on the streets. His rugged good looks and boyish charm combine to create a sensual magnetism heretofore unknown in the anals of popular culture. Not just a composer, not just a performer of compelling intensity, Rudy Keen is a rock icon, a movement in and of himself.*

Maybe *movement* was the wrong word. *Movement* sounds like something you flush. Maybe I should've said trend, or *revolution*. Not that it matters. There never was an album. I'll get to all that in a while.

So where the hell did I leave off? Oh yeah – the turning point. They drew up a new contract *without* Sal's name on the song credits. And I asked for a five hundred dollar advance. You would've thought I'd asked for the Brooklyn Bridge, the way they reacted. I practically had to guide Sherm's hand with my own to get him to finish signing the check.

The two of them traded nervous glances with each other. Sherm had a Gelusil mustache on his upper lip. I felt a little bad about how hard I'd been on them, so when Sal asked me to do him a favor, I said I would. He pulled a brown paper bag that was taped shut out of his desk and handed it to me, said he wanted me to bring it to a DJ by the name of Shaky Baxter, over at Radio Station WPUD.

He'd do it himself, he said, except that it was a good opportunity for me to introduce myself and plug "Bop-Sha-Bop." I had nothing else to do anyway, and it sounded like a good idea at the time.

"Why do they call him *Shaky*?" I asked.

"Wait till you hand it to him. You'll see why."

On my way out of the office, I stopped and rattled the bag. "Say, what's in here?" I said.

Sherm looked at Sal. I wanted to tell him to wipe his lip, but he might've gotten embarrassed.

"Lox," Sal said.

"Lox?" I said.

"Yeah. Lox. He's crazy about them. Comes from a long line of salmon fishermen. Makes him feel at home."

Only me. I'm telling you, only me. I'm the only guy I know who could have two hit songs published and still go walking out of a big business office with a goddamn paper bag full of lox.

Before I left the waiting room, I went over to Lisa's desk. She was sort of fixing herself up, checking her lipstick in a compact mirror.

"What's eating them?" I said, tilting my head back toward the inner office.

She looked to her left, and then to her right, and then closed the compact. "I'm not supposed to tell you this," she said. "But I think they're kinda worried about the business."

"How come?"

"Well, between you and I and the lightpost [she meant between you and *me* and the *lamppost*, not you and *I* and the *lightpost*, but she was from Jersey], two of their biggest writers have just left them and signed with other publishers."

And I said, "Yeah?"

"Uh-huh. And keep this under your cap, too [she meant *hat*, keep this under your *hat*, not *cap* – but I told you, Jersey]; they've been getting pressure to sell out to a big firm."

"Really? What kind of pressure?"

Lisa pressed her lips together the way girls do when they put on lipstick. "I'm not supposed to tell."

"Well, you weren't supposed to tell me the first part, either."

"This I'm *really* not supposed to tell. It's got something to do with guys in dark suits."

I was so naive I couldn't figure out what she was hinting at. The first thing I thought was, *Priests? Why would priests want to buy K.O. Publishing?* But everything makes sense to me now.

♪　♫　♪

Radio Station WPUD. Their slogan was printed on a banner that hung on the reception room wall: THE BIG PUD ROCKS NEW YORK. I found out soon enough why they called that guy Shaky Baxter. He was one shaky bastard. He nearly couldn't hold on to the bag when I handed it to him. I'll bet his record collection was pretty scratched up. And you know what? When I told him who I was and which song I'd written, he didn't even care. All he did was look at the bag real close in his crazy shaky hands, and say, "You didn't open this up on the way over, did you, kid?"

I said, "Hell, no. I get all the lox I want for free, from my Uncle Myshkin."

He swung his head around at me real fast and said, "Lox?"

"Yeah," I said. "Isn't that what it is?"

And he just crumpled the brown bag up and stuck it under his twitchy arms. "Yeah, lox. See ya."

"Don't you even want to interview me for your show?" I asked him.

I guess he didn't. He just looked at me like, You? Who are *you?* The bastard. The shaky bastard. I kind of hoped he'd rattle himself to pieces.

That night at home I was playing "Moonlight Sonata" on my violin, just to keep Ma from getting suspicious about what I'd been up to. I'd completely forgotten about that rude disc jockey, when there was a knock at the apartment door. Ma answered it, and a few seconds later she called out, "Rudolph, someone's here to see you. A Mr. Bailis."

I put the violin down and went to the front door, thinking it was probably another agent who wanted to sign me. Mr. Bailis was a big guy in one of those dark suits I'd been hearing about.

"Rudolph Kearns?" he said.

I wondered how he knew my real name. Everybody in the business called me Rudy Keen.

"Yeah?" I said.

"Is there someplace we can talk?"

I pushed him into the hallway and closed the door behind me.

I didn't want Ma to hear anything about rock and roll.

The guy reached into his suit coat and pulled out a badge. Fuckin' A, he was a G-man. FBI, baby.

"What do you want?" I said. "I didn't do nothing. Honest."

He just poker-faced me, like he thought he was Dana Andrews or someone, and real smooth-like he said, "What was in the bag today?"

"Bag?" I said.

"Don't play dumb with me, Kearns. You know which bag I'm talking about – the one you carried from the Brill Building to W-P-U-D."

"Oh," I said. "*That* bag."

He stuck his badge back in his suit pocket. "Yeah – that bag. What was in it?"

"Lox," I said.

"Lox?" Jesus, everybody always said it like that, like they'd never heard of lox before. How can you live in New York and be salmon-deprived? Then he grabbed my shirt by the collar and slammed me up against the wall. He was choking the shit out of me; I could barely even breathe. "You mean herring, don't you, Kearns? *Red* herring." Lox, herring – red, green ... who gave a good goddamn? All I knew was, I couldn't breathe.

Then he said, "You know what you can get for payola? Felony. Twenty years in the can. You want your mother to have to live with that? A nice Jewish boy like you?"

He let go of my collar and tapped the brim of his hat back. I rubbed my throat with my hand. For a second I thought I'd swallowed my Adam's apple.

"I swear to God," I said, in this real squeaky voice, "it was just a bag full of lox."

"Who gave it to you?"

I didn't want Sal to get in any trouble, so I lied. I said no one gave it to me, that I bought it at some delicatessen in Manhattan. You've got to remember, all this was happening out there in the hall, where it was real dim. There was only a sixty-watt bulb on the ceiling, and I felt like one of those guys on "Mickey Spillane Theater." You know, one of those guys that gets beaten up all the time till he folds and tells the detective everything he wants to hear.

He reached back into his suit again, and this time I was afraid he was going to pull out a gun. I closed my eyes real tight and then peeked a little. No gun – just a cigarette. He stuck it in his mouth and let it dangle out of the corner, then he struck a match, lit the cigarette, and threw the match at me.

"I'm watching you, Kearns. Just remember that. I see everything you do. I know everything you're thinking."

No he didn't. Just then I was thinking I was going to shit in my pants, and if he would've known that, he wouldn't have been standing so close to me. I watched him walk away. I leaned against the wall until I heard the downstairs door slam.

When I went back inside the apartment, my mother said, "So who vas that, that nice man?"

"Him? Oh, just a talent agent. My name's getting around."

"Just dunt sign anything till your Uncle Zollie reads it over first. Remember, Rudolph."

I said, "I'll remember, Ma."

That son of a bitch Sal, I thought. *That son of a bitch.*

3 'Whoa Baby, Whoa'

I couldn't sleep for nights – *nights*. I kept wondering if that FBI guy was outside the apartment door, or in front of the building, at the end of the block, or maybe in my closet. But I had a career to think about, so I made an appointment with the next agent who called. His name was Preston Allerton, and he was with Tal Ltd., a big outfit here in New York. He said I had the potential to be a driving force in the industry. Really, he said that. It was almost as if he'd been reading my imaginary liner notes. So I thought, *This is the guy I want.* He told me to put together some material and rehearse for a record audition.

And I said, "Just like that?"

And he said, "Just like that. I'll get you right in the front door."

Another reason I liked him was he didn't call me *baby* all the time, like a lot of *shnorrers* in the business. He had a nice distinguished voice and he was educated, you could tell. His name sounded like it had just been printed on a Harvard diploma – *Preston Allerton.* He said he'd give me a while to come up with a song I thought would be a hit. I called him back two hours later.

"I've got that hit for you, Mr. Allerton," I told him.

And you know what he said? He said, "What took you so long?"

I had an appointment for the next day to sign management papers and an audition for a label. The song I came up with was easily my greatest work so far – maybe ever. I called it, "Whoa Baby, Whoa." It was a rocker with a very innovative bass line – sounded a little bit like "Day Tripper," which is why I got suspicious when I heard The Beatles do that song seven years later. Lennon nicked pieces from other artists in his time – like "Run For Your Life" – that was taken from "Baby Let's Play House," by Presley. I thought it would've been nice if he'd at least given me some credit – but I'm getting ahead of myself. The song went like this:

Whoa baby, whoa.
You're causing a show.
There's people around.
And nowhere to go.
Whoa baby, whoa.
You gotta take it slow.
We've got an audience.
And I'm ready to blow.

I knew it was a hit the minute I wrote it. Instinct. A hit just feels like a hit. There's nothing else to compare it to.

Now, it would've been a mistake to just walk into an audition looking like Little Rudy Keen, so what I did, I worked on the old image. I had Jimmy Salvo's mother run up my blue jeans on her sewing machine so they'd be skin-tight. No kidding, when I put those things on they looked like Levi epidermis. (That's skin, *epidermis*, in case you don't know. It sounds dirty, but it's just skin.) Next – I went out and bought a black leather vest and a wide black belt with a huge silver buckle shaped like a guitar. The final touch – and this is beautiful, just beautiful – I got a tattoo for my arm, just under the rolled-up sleeve of my white t-shirt. It wasn't a *real* tattoo, just the kind you put on with a patch and a wet washcloth. I didn't want to give my mother an instant stroke or anything. She was always going on about how you shouldn't defile your body, and how you couldn't get buried in a Jewish cemetery if you had a tattoo. She used to tell me that if I ever got a tattoo, they'd have to cut my arm off first before I could be buried in a Jewish cemetery, and then my arm would be buried all by itself, with the dead gentiles. And they don't even give you a marker – you know, a tombstone – for just an arm. People would walk over the ground above my arm and never know it was six feet down there. That's why I went with the washable tattoo. Bought five of them, exactly the same kind – a snake coming out of the tailpipe of a Harley Davidson. Very tough. Very cool.

When I left the apartment the next morning I was Rudolph Kearns, wearing a blue suit and carrying a violin case. But after a quick stop at Jimmy Salvo's place, I was transformed into Rudy Keen, Teen Idol. I had to put on two tattoos because I fucked up the first one; I put the snake on upside-down. It looked cool, but it was on its head. Then I hopped a D-Train to Manhattan, carrying my guitar, and admiring my new tattoo, knowing that if anything happened to me, like if some robber shot me or the train crashed, no one would saw off my arm.

Tal Ltd. was in a swanky building on Fifty-third Street, and it made Sal's joint look like a latrine. They had gold records on the wall, and just as you walked in you saw a giant picture of Buddy Holly and his entire bow tie. *Jesus Christ*, I thought, *Buddy Holly – the best songwriter in the business, bar none*. Except maybe me. I wondered if he was in there, in person, and if I'd get a chance to meet him.

Preston Allerton was a guy in his thirties with a very neatly trimmed beard and a gray suit. And what an office he had. What a view. You could see all of Manhattan from there. There was a bar in the corner, and a hi-fi, and a portable putting green and putters. There was lots of brass stuff and black wood furniture and little chotchkies like from Africa or someplace southern like that. He even had a chrome and glass toothpick dispenser on his desk. Class. After I sat down, he picked up a copy of *Billboard* and tossed it over to me.

"Rudy, 'Bop-Sha-Bop' is number seventeen this week. You must be very pleased."

I didn't know that. I hadn't checked the trades lately. I was too freaked to go out of the house, because of that FBI bastard.

I said, "Yeah. I'm pretty pleased, I guess."

Then I noticed he was staring at me, at my face, He tilted his head a little. He narrowed his eyes. "I think we'll be able to market you, Rudy. We'll need publicity shots, of course. I'll arrange for those. Let's wait a while on that, though. You'll need to grow some sideburns."

I reached up and felt my face where there were no sideburns. There were no sideburns because I couldn't *grow* any. I hadn't started shaving yet. But you don't think I told *him* that, do you? I figured that was why they'd invented eyebrow pencils.

"All right," I said. "Say, listen. You know that picture in the front ..."

"And you'll have to dye your hair black, Rudy. That shouldn't be a problem, should it?"

"My hair?"

"Rudy, yes. Your hair."

"What's wrong with brown? Brown's not good?"

He folded his hands in front of his face so that just the fingertips were touching. "No, Rudy. Brown is terrible. The public has been conditioned to expect a rock and roll star to look a certain

37

way. Elvis conditioned them. Rudy, is Elvis's hair brown?"

"No."

"That's right, Rudy. It's black."

"Okay. If you say so and everything. Listen – about that picture in the ..."

He was leaning over his desk, looking at my legs then.

"What's wrong?" I said.

He leaned back in his chair and wrote a note to himself on a little pad on his desk. "The blue jeans. They've got to go."

"They do?"

"Absolutely, Rudy. Rudy, you don't want to look like you just stepped off a tractor, do you?"

"Well," I said. "I – "

"Certainly not," he said, and wrote another note. "We're going for a more polished, worldly look. You want to appear romantic, am I right?"

"Me? Romantic? Sure."

"All right then, Rudy. The jeans are as good as in the trash. We'll order you some custom-tailored slacks. Now about that tattoo–"

I rolled up my sleeve and turned my arm toward him. "Pretty cool, huh?" I said.

"Tattoos are absolutely no-no in this business."

"It makes me look tough, though."

"It makes you look like a convict. Rudy, let me ask you something. What parent is going to allow his or her kid to hang up a poster of someone who looks as though he just escaped from a penitentiary?"

"Poster?"

He smiled and almost damaged my retinas. Preston Allerton had the whitest teeth I'd ever seen, about a million of them. "Rudy Keen posters. Every girl in America will have one."

I'd been getting pretty pissed-off at him, criticizing the way I looked and all, until I heard about the poster. "Yeah," I said. "Yeah, I can see them now – taped on the walls above their beds while my records play on their hi-fi's."

Preston said, "So Rudy, no short sleeves for you. We've got to hide that ... that *thing*. What is it, a snake?"

"Yeah. It's a snake coming out of a motorcycle tailpipe, see? It's a cobra. You can tell, on account of the way the neck is – "

"Yes, I see. Long sleeves, Rudy."

"Oh, I can wear short sleeves. It just washes off. Watch."

I licked my thumb and rubbed the tattoo, but instead of coming off, it smeared and the rear wheel sort of ran over the snake.

"It's not real?" Preston asked.

"No. Hell, no. What – you think I want to have to get my arm cut off and have it buried with the *goyim*, miles away from the rest of me?"

His mouth sort of fell open then, and he said, "What?"

"Nothing," I said. "It's hard to explain. Never mind."

He stood up and sat on his desk halfway, like only half his ass was sitting, and the other half was still standing. "Well, Rudy, other than those minor adjustments, I like your look. Now, I believe you have some material you want me to hear."

I'd been trying to ask him since I got there if Buddy Holly was in the offices somewhere, and if I could meet him. But he was so pushy and in charge. Preston was one of those very in-charge kind of guys, so I just shut up and opened my guitar case and played him three numbers – "Bop-Sha-Bop," "Radda-Radda-Ready," and "Whoa Baby, Whoa." When I finished, he didn't say anything. He had his chin balanced on his hand and just sat there like a stone, a stone with half its ass on the desk. Finally, he said real serious, "That is very, very commercial material. Rudy, you have a knack for this." He stood up and paced on the carpet. "Has anyone brought to your attention the fact that your lyrics are highly indicative of sexual repression and preoccupation?"

"Whadaya mean?"

"How can I say this nicely? Take that last song you just played. That line, 'We've got an audience, and I'm ready to blow' – it strongly suggests premature ejaculation."

I couldn't understand why people were always telling me this kind of stuff. "Look," I said, "it's just a rhyme. I can change it."

"And what was the other lyric? Oh, yes – 'You make me want to pop.' In every song there is a girl who brings a young male to climax."

"Not in 'Radda-Radda-Ready,' there isn't. There's no premature whadayacallit in that one."

"No – I noticed that. You seem to have kept your obsession under raps in that one. Still, one has to consider that the singer is radda-radda-ready, so anxious he can barely express how ready he

39

is."

This guy was worrying me. "What do you mean by *obsession?* You mean like I'm a maniac?"

"I'm not saying it's *bad,* Rudy. Most teenagers who listen to this kind of music are sexually preoccupied. That is highly favorable to you on the relatability scale."

"But you said I had an *obsession.*"

"It was just an observation, and a poor choice of words. An *interest* is what I meant. Now, shall we take care of the paperwork and get you over to your audition?"

Boy, I don't know. One minute someone tells you you're going to be a star, and the next minute you're an obsessed bastard. Then I remembered what I'd been trying to ask him all morning.

"Yeah, yeah. I'll sign in a second. But listen – I noticed you've got a big picture of Buddy Holly in the waiting room. Is he around here somewhere? You think you could introduce me to him?"

Preston had just taken a big stack of papers out of a desk drawer, and then slammed the drawer shut. "Buddy? Buddy's finished."

"What?"

He divided the papers in front of me into three stacks. "Have you heard any Buddy Holly tunes on the radio lately, Rudy?"

Come to think of it, I hadn't. He grabbed a chart from a tray on his desk and showed it to me.

"Here are Buddy's releases for this year, starting with 'Maybe Baby.' Does a certain downward trend seem to be occurring with his record sales?"

I looked at the chart. "But 'Maybe Baby' made number seventeen. That's where my song is now."

"This is your first time out. Buddy has already had two number one records and lots of promotion. Read on from there. 'Rave On' only went as high as number thirty-seven. There's a slight improvement with 'Think It Over' – that went to twenty-seven. But then he did a Walden Cassotto number called 'Early In The Morning.' That barely hit thirty-two. And the new one-'It's So Easy' – that didn't even chart. Rudy, this business moves fast. If you can't keep up with it, you're gone. I wouldn't be surprised if Buddy becomes history in five months. Now, we're going to be late for the audition unless we take care of these contracts."

The whole time I sat there signing the papers (in triplicate) all

40

I could think about was my hero being a has-been. How did that happen? Those were great songs. Buddy was a great singer. And what the hell was he doing recording a Cassotto song when he could've easily written a better one himself? Then I worried about being a sex pervert. If just one person had told me that, then I wouldn't have let it bother me so much. But two people had said it, and Preston knew what he was talking about. He was an analytical guy. He knew about things like repression and obsessions and preoccupation and popping and stuff. And then, just as we were about to leave, he stopped me.

"Wait a minute, Rudy. You can't show up looking like *that*."

"I can't?"

He pushed a button on his intercom and said to his secretary, "Helen? Do we have a trench coat around somewhere?"

I said, "*Trench* coat?"

A second later this blond with five miles of legs and a really tight sweater walked in and handed him a trench coat. She had this wide belt around the smallest waist in the world, and these big pointy ... but that's not important. Preston held the coat open and started putting it on me.

"I can't perform in this," I told him.

"Rudy, a professional can perform under any circumstances. Let's get over there and show them just how professional you are."

Don't even picture it, please. I'm embarrassed. We walked two blocks down Fifth Avenue, and I was carrying a guitar and had a tattoo of a motorcycle running over a snake on my arm underneath a trench coat that was too big for me, and my blue jeans were so tight that my legs started to fall asleep, and my high-heeled boots made me wobble.

And can I set the record straight again, just one more time? When I wrote those songs I wasn't thinking of sex at all. Not at all. Furthest thing from my mind. Maybe you could consider the lyrics a little suggestive. *Maybe*. But all I'd been trying to do was come up with rhymes, You know, *wop-pop*. *Show-blow*. That's the truth, and I knew it then, too – only I couldn't help thinking that maybe I really *was* obsessed and out of control, and that I'd never be able to stop subconscious-like writing about popping and blowing all over the place. What an awful time for an audition.

Before I knew it, we were standing in front of an office door that said Caboose Records.

"Caboose?" I said. "I've never even *heard* of Caboose Records."

"Oh, they're going to be very big, Rudy. Big money behind them. You'll be the lead act."

"But what about Decca or somebody?"

"Decca owns Brunswick, and Brunswick has Buddy."

"Well, how about Columbia, or some label I've at least heard of?"

"Columbia doesn't sign rock acts, Rudy. Now relax and play your songs exactly like you did for me."

Two guys ran Caboose Records, and they sure were glad to see Preston. They shook his hand and treated him like a big shot. Then they looked at me, eyeing my trench coat up and down. One of them said, "Preston, I don't understand. You tell me to get ready for a new performer, and then you bring me a flasher?"

Preston said, "Sam, this is Rudy Keen. Don't let the trench coat fool you. He's the next Elvis. Rudy, I'd like you to meet Sam Henderson, President of Caboose Records. And over here is the head of A and R – Hoyt Seamen."

I shook hands with them, but all I could think of when I heard the name *Hoyt Seamen* was little injured sperms, swimming around with crutches. *Christ*, I thought. *I* MUST *be a pervert.*

They *shmuzed* for a while and then took me to a room with a piano in it. Henderson and Seamen didn't look any too convinced about me. I played "Bop-Sha-Bop" on the guitar and worked up such a sweat in that goddamn trench coat that I right then and there took it off and threw it on the floor. Then I went to town on the piano and played "Radda-Radda-Ready" and "Whoa Baby, Whoa."

I won 'em over in no time. Sam said to Preston, "I gotta have him. Where does he get his material?"

Preston said, "Sam, that's the best part. He writes it. Every one of those songs is a Keen original."

Sam's eyebrows shot up when he heard that. Hoyt said, "Publishing," and smiled. "Collection rights."

"That's right, Hoyt," Preston said.

They offered me a three-record deal, with an option for an album. Preston kept trying to get them to sign the album on the spot, but they said no, they had to see how the sales went first.

"Can you imitate other performers?" Hoyt asked.

And I said, "Well, sure. But I prefer to sound like myself."

"That's good, Rudy," Sam said. "Mark of an original talent, But if you *wanted* to write a song that sounded like somebody else's, would you have a problem with that?"

"No. No problem. I wouldn't *like* it very much, but I could do it."

So then Hoyt, he started calling out names of acts to see if I could write something like they would.

"Jerry Lee Lewis," he said, and I whipped up a copy of "Whole Lotta Shakin'." Sam and Hoyt looked at each other and nodded. "The Everlys," Hoyt said next. So I gave them something close to "Wake Up Little Susie."

"The kid's a natural," Sam said to Preston.

"The Crickets," Hoyt said.

"You mean *Buddy Holly*," I said. "Buddy writes and sings all their stuff."

"Holly-shmolly," Hoyt said. "Just give me a Crickets copy."

He was supposed to know something about the music business, and he didn't even know who had all the talent in that group. But just to cinch the deal, I did a variation on "That'll Be The Day." They went nuts. I was scheduled to cut my first single in two days, and Allerton got a three thousand dollar advance that he said would go into a special account for me, after he took out his percentage.

I'd forgot how hot it was outside. When Preston and I walked out of the revolving door on to Fifth Avenue, it was like hitting a wall. The first thing he said to me when we were outside was, "Well, Rudy, how does it feel to be on your way?"

I just sort of lifted my hands in the air and said, "I don't know."

It was noon, and crowds of people were standing in lines in front of restaurants, waiting for seats, and taxicabs were stuck in the middle of intersections honking their horns. Preston looked kind of funny at me, concerned-like. "Rudy, is there something you're not happy with?"

"Yeah. Yeah, there is. I'm not crazy about that imitating stuff they wanted me to do."

Preston smiled his Frigidaire smile for a second. "They just wanted to see if you could compete, that's all. Rudy, this business gets swept up in trends. The ability to imitate a certain sound can be a life preserver."

"I don't want to imitate anybody, though. I don't need a life preserver – I can *swim*."

"Now don't go getting over-confident."

"I'm not. But half the time I didn't know what those guys were talking about. One of them said something about collection rights."

"That was Hoyt Seamen."

That guy was going to have to change his name before I could work with him. Every time I heard it, it sounded like a medical condition, and then I'd think things like –

Remember, Geritol will improve tired blood cells, but it won't do a thing for Hoyt Seamen.

"What are collection rights?" I said.

"Just a minor contractual detail. Don't trouble yourself about it. I'll write up the papers this afternoon and make sure you get the best deal possible. Now – are you satisfied?"

It was so hot my tattoo started to melt and run down my arm.

"Yeah," I said. "A few concert dates wouldn't be a bad idea, either. Maybe Carnegie Hall. And TV too – Ed Sullivan, American Bandstand."

"Whoa baby, whoa," Preston said, and then laughed like a hyena. "Don't get ahead of yourself." Then he waved and disappeared into the crowds of people who all moved together down the sidewalks like they were on a conveyer belt.

I stood around watching them for a while. I didn't know who they were, and I didn't know where they were going, but they sure were in a hell of a hurry to get there, wherever it was. But I didn't have *anywhere* to go, except Jimmy Salvo's apartment, to turn back into Rudolph Kearns. Isn't that something? Here I had a record deal, and all I could look forward to was switching back to my secret identity. If I could've hung out with Clark Kent in a bar somewhere, we would've just sat there looking depressed, slugging back drinks, him with his hat on crooked, and he'd say, "I can't stand being this guy," and I would've said, "I can't stand being *this* guy, either, and at least you can grow sideburns if you feel like it." Then what we would've done – we would've gone out back behind the bar and switched into our hero clothes, "Look at this goddamn cape, would ya?" he'd say. "Finest Kryptonian broadcloth." And I'd say, "Yeah – dig this guitar-shaped buckle," But sooner or later we'd have to put on our stupid regular clothes and be regular guys, no matter how much we didn't want to.

I'm almost digressing again. (Between you and me, I always thought his cape was kind of on the faggy side, anyway.)

So where the hell was I going? Oh! So I was standing there on Fifth Avenue, when all of a sudden Brenda's face floated across my mind like a cloud. (I like that – that's sort of poetic, 'like a cloud, a soft cloud, a beautiful cloud, a very wet cloud.') I reached in my pocket and felt the wad I'd been hiding ever since I cashed that five hundred dollar check from K.O. Publishing, and I thought, *Why not?* I could just hop in a cab, pick up some flowers, and go meet Brenda at Schrafft's. What was to stop me? Nothing. It's funny; if you've been a nobody all your life, you kind of still think like a nobody, even when you're a somebody.

So that's what I did. I hopped in a cab and had the driver pull over near an old lady who was selling roses on a corner, and she wrapped up twelve of them for me while I was hanging out the window and everybody was blowing their goddamn horns for us to get moving again. I was so excited to tell Brenda about my record contract and the posters, I was practically peeing in my pants ... until I walked into Schrafft's. Son of a bitch – wouldn't you know it? Right there, leaning over the counter, was *Sal*. He was talking kind of quiet to her in his quiet swine voice. I don't know what she saw in that guy. I honest-to-Christ don't.

"Rudy – hey, Rudy!"

It was too late; he'd seen me. I ducked in a booth and shoved the flowers in next to me. That's all I needed – for him to find out that I'd bought his girl flowers. He walked down the aisle and sat on the seat across from me.

"I've been lookin' all over for you. Your mother says you're not home. She thinks you're with Paul Whiteman or something."

"I told you not to call my house," I said.

He lost his smile but fast. "Look, babe. You've got to check in with me once in a while. We're runnin' a business."

He probably just needed some *schlemiel* to carry brown paper bags to disc jockeys. "I don't think I want to write for you anymore," I said.

His head jerked back like I'd just tried to hit him when he heard that. I wish I would've.

"Whadaya mean? What's the matter?"

"What's the matter? Would you like to know what's the matter?"

45

"Yeah! That's why I just said, 'What's the matter?'"

"I'll tell you what's the matter," I said.

"I hope to Christ you do so I can finally find out what's the matter!"

"This is the matter – an FBI agent followed me home last week after I gave that package to that Shaky Baxter bastard. He followed me home, knocked on my door, talked to my mother, and nearly choked me to death. Told me I could do twenty years for payola."

You know how they say, " ... and then his face went white," but they're exaggerating, because it's just an expression? Well, Sal's fucking face went *white*, and I mean *white* – no exaggeration. For a second he looked like he'd been embalmed with Clorox. And here's something weird – I noticed the end of his tie was all burned. Looked like charcoal.

"There must be some mistake," he said, but he couldn't look me in the eye when he said it.

"The FBI, Sal. *Baby.* Why did you set me up like that? Can't you find anybody else to make your crummy payola drops for you?"

"I don't know what you're talking about."

"Sure you do. What was in that bag, Sal?"

"I told ya. Lox."

I kept sticking it to him. *Let him sweat*, I thought. "It wasn't lox, Sal."

He looked away and rubbed his stupid chin, and then he put his hands up in the air, like he was surrendering. "All right, already. You got me. It wasn't lox."

"What was it, then?"

He looked me dead in the eye, and then said, "Kreplach."

Can you believe the *nerve* of that son of a bitch? "Kreplach?" I said. "What kind of an idiot do you take me for?"

"On my grandmother's grave, I swear," he said, touching his heart and looking like he might cry, because he was thinking of his grandmother, buried in some gentile cemetery, where there might be a few Jewish arms with tattoos thrown in without tombstones.

I said, "Why would an FBI agent follow me all over town and then choke me outside of my apartment if all I was carrying was kreplach?"

He shrugged. "Go figure. The FBI – what do they know? Jewish food, dope – it's all the same to them."

Just to show you I was as naive as I told you I was back in those days, listen to this: I started thinking, *Well, maybe he's telling the truth. He did give me my first break.* So I softened. I said, "Okay – but no more paper bags, Sal. I'm a writer, not a caterer."

"Anything you say, sweetheart. And you're right. You deserve better." His eyes shifted to my arm for a second. "Nice tattoo, by the way. Real nice. What is that? Looks like a reptile in a road accident."

"It was a snake. He used to be coming out of the tailpipe, but I smudged it by mistake, and now the goddamn axle – see?"

"Yeah." He tried to smile again, but he couldn't quite get the corners of his mouth to go along with it. "Say," he said, "you didn't tell that FBI guy who you were carrying that bag for, did you? I mean – it was only kreplach, and I don't care who knows that, 'cause it's still a free goddamn country, and if you feel like giving somebody kreplach, you can give them all the kreplach you want. Buckets full, if you feel like it. Truckloads. I'd like to see somebody try and stop me if I wanted to fly in cargo planes filled with the crap. Or oceanliners, or ..."

"I get the idea, Sal."

"But you didn't, did you? Tell him, I mean."

"No."

"He didn't ask?"

"Oh, he asked. I told him I picked up the lox at a deli."

He sat back in the booth and then sighed. "Thanks, babe. You know, when I'm in a spot I know I can always count on old Rudy." He sat and looked at how polished his nails were. "And I'm in a spot."

"What kind of spot?"

"I need a new song as soon as I can get one."

"Oh, I've got one," I said.

"That's great. Let's go back to the office and – "

"But I'm recording this one myself."

His mouth fell open. Every two seconds that guy was either turning white or looking like he'd just thrown an embolism. "*You?* You haven't even got a record contract."

"Sure I do."

"With who?"

"I think you mean, with *whom*. With Caboose Records. Signed with them this morning."

Did you ever see someone try to add up a grocery bill in their mind at the check-out counter *before* the checker does? And their

47

eyes sort of get that far-away glaze, and they look stumped as hell? That's how Sal looked, like he was adding up his groceries. He shook his head a few times and said, "How? How did you get a recording deal?"

"I signed with Tal Limited. They're my new agents."

"You what?"

"A guy named Preston ..."

"*Allerton?* You signed with Preston He's-An-Asshole-I-Hate-His-Fucking-Guts *Allerton?*"

"I'm not sure about his middle name. Could be the same guy."

He was leaning over the table and shaking, like he was trying to force himself not to kill me. So I said what's wrong with that, I can sign with who I want, and he told me that Tal Ltd. owned Blue Rose Music, and that they'd want my publishing rights, only they couldn't have them, because *he* owned them, and he'd keep owning them for the next five years. Then he called me an ungrateful bastard while he kept sticking his fat finger in my face. He said if I published with Blue Rose, he'd have my legal ass on a platter and sue me up the wazzoo.

How do you like that? Instead of being happy I was getting somewhere in my career, he did a one-man impersonation of Hiroshima. He was bent so far over the table by the time he was through screaming at me, that our faces were practically touching. And that's when he saw the flowers. He looked at me, then at the flowers again, and then at Brenda, back at the counter. He slammed his fist down on the table and the silverware rattled, and then he ran out of the place so fast and angry I thought for a minute he was going to jump through the glass door instead of opening it first – which would've been okay with me, because I wouldn't have gotten up to help him, even if he was lying all bloody and cut up on the sidewalk. I would've just left him there with his goddamn manicure and his burnt tie, so all the New York pedestrians could trample him on their way to wherever they're always going, but nobody knows where it is. And don't think they wouldn't have.

But he opened the door, the bastard.

Brenda walked over to my booth to see what the hell had been going on. We'd been pretty loud, Sal and me. We'd caused a scene.

She said, "Rudy, is something wrong?"

I was tempted to tell her I'd never been with Sal on those nights I'd said I was, but then I would've looked like as big a liar as

48

he was. My mother used to have a Yiddish expression for the kind of situation I was in. The translation goes something like, "If you tell a lie for someone else and get found out," I can't remember the rest, exactly. " ... then you're an asshole," or something. Something like that.

So I told her what happened, and about how he was going to put my wazzoo on some kind of platter. Brenda made me scoot over in the booth so she could sit down, and she started talking about Sal as if he was some poor orphan who we all had to look out for. It was pretty obvious she bought all the bullshit he was always giving her. You take a nice, sweet girl like Brenda, and she'll believe all the lies some jerk gives her every time. She said I should take it easy on him, that he might lose his publishing business – the same routine Lisa, the receptionist, had given me. She went on and on about how much pressure Sal was under.

"You don't know the whole story, Rudy. Sal doesn't want you to. But he tells me everything. He's just found out there's a new publishing group in town, and they're stealing all his best writers away. He's probably worried that he's going to lose you, too. He needs friends right now."

That's not what he needed, I knew what he needed. He needed an enema – for his *head*. But I didn't want to talk anymore about Sal and his goddamn problems, so I picked up the bouquet and gave it to her. I wish you could've seen her face whenever she was surprised and happy. It glowed like the Hudson at sunset, except it was a lot cleaner. She kept asking, "For me?" Girls are funny. You give them a bunch of flowers and they'll always say the same thing – "For me?" – like maybe you accidentally gave them to the wrong person.

"Congratulate me," I said. "I got a record contract."

She was so happy and excited, she hugged me. Wop, wop, wop – I was ready to pop. And while she was smelling the flowers, I was smelling her. You know how it is when you're close to a girl for the first time, and you can smell how good they smell? There ought to be a law against girls smelling like that, because it can make you lose your senses, all your brain cells and crap. I'd lost so many brain cells I was ready to propose to her.

Then she said I was probably going to paint the town red that night, and I said yeah. She kept asking me who the lucky girl was, until I finally had to admit I didn't have anyone to go out with. Then she patted my back and said, "Aw," and told me if I stuck around till

49

her shift was over, *she'd* go out with me.

I was in Teen Heaven, with a Teen Angel, drowning in a Sea Of Love. Of course, she only made the offer because she felt sorry for me, but I didn't care. I waited around for her for three hours and drank about fourteen sodas and became very familiar with the bathroom.

We took a bus to a Loew's Theater on Broadway and Ninety-sixth Street. It felt great to have Brenda hanging on to my arm as we walked down the street, but I wished I'd left my damn guitar at home. It kept getting in the way. *Twice* I goosed her with it by accident. I kept saying, "Oh, jeez, I'm sorry," but she was pretty cool about it and forgave me each time. This theater we went to showed old movies, classics. I can't remember which one we saw, but after the show, Brenda asked me if I wanted to go get a drink to celebrate. I said sure, that we could go to this little restaurant across the street, but she didn't think that was such a good idea, since Sal went there a lot.

And I said, "So what?"

And she said, "He's very jealous, Rudy. He might get the wrong idea."

"Yeah?"

"Oh. Yes."

So then I said, "Just how jealous *is* he?"

She said I had no idea, that once he caught a guy looking at her, just *looking* at her, for Christ's sake, when they were standing in a line at a Broadway theater, and he almost tore the guy's head off. She had to stop him.

Well, that was great. He'd seen those flowers; he knew they weren't for him. What was I going to do now?

We ended up at a soda shop (just what I needed, my fifteenth soda), and in-between trips to the bathroom, Brenda talked about my future in show business, and how I'd have a mansion with gold records on the wall, and she'd be able to tell everybody that she knew Rudy Keen when he was a nobody.

"Is that what you think I am – a nobody?"

Her eyebrows jumped up and her mouth made a little "o." "That's not what I meant, Rudy."

But I knew what she meant. She meant just what she said, and she was right, too. So far, I was still a nobody. So then I wanted to impress her. "Hey," I said, "you wanna see something?"

I rolled up my sleeve to show her my tattoo. She looked at it for just a second, put her hand up to her mouth, and then she said, "Oh my God! Is that legal?"

I didn't know what the hell she was talking about until I looked at it myself. It had smudged some more, and the snake had lost one of its eyes. Holy *Christ*! Now it looked like a gigantic *penis*. I rolled down my sleeve real fast. I didn't want to get arrested or anything.

I walked her home that night. The stars were out, but fat chance of spotting one in Manhattan. Too many lights, too much neon. We held hands. I was so far gone over Brenda I didn't know what I'd do without her. But while I was asking her what she thought I should wear on "American Bandstand" – a leather jacket, or a classy suit, like Freddy Cannon, I saw that she wasn't paying any attention. Her eyes were all red, like if she didn't close them, she'd bleed to death.

"Hey, Brenda," I said. "What's the matter?"

"Hm? Oh, nothing."

"It was a *snake*, the tattoo. I promise. It's just smudged, is all. It's not what it looked like."

She said it wasn't the tattoo. It was Sal again. The son of a bitch was ruining things for me even when he wasn't around. She told me he was in trouble, real trouble. He'd been asking questions about this new publishing company, Stek-Circ, Inc., and apparently he'd asked too *many* questions. He started getting threats – in the mail, over the phone. She was afraid someone was trying to kill him. A few nights earlier, his apartment caught fire. Almost everything he owned burned, and if he hadn't woken up, he would've suffocated while he slept, or else he would've been one well-done Italian roast.

The barbecued tie – now it made sense.

I said, "But who'd want to kill Sal?"

There was a stupid question. Sal was a swine. Probably everybody who knew him wanted to kill him. What I meant was, Who'd actually *do* it?

Brenda said, "Someone who wants him out of the business in a hurry. Someone from Stek-Circ."

Over the years I've wondered a lot of times just exactly when I started to suspect that something fishy was going on, something big. It was *then*, right then when I heard about the threats, the fire in Sal's apartment, and when I saw how frightened Brenda looked. I'll never forget her eyes – scared, like a rabbit in the jaws of a fox.

Hey – I like that. That sounded kind of poetic, like Mickey Spillane. *Scared, like a trembling rabbit in the slathering jaws of a rabid fox.* I could work that sentence a little further, but you don't want to ruin it. Damn, I'm good.

But that was just the tip of the rock-and-roll iceberg. I had no way of knowing then what kind of trouble was ahead – for all of us.

I said goodnight to Brenda at the entrance of her building. I told her everything would be all right, and not to worry, and she kissed me. Just a little kiss, but it meant the world to me. I floated down the steps and onto the sidewalk near the wrought iron fence there. That's why I didn't notice him at first, not until he said, "Have a nice time, Rudy?"

It was Bailis, the FBI dick.

"*Oy!*" I said, "Where did *you* come from? What're you, nuts? You can scare a guy to *death*, sneaking up on him like that."

He lit a cigarette and blew smoke out of his stupid nose. "She's quite a piece. Quite a cute little piece."

I said, "You leave her alone. You just shut up about her."

"She's Sal DeGrazzia's girl, isn't she, Rudy?"

I started walking fast, hoping he wouldn't follow me. But he did, the dick. It's what he did for a living.

"You're both getting some, aren't you?" he said.

That did it. I spun around and said, "Quit following me! Don't you have anything better to do? Isn't there an FBI agent ball you can go to or something?"

Bailis took the cigarette out of his mouth and started twirling it around in his hand, like he was writing something in the dark with the orange burning part. "I see you everywhere you go. I know what you're thinking."

So what – you think I was going to stand around and listen to more of that shit? He was making me paranoid as hell. I took off down the street. I ran until I could feel my heart throbbing in my ears, hating that bastard and the dirty lousy way he'd talked about Brenda. When I got to Broadway I hailed a taxi, and when it pulled up to the corner, I threw my guitar in first and then *dove* in after it.

"Where's the fire, Mack?" the driver said.

"Brooklyn," I told him. "Bay Ridge. Hurry!"

I checked out the rear window to see if Bailis was following me. It didn't matter – he knew where I lived. He'd find me. And here's the lovely part ... it was too late to go back to Jimmy Salvo's place and pick up my suit and violin. I had to sleep on the fire escape of my building, using my guitar case for a pillow. And the hell I caught from my mother the next morning for staying out all night, *please*. I don't even like thinking about it. She should have only known I'd been out with a *shiksa*.

It was a lonely night out there on the fire escape, and it wasn't my last one. That was the night I started running, and I've never stopped, till now. Now there'll be no more running. I'm going to tell everything – about what happened to me, and Brenda, and Sal, and Bobby Darin, and all the other great rock artists, especially Buddy Holly. I'm going to blow the lid off the biggest scandal in entertainment history. I'm going to take the bull by the horns and nip it in the goddamn bud and throw away the key. Let them try and stop me now. Let them.

4   'Oh, Brenda!'

My days of quick changes at Jimmy Salvo's apartment were over. Now Preston sent a car to pick me up every morning and take me to rehearsals, or photo sessions, or to a tailor for measurements. I had this crazy driver, Reinhardt. I don't know if that was his first name or his last; everybody just called him *Reinhardt*. I think he used to be a Nazi – he always zeigheiled me. He kept telling me about these whorehouses he knew about, and how we should stop in at one before we went to the rehearsal hall.

"C'mon, kid. No one'll ever know."

"Naw," I'd tell him. "I got work to think about."

"Quick stop, get yer whistle cleaned."

"My whistle *is* clean."

"You know what I mean."

"Just take me to the hall, Reinhardt. You can stop in at one after you drop me off. I'll tell them I sent you on an errand."

"Thanks, kid. Sure you don't wanna come?"

"I'm sure."

"The poisons'll back up in yer system, you know."

"I'll take that chance."

"Shouldn't take chances with poisons. You know what'll happen?"

"What?"

"One minute you'll be on stage singin', and the next, you'll just keel over. Coroner'll come in, examine you, and tell everyone it was backed-up poisons that got ya, 'cause you didn't get your whistle cleaned."

"Let me worry about my own goddamn whistle, will ya?"

"It's *your* whistle."

"Thank you."

And there was no way to keep what was happening from my

mother. One day her son's hair was brown, the next, jet black. Memphis pitch. I made the mistake of going into the kitchen one morning for a cup of coffee, and she screamed, "Agh! Your hair! Vot happened? You shampooed vit iodine?"

And when the packages started arriving at the apartment, the game was over. There was no other way to explain two-hundred dollar suits, sweaters, custom slacks and imported shoes and boots. She thought I'd joined the Mafia.

"Rudolph, vot is it? Is it gambling? Dope?"

So I had to tell her. "I signed a recording contract, Ma. I'm making records now."

"Vit Paul Whiteman?"

"No, Ma. Just me."

"Vot – records vit just vun violin? Vot kinda records are those?"

"No violin, Ma."

"Vot, den? Piano?"

"I'm singing rock and roll."

"*Oy!*"

"Knock it off, Ma. They're good songs."

"Don't give me no *bobbeh meisseh*! Up there vit those tight pants, so you can practically see the moons of yer *tochkes*!"

"The *what*?"

"The moons – the moons of yer *tochkes*. Vit the sheeksas screamin' like dey do for that hillbilly, Elvis Pretzel!"

Every morning it was like that. One time I woke up and she had Rabbi Kaufman in the kitchen waiting for me, with a pep talk about what it meant to be a *mensch*, and how the world of show business was the first step on the heathen path to Sodom and Gomorrah – which was pure crap, because I'd never had either of those diseases. I had to run a gauntlet just to get out of the goddamn apartment, and then my mother would sit in one of the Morris chairs and hang her head like a martyr, mumbling, "Tank God yer faddah can't see you now. It vould keel him."

She'd always pull my father into it. That's when I'd make my escape. I sure didn't want to talk about *him*.

♪　♫　♪

I think it was late August or September. Everything from back then is fuzzy, and no one wrote the dates down, so I'm guessing.

That's when I recorded "Whoa Baby, Whoa." I'd never been inside such a studio. Big control room, huge studio. I had a fourteen-piece band waiting for me. For *me*! And get this – Eddie Cochran on guitar. If I'm making this up, I hope to drop dead (not necessarily right now). Before we put down an instrumental track, Eddie and I had a jam session with "Summertime Blues." That guy could really play.

And you could've knocked me over with a matzo when I saw who they had in the background chorus – Walden Cassotto. Except everybody was calling him *Bobby* now.

"It's the one decent thing Sal DeGrazzia ever did for me," he said. "He came up with my stage name – Bobby Darin – and that's what they call me on my new record."

I said, "What are you talking about? *I* came up with that name! The same day you recorded 'Early In The Morning.'"

"*You* did?"

"Yeah! I told Sal, 'Why not call him Bobby Darin,' and he said there were already too many Bobbys out there."

"That son of a bitch charged me five hundred bucks for that name."

"I would've given it to you for free, or at least wholesale."

"That son of a bitch," he said. "I told him my middle name was Robert, and then he said he could make something out of that, but if I liked it, there'd be a fee."

Oh, how I hated Sal. The swine. The *chozzer*.

But listen, we made rock and roll history that day. For two hours we jammed, and the engineers let the recorders roll. Try to find those tapes today – you can't. They're gone. When I tell people what I think happened to them, they tell me I'm crazy. "Conspiracy theory," they say, and then they laugh. All right, already. So laugh. Just wait till you read the rest of this incredibly fascinating book. Read it all the way to the end, then we'll see who's nuts. (And buy extra copies for your friends and relatives, because if you just *tell* them about it, they might not believe you. They'll just laugh and tell you you're crazy. People need to read it in black and white for themselves. And don't wait for the paperback; buy the trade edition. Paperbacks fall apart and the pages turn yellow. And the paperback company makes me wait an extra six months for royalties. Yeah, yeah – I know. The trade edition costs more money, but what are you – a cheapskate? You want your friends and relatives to talk behind your back about how cheap you are? Of course not. Get to the book store now. I said, NOW. Hurry. Some of them close early.)

So where the hell was I? Oh! I know. Then Sam Henderson of Caboose Records came in and told me I needed a song for the flip side. But I didn't *have* a song. I'd been so busy with photo sessions and tailor appointments, and dodging Ma and Rabbi Kaufman, I hadn't had time to write. So I asked everybody to leave the studio for a half hour while I came up with something. What I came up with was a ballad. Take a look.

"Oh, Brenda!"

Copyright 1958, by Rudy Keen

> I never told you,
> What you mean to me.
> I never dreamed,
> Just what a love could be.
> Secret yearnings,
> My heart is learning
>
> How it feels to hide,
> Love deep inside.
> Oh, Brenda! It's you.
> Oh, Brenda! It's true.
> But the secret stays with me,
> My private misery.
> When I see your lips,
> Something starts to drip.

"You can't sing that," Sam told me when I played him the song.
"Why not? It's how I feel. I always write about how I feel."
"It's beautiful, Rudy, that first part. It's all about unrequited love. Stop while you're ahead. You don't need that 'Something starts to drip' part. It's obscene."
"No, it's not. I didn't say *what* starts to drip."
"People will know. For Christ's sake, Rudy! What else drips?"
"Hearts. Hearts drip blood when they're broken."
"'When I see your lips, Something starts to drip' – now listen,

either the singer has salivary gland problems – which is disgusting to begin with – or else he's having an orgasm."

It was around that time I decided that everybody in the music business had sick, dirty minds. All they ever thought about was sex. I don't know how they could've read sex into that love song, but I took out the last two lines anyway, because Walden, I mean *Bobby*, nodded and said it was probably a good idea not to have anything dripping in the lyrics. Boy, I'll tell you. So much for freedom of speech. But I did learn one thing when I wrote that song. I learned how I really felt about Brenda. When you have to write something spontaneous-like, the truth always comes out. I loved Brenda, and there was no way I could tell her. She had Sal (the swine), she was older than me, and besides – to her I was just Little Rudy.

We were all pretty sure we had a hit when we finished that session, especially Hoyt Seamen. (I won't make fun of his name, but you go ahead and try it. Make some comment up yourself. It's fun.) Hoyt said it might be a double-sided hit, but he wanted to put strings on "Oh, Brenda!"

"No way," I said. "This is a rock and roll ballad, not a Tony Bennett song."

"I just want to fill it out, Rudy. What do you have against violins?"

"You mean, other than the fact that I was forced to learn how to play the violin when I was three, and had to take lessons twice a week, every week, with four hours of practice a day, and my fingers used to bleed and I'd *still* have to keep playing, and all the kids who played saxophone were considered cool, and me and one other kid named Oliver Goldstein were called *violin pussies* and beaten up on the playground every Tuesday and Thursday? Well, other than that – I've got nothing against violins."

And Hoyt said, "All right. Have it your way. I just don't understand why a newcomer who calls himself *Rudy Keen* should doubt my expertise, after all my years in the business."

And I said, "Hey – you know what you get when your underwear are too tight?"

All the band members called out, "Hoyt Seamen!" (You should've too, if you've been paying attention.)

Hoyt was pretty pissed. He ran off to the control room while the rhythm section made up a song about his name.

♪　♫　♪

Bobby and I went to a little bar in the Village afterward. Some blues player was on the stage, playing a Robert Johnson song.

"Do you think I've got a chance?" I asked Bobby. "I mean, being up against all those big name acts?"

"Don't think of the stars as competition. They've just been at it longer than you have. You'll be surprised when you see how much they want you to make it. Everybody helps everybody else. It's like a community."

"Help me out, then."

Walden smiled and sipped his drink. He hardly ever finished a drink, just let it sit in front of him a long time. "I've already helped you. I sang on your song."

"I've got to get on a tour, though."

"Don't you have an agent?"

"Yeah, I do. Preston Allerton. He's with Tal Limited."

He grabbed his chest when I said that, and his face sort of froze.

"What's wrong?" I said.

"Nothin'," he said. But I could tell something about Allerton bothered him. He was huffing and puffing and he got real pale. I didn't know it at the time, but Bobby had a bad heart. It's what kept him out of the Army. I got rejected by the draft, too, but I'd prefer not to talk about it.

I nudged his arm and said, "Do you know something about Allerton? Huh?"

Walden spun his glass and looked at it. "There's a lot of bastards in this business, Rudy, mostly on the management side. Some you learn to stay away from. Some you learn not to say anything about, if you want to stay healthy."

"What'd Preston do to you?"

"He didn't do anything, except screw me royally out of collection rights for a few songs."

Then I remembered what Henderson had said about collection rights the day I signed with Caboose. "What're collection rights?"

He took a few deep breaths and slugged back some of his drink. "He didn't tell *me* what they were, either. That's why he owns the rights to 'Now We're One' and a few others. Collection rights allow the owner to put your cuts on an album of various artists' releases. They attract a bigger buyership with the more acts they can feature. The problem is, the artist and composer get a much smaller chunk of the royalties than they normally would, which means more of the profits go to the owner of the collection rights. Preston and his outfit don't even wait for a song to live its lifetime before they issue the collections, so the performer competes against himself for sales. If Preston puts out 'Whoa Baby, Whoa' on a collection at the same time your company releases the single, he's hoping the album sells as well or better than your single release."

I said, "Nobody told me this stuff."

"Hey – nobody wants you to *know* this stuff."

"What'd you mean about staying healthy?"

He looked down at the bar and grabbed his chest again. When he caught his breath, he said, "Let's just say that Tal Limited isn't afraid to use persuasion if they don't get their way."

Damn. Payola. FBI. Men in dark suits. Collection rights. Persuasion. I was just starting to get a picture of what was going on in the music industry.

Then he started talking about this tour he had coming up – *The Biggest Show Of Stars For 1958*. It opened on October third, I think, in Worcester, Massachusetts. I asked him who else was on it.

"Frankie Avalon."

"Shit," I said. "Who else? Don't say Pat Boone."

"No, but there's Bobby Freeman."

"Oh, he's good. 'Do You Wanna Dance' – hot record. Go on."

"Uh ... Clyde McPhatter."

"Clyde's cool. Great pipes."

"Um ... Dion And The Belmonts."

"Yeah? Are they headlining?"

"No. We've got Buddy for that."

"Buddy? You mean, Buddy *Holly*?"

"Sure."

Well, that was that. I told him he *had* to get me on that tour, because I had to meet Buddy, my idol. "Please? Come on. I'll do anything. I'll write you a song for free. Please? Whadaya say?"

He promised he'd talk to the promoter. They needed someone to open the show anyway. No one wanted to be the opening act; there were a lot of egos in the business. And then I told him what Preston had said to me about Buddy, about how he'd be history in five months.

Bobby said, "That bastard. He said that?"

And I said yeah, he did. For the next few minutes we talked about why Buddy's records weren't selling much anymore.

"Everybody has ups and downs," he said.

See, Bobby never liked to say anything bad about another performer. It's just the way he was. But I had my own theory on what was happening to Buddy's career. Let's talk about appearance. When Buddy first hit, nobody knew what he looked like. When you don't know what somebody looks like, and all you hear is his voice, you can imagine him to be any way you want. But now there were Buddy Holly fan club photos and record jackets, and he'd done Sullivan's show twice. Now, I'm not saying Buddy was funny looking, or a bug-eyed geek. I'm no one to talk. Next to me, Buddy looked like Tony Curtis. But somebody'd given him the advice to make his glasses his trademark. Does that sound like good advice to you? If you had a record out, would you want your audience to picture in their heads a pair of singing eyeglasses? I don't think so.

But I digress.

Bobby still had the same goddamn drink in front of him when he said this to me: "If I tell you something, would you promise to keep it to yourself?"

"Who, me? I'm the best secret keeper around. Everybody tells me stuff they don't want other people to know. For instance, this girl I know, Brenda, she told me ... oops. I forgot. I'm not supposed to tell."

"Come on, Rudy!" Bobby said, all excited and everything. "You've got to *promise*."

"All right, already – I promise!"

Well, old Bobby told me something I've never repeated. I've kept that promise to this very minute. Now I'm going to blow it to hell, but I think he would've wanted me to. Or maybe not. But it's not like I'm going to hear from him about it, either way. He told me (forgive me, Bobby, and *alavasholem*) that Buddy had lost confidence when his sales hit bottom. He moved to New York to work on promotion and to get better studio production quality. At first he thought he should go mainstream, and he did, a little. But then he had a change of heart. He hid out for a few months and came up with some songs that had a whole new sound, a sound that he hoped would help him make a comeback, maybe the biggest, most spectacular comeback ever.

I said, "What's it like, this new sound?"

"You've never heard anything like it before."

That's what he said to me. So then we both knew Buddy's secret. We didn't know how it was going to happen, and we didn't know when it was going to happen, but we knew Buddy was going to strike again. I can prove all this, you know. I've got facts and proof, which I'll get to later. But if I told you the titles of some of those songs Buddy wrote, you'd faint right now. You'd just keel over and pass out and drop this book and probably lose the page you were on. Or else you'd tell me I'm full of shit and ought to see a rock-and-roll psychiatrist. But hold on. There's a time for everything, and it ain't time yet.

Just before we left that little bar, Bobby asked me what I thought of his new record. I didn't even know he *had* a new record.

"I haven't had much time to listen to the radio," I said. "What's it called?"

"'Splish-Splash.'"

Goddamn. I knew that record. As a matter of fact, I was pretty pissed about it. It sounded almost exactly like "Bop-Sha-Bop."

"That's *you?*"

"Yeah," he said. "You like it?"

"Well, yeah, I like it. That's why I wrote it."

"What're you talking about?"

"Come on, Walden – I mean *Bobby*. That's 'Bop-Sha-Bop' all over again."

"You think so?"

"Well, of *course* I think so. In the first place, they're both named after sounds instead of words. Do you know what I mean?"

"Onomatapoeia?"

"No thanks. I just went. But if you have to – "

"No, that's what they call words that sound like the noises they represent."

"Oh. Sure, I knew that. I practically invented that imawannapeea stuff."

"*Onomatapoeia*," he said.

"Well, make up your mind. A second ago you said you didn't have to go."

You didn't know that I wrote "Splish-Splash"? Oh, yeah. That baby's mine. But I didn't make a big fuss about it. After all, Bobby had sung background on my record, and he was going to help me meet my hero, Buddy Holly. Besides, when you've got as much talent as I have, you don't mind spreading it around among friends. It's all rock and roll under the bridge, is the way I look at it. (Royalties would be nice, though.)

When we were outside waiting for a taxi, he turned to me and said, "So when do you think I could have that free song you promised me?"

Jesus Christ, I thought. *I didn't think he'd hold me to it.*

"When do you want it?" I said.

"No hurry. Day after tomorrow is fine."

The day after tomorrow! Some notice. So I went home and wrote this song about a farm girl who always meets her boyfriend in the barn, and they have a lot of fun with dairy products together. I called it, "Cream Lover." Bobby liked it, but he was afraid it would get banned. He changed it to "Dream Lover." That's where that song came from, so help me God. I practically made his career. It was one of his biggest hits, but between you and me, I liked my version better.

♪　♫　♪

I used to think music business news went out over some kind of wire service. Everybody knew every move you made. Two days after I recorded "Whoa Baby, Whoa," Sal was on the goddamn phone asking for the lead sheets.

"I want those sheets in my office by noon today. You understand?" He'd called me at home again. He knew I hated that, but he did it anyway.

I said, "Yeah, yeah. I understand. Don't get your nuts twisted in a knot."

"Look, Keen. In case you go getting any ideas about publishing with Blue Rose, let me just remind you about a certain exclusive contract you signed."

"I *told* you I'd bring the lead sheets over. What more do you want from me?"

There were a few seconds of silence. "I'd like you not to bring flowers to my girl."

See, that's what was really bothering him. Remember when he went nuts that day at Schrafft's when he saw the stupid flowers?

"Like *you'd* bring her any," I said, and hung up. That made me feel pretty cool, talking to him like that. Then I spent the next hour wondering when he'd get around to breaking my neck.

And that same day, Preston called. *He* wanted the lead sheets, too. Christ, was I in a bind. I told him, "Look, I can't publish with your organization."

And he said, "What do you mean, can't?"

"I'm sorry, but I've got an exclusive contract with K.O. Publishing."

"You never told me that, Rudy."

"Well, you never asked."

"Contracts were made to be broken, Rudy. We can have our legal department look into it."

"No," I said. "You don't understand. I gave them my word. I can't go back on it."

"Rudy, I'm sorry to have to tell you this, but without publishing interest, Caboose is highly unlikely to give your records any promotion. What you need is my name on those songs along with yours, because people in the industry know me, and will be more inclined to give you air time."

Now, where had I heard *that* song and dance before? And here's a funny thing – if Blue Rose was a division of Tal Ltd., why did Caboose give a shit about the publishing end? Unless Caboose was somehow related to both Blue Rose and Tal Ltd.. Are you catching on?

"I'm sorry, Preston," I said. "I gave my word."

He waited a second, and then said, "Rudy, I'm very disappointed to hear that. Very disappointed." And then the phone clicked and was dead.

No kidding, he was disappointed. Of course he was disappointed. I'll tell you why he was so goddamn disappointed – it was because he saw the publishing money fly out the window. Bobby had been right about him. He was just like every other two-bit *shtarker* in the business. But I needed an agent. What the hell could I do?

So I hopped the D-Train and took the lead sheets to K.O.. When I walked in, the place was empty. No desperate songwriters pissing nervously down the pegged legs of their pants in the waiting room. No Lisa. Not even any Sal, just Sherm. I knocked on his office door, which was part-way open, and he looked up like he was surprised to see me.

He said, "Oh, hello, Rudy."

I walked in and sat down. "Where the hell is everybody?"

Sherm had his hands folded across his middle – he had kind of a paunch – and he swiveled in his chair a few times. "I guess you haven't heard, then."

And I said heard what, and he said about the business, and I said what about the business, and he told me that it looked like it was finished, that they weren't buying any new songs, and he had to let Lisa go.

"You're joking," I said.

And Sherm said, "I'm afraid not. K.O. has been K.O.-ed."

Well, hell. I didn't know what to say. I just sat there looking at the lead sheets.

"What do you have – new songs?"

"Yeah. Sal called and said I'd better get them down here *toot sweet*, whatever that means."

Sherm stood up and walked over and took the sheets out of my hand. He looked them over and then gave them back to me. "Are these for your new record?" he asked.

I told him yeah, that my agency wanted me to publish with one of their subdivisions, but I was sticking to my agreement with K.O..

"That must've made them happy," he said, and smiled.

"Oh yeah. They're so thrilled they're ready to let my record flop. Said I wouldn't get any promotion unless I published with them, but I gave my word to you and Sal. I'm no double-crosser."

Sherm pushed some papers out of the way and sat down on top of his desk. "You want some advice, Rudy?"

"Who, *me*? Sure." Sherm was kind of a fatherly guy. He was the calm one in the organization, if you could call that joint an organization, and I guess you couldn't anymore.

"Go ahead and give them the songs."

Do you get that? I didn't get it. I said, "Shit – I can't do that. Sal keeps saying he's gonna put my wazzoo on a platter or something."

Sherm sat very still and looked very kind of *knowing* at me. "You're young, Rudy. You've got a career ahead of you. With the right promotion, you could make a lot of money with those two songs. Take the money, Rudy."

"But what about Sal?" What about my wazzoo, for that matter?

"I'll take care of Sal."

"He's gonna be pissed, Sherm."

Sherm laughed. "Like he won't be pissed if he sees a lead sheet titled 'Oh, Brenda!' I'll take care of Sal. Don't worry. Go out and make those songs hits."

I stood up and headed for the door.

"Oh – and Rudy?" Sherm called out.

"Yeah?"

"That's a nice song, that Brenda song."

I didn't know how he knew that just from looking at the lead sheet, but I said, "Thanks," anyway.

"Going to put some strings on it?"

That was exactly what Hoyt wanted to do. How would he know something like that?

"No – I ... no. I don't like strings."

"Too bad," he said.

And that was that. I left the Brill Building kind of confused.

Get this. I walked over to Preston's office, all right? I figured he'd be happy now that he could have the publishing rights. Reasonable assumption, wouldn't you say? But he *wasn't* happy.

"How old are you, Rudy?" he said.

"Eighteen," I said.

"Let's see your driver's license."

"Uh ..."

"Well?"

"I ... I haven't exactly got one."

"Oh? What exactly *do* you have?"

I hated having to admit that I couldn't drive. There was only one thing I hated more than having to admit that, and that was having to admit I was seventeen. I graduated early because I skipped third grade. I used to be bright – had an I.Q. of 160. Don't ask me what happened.

"Our legal department checked your birth certificate at City Hall. You are seventeen years of age. Your signature on those contracts is invalid."

"I gave you my word. My word is good."

"Not good enough," Preston said. Then he handed me a whole stack of *new* contracts.

"What do you want me to do with *these*?" I said.

And you know what he said? He said, "I want you to have a parent sign them, and then bring them back to me."

66

Christ! Can you see that? Can you see me going to my mother and saying, "Ma, could you please sign these papers so I can sing rock and roll and wiggle my hips in pants so tight you can see the moons of my *tochkes?*"

So I said, "I can't."

And Preston said, "You *have* to."

And I said, "But I *can't.*"

And then he leaned over his desk, holding himself up by his hands, and said, "That's too bad, Rudy. Especially considering the five thousand dollar advance check I have for you, and the date I just made for you to open the Biggest Show Of Stars Autumn Tour."

Well, *schtup* me! Now I had to do it. *I was going to play on a tour with Buddy Holly!* I could see the marquee already:

BIGGEST SHOW OF STARS! FEATURING BUDDY HOLLY, WALDEN CASSOTTO – NO, MAKE THAT BOBBY DARIN, WITH BOBBY FREEMAN, DION AND THE BELMONTS, CLYDE McPHATTER, AND THE SLIGHTLY SEX-OBSESSED MUSIC OF TEEN SENSATION R U D Y K E E N ! ! ! ! ! ! ! ! ! !

I'd walk on stage and the crowd would go wild. Teen-age girls would rip their bras off and throw them at me. Some girl named Louise, with real big tits, would lean over to her friend, Connie or somebody, and say, "I can see the moons of his *tochkes!*" At the end of the show all the stars would be waiting backstage to congratulate me, and to make me the new headliner. Then the marquee at the next stop on the tour would read:

THE FABULOUS SEX SYMBOL RUDY KEEN! IN PERSON! WITH SOME OTHER GUYS WHO ONLY WISH THEY WERE AS GOOD.

I snapped out of it as Preston picked up the pile of contracts. I snatched them out of his hands, and as I went running out the door, I said, "I'll be back as soon as I can!"

"I want that signature notarized, Rudy."

"Yeah, yeah, yeah!" I said.

It was two hours later. I was leaning over the table in the kitchen of our apartment, saying, "*Please,* I don't want to hear anymore about having to get my arm cut off and buried with the *goyim*, or about Gary Goldfarb's career as a goddamn accountant and his lovely co-op on Seventy-first Street. Please just sign the contracts, Ma. I'll promise you anything. *Anything.*"

Ma was sitting at the table, staring at the big mess of contracts as if they were some horrible non-kosher food – *cheeseburgers*, maybe. After a long time, she lifted her head and said, "Any-ting?"

"Yes! Yes! Yes! *Any-ting.*"

"All right, then."

"You'll sign them?"

She nodded. "But I vont you should go back to the *yeshiva.*"

"Ma! I'll be on the road!"

"So ven you get back from the road, you go to the *yeshiva.*"

What – you think I didn't promise? I would've promised my left nut to get on that tour. (There's a stupid expression for you. Why is it always the *left* nut everybody promises? It's not as good as the right nut? But I digress.) One day I'd be a rock and roll star, the next – I'd be sitting in the *yeshiva*, wearing a yalmuke, reading the Torah and whistling "Hound Dog." They could've made a movie about me – *I Was A Teen-Age Schizophrenic Jewish Idol.*

♪　♫　♪

Do you know what I did with the five thousand dollars? I went right out and bought a black Thunderbird. Yeah! I didn't even have a driver's license, and I'd never been behind the wheel of a car before, but that didn't stop me. I had this manic rush going – freedom! Success! Fame! I drove through Central Park all day before I discovered I'd had the T-Bird in low gear the whole time. Then I put it in drive, and WHOA! I must've done a hundred past the zoo. Freaked out a zebra.

When the thrill of the car wore off, guess who was on my mind? Who else? Brenda. I started singing that song I wrote about her, and pretty soon I couldn't think of anything but her. I drove over to Schrafft's and parked the car illegally. I didn't care. The damn thing didn't have any plates. Anyway, this girl who was working the counter told me Brenda had called-in sick. She wouldn't give me her phone number, so I asked her if she'd at least *dial* it, and then hand me the phone. She said okay, but then she got busy, and I ordered a sandwich, and of course by the time she got around to handing me the receiver, my mouth was full of food and I had nothing to wash it down with. Brenda kept saying, "Hello? Hello? Who *is* this?"

"Wooo-dee."

"Who? I can't understand you."

I forced it down dry and almost ruptured my throat. Oh *God*, did it hurt. Then I couldn't talk at all; all I could do was gurgle into the phone like a brain-dead *schlemiel*.

"Aghl-aghl-aghl."

Brenda went nuts. "Look, I don't know who you are, but I told you last night never to call me again, you pervert. I don't appreciate this kind of call."

By then the waitress had finally brought me a glass of water and I was able to put out the fire in my throat. "Don't hang up, hey. It's me. It's Rudy."

"Rudy? *You're* the pervert who keeps calling?"

Apparently I was *one* of them. "No – you don't understand. I was choking on a sandwich."

"Oh, thank God you called. Can you meet me ... soon? Say in about a half hour?"

"Well, sure. Sure I can. Why? What's the – "

"Go to that little restaurant on Ninety-sixth and Broadway. Hurry, Rudy."

"Isn't that where Sal hangs out, though?"

"Just hurry, Rudy."

So I said okay, I'd meet her, and I got her phone number before I hung up. Wrote it on my wrist.

I remember I was so worried about her that I was shaking. What was all this about? I blasted my way uptown. Even though it was only my second driving experience, and even though I didn't know Jack shit about the rules of the road, nobody knew the difference. Hey – it was New York, all right? In New York, *everybody* drives like me. When I got there I parked the T-Bird right in front of the restaurant. Man, I knew she was going to die when she saw it.

I took a table with a view of the door so I could see her when she came in. Seven o'clock – no sign of her. I ordered cheesecake. The cheesecake was okay. Seven-thirty – she still hadn't arrived, so I asked the waiter for a beer.

The waiter said, "May I see your driver's license, sir?"

What was it with everybody and driver's licenses? "Look," I told him, "I want to *drink* it, not take it for a spin around the block. Just bring me a beer."

And hot damn, he did. I didn't look old enough to go on most of the rides at Coney Island, but I got served. Must've been the way I was dressed – very sophisticated. Plaid sport coat, pink Italian slacks, tan suede boots. The beer was a bad idea, though. I got drunk on half a bottle.

Eight o'clock – no Brenda. Now I was getting worried. I got up and went to the pay phone near the bathrooms and dialed her number. No answer. I thought maybe she was on her way over, so I sat down again and watched the door. One minute, two minutes, three minutes – and then guess who walked in? Sal, the bastard. What were the odds? I mean, what were the *odds*? He breezed through the room with that macho swaggering bullshit of his. He was about to sit down at a table, until he spotted me. Then he pushed his jaw forward and tossed his head back like a pit bull with a stiff neck, and did his fascist shuffle over to where I was sitting.

He said, "Mr. Fancy Clothes. Look at you. Ain't you somethin'? Imported threads from Modena. How'd you afford those, Rudy? Sell out the guy who gave you your big break?"

I didn't even give a damn that people were staring. I stood up and squared off with him. It was really a stupid thing to do. The top of my head came up to the middle of his chest. We looked like before-and-after pictures of a pygmy who'd been given the growth hormone. *Oy*, was I drunk.

"You didn't gimme any goddamn break," I said. "All you did was steal half my songs and half my goddamn *gelt*."

He looked like the fucking Incredible Swarthy Hulk. He bent his head down and gritted his teeth. "Weasel," he said.

I was swaying a little – either that or there was some unusual geological activity in New York, that night. I moved in on him until my nose was nearly touching his tie. "Ass-grabbing swine," I said.

He may have been getting ready to hit me, in fact, I'm *sure* he was getting ready to hit me, but the waiter got between us and said, "Gentlemen, is there some problem? Hm?"

Sal looked around and saw everybody gawking at us, and then he straightened the crease in his pants by tapping it a few times. "No. No problem," he said, and then he stomped on my foot as hard as he could. Christ, the *pain*! I thought I'd lost all my toes. I could picture them, all cut off and scattered around the inside of my boot. But I was so *shikker* I didn't even scream. He was on his way out of the place, but before he left, he turned around and flipped me the Italian bird – his hand under his chin, you know.

I wondered if it was just a coincidence that he'd shown up when I was supposed to meet Brenda, or if he'd somehow found out about our date, and kept her from coming. Maybe he'd scared her, or threatened her. Because by nine o'clock, Brenda hadn't come through the door. I tried wiggling my toes, but I couldn't feel them. I was sure they'd been amputated. But what was I supposed to do – take my boots off at the table and count them? I finished my beer and ordered another. I couldn't have counted if I'd wanted to. Ten o'clock. Eleven o'clock.

Hey man, she never showed.

♪ ♫ ♪

"Rudolph? Rudolph! Vake up. Some *farshlugenah* Nazi vit a cap on is here, and he sez yer late for the tour."

"Huh?"

The next thing I knew, Reinhardt was in my bedroom shaking hell out of me, trying to get me up.

"C'mon, Keen. Mr. Allerton's been lookin' for you for days. Where've ya been? The tour leaves in an hour, and yer holdin' up the goddamn bus."

It all started coming back to me, slow-like, in a fog. After Brenda didn't show up that night, I'd gone on a binge. It's how I learned to stay away from alcohol. *I can't drink.* I told you, I get nuts on one beer. A six-pack could keep me drunk for a week.

I said, "Where's my car?"

"What car?" Reinhardt said.

"My Thunderbird. My Rudymobile."

"When was the last time you saw it?"

I had no idea. Two days? Three? I thought for a second while Reinhardt rolled up the window shade. Agghh! Solar torture. "I don't know," I said. "I parked it somewhere in Manhattan."

Reinhardt said, "*Where* in Manhattan?"

"Fuck if I know. Hey – pull the shade down, will ya?"

"You gotta get movin', Rudy. The bus is waitin' and you look like shit."

You knew you were in trouble if Reinhardt thought you looked

71

like shit. The guy was a walking ad for pockmarks. Some way to start a career – I was hungover, late for my first tour, I'd lost my brand new T-Bird, and the girl I loved had stood me up. I pulled my hand out from under the covers to see if her phone number was still on my wrist, but it wasn't. I must've washed it off. Or maybe I just *drooled* it off.

On the way into town I asked Reinhardt where my guitar and stage clothes were.

"In the trunk. Say, kiddo – as long as yer late anyway, what say we stop off and – "

"I don't want to hear about any whistles!"

"Take it easy. Take it easy," he said. He drove on and kept checking me in the rearview mirror. Then he said, "Yer all tied in knots. Tense. That's what the poisons'll do to you, make you all edgy. It's the poisons, I tell ya."

"You think so?"

"I *know* so. It's not up to me, but if *I* was goin' on my first national tour, *I* wouldn't want to take a chance that my poisons might mess up my performance."

Holy shit, I thought. *Wouldn't it be something if I went out in front of all those people and bombed, all because of my poisons?*

What—you think I'm *proud* that I listened to him? I'm not *proud* of it. But I was only human. All right, maybe a little *more* than human because of the genius IQ thing, but still human. Christ, that place smelled like a cheap whorehouse. The place *was* a cheap whorehouse. Flocked wallpaper, plastic flowers in ugly vases. She was pretty good looking, my rent-a-girl, Avis, or whatever her name was. But a little too ready? Jesus. "Ooh," she told me, "ooh, someone needs to relax."

"It's the poisons," I said. "I'm only here to get them removed."

And she said, "Come again?"

Again? I thought. *What does she mean*, again?

She was all over me. She started unbuttoning my shirt, and saying I was going to see fireworks, that it was going to be like the Fourth of July or something. She was very patriotic, for a slut. And what do you know – she was right. By the time she was on the third button, there were skyrockets and marching bands, Roman candles and "Stars And Stripes Forever." I was the John Philip Sousa of love.

I got out of bed, buttoned my shirt back up, and said, "Thanks."

That's when she went postal. "Thanks? Thanks for *what?* I didn't even get your shirt off!"

"But everything else got off, so – "

"What about *me?* Ain't I supposed to get no pleasure?"

Have you ever heard such *chutzpah* in your life? I apologized, but that wasn't good enough for her. She kept criticizing me. Called me *Minute Man.*

"Look," I said, "quit calling me that. In the first place, you don't mean '*Ain't I supposed to get no pleasure.*' That's a double negative. It's '*any* pleasure.' And in the second place, who's the whore around here, you or me?"

And she said what did I mean by that, and I said I meant that *I* was the customer, not *her.* Then she threw a pillow at me and kicked me out of the room. "Minute Man," she said again, and slammed the door.

I would've been better off with my goddamn poisons.

I waited out in the hallway for Reinhardt to finish. I don't know what the hell was going on in his room, but they had Wagner on the record player and a few times I thought I heard whips cracking. I'm willing to bet he learned how to be a chauffeur by driving in a *panzer* division. I'll give you odds, in fact.

I was the last one on the tour bus. They'd held it for me. While Reinhardt loaded my stuff in the luggage compartment, Preston was waiting for me at the door, tapping his foot.

"I hope it wasn't inconvenient waking you up for your first tour." Sarcastic son of a bitch.

"At least my whistle's clean," I said.

"I won't even ask what that means." He handed me an envelope. "This is your itinerary and song list. Your record, in case you're interested, was released six days ago and has yet to chart. It's up to you to make it a hit. Make sure you bring the house down when you play. Do you understand?"

I nodded and got on the bus. The driver started to close the door, but I banged it open because all of a sudden I remembered about my T-Bird. I asked Preston if he could have somebody find it, and he gave me a prissy little snotty look and pulled a pen and a pad from his suit coat and asked what the license number was, and I told him it didn't have any license plates, and he looked like he wanted to kill me when he asked where he should start looking, and I said Manhattan, and his eye started twitching and he said, any particular part of Manhattan? and I said if I knew *that*, the goddamn car wouldn't be lost.

Then the bus driver, the rude bastard, he closed the door right in my face. I turned around and saw all the performers and musicians staring at me. None of them looked too happy.

"*That's* the little prick we've been waiting for?" I heard someone say. I started walking down the aisle, but no one would slide over in their seats to make room for me.

"Hey, Rudy! Back here!"

It was Walden. Man, was I glad to see somebody I knew.

"Howsa boy?" Walden said.

"I'm a little late."

"I noticed. *Everybody* noticed."

He wasn't kidding. They were all turned around in their seats, looking at me the way the kids on the playground used to, just before they beat the shit out of me and kicked my violin around.

I said, "Hey, Walden – "

"Shhh," he whispered, holding a finger in front of his lips. "It's *Bobby*, remember?"

"Oh, yeah. Right. Listen, Bobby – you won't believe what's happened to me in the last week. I bought this car, see, and Sal's girl tells me over the phone she's got to meet me, but when I go to where she tells me, Sal (the swine) walks in and we nearly get into a fight, and then I got drunk and lost my car, and I washed Sal's girl's phone number off my wrist, and then my mother wakes me up, and the next thing I know, Reinhardt's got me in a whorehouse to get rid of my poisons, and then I hear whips, and ..."

"Who wound Junior's rubber band so tight?" some guy sitting behind Bobby said. I was about to tell him to fuck off, until I saw he was wearing these big, black, ugly spaceman glasses, lenses that made his eyes look like *bowling* balls, for Christ's sake, and I nearly lost my breath.

"*You're Buddy Holly!*" I said.

"I know."

"*You're Buddy Fuckin' Holly!*"

"I know," he said again. "Who the hell are *you?*"

Walden introduced us, and I forgot to let go of his hand after I shook it. He had to pull it away from me.

"Don't mind Rudy," Bobby said. "Sometimes he's like an album track playing at seventy-eight. This is his first tour."

74

"W-a-a-l-l," Buddy drawled, "that's what we're gonna call you from now on, Rudy – Mr. Seventy-eight RPM." He leaned his head back against his seat, closed his eyes, and fell asleep. Slept for the whole rest of the trip. What a pro. He even *snored* on key.

And that's how I met Charles Hardin Holly. It was one of the most important days of his life – believe me.

♪   ♫   ♪

Late that night I was standing outside of a motel in Worcester, Massachusetts, lonely as hell. I was thinking about home (even Brooklyn looks good from a distance), and Brenda, and wondering why she'd stood me up that night. I went over to the soda machine to get a Green River, but the goddamn thing ate my dime and wouldn't give me the bottle. I kept yanking and yanking on it (the bottle), and mumbling, "Dirty stupid son of a bitch bastard machine," when someone dropped another dime in and I fell over on my ass when the bottle slipped out. I looked up and saw Buddy. He crossed his arms, leaning against the side of the motel. I remember this real well. I can even tell you what he was wearing. He had on a salmon-colored t-shirt and tan wrinkled pants. Two-tone shoes – real gone. He looked like a record cover come to life.

"Thanks," I said.

"You're gonna pee all night."

"I can't sleep anyway," I said.

Buddy stood away from the wall and put an arm around my shoulders. "Stage fright, or homesick?"

"Who, *me?* Neither. I'm a professional, man." I opened the bottle and it erupted. Buddy jumped out of the way as it sprayed all over me – my face, my shirt, my pants. What a dripping mess. I looked like I'd just taken a *swim* in a green river.

Buddy smiled and lowered his head. "Sure you are, Seventy-eight."

How humiliating. I put the bottle down and started wringing out my shirt. "Buddy," I said, "when you were new at this, I mean brand new, did it take you a while to catch on?"

"Naw. I've always been pretty good with a pop bottle."

"That's not what I meant. I meant getting along with the other acts, and understanding all the contracts you have to sign."

"Why, sure. But once you start doing the shows, y'all become a team. Of course, the guys might take to you faster if you stop making the bus driver pull over every fifteen minutes for pisscall."

"I can't help it," I said. "I've got a very weak bladder."

Buddy laughed. "You'd never know you had one at all. Now, 'bout the business – don't you have management?"

"Oh, yeah. I've got a big company behind me – Tal Limited."

When I said that he sort of moved backwards and wrinkled his forehead. "Not Preston Allerton, I hope."

"Why – you know him?"

He shook his head and kicked at some pebbles on the ground. "*Know* him? You don't forget a guy who steals publishing and collection rights out from under your nose."

Shit. It was just like Bobby said.

"He *stole* them?"

"Waaall," Buddy said, "it looked legal on paper, but it amounts to the same thing. That ole boy is lower than a nightcrawler's ass durin' a drought. I'll bet he told you his name should be on your songs so the stations will play them. Am I right?"

Right? He might as well have been a psychic. "But what should I do?" I asked.

"I don't know, Seventy-eight. If I were you, I'd have a lawyer look over those contracts and try to break 'em somehow. Till then, I wouldn't feed him any more material, 'cause he'll own whatever you give him."

I felt sick about how stupid I'd been. I think Buddy must've known, because to cheer me up, he asked me did I feel like playing some guitar with him. Did I *feel* like it? I would've traded my T-Bird for a chance to play with Buddy – if I'd known where it was.

We went back to his room and he pulled out two acoustic six strings. He had the most beautiful Gibson model I'd ever seen. Man, it was a fine guitar. Sounded like an organ, it rang so nice and sweet. He played "Not Fade Away," and I joined in, singing the background vocals and strumming the Bo Didley rhythm part. Then I played "Twenty Flight Rock," an Eddie Cochran song, and Buddy sang the last line of the chorus. When I went into "Bop-Sha-Bop," Buddy cracked up.

"I can't believe they let you keep that part in – 'You make me wanna pop.' They banned that song in Lubbock."

"They did? Why?"

He laughed and laughed. "See, they don't 'low no poppin' on

Lubbock radio."

Which is why I was glad I was from New York. You can pop all you want, there. But it hit me then how far I'd come – I was in a motel room with Buddy Holly, the night before my public debut. There'd be spotlights, crowds, All at once my legs went numb and I felt like I'd turned to stone.

Buddy looked at me. "Nervous?" he said.

"Scared to death," I said.

He let one arm hang over the neck of his Gibson. "Look here – the walk out to center stage, after they announce your name and the audience is cheerin', that can be the longest walk of your life. But what happens is, the band kicks in, and all the faces out there fade into a haze. When you start singin', the music grabs you, gives you the *all-overs*. You feel it all over, and pretty soon you become the song ... ."

♪ 🎵 ♪

"Ladies and gentlemen, cool cats and pretty kitties, here he is now, from Brooklyn, New York, the newest teen rage, *Mr. Rudy Keen!*"

It was just like Buddy said it would be, the next night, when I walked out to center stage. It was a long, slow walk, and the crowd was losing their minds. The band hit the introduction to "Whoa Baby, Whoa," and I screeched out a riff on my new Rickenbacker guitar. I stepped up to the microphone, sang the first line – and all I remember is a flash, a blinding blue jolt of electricity. When I woke up, I was in the Worcester Memorial Hospital emergency room. A nurse said, "He's coming out of it."

I thought I was dreaming. I figured I must've gone out with the band after the show and gotten so drunk I couldn't remember doing my set.

"What's going on?" I said.

A doctor walked over and shined a little flashlight in my eyes.

"Ow! Turn that goddamn thing off! What's going on?"

The doctor said, "You've had an accident."

"An accident? That's impossible. I was on stage. I was playing my guitar."

"That's right, Mr. Keen. You were playing your guitar, until you electrocuted yourself with it."

I still can't believe it. All these years later and it still seems like a dream. Something was wrong with my patch cord. It shorted out all the electricity in the auditorium – the lights, the sound system. My first public appearance, up in smoke.

They made me stay in the hospital overnight, and the next morning Bobby came by and asked me how I was doing.

"I'm fine, except my eyebrows. They got singed off. The doctor says they might grow back. Or they might not. Do they look funny?"

Bobby flopped a newspaper on my bed. "Page forty-seven," he said.

He didn't say whether they looked funny or not, so I guess they did. I opened the paper to page forty-seven. There was a review of the concert.

WATTS HAPPENIN', BABY!

It's certain that the teens in attendance weren't prepared for the electrifying performance they witnessed last night at the Worcester Auditorium. Billed as "The Biggest Show Of Stars Of 1958," audience members say it was indeed, as newcomer rocker Rudy Keen turned himself into a supernova, four seconds into his set.

"There was this blue explosion, then everything went dark and quiet," says Mary Tepper, 16, of Boston. "I closed my eyes, but I couldn't stop seeing that bright blue light. I thought I'd been blinded."

A faulty electrical cord is being blamed for the musical fiasco. It seems that Keen was unaware that the insulation of his guitar connection had been worn away, transforming him literally into a real live wire. Headliners found it impossible to follow Keen's act, for power still has not been restored. Keen himself is hospitalized in good condition.

It was a mostly silent night, last night, at the Auditorium, but fans are not likely to forget the four-second debut of Electric Rudy Keen.

"The publicity might be good for you," Bobby said.

I just stared at the newspaper.

"A lot of times we don't even get reviewed."

Son of a bitch, I thought.

"They spelled your name right, Rudy."

It was over on page forty-eight, a little news item near the bottom of the page.

MISSING WAITRESS MET WITH FOUL PLAY

Some clothing and personal items belonging to Brenda Taylor, 20, of New York, were found alongside the banks of the Hudson River, Tuesday. Taylor had been reported missing by her employer, Schrafft's Restaurant, several days prior to the discovery.

"It doesn't look good," said Detective Eugene Seymour. "There are signs of a struggle – ripped clothing and what-have-you." Police later confirmed that an anonymous caller claimed to have witnessed a heated bout at the location where the clothing was found. The attacker apparently beat the young waitress and then threw her into the river.

No trace of her body has yet been found.

I let go of the paper. I'd never felt so empty inside. He'd gone and done it. He'd really gone and done it.

5   'Jelly Baby'

10/19/58

Dear Rudy,

I'm sorry it's taken me so long to write, but I haven't had a free second until now. The tour was a real wringer. The bus was an old heap, and the kid who replaced you, Derek Halloway, was a pain in the ass. I hope your recovery is coming along fine. Bobby told me about your eyebrows. Don't worry; they'll grow back. How come I know is this: I once had a mutt that got too close to an incinerator, and fifty percent of his fur got scorched off. It took two of us to put him out - the fire, I mean. We had to roll him up in a towel. Boy, when that old doggie went up in flames, I thought I'd just about seen everything - until I caught your act. Anyway, in a couple of months you never would've known it. All the fur grew back. Except in a few places.

Everyone's still talking about how you set the stage on fire. Laughing about it, mostly. They all hope you'll be joining us for The Winter Dance Party Tour. (They're not calling you Seventy-eight no more. Now you're *Electric Rudy*.) Don't worry about having to listen to 'Didi Dinah' every night. Frankie can't make it. Neither can Bobby, but Dion and the guys will be back, and I know you like them. Oh - and listen, The Big Bopper is signed, so advance warning. No jokes, please. He can't help being a big goof.

About the business we discussed at the motel that night - I hope you've had a lawyer look over your contracts. Since we talked, I've been hearing similar complaints about one P.A. (initials) from Sam Cooke and Eddie Cochran. Sam got out of his legal mess with P.A., but Eddie is still under obligation. I mentioned your problem to both of them, and they'll be happy to meet with you. Enclosed are

80

numbers where you can reach them.

I'm going into the studio at the end of the month, or early in November. Hope you can be there. For now, all the best, and remember that mutt I told you about. (Although when the fur grew back, it did look a might scruffy, but no matter.)

Sincerely,

Buddy Holly

I keep that letter in my wallet. It's pretty much falling to pieces by now, but it's the only letter Buddy ever wrote me (except for one little note I'll tell you about later), and I like to have it close by.

Brenda's death knocked me for a loop. I know I wasn't her boyfriend or anything, but I loved her. For the first week I was home, all I did was stay in bed. What finally got me up and around again was my mother's chicken soup. I couldn't stand another spoonful of it – so I *had* to get out of bed.

There was an announcement in the newspaper about a memorial service for Brenda, so I called her family and asked if I could come. They said yes, that anyone who was a friend of Brenda's was invited. They sounded like nice people. But the day before the service, I got this idea. I thought I'd stop in at the central police headquarters in Manhattan and talk to the guy who was handling the investigation of Brenda's murder. I'm always getting ideas like that. What I should do is just ignore them, but I don't. And did I ever get looks at that goddamn police station. You'd think they'd never seen a guy with no eyebrows before. But I didn't care. I just wanted to get Sal's ass locked up, and fast.

This one officer took me back to Lieutenant Detective Seymour's office. I had to wait forty minutes till he opened his door and asked me to come in.

"I understand you want to see me about the Taylor case," he said.

And I said, "That's right. I know who did it."

He'd just picked up a pencil and was about to write something down, but he stopped. He started twirling the pencil around with his fingers.

"You do, huh? And just how do you know that?"

"Because she was dating a bastard, that's how. Sal DeGrazzia. He's the bastard you want."

He tapped the pencil on his desk. "We know who Sal DeGrazzia is. We're looking into him. Do you have anything else to go on – besides him being a bastard?"

"Yeah – he saw me bring flowers to Brenda one night, and he threatened me. He just went nuts. And another time – just before she got killed, she called me. Said she had to meet me in a hurry, at a restaurant on Ninety-sixth and Broadway. She never showed up, but Sal did. He told me to stop bringing her flowers. Brenda told me herself that he was a real jealous son of a bitch, and – "

"*She* said he was a son of a bitch?" he interrupted me.

"No. She didn't use that kind of language. She was a real classy lady. An angel. She had these big – "

"Who called him a son of a bitch?"

"I did. Just now. You got to pay more attention. Anyway, you didn't know Brenda. She was beautiful. She had these gorgeous big, and I mean *big* – "

But he didn't want to hear about Brenda and all the things she had that were so big, like her eyes, for instance. I don't know how the legal system in this country ever got so screwed up. There I was, an innocent citizen, trying to do my civic goddamn duty – and Lieutenant Seymour started questioning *me*. He wanted to know where *I* was the night she disappeared. I told him – at the restaurant. But then he said no, where did I go after I left the restaurant, and I said I don't know, and he said why don't you know, and I said because I got drunk.

"You got drunk? Where did you get drunk?"

"I started at that restaurant, and then I went someplace else."

He leaned over his desk and looked at me with his rivet eyes, like he was going to fasten me to the wall with them. "What someplace else – what was the name of the place?"

"Hell if I know. I just told you. I was drunk. I even forgot where I parked my car."

"You were *driving*? You were driving drunk?"

"Yeah. But with me you wouldn't know the difference."

Boy, was he ever a suspicious son of a bitch. He made me tell that story over about a thousand times, and then he asked me if I'd take a lie detector test. Yeah! He thought I was lying,

"Me?" I said. "Why *me*? Why aren't you out there arresting Sal DeGrazzia?"

"You sure want to see him put away, don't you?"

"You're goddamn right I do. He's a murdering bastard, I already told you."

I had to agree to the stupid lie detector test, because once they ask you, if you say no, you look guilty. They took me down some stairs to another office and hooked a bunch of wires up to me. It made me kind of nervous, the wires – ever since that stage incident, I didn't trust electricity. Then I heard Seymour whisper to a sergeant, "I think we've got a new slant here, see? Love triangle." He scribbled some stuff down and handed it to the guy who was working the machine. Once the paper started rolling, the lie detector guy asked me a bunch of dumb questions.

"What's your name?"

"Rudy Keen."

They both looked at the machine, and then at each other.

"The machine says you're lying."

"Oh – that's my stage name. Ask me again."

"What's your name?"

"Rudolph Kearns."

"It says you're lying again," the guy said.

"It does? Oh. I know. I'm not supposed to tell anybody, but we had it changed from *Kearnstein*. Go ahead. Ask me again."

The guy was practically pulling his hair out. "I'm *not* gonna ask you again. I don't really give a damn who you are. Tell me where you live."

"In an apartment."

He was tapping his fingers on the table and looked like he wanted to shoot me. "I meant your *address*."

"Forty-seven twelve McKinney."

"What's your occupation?"

"Teen idol."

"*What?*" They really should've gotten that guy some blood pressure medication. He was going berserk. I think he'd been around that crazy machine too long.

"I'm a rock and roll star."

They looked at the needle on the paper. Nice and easy lines, it was drawing. "Says he's telling the truth," the machine guy said.

83

"Of course I'm telling the truth. Haven't you ever heard 'Bop-Sha-Bop'?"

"No."

Squares. They probably still listened to Guy Lombardo.

"What happened to your eyebrows?"

"Look – I'd rather not discuss that. It's embarrassing."

"Just answer the question, Keen, or Kearns, or Kearnstein, or whoever the hell you are."

What could I do? "I electrocuted myself onstage at the Worcester, Massachusetts Auditorium and burned them off."

The lie detector guy looked up at Seymour and said, "Hey! I read about him in the newspaper. He's the guy."

"What guy?" Seymour said, stubbing out a cigarette.

"The one who fried himself onstage with his guitar and blew out every transformer clear to Boston."

"Oh, a troublemaker, huh?" Seymour said.

"It was an accident," I said. "See, if you play electric guitar, you've got to make sure the insulation on your patch cord – "

Then Seymour said it was all because of rock and roll, that it was going to ruin the country one way or another. He called it *animal music*. What a *putz*.

But the lie detector guy was pretty impressed with me all of a sudden. "Hey, can you get me Frankie Laine's autograph?"

"Who?"

"Frankie Laine. You know – the singer."

"No."

"And you call yourself a star."

I was losing patience with these two. *Frankie Laine*, for Christ's sake.

You should've heard what they asked me then – stuff that had nothing to do with Brenda or her murder. I found out later it was to see what the needle looked like on the graph when they knew I was telling the truth. But at the time, I thought they'd lost their minds.

"How many eggs are in a dozen?"

"Huh?"

"Answer the question."

"Twelve. But ..."

"Who's Dinah Shore's sponsor?"

"Come on," I said.

"Who *is* it?"

84

"Chevrolet. Everybody knows that."

"Who's buried in Grant's tomb?"

"Dinah Shore."

Seymour said, "Keen, I'm warning you."

"Or it could be Frankie Laine."

"Where's the Eiffel Tower?"

"Why – is it missing?"

"Quit wisin' off!" Seymour shouted.

"I can't help it!" I said. "He keeps asking me these stupid questions!"

But then the lie detector guy asked me this one: "Were you Brenda Taylor's lover?"

I sort of tranced out. I saw Brenda in my head, that pretty face, that nice smile, those big –

"Well, were you?" he asked again.

"No."

They both looked at the needle, and then back at me.

"Did you ever have sex with Brenda Taylor?"

What a thing to ask! They shouldn't have gone around asking people personal questions like that, especially about a sweet girl like Brenda. I said *no*, and the goddamn lie detector said I was lying. At first I thought it was broken, but then I remembered a couple of dreams I'd had about Brenda. I won't go into them here, but maybe the machine couldn't tell the difference between what I did in my dreams, and what I did in real life. Ask O.J.. He'll tell you what kind of shit dreams and lie detectors can get you into.

"Did you kill Brenda Taylor?"

"Of course not!" I said.

That's when it dawned on me what kind of a jam I was in. They really thought *I* did it. I wouldn't have hurt a hair on her head ... or anywhere else on her body, for that matter. She was my teen dream, my first love. The two of them huddled over the paper that came out of the machine and started putting pencil marks on it while I sat there with a bunch of wires stuck to me, looking like a sprouting potato.

"Hey," I said. "Can I go now, or do you still think I took the Eiffel Tower?"

The lie detector guy took the wires off me. Seymour folded up the graph paper and sneered. "A guy in your shoes oughtn't to crack so wise, Keen." He took a cigarette out of a pack in his shirt pocket and lit it. "You liked that Brenda babe quite a lot, didn't you?"

"Yeah, I did. Can I go now?"

He tilted his head while he looked at me, the way a cocker spaniel does when he can't figure out which hand the Milk Bone is in. "Sure. Sure, you can go. We'll be seein' you again, though. I wouldn't leave town, if I were you. And I'd get myself an attorney, too, see?" I stood up, but Seymour wasn't finished. "Oh – and Keen? Tell me something."

"What?"

"How did it feel, all that electricity goin' through you?"

I know what you're thinking. You're thinking, *Cripes Rudy, that was a pointed reference to the electric chair* – and it was, too. But I kept my cool. I said, "Well, to be honest, it made me feel stupid. Very stupid. Kind of like what it must feel like to be a cop, I guess."

I figured, what the hell, I couldn't be in any more trouble if I tried, so I should at least keep my self-respect.

♪　♫　♪

"*Oy, vey iz mir!* Aren't you a *shemen zikh*? Vot kinda *pek'l tsuris* have you got yerself into now?"

That was my Uncle Zollie, the lawyer. I was over at his house, and I'd just shown him my contracts with Tal Ltd., and told him about the mess with the cops. He was holding his head in his hands and walking back and forth across the vinyl runner he kept on his new carpet. It was a really ugly carpet. Maroon.

"But you can help me, right?" I said.

"You've become a *shklaf* to a *shtarker*. I can't touch these contracts! They're iron clad, I tell ya! And you could go to de 'lectric chair – over what, a *shiksa*?"

Uncle Zollie couldn't help me.

♪　♫　♪

"... and though I walk in darkness through the valley of the shadow of death ..."

Park Hill Cemetery, New Jersey. It was a cold, gray day, and the preacher was depressing everybody with Psalm 23, the one you always hear in the movies when everybody's crying and sniffling. Listen, if *I* were a preacher, and *I* had to face a bunch of people who

86

were real sad because someone they loved was dead, I wouldn't read that shit. I'd say something to cheer everybody up, something like, "Free drinks in the lobby!" But they always read Psalm 23, the bastards. Sometimes I think they *want* everybody to cry their eyes out.

"The Lord is my shepherd ..."

But it was a nice service, in spite of the preacher. I met Brenda's mother and brother and sister and a zillion aunts and uncles, and I told them all how sorry I was, and how much Brenda meant to me. Her sister, she said Brenda had told her about me.

"Yeah?" I said. "What did she say – did she say I was handsome? Sexy?"

She took a handkerchief away from her nose and said, "She mentioned something about a sweet little fellow named Rudy Green, who played the guitar. I can't remember all of it – something about a tattoo."

But I didn't want to get into that, did I? Especially since I was standing in a gentile cemetery. I didn't bother to correct her about my name, either – I just grabbed my arm and held it good and tight, and sort of hung out with the family there on the lawn. There were flowers all over the place. I'd personally sent a big arrangement myself. It was shaped like a cupid – remember that charm she used to wear? And in the middle of all the flowers, in a little brown box with the lid open, were Brenda's sweater and shoes. That's all of her they had to bury. It didn't look like a funeral; it looked like a Salvation Army donation.

Everybody started doing this cross thing with their hands, and I didn't know how to do it, which hand to use and all, so I tried to fake it by touching myself all over – when all at once Brenda's mother gave out a "Huh!" and looked like she was going to collapse.

"I'm *sorry*," I said. "I don't know which parts you're supposed to touch, honest."

"It's him," she said, pointing. "That *man*."

I turned around and saw Sal DeGrazzia hiding behind a tree in the distance. That guy had raw *chutzpah*. First he kills her, then he crashes her funeral.

"I'll take care of him," I told Mrs. Taylor.

When he saw me walking toward him, he stepped out from behind the tree and just stood there looking like a dick. A *worried* dick. I went right up to him, grabbed him by the lapels of his pinstripe suit, and tried to push him over. I couldn't, though. The big slob outweighed me by a hundred pounds.

"You've got a lot of nerve showing up here, you son of a bitch."

"Rudy," he said, "take it easy. I've got to talk to you."

I grabbed his lapels tighter and gave him another shove, but he didn't even budge. He was built like a brick shit house. (And would somebody mind telling me what a brick shit house *is*? People talk about them all the time, like everybody's got one, but has anyone ever *seen* a brick shit house?

"We should have a barbecue today, don't you think?"
"Okay. Where do you want to have it?"
"How about out by the brick shit house?"

I don't think they exist, And actually, he was built more like a concrete shit house, but you don't see any of those, either. I'm not going to digress about it, though.)

So then I said, "You cheated on her, and you treated her like *shmutz*, and then you finally killed her. Why are you here, Sal? Haven't you done enough to her? You want to ruin her funeral too?"

"You moron," he said. "It wasn't me; it was them."

I backed off and took a running start and dug my shoulder into his rib cage. The big bastard wouldn't fall over.

"Them who?" I said.

"You mean *whom*. I'll tell you whom – the same guys who put me out of business. The ones that set my apartment on fire. Killing Brenda was just a way to get to me." He rubbed his forehead with his hand and then loosened his tie. "Don't you think I loved that kid? Sure, I stepped out on her once in a while, I admit it. She was too good for me, all right. But I know too much now, and they're after me. They follow me wherever I go. Why, just last night they opened fire on me while I was driving. I was on Riverside Drive, and this dark coupe pulled right alongside of me and some hood started shooting. I ducked, swerved, hit the brakes, and they were gone – " he snapped his fingers " – just like that. I'm telling you, I need help. I need protection. You've got to help me, Rudy."

Of all the slimy lying cowards. It made me sick to see him blubbering like a baby, asking *me* to help *him* after what he'd done. I let go of him, straightened my coat, and hauled off and socked him right in the chin. He fell over like a lopsided loaf of mortadella. Glass jaw. I should've thought of doing that in the first place.

I rubbed my hands together and walked back to the ceremony. Everybody had seen what had happened, except the preacher.

"*He leadeth me on to green pastures ...*"

Brenda's sister clasped my arm and said, "Thank you, Mr. Green."

I whispered, "*Keen.*"

"It certainly was," she said.

♪　♫　♪

"Whoa Baby, Whoa" hit the charts at number 99, stayed there for two weeks, and disappeared. At the same time a collection of songs was issued by Caboose, and "Whoa Baby, Whoa" was included. Preston blamed the lousy chart action on my performance in Massachusetts, but I knew better. I called him and said we had to talk. He told me he could squeeze in a lunch at the Ritz.

"First impressions, Rudy. How many times must I tell you? They mold the public's opinion of you, and then there's nothing to be done."

We were sitting at a table in the Ritz, and it was pretty ritzy, all right. Waiters in tuxedos, long-stemmed roses in narrow little vases.

"But I've got a three-record deal, and so far Caboose has only released one record. I want another one out by the end of the month."

"Can't be done." He picked up a carafe of wine and poured some into his glass. Then he sniffed it. He always sniffed his wine.

"Oh, it can be done. It can be done, all right. And Buddy Holly wants me on The Winter Dance Party Tour. Book me."

He shook his head and smiled at me the way people smile at puppies and cretins. "With that loser? Don't be absurd. Besides, that tour is insufferable. You'll be in farm states, playing to a bunch of cowpokes, snow up to your derriere ..."

"Let me worry about my derriere, okay, Preston? I've been invited, and I want you to book me. And I want a new record. Just do it – don't give me any of this sissy *insufferable* bullshit."

"What do you mean, *sissy?*"

See, Preston was the kind of guy you think might be a faggot, but you can't tell for sure. He certainly was sensitive about the word *sissy.*

"All that high class talk. That's all I meant."

He patted his mouth with his napkin, lit a cigarette, and blew a smoke geyser at the ceiling. "All right. I can get you on the tour and schedule a new recording session. But I'm going to need you to come up with some new songs for other acts, first."

I straightened up in my chair. I'd got my way. "Yeah. That's no problem."

"Now, I want one of them to sound like a Holly song, and another to be instantly recognizable as an Everly Brothers' piece."

"I don't copy other writers."

"You do now. We've had this chat before, and you've already proven that you can do it, so do it."

"But if you think Holly is such a loser, why do you want a song that sounds like one of his?"

"Don't second guess me, Rudy."

I hated like hell copying those other guys, but I didn't have any choice. I knocked off the songs he wanted, and for my record I wrote a classic. I called it "Jelly Baby."

Jelly Baby
c 1958, by Rudy Keen

Jelly in the morning, baby, when it's bright,
Jelly in the evening, sugar, nice and tight.
Jelly in my sandwich, darlin', Jelly in my tea,
Jelly on my bread, and all over me.

Jelly Baby, Jelly girl,
Jelly sway me, Jelly whirl.
Jelly bop and Jelly stroll,
Jelly pop me in your roll.

"I will not allow Caboose to release that song! It's fucking obscene!"

I was having another lovely conversation with Preston. He called me up after he heard the acetate demo.

"What do you mean, obscene? It's a *metaphor*. It's about a girl who's as sweet as a doughnut – that's all."

"I am starting to believe that there is something intrinsically and seriously wrong with you, Rudy. That song might as well be called 'Vulva Baby.' '*Pop me in your roll*' – God! It's bakery pornography!"

"It is *not*. It's a nice little song about jelly, for crying out loud. 'Pop me in your roll,' well – that means like, *let me in your life*. It's figurative, for Christ's sake."

The phone went silent, and for a second or two I thought the line was dead. Then Preston spoke up real slow, real serious. "Do you honestly expect me to believe you don't detect the vulgar references to sex in those lyrics?"

"Yeah, I expect you to believe that, 'cause it's true."

"'Jelly on my bread, and all over me'?"

"See, in that line he's comparing her to a sandwich – "

"God, Rudy."

"A sloppy sandwich."

"You're developing a reputation as a risqué act."

"You know, like a jelly sandwich, and maybe you put too much jelly on it, and it like falls out on your plate, or on your pants or something ... ."

"Just the other day a distributor in Omaha referred to 'Bop-Sha-Bop' as '*that dirty song about cumming.*'"

"Jelly's a natural food, you know."

"Rudy?"

"Huh?"

"Do me a favor. Go out and get laid. Get it the hell over with."

♪　　♬　　♪

"Hold it. Keep it down. We're rolling."

That was the voice of the lady in the control room – the producer's assistant. I was playing second piano, and there was a whole string section set up behind baffles so the sound wouldn't leak over into Buddy's microphone. He cleared his throat, and I hit a C on the piano. He started the song a cappella, and the rest of us came in on the fourth beat.

It was "True Love Ways," a beautiful ballad Buddy had come up with, and I felt sort of honored that he'd asked me to be part of the session. Man, those were great days. I can't believe they're gone for good. Do you know what life is like? It's like something that goes by real fast, only you don't know how fast until it's almost over, like the Indy 500, or a videotape on fast-forward, or my career. Or eating a jelly sandwich – and there's no sexual reference there. Can we please get that straight? And come to think of it, it's like sex, too, the way life goes by so fast. At least for me it is.

We got the songs done in one or two takes, and then Buddy asked me if I wanted to go up on the roof of the building to get some air. It was about one or two in the morning, and it was chilly. The Manhattan wind was like a whip. Buddy had a gray overcoat on, the collar pulled up around his neck. He looked out toward the skyline and then turned to me.

"What did you think of the songs?"

"I liked them," I said, "especially 'True Love Ways.' That's going to be a romantic classic."

"What about the other one – 'It Doesn't Matter Anymore'?"

"It's nice."

"You don't like it."

"It's not that – I just don't see why you need Anka to write material for you when you can write circles around him."

Buddy hugged his chest to keep warm. "If that's true, if I can write circles around Paul, then how come my records aren't selling?"

"Buddy, I don't even know why *my* records aren't selling."

He reached into his pocket and took out some chewing gum. He offered me a piece, but I didn't want any. "You know, Rudy, sometimes I feel like it's a plot."

"Like what is?"

"My sales, man. When all the business guys got involved, all of a sudden the numbers went down. I lost control of my own career. It's like they can make you or break you. Right now it seems like they're all out to break me for good, but I don't know why. It feels like sabotage."

"You really think someone's doing this to you on purpose?"

I can see those big black glasses in front of me even now. He looked me in the eye, just held that pose for a minute, then nodded once. "Yep. Yep, I sure do. Only, who? Why?"

I had two thoughts at that moment. The first was – *Buddy's getting paranoid.* The next was about that new sound Bobby told me Buddy had come up with. I mean ... where was it? As good as "True Love Ways" was, it wasn't a new sound. It was Buddy doing Nat King Cole. I couldn't come right out and ask him about it, though, because it was supposed to be a secret.

Up above, the clouds were racing across the sky. Buddy was

looking at them when he said, "You know why I always wanted to be a success, Rudy?"

"Why?"

"For my daddy. Wanted him to be proud of me. He worked so damn hard all his life, gettin' nowhere at it. I figured I'd go out and make something happen for him in a hurry – just take the world by the tail so fast it wouldn't see me coming. And that's what happened, too. For a while."

I remember thinking it was kind of lonely and nice, old Buddy up on a roof at night, thinking and talking about his father like that.

But then he said this: "What about you, Rudy? You get along good with your daddy?"

"Not so good, no."

"Aw," he said. "That's too bad. What's the problem?"

I sure didn't like talking about it, but he asked. "My father's gone."

"Gone?"

"Left home. He left me and my mother by ourselves."

"I'm sorry, Rudy. Men are funny that way – isn't it the truth?"

"I guess."

"Another woman?"

"No. Say – do you know what a *kibbutz* is?"

"Yeah. It's one of them German sports cars, isn't it? Is that what he's doin' – drivin' around in a fancy new Kibbutz?"

"No," I said. "You don't understand."

"A red one, a convertible?"

Buddy was a sweet guy, but talk about supergoy. "No, Buddy. A *kibbutz* is like a farm or a settlement in Israel. All kinds of people work and live there together. He said it was his mission in life, to help build the homeland. I just wish *I* would've been more his mission in life."

"Waaall," Buddy drawled, slapping me on the back, "maybe you're playin' this rock and roll game for the same reason I am. Think of how proud your daddy'll be someday when he turns on the radio in his *kibbutz* and hears a number one record by his own son."

I didn't say this to Buddy, but it wasn't too likely that they tuned in the Top Thirty Countdown and did the stroll around the tractor in the Golan Heights.

It was cold and we were about to go in, when Buddy asked me if I'd had a lawyer look at my contracts. I told him yeah, but I was locked in.

"Did you talk to Sam and Eddie yet?" he asked next.

"I haven't had any time."

"Make time."

♪ ♫ ♪

So that's what I did. A few nights later I was standing at the bar of a little club in the Village. It was a dark place with an old wood floor. Some girl singer was doing a steamy blues number; I can't remember which one. I just remember she was too *white* for the song. It was sort of like listening to Rosemary Clooney or the McGuire Sisters sing an Etta James number. She was a real Nabisco.

They came in together, Sam Cooke and Eddie Cochran. They were so cool you could feel the breeze, man. Eddie knew me right away, because we'd worked together on "Whoa Baby, Whoa."

"Hey - how're ya doin', Electric Rudy? Sam, I'd like you to meet the eastern seaboard power company's worst nightmare - Electric Rudy Keen. Make sure you're grounded when you shake his hand."

Sam had a look about him that said he was in control wherever he went. I've never seen a guy with so much confidence.

"I understand you're a real show-stopper, Rudy," he said, grabbing my hand.

"It was an accident, Sam. See, my patch cord ..."

Eddie broke in. "Rudy doesn't even let the show start before he stops it. The kid invented the four second concert."

I said, "Eddie - "

"You think that eyebrow look is gonna catch on, man?"

"Cut the shit, Eddie. Buddy told you why I wanted to see you, didn't he?"

"Tal Limited?" Sam asked.

"Yeah. I need some advice."

"I've got some advice for you," Sam said. "Run."

"Whaddaya mean?"

Sam laced his fingers and hunched over the bar. "I got away from Allerton. Eddie hasn't. Tell him what happened to you, Eddie."

Eddie slid a beer in front of me, and I said, "Thanks, but I can't."

"One beer ain't gonna kill you. Now listen, and listen good,"

Eddie said. "Allerton's got me on a three-year contract, and I've tried to get out, but it's solid. A little earlier this year, he was givin' me a hard time about a single release. I gave him a master I wanted to be an A side, and he didn't think it was good enough. I wouldn't give in. I told him there'd be no master for the flip unless that song went out as the A side. A week or so went by and Gene and me – Gene Vincent, you met him?"

"Not yet," I said.

"I'll introduce ya. Anyway, Gene and me were drivin' across the desert to Vegas for a show, when we had a blowout. I got out of the car to change the tire, had the wheel off and all – and out of nowhere this new Ford comes at me like a jack rabbit with Goodyears. Must've been doin' around a hundred – almost ran me over. Came so close it knocked the jack out from under the car and smashed the rear fender. When Gene and me took a good look at the old tire, we found three eighth-inch nails stuck in it, all in a row. Somebody wanted us to have that blowout, Rudy."

"Is that *it*?" I said. "A blowout?"

"We got us a skeptic on our hands, Sam," Eddie said. He started tapping his fingers on the bar and eyeing my beer bottle. "You know, that beer ain't gonna drink itself."

"I'll get to it," I said.

He scratched his chin and then waved at the bartender for another drink. "There's more. So I get home from the Vegas show, new tire on my car, and what do you know – someone's broke into my place. Do they take my electric equipment? No. Guitars? No. Jewelry – it's all there. But my lead sheets and all my demo tapes – gone. Can I prove Allerton did it?"

"Can you?" I asked.

"No. But ask me what I think. Your turn, Sam."

Sam was listening to the singer. She was busy ruining "Don't Start Me Talkin'." Sam just shook his head. "Man, she's got about as much soul as a day-old Jell-o mold." He put his hand on my shoulder and said, "Listen, Rudy. Allerton handled some of my business when I was just breaking into the business. When I landed a deal with a bigger outfit – on my own, by the way – he took some of my old masters. My attorney sent him a letter that said I was going to sue for control of those tapes and some of my publishing rights. A week later, in Chicago, in an alley behind Mr. Kelly's, a couple of thugs roughed me up. They told me I'd be dead if I made any trouble. Said

95

it just like that – I'd be dead."

"So what'd you do?"

"I called the motherfucker's bluff and sued anyway – and I won. I won't have a thing to do with Tal Limited, or any of their subsidiaries, and their subsidiaries must be breeding at night, man. They own almost everything – promotion agencies, record labels, publishing companies. But even so, it still isn't over. I can't say for sure that Allerton's behind it all, but things keep happening."

I didn't know what the hell he was getting at. "What kinds of things?"

Sam and Eddie traded looks, and then Eddie said, "You want to show him?"

Sam said, "Not here. Follow me."

So we all walked across the club to the men's room. It was a tiny little room with one john, and apparently everybody who used it had lousy aim. Sam locked the door and took off his suit coat and started unbuttoning his shirt.

"Wait till you see this," Eddie said,

I was kind of afraid of what he was going to show me for a minute.

"My business with Tal Limited ended over a year ago," Sam said, popping out his cuff links. "One day about six months later, I was walking out of my apartment building. It was two in the afternoon. Bright sunny day, people on the street. The moment I stepped onto the sidewalk, something knocked me over with the force of a train – knocked me right on my ass. I felt this warm spot on my shoulder, and I went to touch it – blood. I'd been shot." There it was, just like he said, a dark round bullet wound. "Shot by a sniper in broad daylight."

"*Oy*," I said. I'd never seen a bullet wound before. I almost passed out.

Somebody started knocking on the bathroom door. "You guys havin' a *convention* in there, or what?"

"Cross your legs. We'll be out in a minute," Eddie said.

"So what're you guys trying to tell me?" I asked.

Sam smiled as he put his shirt back on. "What are we trying to tell him, Eddie?"

"Oh, I dunno. Look both ways before you cross the street. Think about leavin' the country."

"I'm serious," I said.

Sam said, "So are we. Rudy, what if your electrocution wasn't an accident?"

(*We are now entering my mind at that very second. My mind is a mostly empty place - except for a blue electrical flash. I'm reliving my electrocution. The world stands still and goes black. I come to. It dawns on me for the first time:* **Hey, you** *putz* **- SOMEONE WANTS YOU DEAD!**)

"But why *me*?"

Eddie slouched over and looked me in the eye. "Did anyone ever show you that patch cord?"

"No."

"Was there an investigation?"

"Well, no, but ..."

"Who owns your publishing rights?"

"Tal Limited."

"And your collection rights?"

"Tal Limited."

"Me too - they've got some of mine. How about you, Sam?"

Sam let out a little grunt. "A few, maybe. Some I couldn't get back from them."

"Now lookee here," Eddie said, waving a finger at us as he talked. "All three of us have had close calls, and we've each of us signed away rights to Tal Limited. I wonder how much more our recordings would be worth if we were dead? And what would they call an album collection of our cuts - *Teen Heaven*? Man, don't you see?"

"Wait a minute," Sam said. "You know I don't believe it's a coincidence that we've all nearly been offed. Not for a minute. But I think after they miss one of us, they just go to the next. Allerton wouldn't dare kill all three of us."

I said, "What makes you think so?"

"Come on. Wouldn't it look a little suspicious if three rock and roll stars died, one right after the other? It would be obvious to everyone. He knows it."

"I wouldn't put anything past him," Eddie said. "Not even that."

The guy was pounding on the door again. "I hope you boys are havin' a good time in there."

Sam's eyes got wide when he heard the word *boys*.

"Oh, we are," Eddie yelled back. "But we're gonna have a much better time when we come out and kick your ass around the bar."

The knocking stopped.

I was pretty worried. I think we all were, but the other two didn't show it as much. "Can't we *do* something?" I said. "Can't we go to the police?"

Sam said, "Picture the headlines, Rudy – **'THREE CHICKENSHIT ROCKERS WITH ABSOLUTELY NO PROOF ACCUSE MANAGER OF MURDER CONSPIRACY.'** I figure the defamation suit will be filed within an hour, and then I'll meet up with another sniper. No, sir. You go if you want, but leave my name out of it."

He was right – I knew he was. Besides, look what happened the last time I'd gone to the police.

"What should we do, then?" I said.

Eddie helped Sam on with his suit coat. "Well, since we can't prove Allerton's behind it, we're goin' back to the bar and finish our drinks. Then we're gonna be very careful. If anything happens to one of us, he'll let the other two know. Unless he's dead. In that case, the other two will read about it in the paper."

What a comfort THAT was. Thanks, Eddie! He had me so jittery I did something I never should've done. I finished the whole beer and then had another. I've told you – with *my* system that's the same as being pumped full of goofballs. I kept buying Sam and Eddie drinks because I didn't want to be by myself, but finally they said they had to go. That left me alone at the bar, and I started thinking about Brenda, and how much I missed her. The next thing I knew, I was in a cab headed uptown to Sal's apartment to beat the shit out of him. Christ, was I drunk. *Shikker* to the hilt. Even the cabbie knew how gone I was. He kept turing around to look at me, saying, "You all right, fella?"

"You goddamn fuckin'-A better believe I'm all right, boy."

"Maybe you'd better stop off for some coffee. Make you feel better."

"Nope! Nope-a-roonie, baby! Gotta break some bastard's dirty stinkin' neck, an' then I'll feel a *lot* better, by Christ."

What a waste-oid I was. I hardly remember anything else about that night – just two things. First, I couldn't count my money, so I just handed the cabbie my whole wad. I'll bet I tipped that guy four hundred bucks. And second, I remember walking into Sal's apartment. Don't ask me how I got past the doorman. Don't ask me if there *was* a doorman. All I know is, I was pounding on Sal's apartment door and it opened all by itself, like he'd forgotten to shut it or something. I stumbled inside, yelling a lot of stupid drunken things. "Come out and fight me like a goddamn man, you swine!"

Boy, it was dark in there. Spooky. The city lights were shining through the windows, making blind-slat shadows over the furniture, the floor, everything. And there in the middle of the living room, stretched out on the carpet, was Sal.

"Get on your feet so I can knock you down, you big bastard. C'mon, hey!"

Then I kicked him. He didn't move. I figured he was sleeping, right? I thought that maybe he'd gotten drunk too, and passed out on the goddamn floor. I ran my hand along the wall, looking for a light switch, and knocked a bunch of crap off a shelf. When I found the switch, I clicked it on and just stared at him for about a minute or so. His eyes were wide open and there was a hole in his forehead.

"You got a fuckin' hole in your head," I said. I walked around him a few times, kicking him once in a while to see if he'd move. He didn't.

I heard a match light behind me. When I turned around, I saw someone standing in the doorway, lighting a cigarette. Guess who?

"Nice night for a murder," agent Bailis said. "Eh, Rudy?"

6   'Buddy In The Sky With No Glasses'

"Turn up the heat!" someone in the back of the bus shouted.
"It don't go no higher" – the bus driver.

It was January 21, and the whole world was white, snow
everywhere you looked. When it was cloudy you froze; when it was
sunny you froze and went blind from the glare. We were on our way
to George Devine's Million Dollar Ballroom in Milwaukee to kick off
The Winter Dance Party. Some party.

We weren't even out of Pennsylvania when my fingers went
numb. I rubbed them together inside my coat pocket. Some of the
guys in the band were listening to the radio. Everybody else was
sleeping. I was tired, but I was afraid if I fell asleep I might freeze to
death and never wake up, or that my mouth would fall open and my
tongue might hang out and get stuck to the metal seat back.

The bus hit a bump and knocked a magazine out of the Big
Bopper's hands. Poor guy. Somebody always had to pick up stuff he
dropped, because he could barely bend over.

"Here you go, J.P.," one of Buddy's sidemen said, handing him
the magazine.

"Thanks. Are we there yet?"

"Not yet, J.P.. Should be any year, now."

Pennsylvania was growing.

I'm not saying I was the saddest guy in the world, but you
wouldn't have wanted me to show up if you were having a good time.
I had *tsuris* up to my chin. Ever since Bailis arrested me that night at
Sal's apartment and brought me in for questioning, my life turned
into one long interrogation, first with the FBI, then the NYPD. After
a few days, the FBI admitted they didn't think I murdered Sal – no
weapon, plus Bailis saw me go into his apartment, so I wouldn't have
had time to do it. But when the cops got their hands on me, they
kept me in a cell for a week. They'd tracked down my cabbie and got
him to sign a statement saying I was drunk and threatening to break

some guy's neck. (He did that to me – can you imagine? And after a four hundred dollar tip!) Lieutenant Seymour was convinced I killed both Sal *and* Brenda. He kept telling me I was a maniac, that the streets weren't safe with me on the loose – which only would've been true if I were driving. But then – get this. Guess who bailed me out? *Preston Allerton.* He hired an attorney to give the cops a lot of shit about my rights, and a detective to get me an alibi.

"Rudy," he said, in that less-than-manly way he had, "we're going to find out which bar you were in the night Brenda disappeared. Somewhere in Manhattan is a person who can clear your name."

So I changed my mind about Preston trying to kill me and Sam and Eddie. Why would a guy, who supposedly wanted his acts to keel over, go out of his way to save one of them from the chair? That wouldn't make sense. I started thinking that we'd all gotten ourselves nervous about nothing.

The day they let me out of jail, Uncle Zollie was visiting me. He was hurt that I was using another attorney.

"Suddenly I'm not good enoff to defend the great Rudy Keen? Huh?"

"It's not that, Uncle Zollie," I told him.

"Vot, then?"

"This guy's an expert."

"So too am I!"

"He's had a lot of experience in this sort of thing."

"Me too, I've had experience," he shouted.

"And I'm getting him for free."

"Oh, vell," he said, shrugging, "you didn't tell me."

And just then, Preston and Josh Silverman, my lawyer, showed up at my cell door with Lieutenant Seymour, the idiot. Seymour opened the door and said, "You'll be back in here before long, Keen."

Josh wagged his finger at Seymour and said, "No he won't, because you haven't got a case, Mr. Important Lieutenant. You've got no body for the Taylor case, and you've got no weapon for the DeGrazzia murder."

Uncle Zollie pulled me by the ear and scolded me in Yiddish. "*Vilstu zayn dos vos du bist nisht, vestu oykh nisht zayn vos du bist yo.*"

And I said, "Yeah, yeah, yeah."

He'd just told me, "Try to be what you're not, and you end up fucking yourself," or something like that. I really didn't know what the hell he was going on about. Sometimes I thought Uncle Zollie was a noodle short of a full kugel. I mean it. On the way to Preston's car, Josh was trying to give me some important legal advice, when Uncle Zollie interrupted him and asked me if I'd heard the one about the rabbi and the uncircumcised dwarf. My life was up for grabs and he wanted to tell jokes. My family – go figure.

I had a lot of time to think when they had me behind bars. I guessed that maybe Sal hadn't been lying about those guys being after him. But how was I to know? How the hell could anyone know what to believe anymore? And who were these guys? Men in black suits? And was Sal also maybe telling the truth when he said he didn't kill Brenda? Round and round the questions went – but I had no answers. It just about drove me *meshugge*.

A few days before the tour started, I was up at Tal Ltd.'s offices talking to Preston about my publicity campaign. "Jelly Baby" was released that morning, and he'd wired in fan club news to all the local papers in the towns where we'd be playing. Luckily, he'd managed to keep my arrest out of the media. A little money here, a little money there ... you know. There was a grand jury looking into me, but Josh had been telling me for weeks, "You're off; it's a sure thing." The story changed when Preston got a phone call from him just before I left the office. He didn't look happy when he hung up.

"The police have recovered your Thunderbird."

"Great!" I said.

Preston shook his head. "Not great, Rudy. It was parked across the street from Brenda Taylor's apartment building."

I didn't think I would've done that. I didn't think I would've gone over to Brenda's place all smashed out of my head, uninvited. But I couldn't remember. *Why did I have to get so drunk?* I wondered.

One thing bothered me the whole time I was on that tour – If my car was parked across the street from Brenda's building all that time, from October to January, why did it take the cops so long to find it? Okay, so they're incompetent. That could explain it. But *all that time*? Yeah, I know – the police department is a bureaucracy. Even so – four months?

♪ 🎵 ♪

We were still in Pennsylvania when the bus broke down. All the guys in the back started bitching and moaning – "Oh, man! Oh, shit!" All of that. Buddy got up to go see what the problem was, and I followed him.

We were stopped on a bend in the road. You could only see about fifty feet in front of you and fifty feet behind. The bus driver had the engine panel open, and he was wearing gloves with the fingertips cut off them. His fingers stuck out and looked all pink and frostbitey. Snow kept smacking him in the face as he leaned over and stared at the engine.

Buddy closed his overcoat and walked up behind him. "What all seems to be the matter?"

The driver didn't look at him. He just kept staring at the engine. "Broke down."

Buddy's glasses had Jack Frost lines on the bottoms of the lenses – *that's* how cold it was. "What I meant," Buddy said, "was *why* did it break down?"

"Don't know."

My high-heeled boots were slippery on the snow and ice. I almost fell on my ass just standing still. Buddy walked over to me. "You know, if I didn't need the money so damn bad, I never would've booked this tour."

"Ask him if he can fix it," I said.

So Buddy walked back to the driver, who wasn't doing anything but staring at the goddamn engine. "Can you fix it?" Buddy asked.

"Don't know."

Maybe you've seen pictures of Buddy looking this way. He had this look, this kind of hopeless look once in a while, his eyebrows both raised and his mouth shut tight in a frown. That's how he looked then. You could almost hear him counting the miles to Milwaukee. And inside the bus Valens and some of the other guys were playing their guitars and singing a song:

> This bus don't rock,
> This bus don't roll.
> Don't give a fuck,
> 'Cause it's so cold.

"I'd better go back in and calm the fellas down," Buddy said. "As long as we're stuck, why don't you take a whizz and save us a stop down the road, Seventy-eight."

I was always getting razzed about that – and I'd only made the driver pull over *once* since we left Manhattan. But it was a good idea, because I really *did* have to go, so I went over to the side of the road and pulled my zipper down. NO PENIS! WHERE DID IT GO? Does that ever happen to you when it's real cold – you open your zipper and there's no penis? I mean, if you're a guy and everything. If you're not, I guess you're used to it.

"Hey, Rudy."

Christ. It was hard enough trying to take a piss out there in the cold without getting interrupted. I looked over my shoulder and saw the Bopper waving at me through an open window.

"I'm a little busy at the moment, J.P.."

"That's okay. I won't bother you. Listen – I heard that number of yours that you wrote for the Pigeons. What's it called?"

I wished to hell he'd leave me alone and let me concentrate. "'Radda-Radda-Ready,'" I said.

"Yeah. That's the one. Say now, you suppose you could write a number like that for me?"

I wondered if it was humanly possible to pee outside when it was this cold. "I don't know. We can talk about it when I get back on the bus."

"Maybe a tune with a French phrase in it, ya know? Somethin' like, 'Ooo-La-La-Lula.' Some French words and a girl's name."

I might just pee icicles, I thought. "Yeah – we can talk about it."

"I need a number that'll make the girls go wild and scream every time they hear it."

"Right! Right! Okay!" I didn't have the heart to tell him that the girls screamed for the *singer*, not the song. That poor guy. But meanwhile I was getting frostbite, and I don't think I have to tell you where.

About a minute or two later the Bopper hollered at me.

"Hey, Rudy!"

"What, goddamn it?"

"What's taking you so long?"

"I haven't even found it yet!"

♪　　♫　　♪

104

Now, there was this one guy on the tour that Buddy had warned me about in his letter – Derek Halloway. What a whiny son of a bitch. He'd been booked as an alternate opener and would probably never have a chance to go on, so he played guitar in the band most nights. I didn't like him from the minute I met him. He always had something rude to say, and you could tell he was jealous of all of us. When I got back on the bus he was bitching about the accommodations.

"This is *not* a first-class tour. Everybody in the business knows it. My manager told me personally that the only reason any act agreed to go on it was because they were desperate for money."

"Well, now we know why *you're* on it," Buddy said to him. Buddy could be quite sarcastic when he needed to be.

Derek faced off with Buddy, but then didn't do anything, of course, because he was a chicken shit. He just went and sat down and mumbled to himself like a baby. A little while later Buddy and I went back outside to talk to the driver again. He wasn't looking at the engine anymore. Now he was looking at the road. Buddy asked him if he'd figured out what the problem was.

"Yep."

"Well – can you fix it?"

"Nope."

So I asked the next obvious question. "So what do we do?"

The driver spit (I'm not making this up), and I heard the spit crack before it hit the ground. No *wonder* I couldn't pee in that weather. "Wait here till we can flag someone down. Need a part."

Buddy was running out of patience. "And that part is – ?"

The driver spit again. *Crack!* "Fuel line. Looks like someone slashed it with a razor."

Buddy and I looked at each other. Then he asked, "Looks that way, or somebody actually did it?"

"Don't know."

Buddy pulled me over near a snow bank. "You *did* have that talk with Cochran and Cooke, didn't you?"

"Yeah," I said. "And I know what you're thinking, but it can't be a plot. It's got to be a coincidence."

"How do you *know* that? How do you know for sure?"

I hadn't told anybody in the business about it, except Allerton, but I had to spill my guts to Buddy about the mess I was in back in New York – about how the cops thought I'd killed Brenda and Sal.

I explained that Allerton had saved my ass, had hired people to protect me, and that it didn't add up to a conspiracy.

"Waaall, maybe you're right," he said. "I just don't think I'll ever trust that Allerton, though."

And then he asked me if Brenda had been special to me, and I said yeah, and he asked if it was true love. He talked like that, like the words in his songs. I said no, it wasn't love, probably. It was more like crying, waiting, hoping.

"Hey," he said, "I like that – crying, waiting, hoping."

He sure must have. A few days later he wrote a song with that as the title. (A lot of people think he wrote that *before* the tour, but nuh-uh. He wrote it after he heard me say it. The tape ended up back in his apartment because he always sent home tapes he made on the road. The credits under that song should read *Holly-Keen*, but I don't care. We borrowed little pieces from each other. It all came out even in the end – except for royalties. I got the rock-and-roll shaft instead of royalties.)

Buddy said, "Was she the Brenda you wrote that song for?"

"Yeah, it was for her."

"Aw – I'm sorry, Seventy-eight."

A pickup truck stopped while we were talking and took the driver into town so he could buy a new fuel line. We waited two hours for him to get back, and it took him another hour to fix the thing, and by the time we were rolling, it was on toward ten at night.

We slept most of the next day. *There's* something you'll have no trouble doing in Milwaukee, unless you happen to be on a tour with Derek Halloway and he stops by your room every five minutes to complain about the way everyone treats him, or to tell you how unfair it is that he never gets a chance to open the show. God, what a *kvetch*. I guess I wasn't the only one he bothered, because at two in the afternoon Ritchie Valens and some of the guys in Buddy's group came to my room and locked the door behind them.

"Guess what we've got here?" Ritchie said.

"I don't know. What?"

"Derek Halloway's tuxedo pants. Guess what else we've got?"

"Lice," I said.

"No – a seam cutter. What do you suppose we should do with it?"

I'll tell you what we did with it – we cut the zipper out of the goddamn pants and then hung them back up in his closet. Man, were

106

we bored. That livened up the night, though. We just didn't know what a little prick that Halloway character could be.

I'll get to that in a minute. Right now I want to tell you about a conversation I had with Buddy that afternoon. I'd gone to his room to ask him which song he thought I should open with. I was pretty nervous about the concert, because I'd only had four seconds of professional performing experience, most of which I couldn't remember. Voltage will do that to you. But before I could get an answer from him, he pulled out a hand mirror and looked at himself and asked me if I thought he was geeky looking.

Jesus Christ, why me? Why did he have to ask *me*? I swallowed hard, tried to look as convincing as I could, and told him no, he wasn't.

He dropped the mirror on his bed and looked hopeless. "Be honest with me, Rudy."

"I am. I'm being honest."

He picked up the mirror again and looked at himself. "You call this *handsome*?"

"Well – in a way. In a very peculiar way. Almost."

"Uh-uh, Rudy. Look at me, and then look at someone like Darin. *He's* handsome. He's swarthy, the girls love him, his records sell. I'm geeky."

"Stop saying that, will ya?" I said. "Darin's got that swarthy thing going, okay. But you've got ... you've got – "

"What?"

"You've got something *else* going, is all. You want to talk about geeky? Look at me."

"You're not geeky."

"The hell I'm not. I'm short, my ears stick out. I can't even grow sideburns. Or eyebrows."

"But you've got presence."

"Yeah. Some presence. I plug myself into an outlet and become a human transformer."

I looked at the table and saw a *Hot 100* chart from New York. "Heartbeat" by Buddy Holly was circled in pen at number eighty-two. That's when I knew what all this geeky business was about.

"Buddy," I said. "You can't go kicking yourself about the charts."

He stood up and paced back and forth. "Two years ago I got to number one with a crummy demo. Now I hire top producers and can't crack the top seventy. I sure wish I knew why this was happenin'."

I knew why it was happening. I couldn't tell *him*, though. "Heartbeat" was an okay record, but I knew for a fact it didn't give him the "all-overs." He didn't even write that song. He probably only recorded it because his confidence was down.

I kept reading the chart. "Jelly Baby" wasn't even listed.

"Things could be worse, Buddy. You could have a record that doesn't even *make* the chart, and a grand jury investigating you."

He stopped pacing and looked down at me through those big glasses. Sometimes when Buddy looked at me it was like being studied by a laboratory guy with a microscope glued to his forehead. "I'm sorry, Seventy-eight. I'm bein' selfish, ain't I?"

"No," I said. "You've got problems. I understand."

"But you've got bigger problems. You're worried 'bout gettin' charged with murder, aren't ya?"

"It crosses my mind six or seven thousand times a day."

"Hey, man – " Buddy said, patting my shoulder, "all they gotta do is come up with the guy who really did it and you're off the hook."

"They're not even looking for the guy. They think they've *got* the guy."

Buddy sat down on the bed again and held his fist under his chin like that statue of the guy who's always thinking. You know the one I mean. He's kind of hunched over with his elbow on his knee, naked, and he's thinking real hard – probably about where he left his clothes. I can't remember the name of it. "You got any idea who did it?" he asked me.

"Not anymore. After Brenda disappeared, I thought it was Sal. Now he's dead too. He kept telling me someone was after him, but I thought he was lying."

"He never said who it might be?"

"Nope."

"Not even a name – just a first name or somethin'?"

I started thinking back. "*He* never did, no. But on that last night I saw Brenda, she was telling me about threats Sal was getting. She thought it had something to do with a publishing company that was signing away all his acts. I guess he asked around town about them too much, and they supposedly started a fire in his place or something, but at the time I figured he was making shit up so Brenda wouldn't find out he was stepping out on her."

"A two-timer, huh?"

"Sal? Oh, yeah. He was a swine. You could get trichinosis just talking to him."

"Do you remember the name of the publishing company?"

Everything started to add up. Sal had told me they took care of Brenda to get to him. And when that wasn't enough – they got him, too. I could still see that hole in his head, big as a quarter.

"It was a funny name. I think Brenda said it was Stick-Suck. Something like that."

Buddy said, "Stick-Suck? What the hell kind of name is that? Stick-Suck? That doesn't even make sense." Then he thought some more, and all at once his eyes opened up real wide and his head popped up like a Texas Jack-in-the-box. "Do you mean *Stek-Circ?*"

"Yeah – *that's* it. It was Stek-Circ, not Stick-Suck."

It was a hell of a funny name, Stick-Suck. I wonder what made me think of that? I mean, other than what I'm usually thinking about.

You should've seen old Buddy's face when he found out it was Stek-Circ. He looked like a proctology patient during an exam. He jumped up and went to his valise and started shuffling through a bunch of papers.

"It's here somewhere," he said.

"What is?"

It looked like a newspaper, what he found. He pulled it out of the valise and started turning pages real fast. His hands were shaking. "British charts," he said. He ran his finger down the columns and circled certain songs with a pen. There was one by Eddie Cochran, one by Gene Vincent, an old re-release of Sam Cooke's, and at number thirty-two, my "Whoa Baby, Whoa." *All* of them listed Stek-Circ as the publisher.

I said, "But I never signed any contract with Stek-Circ. How can that be? And am I really number thirty-two in England? Let me see that!"

He let me take the chart. He kept talking to me while I studied it. "Tal Limited can sign your foreign rights to any publisher they want. And someone at Tal Limited is signing them to an English outfit called Stek-Circ. Hell, Rudy. The sky don't gotta fall on you before you see what's goin' on, does it?"

"Whadaya mean?"

"Tal Limited is connected to Stek-Circ, and Stek-Circ had

Brenda and Sal killed."

"Then why don't they just let me take the fall? Why are they trying to prove I'm innocent?"

"Are they?"

"Yeah. I think so."

"You're not in New York. You don't see what they're doing. Maybe they're afraid you'll piece it together and talk. Maybe they want you out of town so they can kill you on the road. Maybe that gas line *was* sliced by a razor, and they were hoping you'd freeze to death – that we all would."

"Knock it off, Buddy. You're scaring the shit out of me."

We were both sweating bullets. Oops – bad choice of words. That makes me think of the hole in Sal's head. Did I tell you it was as big as a fucking *quarter*? It was. You could even kind of see part of his brain leaking out, all gray and bloody and slimy, but I won't go into it because I don't want to make you sick.

Buddy said, "Only Brenda and Sal knew that Stek-Circ was signing his acts away. Only Brenda and Sal suspected that Stek-Circ set his apartment on fire."

"And me. I knew, because Brenda told me."

"But they don't *know* that Brenda told you. You didn't tell anyone else, did you?"

"Nope. Just you."

Buddy took off his glasses and rubbed his eyes. "Somethin's rotten in England – *and* New York. Maybe we should just jump this tour."

Well kids – the story's been told. It's history now. We didn't jump the tour. We should've. But Buddy needed the money; he was flat broke. And we were both afraid we'd never get booked by a big promoter again if we walked out on a signed deal – not to mention what it might cost us in lawsuits. So we went on that night, but not without problems.

This is the part about Derek Halloway I've been meaning to get to. That rock and roll weasel. We'd just arrived at George Devine's Million Dollar Ballroom (which had been over-appraised, if you ask me) when Buddy opened his guitar case, *and every single string was broken*. He took one look at that guitar and said, "What the hell?"

Who comes walking by, just coincidentally at that very moment? Derek. "Must be the cold," he said.

Buddy knelt down and picked up the guitar like it was his run-over puppy. "They're all broken at the same exact place," he said. "The cold didn't have nothin' to do with it. These strings have been *cut*, man."

Fifty minutes till show time. I asked Buddy if he had any spares. He shook his head. "These are special gauge flatwound strings. I meant to pick up an extra pack, but with the bus breakin' down and all, I haven't had time."

"I'll go on in your place, if you want," Derek said.

Buddy turned around toward him and stood up real slow. "Pardon?"

"I said, *I'll* take your place."

I haven't seen Buddy angry too many times in my day – but that was one of them. He gritted his teeth and turned red and walked up to Derek till there wasn't a centimeter between them. "*You'll* take *my* place?"

Derek backed away; he held his hands out to keep Buddy off of him. "O-o-only if you want m-m-me to," he stuttered.

"Listen here, Junior. *Elvis* can take my place. Ritchie and Dion *might* take my place. But you couldn't take my place standing in line at an outhouse."

I knew what I had to do. I threw on my overcoat and said, "I'll be right back."

Buddy ran after me. "Rudy – where in Sam Hill do you think you're goin'? It's fifteen below zero out there!"

On my way out I heard Derek saying, "If he's not back in time to go on, I get to open. It's in my contract."

I flew out of that theater and hit a sheet of ice and went sliding on my ass down the sidewalk. Goddamn high heels. A group of screaming teen-age girls who'd been standing in line came running after me.

"It's *him*!" one of them screamed.

"Who? Who?" another one shrieked.

"I don't know! I've never seen him before! Maybe it's Buddy's ugly cousin or something!"

I got up and ran, playing hopscotch over ice patches. Snow was blowing straight at my face and I could barely see where I was going – not that it mattered, because I knew Milwaukee about as well as I knew Timbuktu. As a matter of fact, I knew Timbuktu *better* than I knew Milwaukee. It's in central Mali, near the Niger River, population 15,000. I'd seen an educational show on TV. But never mind that now. I had to get some Fender flatwound strings. I found a street maintenance guy in an orange parka throwing salt on a sidewalk, so I ran up to him and said, "Can you tell me where there's a music shop?"

He looked at me like I was from one of Jupiter's moons, or Newark, and he said, "Eh? Music shop?"

The wind cut through my coat. "Yeah. You know, where they sell musical instruments."

He just went back to salting the sidewalk and said, "I don't play no instrument."

Did I ask him that? Did I ask him if he played an instrument, or did I ask him if he knew where there was a music shop? I felt like saying, "Really? An obviously gifted son of a bitch like you, and you don't play anything?" But I didn't. It was too cold to go on yapping, and I was turning into an ice statue of myself.

I ran on into the night, into the storm, until I was all alone on a dark street, snow up to my knees, my fingers frozen and numb. I stopped and looked up at the swirling whiteness. I didn't know what else to do, so I lowered my head, closed my eyes, and said real softly to myself, "Please, God. I'm lost and cold. Let me find those strings. Do it for Buddy. *Please.*"

I hadn't noticed it before, but when I wiped some snow from my eyes, I saw a light on in a window across the street. Out of instinct, I walked toward it. The wind kept whipping me, but by then I couldn't feel anything. It was a little storefront shop with a Gibson guitar hanging in the window. "Lonesome Hank's Music Emporium," the stenciled sign read. I rubbed my eyes again because I thought I was hallucinating. There on the door was a little cardboard sign – OPEN. I leaned on the door and it squeaked as I walked in.

I was expecting it to be warm in there. Maybe I was chilled to the bone and couldn't tell, but I would've sworn it was as cold inside that place as it was outside.

"Howdy."

Behind the counter was a man with sad eyes and an even sadder smile – Lonesome Hank. The poor drip. His bastard landlord gave him no heat in the winter and all he was wearing was a thin cowboy shirt.

"Hi," I said, looking around. There was just that one guitar, the one in the window. In the glass display case he was leaning on, there was a package of guitar strings and two or three red and white picks.

That's it. There wasn't another goddamn thing in the store.

"What can I help you with, friend?"

He sure didn't sound like he was from Milwaukee. He sounded like he'd just fallen off the Louisiana Hay Ride.

"I need some strings." I said. "But it doesn't look like you've got much of a selection."

"Well, I guess not. All's I got left is this here one pack. Now, if you're fussy, they might not be what you're lookin' for. But I'll tell ya what – they'll do in a pinch."

He took them out of the case and flipped them over on the counter. *I'll be a rabbi's bastard son,* I thought. The package was marked clear as anything, FENDER FLATWOUND CUSTOM GAUGE STRINGS.

My mouth must've hung wide open. "I can't *believe* it," I said. "These are exactly what I needed."

The sad looking guy said, "Well then, looks like you come to the right place."

The hair on the back of my neck stood up. When I'd first walked in, I'd seen a Gibson guitar in the window, but now it wasn't there anymore.

"Wait a minute," I said. "What's going on here?" Lonesome Hank didn't look so lonesome all of a sudden. His eyes were kind of twinkling, like they were in on a joke, like they were laughing at me. "It's eight o'clock at night, and I'm lost in Milwaukee in a snowstorm, and I just happen to need a set of Fender custom gauge strings, and here you are, with nothing but some picks and one set of strings, and they're exactly what I want. How can that be?"

"Ain't it somethin'?" the guy said. "Would you rather've walked around freezin' all over town and *not* found 'em?"

"Uh – no."

"Well, there you are."

It didn't add up. But I was late and I had to get back. "Look, mister. How much do I owe you?"

He just frowned and shook his head. "On the house," he said, handing me the strings.

And on top of everything else, he was giving them to me for free? I would've paid a hundred bucks for those strings.

"I can't let you do that." I pulled a twenty out of my pocket and slapped it on the counter, but he just pushed it back at me.

"You need 'em – you keep 'em. And take these along, too, why don'cha. Might bring you luck."

He dropped the red and white picks in my hand, one by one. They were the strangest picks I'd ever seen. They looked like they were glowing. Weird, man. I slipped them in my pocket and said, "Thanks."

When I turned to leave (and son of a bitch, I swear this is true), the Gibson guitar was back in the window, right where I'd first seen it. Well, I freaked. I just out and out freaked. I opened the door so fast I practically took it off its hinges, and then I ran the hell away. As the snow surrounded me, I thought I heard Lonesome Hank yell, "Say hi to Buddy for me." But he couldn't have. It must've been my imagination.

I stopped about a block down the street and looked back, but all I could see was snow. It was as if that little emporium had never been there. Talk about a case of the heebie-jeebies! (I'm not crazy about that expression because of the *heeb* in heebie-jeebies, but that's what I had, the old heebie-jeebies.) Sometimes when I look back on what happened that night, I think that maybe I was suffering from cold trauma and dreamed the whole thing. But then how do you explain the strings and the picks? They were real. I read a book by a physicist guy named Stephen Hawking – you know, the guy with ALS who talks through a voice computer. He's a pretty cool guy. Real gone. Someone asked him once what records he'd bring with him if he was going to be stranded on a deserted island, and he said *Please Please Me*, by The Beatles. That's a pretty cool answer for a science cat. Anyway – in this book, which I didn't completely understand (I didn't understand any of it, actually), he talks about wormholes in space. Maybe I slipped into a wormhole in Milwaukee and found another universe. I can't say for sure. I wrote Hawking a letter about it, but so far he hasn't written back, which I understand. I mean, he's a pretty important guy, and typing must be a real bitch for him. I gave him my phone number, so maybe he'll call me someday. One of his assistants could keep switching the phone from his ear to that little computer speaker, and I could ask him once and for all if Milwaukee is a wormhole. I know people who think it is, but I want to hear it from a physicist, someone who works with black holes and wormholes every day. Someone who really knows his holes.

So there I was, out in the middle of a goddamn blizzard, freezing my *pupic* off. I couldn't see where I was going, but I wasn't afraid of getting lost. Not me. I was *already* lost. I ran; I slipped; I stumbled. Pretty soon there it was, up ahead – George Devine's Million Dollar (my ass) Ballroom. When I got inside, there was a lot of confusion – a big fuss going on backstage. Derek was having a fit about something while Buddy was taking the broken strings off his guitar.

"Look at my tuxedo pants!" Derek yelled, holding open his fly. No zipper.

I said, "I think you've got the ballroom concept all wrong, Derek." I tossed Buddy the strings.

"Holy Hunchbacked Hannah, Rudy! Where'd you ever find these?"

Holy Hunchbacked who? I thought.

"Look at my goddamn pants!" Derek kept whining. "I can't go out there with my dick hanging out!"

Ritchie was trying not to laugh. He looked down at Derek's fly and said, "*What* dick?"

I took off my overcoat and grabbed my guitar. This time I checked the patch cord good and careful before I plugged it in.

"What do you think you're doing?" Derek said to me, trying to hold his fly shut.

"I think I'm getting ready to open the show."

"Nothing doing! You were late. My contract specifically states–"

Buddy had had just about enough. He got up and walked over to us and shoved Derek's guitar at him. "Looky here, fancy boy. I'll get you a safety pin for those wide-open pants, but don't make me have to teach you how to keep your lip shut, you understand? Now get up there with the other band members, junior, or you'll be sorrier than a sow in a wet cee-ment sty."

Derek pursed his sissy lips and grabbed his guitar out of Buddy's hand. He wouldn't say anything back to Buddy face-to-face, of course. He waited till he walked away, and mumbled, "I'm gonna call my manager."

Then, just like that, the lights went down.

"What's going on?" I said.

"What do you mean, *What's going on?*" Buddy said. "The show's startin'."

"It can't. I'm not ready."

I could hear the MC. "WELCOME, EVERYBODY, TO THE SCENE OF ALL SCENES, THE ONE, THE ONLY ... WINTER DANCE PARTY!"

115

Buddy said, "It's not like you've got a choice or anythin'."

"But I tell ya, I can't go on yet. I'm not warmed up."

The Bopper was walking back and forth, playing with that phony telephone of his. He kept saying, "Helllllooooo, Baaaaaby!"

"LADIES AND GENTLEMEN, LET'S GIVE A HIGH VOLTAGE ROUND OF APPLAUSE TO BROOKLYN'S OWN REAL LIVE WIRE, ELECTRIC RUDY KEEN!"

The kids were screaming and I felt like I was going to pass out. Buddy whispered in my ear, "Give 'em the all-overs, Seventy-eight," and then pushed me from the wings onto the stage.

My head was pounding and my *kishkes* felt like they were going to take the nearest exit to the floor. I pulled out one of those good-luck picks that Lonesome Hank had given me, raised my hand like a pitcher taking a wind up, and just before I hit the G-chord intro to "Whoa Baby, Whoa," I prayed, "Please, let me be grounded."

Was I scared? Is matzo kosher? I nearly peed in my hand-tailored satin pants. But I didn't, because I knew two things: #1 – stains are hell to get out of satin, and #2 – urine is a wonderful conductor of electricity. Instead I borrowed a few moves from Chuck Berry, strutting around like one of Uncle Myshkin's decapitated chickens. I did some Elvis splits. Ouch. I aimed my guitar at the audience like it was a machine gun and fired off a hot riff. Yeah, man! I just ripped it up. I was a different person out there. Old Rudolph Kearns could never have done anything like that in public, but Electric Rudy could. I wound up my set with "Jelly Baby," and I pointed at a different girl each time I sang, "Jelly on my sandwich, baby, and all over me."

The screams, *oy!* The girls flipped! They loved my music! They loved me! They *wanted* me! And who could blame them? I was so hot, *I* wanted me. As a matter of fact, I've *had* me a few times – but once again, that's another story.

The Bopper and his telephone came out and "Chantilly-Laced" the crowd but good. The kids ate it up, and I was glad for him; I really was. All he had going for him was that corny gimmick, that *farshlugenah* phone. If he were around today, doing Vegas, I'm afraid he'd come out with a fax machine, thinking he'd updated his act.

Ritchie Valens got the joint heated up with "La Bamba." He practically gave all the girls – well, you know – organisms. But none of us did what Buddy did when he hit the stage. He blew everyone away. "Rave On" just about brought the roof down. You've never seen a guy with the kind of energy he had. The crowd was jumping on top of their seats with their hands in the air, shaking and rattling and rolling. And then ... oh, Christ, I almost wish he wouldn't have. Buddy waited for the place to go quiet, stepped back up to the microphone, and sang "Oh, Brenda!" He didn't tell me he was going to do that. I know I wrote that song, but I never really heard the lyrics until Buddy sang them. It was so pretty and sad and blue, it made me see Brenda all over again. I could see the way she looked and all, just like she was standing in front of me, her pretty eyes, her firm hips, her big round knock – I mean, her nice figure. She was the one girl I'd ever loved, and now she was gone. I sat down on a drum case backstage and cried like a baby. When the show was over, Buddy walked by and found me like that. It was pretty embarrassing, but there wasn't a hell of a lot I could do about it. He put his hand on my shoulder and said, "Did ya like it, Seventy-eight?"

And I said, "It was beautiful, Buddy."

"Waall, I had some help from the songwriter."

I hope some of the critics who trashed me back then, who called me a one-hit wonder, a novelty act, a sexual moron – I just hope they're paying attention. Did you guys read that last part carefully? Buddy Holly as much as said that I had written a beautiful song. What do you say to that, you bunch of *shmutz* peddlers? Did Buddy Holly ever tell you that you wrote a beautiful *review*? Do I really need to ask that question? Please. Give me an order of reality to-go.

♪　♫　♪

Okay – so the first night was exciting. But the rest of them? Hell. They were hell, I tell you. That tour nearly killed us. Every night we worked another hick berg. And riding in that bus was like being shipped across the midwest in a Frigidaire on wheels. There was no fucking heat. I've been in warmer morgues. And what an itinerary! This way and that way over the same state lines, day in and day out. Kenosha, Wisconsin; Mankato, Minnesota; Eau Claire, Wisconsin; Montivideao ("Day-o, day-ay-ay-o") Minnesota; Davenport, Iowa (which just sits there like a sofa). What a geographical genius plotted our course. Couldn't they have kept us in one state until we finished all the dates, and then moved us on to the next? At every stop Buddy called New York and bitched about the awful conditions we were living in, but do you think it did any good? He'd lost whatever clout he used to have. They didn't give a shit, is what it comes down to. They just didn't give a shit, not even when he threatened to walk out. "Heartbeat" had sunk to number ninety on the Hot 100 Chart. He was working the worst tour in the country and he had no sales. And to top it off, he caught a cold and hacked and wheezed on the bus at night and couldn't sleep. I thought things had gotten about as bad as they could.

Wrong again.

Let's see, we'd already done Davenport and Duluth, so I think it was in Green Bay, Wisconsin that Buddy got the telegram. We'd just wrapped up the show at the local armory when Buddy pulled me aside, looking ruffled and nervous. Man, he was all shook up. He told me they were going to arrest me, and I said who, and he said the New York cops. He unfolded the telegram and showed it to me. It was from Preston. I guess he sent it to Buddy instead of me so there wouldn't be any evidence that he'd tried to tip me off. Here's what it said:

ELECTRIC DEVIATE EXPECTING GUESTS IN UNIFORM **STOP** GIFT SET OF CUFFS AND ONE WAY TICKET BACK **STOP** KNOW HE HATES SURPRISES **STOP**

I said, "Deviate? What's this *deviate* crap?"

"He didn't want to use your name," Buddy explained. "It's nothin' personal."

"Nothing personal? Did you say nothing *personal*? Are you kidding? The guy called me a deviate, and it's nothing personal? He might as well have called me a fucking pervert!"

"Now, hang on a minute, Seventy-eight – "

"I will *not* hang on! Why should I hang on? How would you like it if he called you *Buddy Deviate*? Would you like that? *Buddy Deviate And The Sicko Crickets*. Does that have a nice ring to it? Huh?"

"I think you're missin' the point, here."

"He could've said *Electric Star*, or *Electric Idol*. Why didn't he say that? The bastard. Always putting down my songs, and they're good, clean, wholesome American songs. I've never written a dirty lyric in my life. It's all in his twisted imagination. Christ, if it were up to him, my record labels would say *Rudy The Deranged Sex Criminal*. But am

I that kind of guy? No. Do I proposition teenage fans? All right – skip that. But do you ever see me in an X-rated book shop? Well, just that once outside of Milwaukee. That doesn't count, 'cause I was lonely. Other than that one time, you never see me in a place like that. *Never.* Unless you want to get picky and count that shop in Newark, back when the tour started. I'd just forgotten to bring reading material, was all. I swear! I didn't know I was going to get a magazine with a bunch of people who had black tape across their eyes."

Buddy took a deep breath and then sighed. "You through?" he said.

"Yeah. Why?"

He whipped that telegram in front of my face and held it there. "Because, gall darn it. The *cops* are comin' for ya!"

There was that to consider, too. The only thing it could've meant was that I'd been indicted by the grand jury. Grand, just grand. Buddy took it harder than I did. I'd been worrying about getting arrested for so long, I was almost glad to get it over with. But I sure as hell didn't want to be seen by all of America on TV in handcuffs as they pulled me off-stage during a show.

Buddy was trying to figure out what to do, and all I said was that Preston had helped me out again, so maybe all that stuff about Stek-Circ was a lot of baloney. You know what he did? He slapped me, right on the back of the head.

"Maybe Preston wants to take you out *himself*, 'cause he's afraid you'll tell the cops everything you know. No sir, we ain't takin' any chances. Now let's you and me think."

So we thought. We decided I'd go on with the tour to the next stop, which was Appleton, Wisconsin, and then I could slip out of town somehow. What we didn't count on was the worst cold spell and snowstorm we'd faced yet. I'll never forget it – the guys in the band huddled under blankets and coats, shivering and turning different shades of blue. You would've thought we were prisoners of war, not recording stars. And then fifty miles outside of Appleton, the goddamn bus broke down again.

Half the guys were already sick with flu and fever, and every fifteen minutes that we sat there on the side of the road, another inch of snow fell. Buddy wouldn't listen to me when I told him not to go outside to talk to the bus driver. He was sick as a dog and shouldn't have been out there in that weather, not that it was much warmer on the bus. I followed him out, and we found a familiar sight

– the bus driver staring at the motor.

"What the hell is it this time?" Buddy asked him.

"Don't know."

Buddy rolled his eyes and walked a few feet away. "I'd ask him if he could fix it, but I'm afraid I'll have to kill him if he says *'Don't know'* again."

I said, "We'll never find out if we don't ask him."

"Okay. *You* ask him."

We walked back to the driver; he was still standing there, still staring at the motor. I think he was *communing* with it.

"Can you fix it?" I asked him.

"No, I'm pretty sure I can't."

I turned to Buddy and said, "See? He didn't say what you were afraid he would." Then I asked the driver, "So what do we do now?"

"Don't know."

Buddy kicked the front tire and said, "Snot."

♪　♫　♪

Things turned ugly fast. The drummer's feet were all frostbitten; he couldn't walk, let alone play drums. The road was snowed in, which meant no traffic, no one to help us. We'd already missed any chance of making the matinee appearance in Appleton – and there went my escape. After about an hour of just sitting there freezing, Buddy called all the guys together in the middle section of the bus for a conference. He said that I was in a jam with the law back east, and that there might be some cops coming around to ask about me. He said he wanted them all to help me out. He'd come up with a plan.

Buddy's Plan: *If* we got rescued, and *if* we lived to see Clear Lake, Iowa, I'd hide backstage under amplifier covers during the concert. Derek would go on in my place. After the show when it was dark and nobody was around, they'd see if they could get me to a train station somehow.

"Why do *I* have to open? I want someone to go on before me." That was Derek.

Buddy adjusted his glasses, gave him a long look, and said, "You give me piles, son. You know that?"

"No, I don't."

"Yes, you do. Real big Texas piles, the kind cattle get."

"But I want someone *else* to open for *me*."

Buddy puffed his cheeks up and blew the air out real slow. "I know you do, Derek. You want a lot of things. You want fans, but you haven't got those. You want talent, but you haven't got that, either. And you want someone to open for you, but it ain't gonna happen."

"Fine, then. But I'm not sticking my neck out for Keen. Why shouldn't I just tell the cops where he is?"

"Oh, I think you know why," Buddy said. "So it's settled. You take Rudy's place; Rudy hides backstage. None of us have seen him since early last week."

The little weasel pulled his walk-away-and-mumble trick again. He kicked at the bus door until it opened and then he went outside to let off some steam, and I mean like literally. He looked like a hot spring in February. I went out too, just to calm him down. I didn't need him squealing to the cops.

"What are you so pissed about?" I said. "All this time you've been wanting to go on, and now you can."

"Give me one good reason I should be happy about replacing a nobody."

Whoa – he was coming on a little strong. "A *nobody?*" I said.

"That's right."

"You mean as in *me* being the nobody?"

"That's right."

"And you wanted how many reasons?"

"Just one," he said.

So I dropped the little bastard. Punched him right in the mouth. Just once, though, because he only asked for one reason.

When I got back on the bus I sat down next to Buddy and he gave me some of his blanket to cover myself with.

"Where's Derek?" he asked.

"He's having a refreshing snow bath. He'll be back soon."

It sure was quiet on that bus. I could hear sleet *tick-tick-ticking* against the windows. I tried to keep my eyes open, but I was getting drowsy.

"Buddy?" I said.

"Hm?"

"Do you think we're going to make it out of here?"

He sat back, blinking at the ceiling, his breath coming out in little clouds. "Oh, I pretty much think so. I don't feature me dyin' on no sorry-ass rock 'n' roll tour in the middle of nowhere."

My feet were numb and my eyelids were heavy, and I could feel myself drifting, drifting off to sleep. I had the craziest dream. I was standing in a snow-covered field, and up ahead I saw something sticking out of a drift, so I walked toward it. The snow crunched under my feet. My footprints glowed red and white, just like the picks Lonesome Hank had given me. I thought to myself, *Why is the snow turning red?* As I got closer to the thing in the drift, I saw that it was Buddy's Fender Stratocaster. I went to pick it up, but then I heard Buddy calling me. "Rudy? Rudy, are you there?"

His voice came from above. I looked up and saw Buddy's face on a cloud. It was huge, like it was part of the sky. I yelled up at it, "Here I am, Buddy! Down here!"

"Where?" he said. "I lost my glasses. I can't see you without my glasses. Where are you, Rudy?"

I waved at him and shouted, "Here I am! Here I am!"

And then the cloud that was Buddy's face blew away, and I was left all alone in the red and white snow.

♪ 𝅘𝅥𝅮 ♪

When I woke up there was a commotion. The guys were all excited. I heard somebody say, "Thank God." Through one of the windows I could see a pickup truck parked next to the bus, and some farmer-type guy standing next to our driver, waving at us to come out.

Buddy whispered to me, "I think you'd better come along, Seventy-eight, 'less you'd rather wait for the State Patrol to drive in some of your friends in blue from New York."

It was a hell of a ride in the truck, wind slicing our faces like a greased switchblade. When we got into town, Buddy called New York and yelled at the promoters, and they chartered another bus for us in Appleton. We slept all the way to Clear Lake and then had to unload our equipment all over again. I was getting damned sick of it. I started thinking maybe I should've become a butcher like Uncle Myshkin.

I'd only been backstage a few minutes when Buddy came flying at me like a lunatic. His eyes looked like big fried eggs behind those lenses. "They're here!" he hollered.

I said, "Huh?"

"The cops! They're here, and they're lookin' for you!"

"*Oy, g'vald,*" I said.

The amplifiers hadn't been brought in yet – no covers to hide under. Buddy was looking around like mad for someplace to hide me, and accidentally ran into a bass drum. He started unwinding the skin keys and said, "Quick – I'll do this side; you take the other."

"You expect me to hide in a goddamn drum?"

"Shut up and unwind these things. When we get the front off, fold yourself into a ball and get inside."

"But my ass will hang out."

"Damn it to tarnation, if you don't get in there, your ass'll be *arrested.*"

Back in 1959 I was a short little skinny guy, but it was still nearly impossible to squeeze me inside a Slingerland. Buddy put the skin back on. He was still turning the keys when I heard a very familiar voice.

"Excuse me, are you Mr. Holly?"

"Yas, yas. Ain't got no time for autographs, though."

"I'll just take a minute of your time, see. I'm Lieutenant Seymour, of the New York City Police Department. I'm looking for someone I believe is with your traveling show. Goes by the name of Keen, Rudy Keen—a.k.a. Rudolph Kearns. Kind of a homely fella. Looks a little like a perv."

Homely? A perv? I wanted to kill him! But I was packed inside that bass drum like a potato latke.

"Keen? Waalll, you're about a week late and a dollar short, lieutenant. Old Rudy jumped tour back in Milwaukee – or was it Mankato?"

"But look, see. His name is on the marquee outside."

"It is? That damn tour promoter. He's supposed to send out new stage billin'. Guess he hasn't got around to it."

Seymour wasn't going to buy that bullshit. I knew that much. I could hear him scuffing up the floor with his flat feet. "You mind if we have a look around?"

"Nope. Just don't get in the way. We got a show to do."

I didn't hear anything else, not for a long time. I kept expecting to be let out, but no one came around. Suddenly there was a little bang on the drum skin and Buddy whispered, "Pssst! I'm afraid you're gonna have to stay in there for the show. The dicks haven't left yet."

"For the show? For the *whole show?* Are you kidding?" No answer. "Buddy, goddamn it! I can't stay in here one more second! Buddy? Buddy?"

I was trapped. You know how it is when you're in an uncomfortable situation and your foot falls asleep? Well, my whole *body* fell asleep. And I'm highly claustrophobic. You could put me in the middle of the Grand Canyon and I'd feel like there wasn't enough room. Then someone picked up the drum – I was being carried to the risers.

"Jesus Christ," one of the stagehands said. "Does this drum feel heavy to you?"

"Yeah," the other one said. "And I thought I heard whimperin'."

"Whimperin'?"

"Yeah. You know, like when someone whimpers."

"That was probably you tryin' to lift it."

The lights went down. While the MC started the introductions, there was a tap on the skin, "I'm sittin' in for Carl. They took him to the hospital for frostbite. Just hold on in there. Put your hands over your ears."

"Buddy?" I said. "Please let me out. I'm claustro – "

But it was too late. **BOOM! BOOM! BOOM! BOOM!** The band had kicked in. I held my hands over my ears just like Buddy had told me to, but I think my eardrums must've blown out during the first eight bars. It sounded like the invasion of Normandy in there, and that goddamn foot pedal was beating hell out of my side. While the music blasted I was screaming, "NOT SO HARD! LIGHTEN UP, ALREADY!" But nobody heard me. During Buddy's set, another guy sat in for him, and Christ, did *he* have a heavy foot. By the end of the show I was nearly unconscious, dripping with sweat, deaf in both ears, sore all over – not even a human being anymore, just a blintz, a jelly blintz. And just when I thought it was all over, the drummer started up again. **BOOM! BOOM! BLAM!**

"NO ENCORES!" I yelled. "THEY ONLY PAID TWO BUCKS TO GET IN – THEY DON'T NEED ENCORES!"

But do you think they heard me? Forget it. *I* couldn't even hear me. I can't say how long I was in that stupid drum; all I know is, it got real cold near the end, and I realized I was being loaded on the bus. I figured they'd forgotten I was inside and I'd freeze to death in the luggage compartment. I thought, Good. *Let me die. It would be a mitzvah.*

But no such luck. All I did was pass out. I came to again when they were pulling off the drum skin. We were in a motel room – I saw Ritchie and Buddy and J.P. peeking in at me. Their mouths were moving, but I couldn't hear a word they were saying. My ears were a disaster, totally shot, and there was blood dripping out of them. They pulled me out, but I couldn't unbend. J.P. got down on the floor next to me and tried to stretch me out flat with his big old hands.

"OW! YOU'RE KILLIN' ME! LEGGO! MY GODDAMN SPINE IS BROKEN!"

Buddy was standing over me and saying something – but I had no idea what. I was living in a silent movie. I pointed to my ears and shook my head, but he kept right on talking. So I said, "I CAN'T HEAR A WORD YOU'RE SAYING. I'M FUCKING DEAF."

Then Buddy cupped his mouth up around my ear. He must've been screaming, but it only sounded like a whisper to me.

"WHAT?" I said.

"I said, we can get you out of (mumble ... mumble ... mumble)."

The second he stopped screaming, I couldn't hear him anymore.

"WHAT?"

"... to Minnesota."

"OKAY," I said. "I HEARD MINNESOTA. WHAT ABOUT MINNESOTA?"

Buddy gave up. He looked frustrated and worried, and that's when J.P. started playing charades for me. He stuck his arms straight out at his sides and ran all over the room. *That's it*, I thought. *The poor bastard has finally looned-out. That's what happens when you let a grown man talk all day on a pretend telephone.*

I said, "I THINK THE BOPPER'S ON GOOFBALLS."

Everybody rolled their eyes and shook their heads. I didn't know what the hell they were trying to tell me, and if you want to know the *emmes*, I really didn't give a shit. I just wanted to get some sleep. I was exhausted. Then somebody handed Buddy a note pad and a pencil. He jotted something down and held the pad for me to read. The pad said:

DO YOU WANT TO FLY WITH US?

I was rolled into a ball and couldn't straighten out, my ears were bleeding and I'd spent the last three hours inside a bass drum. So when they asked me if I wanted to *fly*, I thought they wanted me to take drugs with them. I mean, there was J.P. buzzing around the room, and people asking me if I wanted to fly – what would *you* have thought?

I said, "SHIT, NO. I'M NOT GONNA DO THAT. IT'S HABIT FORMING."

Then I guess I passed out again, because when I woke up the next morning, I was still on the floor in the same spot. Somebody had covered me with a blanket. I was finally able to stand up, and I could hear a little better. I kept snapping my fingers next to each ear to sort of test them out. Then I showered, found my bag on the bed, and changed. When I got out to the bus, one of the guys said, "Feeling better?"

I said, "A little. Where's Buddy?"

He lit a cigarette and told me I must've been out of it the night before. Buddy and Ritchie and The Bopper went on ahead in a private plane so they'd have enough time to have their stage clothes cleaned. Buddy had wanted to take me with them to get me out of town and on a train.

So *that's* what they'd been trying to tell me. Well – it didn't matter. There was no way I could've made a trip like that in the condition I'd been in. I took a seat on the bus and thought about my lousy luck. I'd just have to wait till the next stop to try and catch a train.

When we pulled out, I thought about Buddy on the plane. Buddy loved those little planes. He wanted to get a pilot's license. And if I knew Buddy, he'd probably talked the pilot into letting him fly the thing most of the way there. I all of a sudden got a picture in my head of The Bopper running around the room with his arms out. I'd thought he was pretending to be a bird. A big, weird bird.

When the bus came to a stop next to the motel, I looked to see if there were any police cars around. The band guys picked up their stuff and started filing out, and I asked one of them to go inside and see if the coast was clear. While I was waiting for him to come back, I buttoned up my overcoat and grabbed my bag. It sure took him a long time. For a minute I thought maybe he'd forgotten about me, but then I saw him walk out of the motel. He was walking real slow and sort of looking at the ground with his head down. He stepped up onto the bus and just stared at me.

"Well?" I said. "Is it okay?"

"Rudy, I think ... I think you'd better come inside."

I wish I could remember that guy's name. It was like *Felton* or something. Thin guy. Little pencil mustache. Anyway, I said, "Is it the cops? Are they here, man?"

"No, Rudy. No cops."

"Then what the hell's the matter? Why do you look like that?"

He didn't answer for a couple of seconds. He just swallowed and shook his head and said, "Come inside, Rudy."

Inside the lobby everybody was standing around a TV – a little black and white TV. There was a reporter standing in a field. *It's Minnesota*, I figured. *A field is big news.*

"What's going on?" I said. "Where's Buddy?"

"Shhh," somebody said.

I had to stand right next to the set to hear what the reporter was saying.

"... a chartered single engine airplane that never reached its destination. Authorities have described it as a red Beachcraft Bonanza. The three popular singing stars were on their way to an engagement when the accident occurred near Mason City, Iowa. There is no word at this time as to whether the crash was due to pilot error or mechanical failure. Once again, Buddy Holly, Ritchie Valens, and J.P. Richardson are dead."

I just stared at the screen. They showed a twisted up piece of metal in the snow. You'd never have guessed it had once been an airplane if they hadn't told you. It looked more like a squashed Volkswagen, or a tool shed that had been blown apart by a cyclone.

I dropped my bag on the floor and then tapped my ears to see if I'd heard right. *They're not dead*, I thought. *They CAN'T be dead.* The TV just kept showing the mess in the snow, and then they started playing "Peggy Sue." Two or three of our guys broke down and started crying, right there in the lobby. It's when I heard Buddy's voice that it hit me. I felt like somebody had kicked me in the stomach. I whispered, "*Oy, a broch!*" which means like – a *catastrophe!* The worst thing that could happen.

I sat down in one of the worn lime green lobby chairs and remembered that dream I'd had on the bus a day earlier – the Stratocaster out on the snow, my footprints turning red, Buddy's face in the sky. I'd seen the future. Don't ask me how – I don't understand that stuff very good. I'm not usually very whadayacallit... psycho. Most of the time I can't tell you what's going to happen two seconds from now, let alone twenty-four hours. But when I *am* psycho, I'm *really* psycho. Maybe I'd passed through another wormhole. I don't know. Lately I've been thinking that it could have something to do with that big electric shock I got on stage in Massachusetts, because I've had psycho things happen to me since then, but not before. Maybe I should call up Dionne Warwick on that psycho hotline. She might be able to help me, being in the business and all. I see her on those TV commercials, surrounded by psychos, and I always wonder if they tipped her off in advance about her career ending. "I see no bookings in your future, Dionne. Time to be a spokesperson." Yeah, maybe I'll give her a jingle. When the rates come down. I'm not paying retail.

So where was I? Hotlines, psychos, ugly green lobby chairs – oh. So I was sitting there in the lobby and I had the same feeling I'd had when I first read in the paper about Brenda. What a lousy feeling. You want to help the person who's dead, but you can't. I imagined Buddy lying out in the snow with Ritchie and J.P.. I felt so bad for them, but there was nothing I could do. I sort of let my mind drift while "Peggy Sue" was playing, and I saw Sam Cooke showing me the bullet wound in his shoulder, and Buddy showing me the British trade paper when he'd found out that Stek-Circ owned all our foreign rights, and I remembered Preston Allerton telling me, "I wouldn't be surprised if Buddy was history in five months." That had been exactly five months ago.

It was a set up. Buddy had been murdered.

Was I guessing? Hell no! I *knew* it. But how was I supposed to prove it? And what was I supposed to do about it – kill Preston? I was already wanted for murder. Since I couldn't do anything, I just got my room key and went off to be by myself.

I sat on my bed and felt worse and worse the more I thought about Buddy. I picked up my guitar. Notes and words started coming to me out of the blue. And that's how I wrote my song about Buddy. It wasn't one of those awful tribute numbers. It was a real personal expression of what Buddy meant to me. Maybe you've heard it.

Buddy In The Sky With No Glasses

Copyright 1959, by Rudy Keen

He was just that kind of guy,
Never gave no one no jive.
I think I'll always wonder why,
I saw Buddy in the sky,
With no glasses.

Can he see us when he looks?
How's he gonna read his books?
Maybe you'll see by and by,
Buddy in the sky,
With no glasses.

No glasses, no glasses,
He's up there with the gases.
He sang sweet as molasses,
Always knocked us on our
Asses.
Buddy's in the sky,
But he's got no glasses.

It's amazing how those lyrics have held up after all this time, isn't it? All right, all right. I'll admit it. I'm a sentimentalist. I recorded it later that year. It wasn't a big hit or anything. And I hate to start pointing fingers while I'm writing about Buddy, but does that title sound a little too familiar to you? Hm? Now, I know that John Lennon claimed "Lucy In The Sky With Diamonds" came to him when his son brought home a picture from school. That's a nice story. Okay – I'm a generous guy. I'm willing to give him the benefit of the doubt. It's still a stretch to think that my song didn't influence him. And while we're at it, remember "Judy In Disguise With Glasses," by John Fred and The Playboy Band? I don't know what *his* excuse is. All I know is this – I wrote that song in 1959. Enough said.

I was singing that song when all of a sudden there was a knock on my door. It was Marco, a sax player with the band. I got up and let him in.

"You okay, man?" he asked

"I'm all right."

He just stood there looking kind of awkward-like. His eyes were red. I knew he must've been crying earlier. "Before he left last night, Buddy wrote something on a piece of paper. He asked me to give it to you when you woke up. I'm sorry, Rudy, but I completely forgot about it till now."

"That's okay," I said. "Take it easy, Marco. It's a bad time for all of us."

He reached in his pocket and pulled out a little note written on motel stationery. I didn't open it right away. I wanted to be alone when I did that.

"You know what that promoter wants us to do?" Marco said.

"Bend over so he can screw us better?"

"You got it. He wants us to go on tonight, even after what happened. *And* he wants to subtract Buddy's salary."

Isn't that beautiful? The music business. Bunch of bastards.

"Are you gonna do it?" I asked him.

"We kind of figure maybe the guys would've wanted it that way. Are you goin' on with us?"

"I don't think so, Marco."

"Well," he said, grabbing my hand, "It's been good workin' with you, Rudy."

"Back at you, Marco."

He left and closed the door after him. I sat back down on the bed and looked at the little folded note. I could hardly keep my hands still as I opened it. Then I read this:

Stek-Circ spelled backwards is CRICKETS.

7   'Angel On The Highway'

"Rudy, where are you?"

"I can't tell you that. The phone might be bugged."

I was in a phone booth at a train station in Indiana, talking to Eddie. I called him the first chance I got. I should've called collect. Every three minutes I had to pump a handful of quarters into the goddamn thing.

"You still with the tour?"

"No. I split."

"Good move," Eddie said. "Stay the hell away. Who knows who'll be next?"

There was a guy standing outside the booth, waiting to use the phone. He was making me nervous. I hoped he wasn't a plain-clothes dick, and that he didn't recognize me.

"You've heard about Buddy and Ritchie?" I said.

"I haven't been able to sleep, I'm so sick about it. Ain't it terrible?"

"It's a *broch*," I said.

"Huh?"

There wasn't enough loose change in the *world* to get Eddie through a long-distance Yiddish lesson. "Nothing," I said. "Forget it."

Now the guy outside the booth was pacing and slapping a rolled-up newspaper against his leg. I watched him out of the corner of my eye.

Eddie said, "I guess Sam was wrong when he said they wouldn't dare knock off three famous stars at once."

I hate to quibble, but it was Buddy, Ritchie, and The Bopper, so technically it was two and a *half* stars, not three. But like I say, I hate to quibble. Close enough.

"Listen, Eddie. I haven't got much time, and there's some stuff you should know." I had to catch him up on everything that had happened since we'd seen each other. I gave him a pretty good description of the hole in Sal's head (a quarter, I tell you) when I found him dead in his apartment, and there was always the news about me being wanted for the murder – but that was nothing compared to what Buddy and I had discovered, that the same company that had been after Sal coincidentally owned the overseas licensing to all our songs.

The line went silent for a few seconds. Then Eddie said, "Holy Hunchbacked Helen."

"I thought it was *Hannah*," I said.

"Who?"

"The expression. Buddy always said, 'Holy Hunchbacked *Hannah*'."

"He was from Texas. In Oklahoma it's *Helen*."

"Oh."

Just then the guy standing outside the booth slapped the door real hard with his newspaper. I'd been expecting something like this. I banged the door open and said, "What?"

"I need to use the phone."

"*You* need to use the phone? And what does it look like *I'm* doing – making borscht?"

He gave me a dirty look. "Delinquent," he said, and walked away.

"*Alter kocker!*" I hollered back. I'd been wrong about him. He wasn't a plain-clothes dick. He was just a dick.

"Rudy, you still there?"

"Yeah, I'm here. Jesus – if you're under twenty-one in this country and wear high heels and satin pants, you've got no rights."

"*That will be one dollar and fifty-five cents for the next three minutes,*" the operator said.

I reached in my pocket and dropped about twenty coins all over the floor. I had to bend over to get them, and I knocked my head real hard against the side of the booth.

"Ow!"

"*One dollar and –* "

"I know! I heard you! I'm goin' as fast as I can! I just knocked the shit out of my head and – "

"*... fifty-five cents for the next three minutes.*"

Every time I dropped in another coin, the goddamn phone went, *dong!*

"You there, Rudy?"

Dong! Dong!

"I'm here, already! I've got to feed this *farshlugenah* phone!"

Dong!

"Look, man," Eddie said, "I knew Stek-Circ was my British publisher, but I didn't know this other stuff. Can't you go to the cops about it?"

"I'm *wanted*, Eddie."

"Oh, that's right. Well then, I'm just gonna have to get away from Allerton, contract or no contract."

"No – don't do anything that might give him the idea you know what's going on. Remember what happened to Sal. Remember what happened to Brenda."

"And Buddy."

"Yeah," I sighed. "And Buddy. Now listen to this, Eddie. Just before Buddy got on that plane, he sent me a note. I didn't get it till the next day. It said, 'Stek-Circ spelled backwards is *Crickets.*'"

"Jee-zus! What does it mean?"

"I don't know. But Preston put the screws to me a few months ago to write a Buddy sound-alike song, and Buddy himself was pretty convinced his records weren't charting in the U.S. because of some plot."

"The same thing's happenin' to me! Have you heard my new record, 'Teenage Heaven'?"

Oy vey. I'd been afraid he was going to bring this up. "Heard it? Yeah, I've heard it."

"Well, see – it's only reached number ninety-nine. That's very suspicious, Rudy. What did you think of it?"

"It's, uh – it's got a nice sax solo."

"Yeah, it's rippin', ain't it? So how come it only hit number ninety-nine?"

"Eddie, for Chrissake. It's got the same melody as 'Oh, Home On The Range'."

"Not *exactly.*"

"Yes, Eddie. Exactly. You don't need a conspiracy to explain *that.* I think you ought to go back to the 'Summertime Blues' sound."

"What will I call it?"

"I don't know. Just make it sound like 'Summertime Blues' and call it something else."

"Somethin' else, huh?"

"Yeah. Now, I can't put all the pieces of this thing together by myself. Think about that Crickets-spelled-backwards message, and if you come up with anything, let me know."

"Okie-dokey. Oh! And whatever you do – "

"*That will be one dollar and fifty-five cents for the next three minutes.*"

"Eddie? What were you saying? Whatever I do – what?"

"*... One dollar and fifty-five cents for the next three – *"

"I heard you the *first* time, you A-T and T bitch."

I was digging for more coins when the operator said, "It's a federal crime to use profanity while speaking to a public telephone employee, sir."

"Oh, shit! I thought you were a recording!"

"Now you've done it again. You've used profanity twice."

"I'm sorry! Jesus, I'm trying to get these goddamn coins out of my fucking pocket, and – "

"That is the *third* time you've used profanity while speaking to a – "

What – she thought I couldn't fucking *count*? I knew how many times I used profanity. Not nearly as many as I wanted to. I dropped in a dollar fifty-five, and the phone went *dong! Dong! Dong! Dong!*

"Eddie? Hey Eddie – what were you saying?"

But all I got was a dial tone. He'd hung up. Now I'd never know what it was he'd tried to tell me. I slammed the receiver down, and wouldn't you know it? The phone ate my goddamn change. I dialed "O". I was pretty steamed and I at least wanted my money back.

"Operator."

The same operator! What were the chances?

"Hey, I just got cut off during a long distance call and you didn't give me my money back."

"Oh – it's *you*. Mr. Filthy Mouth."

"Hey, look – I thought you were a recording, all right? Now how about giving me back my dollar fifty-five."

"If you tell me your name and address, we will mail you a refund."

"Name? Address? Uh – you don't understand."

"Name and address, sir."

"Can't you just push a button and return my change?"

"Sir, we don't have any buttons."

134

"Well, you oughta get some. The rates you people charge and you got no buttons. What the hell am I going to do with a check for a dollar and a half?"

"May I remind you of our policy concerning profanity, sir?"

It was obvious I wasn't going to get my money back, and she had no idea who I was, so I figured, What've I got to lose? "Operator?"

"Yes?"

"Eat me."

♪   ♫   ♪

I only mention this next bit because it's another piece of rock and roll history that you'd never have known if I didn't tell you. Eddie took that advice I'd given him about his next record ... to make it sound like "Summertime Blues" and call it something else. It was released later that year, in July, I think. It had that "Summertime Blues" sound, and he called the damn song "Somethin' Else." I didn't mean for him to *literally* call it "Somethin' Else." I just meant he should give it a different title. It's a good thing I didn't say, "Call it any fucking thing you want," or else that would've been the title – "Any Fucking Thing You Want," by Eddie Cochran. Eddie could be a little too concrete sometimes. By the way, that record reached number 58, so I'd shaved off 35 chart points for him over his last release. I'm not trying to be petty or anything; I'm just interested in telling you the truth here, the *emmes*. And who knows all the rock and roll truth? Rudy knows. Trust me, babe.

So what did I do then? Let's see, I think I bought a bag of popcorn and took a leak – but that's not important. It seems to me I bought a train ticket to ... uh, Scranton. Yeah. That's right. Scranton, Pennsylvania. That was my plan – to break up the trip back to Manhattan into little runs, sort of zigzag my way back home. That way Seymour couldn't just go to a station in Iowa or Minnesota and say, "Did anybody buy a ticket to New York today?" and then have somebody waiting for me when the train pulled in. It was a pretty good idea, too, because it worked. The only bad thing about it was I had a lot of extra time on my hands between trains, and at every station there was always a newspaper and magazine stand with Buddy's and Ritchie's faces looking out at me. (It's funny, they never put The Bopper's face on a cover.) Came damn close to breaking my heart all over again. And they'd play their songs over the radio. I'd hear "Oh, Donna" and just about bust out in tears. Or else "Heartbeat" would come on and I'd hear that voice and turn around and expect to see Buddy standing next to me. And isn't it just like the music business to do that – to let a perfectly good song sink until the guy who recorded it died, and *then* turn it into a hit? When he was alive no one was interested. Now they couldn't hear it enough.

When I finally got to New York, it was a sunny, cold day in February. I was *home*, man. Ask any New Yorker how good it feels to come back home after being away. It's the gonest. There's something about the dirty ring in the sky and the noise that really gets to you. But I couldn't go *home*-home. They'd be waiting for me – the cops. I had to live on the streets. I'd used up most of my money on train tickets, and I'd left my stuff with the guys on the tour. I had a spare change of clothes – a t-shirt and a pair of blue jeans and some sneakers, that's it. I'd even given away my red Rickenbacker guitar. Gave it to a guy named Frankie who took my place. I couldn't walk around with a guitar case; it would've been like a neon sign that said, "Arrest me. I'm the guy you're looking for."

I stayed in transcient hotels for the first week or two, but then I went broke. I'd never had to sleep in a park before. I'd never had to ask strangers for food or money, or take a sponge bath in a service station washroom, stepping around assorted bodily waste products. (I know the human body is supposed to be beautiful, but it sure makes some ugly stuff.) I had checking and savings accounts, but I couldn't get to them because I was afraid the police had warned my bank that I was wanted for murder. The minute I tried to withdraw some money – boom! Arrest city. So I got a job in a car wash – which is a lovely way to make a living in February and March. There's nothing like walking around in thirty degree temperatures with soaking wet shoes and clothes. I caught a cold and then a sore throat and then bronchitis. I figured I'd just wait around till I caught pneumonia and then I'd die in my sleep in a subway station, next to more assorted bodily waste products.

One day while I was walking to work, I went past a record store and saw it – an album cover that showed a red airplane failing out of the sky. It was called *Rock And Roll Eternity* – a collection of songs by Buddy, Ritchie, and The Bopper. They'd only been killed four weeks before, and the goddamn album was already on the stands. Those songs never should've been issued. They were early recordings that none of the guys would've wanted anybody to hear. I waited for the record store owner to open the joint, and then I went in and checked out the credits on the back of the sleeve. Every song was licensed by either Blue Rose or Stek-Circ, and of course the label was Caboose. I happened to know that getting an LP edited, mastered, pressed and shipped was an eight-week job, minimum. And here Caboose had done it in half that time. How? You got your detective hat on? Only one way: they must've known that Buddy and the others were going to get killed. And how would they have known that? Don't make me have to lead the horse to the water here and stick his goddamn head in it. *Conspiracy.* Yeah, yeah – I know. I know what you're going to say. You're going to say I'm crazy. What – you think there *aren't* conspiracies? Look what they did to Caesar. Turned his back on his pals for one crummy minute and the bastards shot him. Used a derringer or a musket or something. Look at Marilyn Monroe. Well, you can't anymore, but look what *happened* to her, I mean. And what about Abraham, Martin, and Nancy Kerrigan? The world's filled with conspiracies. There's probably someone plotting to get *you* right now. But don't worry about that until you finish reading this book. (Did I mention it makes a beautiful holiday present, this book?)

So I'd been staring at the back of the album cover for about fifteen minutes when the record store guy said, "Are you gonna buy it, or are you trying to hypnotize it?"

And I said, "Buy it? This piece of *drek*? Are you kidding? This shit? You want me to *buy* it? It's just a cheap trick to make money off of dead guys. You should be ashamed of yourself for selling it!"

Yeah – that's what I told him. Then he threw my ass on the sidewalk. But that doesn't matter, because I got this idea. I knew that if I could prove that Tal Ltd. or Stek-Circ planned the album before the plane went down, it would link them to the crash. Then maybe the NYPD would think twice and investigate them for Sal's murder. That album was the smoking gun. But first I had to find out who called the shots at Stek-Circ, and I didn't know how to do that. What I needed was somebody who knew business and the law – and that was Uncle Zollie.

I called him from a pay phone in Brooklyn.

"Hel-lo?"

"Uncle Zollie, it's Rudolph."

"Vit the red nose?"

"Cut it out, Uncle Zollie. I need help."

When I was a kid he always used the red-nose joke on me. Now I was a disgrace to the family, not only because I was a rock and roll star who wiggled his *tochkes*, but also because I was wanted for murder, which they considered just a little bit worse. I got every Jewish proverb he could remember thrown at me. I stuck it out, though. Nearly made me nuts. When he was all through telling me what a *lemel* I was, I asked him for a favor. On the outside he's boring and annoying, but on the inside he was only a *little* boring and annoying. I said I needed to know who owned Tal Ltd., Stek-Circ, Blue Rose, and Caboose, and if there was any connection between all four of them.

"Can you do that?"

"Can a clock tell time? I'll see vot I can do. Vy you need to know this?"

"Because it might get me off the hook."

Big sigh. "Vare are you?"

"I can't say. I'm hiding."

"Then how am I gonna give you the information?"

"I'll call you. In a week or two."

"You got 'nuff money?"

"I'm okay."

"You got time for a joke?"

"I don't think so, Uncle Zollie." His jokes took three hours to tell. He always got off the track, and I'd heard every one of them before.

"So there's this man who takes his vife on a second honeymoon. Everything vas so romantic – candles at dinnah, vine in crystal glasses. He gets carried avay vit passion – you know how it is – and the last night of the second honeymoon, he makes love to her... *doggie style.*"

"Look, Uncle Zollie, I should get going."

"And in the morning he feels such guilt. Such guilt! He's done a terrible thing! He's afraid to tell his rabbi, but he needs to be forgiven. So he goes to a priest in vun of them confession boxes. You seen 'em?"

"Yeah, I guess. In movies."

"They confess in boxes. And he says, 'Fatha, I've done somethin' sinful,' and the priest, he says, 'Tell me, my son, and I can forgive you.' So the man feels relieved, like he's just taken a varm bath. You know the feeling?"

"I used to."

"That's how he feels. And he says to the priest, 'I made love to my vife doggie style.' Vell – the priest can't believe his holy ears. He says, 'You svine! You're an abomination! Get outa my confession box right now, and take your depraved dirty stories vit you! You make me sick!' Now the man, he feels voyse than evah."

"Uncle Zollie, I've heard it."

"No, you haven't. Shuddup. So the man goes to a minister – differen' religion. Presbylutheran or somethin'. And he says to the minister, 'Reverand, I've done somethin' so awful,' and the minister says, 'There is nothin' so awful that God can't forgive it. Tell me vot it is, and I'll forgive you.' The man's hope is restored! He feels vonderful. He tells the minister, 'I've made love to my vife – doggie style.' Vell, the minister is horrified! He slaps the man across the face and says, 'Get outa my church! Such a disgusting thing, you'll boyn in hell forevah, you *chozzer!*'"

"Wait a minute," I said. "The minister calls him a *chozzer?*"

"Maybe not a *chozzer*. I'm embroiderin' a little here. Okay, Mister-von't-let-me-tell-a-joke?"

"But I tell ya, I've heard it before."

"No you haven't. So the man is consumed vit guilt, at the end of his rope, eatin' his own *kishkes* out vit remorse. He's got no choice; he's gotta see the rabbi. He says, 'Rabbi, I've done the most awful thing. I'm an abomination, a disgrace to mankind. You gotta help me.' And the rabbi says, 'So tell me, already.' The man says, 'I'm so ashamed. I made love to my vife.' And the rabbi says, 'So?' The man says, '*Doggie style.*' He closes his eyes, vaitin' to be thrown out of the temple, to be slapped across the face again, but the rabbi just says, 'So? You're forgiven.' Vell, the man can't believe it. It vas so easy! He says to the rabbi, 'Just like that? But I vent to a priest and he kicked me outa his confession box. I told a minister vot I done, and he said I'd boyn in hell forevah.'"

I interrupted him. "And the rabbi said, 'So what do goyim know from fancy fucking?'"

There were a few seconds of silence, and then Uncle Zollie said, "You've hoyd it before?"

"I *told* you I'd heard it before."

"You could've at least pretended you hadn't."

"Why should I pretend?"

"A *mensch* would pretend."

♪   ♫   ♪

In a little less than a year I'd gone from being a nobody to a star to a bum. I'd been framed, I was a fugitive, and my future depended on Uncle Zollie playing Mike Hammer. I lived in a subway station and my overcoat was my bed. If I so much as saw a cop, I'd have to try not to piss in my pants, and then get lost in a crowd. My life kind of ended back in that field in Iowa, where Buddy's ended. Days went by. I stayed sane by writing songs in my head while I vacuumed Cadillacs and cleaned their wheel covers. After two weeks, I called Uncle Zollie again to see what he'd found out.

"*Blaybt a kashe,*" he said.

"Huh?"

"Eh? Already you forget? Too long away from home, Rudolph. You're losin' the language."

"So what does it mean?"

"It means I haven't figured it out yet. Tal Limited owns Blue Rose Music – so much I know. I checked ownership registration to see who owns Tal Limited. You von't believe – Hogarth Interiors of London. Vot the hell kinda entertainment organization you vit? A bunch of *fagelah* vindow trimmahs?"

"Who owns Hogarth Interiors?"

"*Blaybt a kashe.* I got no idea."

"What about Stek-Circ? All my British records are licensed through them."

"I got nothin'. You vant I should keep lookin'?"

"Yeah. Please."

"So I'll keep lookin'."

"Thanks, Uncle Zollie."

"Did you hear the one about the rabbi who goes into a bar vit a midget on his head?"

"Yes."

"You sure?"

"I'm sure."

"Hm," Uncle Zollie said, clicking his tongue a few times. "Here's vun – there vas a priest, a hookah, and a duck ..."

"Oops! The operator wants another dime. Gotta go."

And then I wondered – a *duck?*

♪ 𝅘𝅥𝅮 ♪

It was a day in April – I'm pretty sure it was April because I remember thinking that soon it would be warm enough to sleep in the park. I was vacuuming the carpet of a Dodge, and the manager of the car wash had the radio on. A song started playing. At first I thought it was Buddy – I could barely hear over the whine of the vacuum. I turned off the power, listened carefully, and ... son of a bitch! It was the Holly copy I'd written for Preston, a tune called "Ready For You Right Now." Whoever the singer was, he'd copied every one of Buddy's vocal tricks, the hiccupping, the snappy little falsetto at the end of the lines. When it was finished the DJ said, "That's number thirty this week on our Hot Record Survey, 'Ready For You Right Now,' by Derek Halloway. I've got a hunch we'll be hearing a lot more of that young man soon."

And I thought, *No you won't, because I'm going to wring the bastard's neck.*

The weasel had a hit with my song. Only one person could've given him that material – Preston Allerton. The coincidences were multiplying. First Preston predicted that Buddy would be history in five months, and a few weeks after the plane crash a collection of Buddy's material is on the market, and then a Holly imitation hits the charts. That was the straw that fractured the camel's vertebra, baby. I threw down the vacuum hose, walked out of the car wash, and never once looked back. Well – okay. I looked back once, just once, when the owner of the Dodge started screaming at me.

"Where are you going? Look at my car – it's filthy!"

And I said, "You're right. How dare you bring in a mess like that?"

I ran to a record store (a different one; I didn't need to get my ass thrown on the sidewalk again) and bought the record. The publisher? Any guesses? Stek-Circ. All that time I'd been wondering who could've found out about the last minute flight soon enough to have it sabotaged. Derek Halloway, that's who. He was the Stek-Circ connection. Remember when he cut the strings of Buddy's guitar and then wanted to replace him? Oohh – and this is what really got me dark, what really lit my fire, man. On the record label, right under the song title, the credits read: "Allerton-Keen", like we'd collaborated. I wanted to kill. But it's a sin to kill, and I could just see me getting kicked out of a confession box.

I jumped on a subway to Manhattan, looking like something that had just crawled out of *The Night Of The Living Car Wash*, and smelling like I'd just swum in a river of Simonize. I must've even looked worse than I thought, because while I was waiting to cross Fifty-third Street, I thought I felt rain, and when I held my hand out to check, some business dork stuck a dollar in it, "Get a hot meal," he said.

"With a fucking *dollar*?" I said. "What – I should buy a can of beans and a match?"

I started having second thoughts in the elevator. *What if Allerton picks up the phone and calls the cops? MURDER ONE. Yikes!* But every time I thought of that Halloway bastard having a hit with my song, and Allerton's name under the title, I didn't care what happened to me. So take me to prison. Get it over with. At least I'd get a shower. At least I'd have a mattress. I just hoped it wouldn't have crabs.

The elevator doors opened and I walked right into Tal Ltd.. The snooty receptionist looked up at me and her mouth kind of fell open. "Uh – deliveries are in the rear," she said.

"I want to see Preston Allerton, and I want to see him now!" You've got to take command when you to talk to those people.

"I'm sorry, sir, but – "

"I'm not taking *no* for an answer! I want to see Allerton *now*."

"But sir – "

"Either Allerton comes out here this minute, or I'm going back there. Do you understand?"

I had her pretty intimidated. She got off her chair and started inching backwards. "I'm sorry, sir, but Mr. Allerton is no longer with us."

"Huh?"

She stood behind her chair, jittery as hell. "Mr. Allerton is no longer with Tal Limited, but if you'd like, you can speak to his successor."

That sucked. "Successor?"

"Yes, sir."

Boy, just when you think you're batting a thousand. "Yeah, well – okay."

She buzzed the intercom and a moment later some guy said, "I

142

told you, no interruptions."

"There's someone to see you, sir. He's looking for Mr. Allerton."

"Well, tell him Allerton doesn't work here anymore and get rid of him."

The receptionist shrugged at me like she didn't know what to do next.

"Tell him Rudy Keen is here," I said.

She was a tall, leggy thing. Gray flannel, lilly of the valley perfume. I tried to give her the eye, but she was too distracted to catch it. She pushed the button and introduced me, and the private office door just about exploded open.

"Rudy?"

Holy balls – it was *Sherman Katz*, Sal's old partner from K.O. Publishing.

"*Sherm?*" I said.

"Rudy, in God's name, what's happened to you? Where have you been?" He put his arms around me and hugged me, and then pushed me away real fast. "Jesus, you *stink*."

"It's nice to see you, too."

"I've been worried sick about you. I couldn't find you after the tour. There was even a rumor that you went down with the plane – that you disintegrated."

"No, that was my career that disintegrated," I said. "How did you end up here? What happened to Allerton? And where are my royalty checks?"

Sherm stuck his hands in his pants pockets, spread out his suitcoat, and with a big smile he said, "Me? I got lucky. Allerton got unlucky. They hired me for my years in the business and my client relationships."

"And my royalty checks?"

He wiped a smudge of dirt off my face with a handkerchief and then threw the handkerchief in a wastebasket. "Not to worry. Everything's being looked after. Right now we have to clean you up. You've got a career to get moving. I can't tell you how much I've looked forward to working with you, Rudy. You know, after being there at the start of your success."

"Career?" I said. "Aren't you forgetting a few things?"

Sherm looked confused. "What things?"

"To start with? Well, to start with, being wanted for murder."

The receptionist gasped and put a hand up to her mouth.

"Wanted?" He looked at the receptionist, and then held out his hand toward the door that used to belong to Preston. "Rudy, why don't you step into my office."

I gave the leggy chick the eye again, real suave, and walked slowly into Sherm's office. It was all changed – new furniture. Sherm closed the door and leaned against it.

"Rudy," he said, "you haven't been wanted for murder for months now."

"I haven't?"

"No. Why didn't you call in?"

"'Cause I didn't trust Preston, and I was afraid the phone might be bugged."

"And look at you – you been living on the streets?"

"Not exactly. Kind of under them."

First he shook his head, then he loosened his tie and opened his collar button. "For crying out loud, Rudy. The detective Tal Limited hired turned up three witnesses who were in the same bar as you the night the Taylor girl disappeared. They testified at the last minute in front of the grand jury – one of them had even taken a picture of a friend, and you showed up in the print – asleep on the bar, drooling. The charges were dropped."

"What about the other murder?"

"Sal? They dismissed all of that when the Taylor connection was scuttled. No evidence. No motive."

All that time in the car wash, in the subway. "You mean I've been living like a fucking bum for three months for no reason?"

"Not quite," Sherm said. "For about two weeks they were still looking for you. You've only been living like a fucking bum for no reason for two and a half months."

Some comfort. But it was good to know I was safe, that my name had been cleared. And it was great to be back with Sherm. I always liked him. He made me feel like I had a father. Not long distance, living on a kibbutz halfway around the world, but right there in New York.

Sherm – he wanted to talk about my career, but I had something else in mind.

"Wait a minute, Sherm. Man, have I got news for you. *Big* news."

He sat down behind his desk and got real serious. "All right.

Let's hear it."

"Just between you and me? You promise?"

"Of course. I'm your personal agent now."

"Okay." I pulled the Halloway record out of my jacket pocket and tried to break it in half, but it just bent. I threw it on his desk. "Look at that. Look at that piece of *drek*."

He picked it up, read the label – he had to turn it around because it was all bent – and then he just dropped it back down in front of him. "I know what you're going to say. That was Preston's idea. I thought it was wrong when I heard about it, but I wasn't with Tal Limited when the decision to release it was made."

"He forced me to write that goddamn song, Sherm. He never told me he was going to give it to that little bastard, or issue it right after Buddy died, with that stupid copycat vocal."

"I know, I know. It was in very bad taste."

"And he put his name on the credits! He didn't write one lousy word or note of it."

Sherm looked down at the record. "I suspected as much. It's what Sal used to do to you."

"That's not the worst of it," I said.

"No?"

"No. Hold that label up to a mirror and read the publisher's name."

"What?"

"Just do it."

He found a hand mirror in a drawer and then unbent the record and held the mirror up to it. "Yeah? So now what?" he said.

"What does it say?"

"Rudy, is this a joke? It doesn't say anything. All the letters are backwards."

I took the mirror and record from him and tried it myself. Damn. He was right. I thought that if you held it up to a mirror, then Stek-Circ would come out backwards, but it doesn't work that way.

"All right," I said. "Give me a pen and a piece of paper. Watch this."

I spelled out criC-ketS on the paper and slid it over to him. He looked at it and said, "So?"

"So? That's Stek-Circ spelled backwards."

"And?"

Boy – you had to explain *everything* to him. "And this: Buddy

145

Holly of The Crickets dies, and a few weeks later a Holly copy is released and published by a company that just *happens* to be Crickets spelled backwards."

Sherm was rubbing his chin with his hand. "Rudy, forgive me. I don't get it."

This was making me *meshugge*. I stood up and started walking back and forth in front of his desk. "What don't you get, Sherm? That plane crash wasn't an accident. I think someone from Stek-Circ had Buddy and Ritchie killed. And The Bopper, too."

Sherm looked up at me kind of funny, like he thought I'd blown a gasket. "Rudy, that's quite a leap you're taking there."

"Is it?"

"Yes. We license a lot of material through Stek-Circ. They're good business partners."

I leaned over the back of my chair and said, "Did you know that Derek Halloway, the little putz who made that record, sabotaged Buddy's guitar in Milwaukee and said he wanted to take Buddy's place?"

"Look, Rudy. A lot of acts wished they could've taken Buddy's place. And no, I didn't know about the guitar incident. What exactly happened?"

"The little weasel cut all the strings so Buddy wouldn't be able to go on."

"Are you sure it was Derek?"

"Oh, yeah. I'm sure."

"Did you see him do it? Do you have any proof?"

"Proof? Well ... no."

"Do you know anything about the aircraft having been tampered with?"

"Uh – not yet."

"Well, Rudy – "

"Sherm, you gotta believe me. I think someone at Stek-Circ did it. *And* I think they had Brenda and Sal killed, too."

Sherm was rubbing his forehead now. I think I was giving him a headache. "Brenda and Sal?"

"Yeah. Brenda told me before she disappeared that Stek-Circ was after Sal – that they set his apartment on fire."

"I remember the fire, but Sal told me it was because of a short circuit."

"He did?"

"Yes."

That didn't figure. Why would he tell Sherm one thing and Brenda another? Of course, he was always lying to Brenda, but usually about stepping out on her – not about guys trying to kill him.

"All right," I said. "I got something else. Sal told me before he died that someone shot at him while he was driving on Riverside Drive."

"Did he say they were from Stek-Circ?"

"Damn it, Sherm! Why won't you believe me?"

"I'm just trying to be logical about it. So far all you've got is a bunch of maybes – and you know yourself how it feels to be accused of something you didn't do when there's no proof you did it."

I couldn't understand it. It all made sense to me before I told Sherm about it, and now it didn't seem to make any sense at all. I thought, *Could I have been this wrong? Am I making it all up?*

I slumped down in the chair. "What about *Rock And Roll Eternity*, that album collection?"

"What about it?" Sherm asked.

"How did it get released so soon after the accident?"

"That had nothing to do with Stek-Circ. They're just the publishers. It was a Caboose Records project, headed by Hoyt Seamen."

There's a name I hadn't heard in a long time. Tell me it doesn't sound like a male reproductive problem. Go ahead, tell me.

"But how did he get it out in three or four weeks?"

"Caboose had the collection rights. With the new technology, it doesn't take any time at all to press and ship an album these days."

"It doesn't?"

"No."

Shit. I was wrong again. "All I know is, Buddy thought that Stek-Circ was behind what happened to all of us."

"Rudy – you're talking in circles. All of who?"

"You mean *whom*. You should say all of *whom*, not who."

"All right, already! All of *whom*?"

"Buddy, for one. He blamed Stek-Circ for the bus breaking down all the time, and for his records slipping down the charts."

"But Rudy, Stek-Circ isn't in the bus business, and Buddy's career had been lagging for some time. It's only natural to want to blame someone else for a thing like that."

"Well, Eddie will tell you."

"Eddie whom?"

"Now it's *who*. Eddie *who*, not *whom*. Eddie Cochran."

"What happened to Eddie?"

"Someone tried to run him over while he was changing a tire on his way to Vegas."

"Eddie told you Stek-Circ was behind it?"

"At first he thought it was Preston Allerton and Tal Limited. So did Sam."

"Sam? Sam ... *who*?"

"Sam Cooke. Showed me his hole in a men's room. A *bullet* hole, I mean. Right in his shoulder. Sniper shot him."

"Are you telling me that Eddie Cochran and Sam Cooke believe that our organization is trying to kill them?"

"Uh – huh. Gene Vincent, too."

"Gene told you that?"

"No. I've never met him. Eddie told me about Gene."

Sherm stood up now, and *he* was pacing this time. He took a bottle of Gelusil out of a drawer and started gulping it down, just like he used to when he worked with Sal. He tried to hide a few burps, but you can tell when someone's burping and trying to hide it. They get a funny look on their face.

"We certainly don't want to be putting off talent of that magnitude – Cooke and Cochran. We can't have it."

"So what are you going to do?" I asked.

Sherm sat back down and tapped a pencil against his desk blotter. "I'm going to conduct an investigation of my own. Rudy, you have my promise that if anything like a plot exists, and that if Stek-Circ or anyone at Tal Limited is responsible for it, I'll go to the authorities. Now, your career is already on the line. Let's not complicate things by making false accusations against an otherwise respectable company. I want you to give me your word that you'll keep quiet about all this until I've had a chance to find out as much as I can. Will you do that?"

"Okay. Thanks, Sherm."

"For nothing. Listen Rudy, you come first around here. I want you to remember that. And if you have any more information about Stek-Circ, pick up the phone and call me. Don't hesitate."

"I will."

"Good boy. Now let's make Rudy Keen a household name. You need a new record. And you're going to England for a series of concerts."

"England?"

"You bet. You're first two releases are doing very well there. Let's capitalize on it."

"But how will I get there?"

Sherm just looked at me, blank-faced. "Why, you'll take a plane."

A plane? After what just happened to Buddy and Ritchie? (And The Bopper?) "Geez, I don't know, Sherm."

"You don't *know*? You don't know you want to be famous and make a million dollars?"

"A million dollars?"

"It's within reach, Rudy, if you're willing to reach for it."

A million dollars. "Well, I guess I could take a plane."

"It beats swimming. Now – you got any new material?"

Did I have material? Did the Pope have a funny hat? We walked over to the rehearsal room and I sat down at the piano and played him "Buddy In The Sky With No Glasses." It knocked him out.

"Rudy, it's beauty-ful. I love it. Now how about a car crash song."

"Car crash song?"

"They're going to be very big."

"You want me to come up with something right now?"

"I've seen you do it before. Go on. Give it a shot."

I played a C chord and let it roll a little bit. "That'll be the introduction, take it down to an A-minor. But it should be on a guitar."

"Okay. Give it some melody and words."

"Uh ... how about this. 'Linda had no license / Linda couldn't drive / If I had only known it / She might still be alive.'"

"Socko!" Sherm said. "Keep going."

"All right. Let's see. 'Her face is in my memory / Her head on the median strip. / Her arms are on the shoulder / But I can't find her hips.'"

Sherm frowned. "A little morbid, maybe. Make it more romantic."

So I warmed it up a bit. "'She's an angel on the highway / A ghost out on the road. / I guess she didn't see the sign that said / Caution: Wide Load.'"

"I like it! I like it! That'll be the title – 'Angel On The Highway.'

Give me another verse."

Now I was really into it. "'She's an angel on the highway, / An angel in my heart, / She used to be my baby, / But then she came apart.'"

I don't want to brag – but how many times did I make entertainment history? Look at those lyrics real close and you can see how they marked my growth as an artist. Did you notice? Not one reference to ejaculation. I think I'd finally cleaned out my subconscious. It felt empty, anyway. And not to show off or anything, but two decades later in an article about 1950's music, *Billboard* said, "'Angel On The Highway' was undoubtedly the most sublimely insipid car crash song ever written." Hey – when you're hot, you're hot.

Anyway, things were happening for me again, baby – just like in the old days. I was in the groove. Sherm booked studio time for me and bought an airline ticket to London. I was supposed to leave in five days – practically no notice. And Ma was so happy I was home. It was kind of touching, for about three minutes. Then she started making me nuts again.

"I got chee-ken zoop for you. Come in the kee-chen."

"I don't want chicken soup, Ma. I need a suitcase."

"A zootcase? Vot for you need a zootcase?"

"I'm going to London."

"London?" She repeated everything I said. "London? But you just got home. Vot – you got *shpilkes*?"

I'd heard that expression all my life, and I still had no idea what a *shpilke* was. You never see a *shpilke*. Nobody I know was ever hospitalized for them. So I said, "Ma – what the hell are *shpilkes*?"

"*Shpilkes* are vot make you go to London ven you just get home. At least sit down and nosh. Uncle Myshkin sent over some lovely gefilte fish."

"I can't, Ma. I've got a European concert tour coming up."

She held both of her hands to her face and said, "Rudolph, it's true?"

"Yeah. Pretty cool, huh?"

"Thanks God! It's vonderful!"

"So I haven't got time for gefilte fish."

"Thanks God! Of course you got no time for gefilte fish. No vonder you got *shpilkes*. You gonna play the violin for the Queen!"

Oh, boy. "No, Ma. I'm not playing the violin for the Queen."

"So not the Queen. So vot? She's just a *shiksa* vit a crown."

"I'm not playing the violin at all."

Her face fell about a mile. "You're not vit the rock and the roll again."

"When are you going to understand? This is what I want to do!"

"So now you're gonna be a *een-ternational* heep shaker?"

"For your information, Ma, rock and roll isn't just wiggling and shaking and noise. It's a legitimate art form. You make it sound like I'm in a carnival or something."

"You gonna wear tight pants?"

"Well, yeah. I guess."

"Blue jeans?"

"No, satin."

"*Oy!* Like a *fagelah!*" That was nice. In case you've been wondering, *fagelah* is Yiddish for *faggot.* "That's the kind of life you vant – to be a rock and roll *fagelah?*"

"And what – the violin is supposed to be *manly?*"

"It's good enough for Itzhak Perlman."

"Itzhak Perlman doesn't *rock*, Ma."

"Of course he don't rock. He's no *fagelah!*"

Can I make a statement here? Can I just say something? When Elvis started wearing his hair long, all you used to hear was faggot, faggot, faggot. And a few months later every guy in the country wanted to look like him. Same with the Beatles. So let's get it straight – *Rock and roll is a very masculine lifestyle.* Ask anyone who's ever lived it. Except maybe Little Richard. Or Elton. Or Bowie. Or Mick. Or Boy George. Or Michael Jackson. Or Billy J. Kramer. On second thought, don't ask anyone. Just take my word for it.

♪ ♫ ♪

Before I left the states I had time to catch up with some old friends. I called Sam Cooke and told him I was in town, and he said we should meet up somewhere. I thought he meant a bar or a restaurant. But he told me he was going to a steam bath that afternoon with Bobby Darin, and he asked me to come along.

"A *shvitz?*" I said.

"No, man. They won't let you do that there."

"That's what we call a steam bath, Sam. Why a steam bath,

anyway?"

"Oh Rudy, you should try it. There's nothing like a steam bath. It relaxes you and opens up your pores."

"Yeah?"

"Oh, yeah," Sam said.

"That's good – getting your pores open and everything?"

"Hell, yes. You know how much dirt and oils and bacteria and junk you got trapped in your body 'cause of closed pores?"

"No. But please don't tell me."

"A lot. A lot, Rudy. And a steam bath will put lead in your pencil."

"What pencil?"

Sam said, "I *mean*, it's good for your sex life."

"I'll be there in a second."

Well, Sam wasn't kidding. The steam bath was real relaxing. And could that guy give a massage! Sam was the best. We all just had towels on, and steam was pouring out of everywhere, and boy, were our pores ever open. Bobby was lying on a bench and Sam was working on his shoulders. They talked for a while about the plane crash and how much they missed Buddy and Ritchie. (And The Bopper.) Both of them agreed with me that the crash was no accident, and that Allerton had something to do with it.

I said, "Wait till you hear the scoop. Allerton isn't with Tal Limited anymore. He split. My old publisher Sherman Katz took his place."

Bobby said, "Get out. Sherm?"

"You trust this Sherm?" Sam asked me.

"Oh, yeah," I said. "Sherm's a good guy. I'm just surprised he got mixed up with an operation like Tal Limited."

Bobby said, "It's just like that son of a bitch Allerton to skip out after the dirty work is done. He's in hiding, I'll betcha. Oh, Sam. That's good. That's great."

Then it was my turn. Sam went to work on my spine while he hummed "You Send Me." That just shows you how manly rock and roll artists really are. There we were, all being manly. Man, were we manly, sitting around in towels, sweating our asses off, massaging each other. While Sam tried to rub out a tight muscle in my back, I told them about how Stek-Circ spelled backwards was Crickets, and about them owning Eddie's and Gene's and my foreign rights.

"I don't like it," Sam said. "It's like Buddy was on their agenda.

I'm willing to go public about the crash being a plot, but not until we have proof."

"I got somebody working on that," I told him.

"Good. You get the proof, I'll testify with you. How's that spot right there?"

"A little lower," I said.

"There?"

"Oh, man! Oh, yeah!"

Yeah, it was a very masculine moment, all right, the three of us putting lead in our pencils. Except they had dates to use their pencils on. Me – I went home with mine and wrote notes to myself.

♪　♫　♪

When I landed at Heathrow International Airport in London in April of 1959, I had the mother of all hangovers. It's a long story, and you know how I hate to digress. I guess I was just nervous on the plane, expecting it to crash any second, and so I had a few too many cocktails. I got totally shit-faced and started bragging to the stewardesses about being a famous rock and roll singer. They didn't believe me. The last thing I remembered before I passed out, I was singing "Bop-Sha-Bop" in the washroom, with my head in the aluminum toilet. I wasn't puking, though. I just needed reverb.

I didn't wake up until pretty late the next afternoon. At first I thought I'd only *dreamed* about flying to London and singing with my head in the toilet. I opened my eyes and saw a strange bedroom – funny wallpaper with flower designs, old-fashioned furniture. I held my head for a minute and hoped I hadn't picked up a senior citizen and gone back to her place. After a few drinks, I'll do anything.

But it was no dream. I was really in London. My flat was on a narrow little street off of Draycott Avenue, not far from Lennox Gardens. I found out later that there are a lot of gardens and what they call *squares* in that part of town. There was Sloane Square and Cadogan Square and Thurloe Square – they're really small parks, but the Londoners call them *squares*, because it's a national rule or something to call everything by the wrong name. When I got to know the place better I sometimes took walks through them, and they were always filled with nannies strolling babies in carriages, and old guys with not so many teeth just hanging around on benches. The old guys would talk to me if I sat down next to them, but I could never understand half of what they were saying because they liked to suck their gums a lot and make sickening sounds. I quit going after a while.

So on that first afternoon I took out my address book and looked up Eddie's number. I was supposed to open for his show on Saturday, and I thought maybe I should get in a few practice sessions with his band. But when he answered his phone, he was almost hysterical.

"When did you get in?" he asked, real fast.

"Last night. I've got a little place in Chelsea. Looks like Mamie Eisenhower decorated it."

"Rudy, I gotta talk to you. I gotta talk to you soon."

"Okay, so talk. What's gotten into you, anyway?"

"Not over the phone, man. I'll meet you at a restaurant called Gavver's. But you gotta take the exact route I give you. You're gonna be jumpin' subways like a purse snatcher, just in case they try to follow you."

"In case *who* tries to follow me?"

"No time for that now. Write down these directions."

Man, was he wound up. He made me write down the names of all these underground stops and then hung up. I didn't know what the hell was going on.

I got lost no fewer than five times – felt like a goddamn rat in a maze. I think I got on the Picadilly Line at Knightsbridge. I was supposed to get off at Green Park, but I missed my stop and ended up at Leicester Square. So then I had to take the Picadilly back to Green Park and get on the Victoria Line. I took that to Victoria and then changed to the District Line and got off at Sloane Square. The whole trip took me over an hour, and I could've walked to Sloane Square from my flat in fifteen minutes. Eddie, the crazy bastard. He had me going in circles.

I got a lot of stares at the restaurant. You would've thought they'd never seen a rock phenomenon before. I was looking pretty cool, if I do say so. I had on a black leather jacket with silver studs and my favorite purple pants. I ordered lamb and had a Coke (warm, of course – England hadn't invented the ice cube yet). I was just being served when Eddie and another guy walked in. The other guy had a limp.

"Pay up and let's get out of here," Eddie said.

"But I just got my dinner."

"Don't matter. Pay up and let's boogie. I got the car out front."

I was pretty disgusted with him by then – all that chasing around and then not being able to eat. I stuffed a chunk of lamb in my mouth, dropped some of that pretend money on the table, and followed the two of them out the door.

The car was backwards. I mean, the steering wheel was on the right, and I had to sit on the left. Eddie laid rubber. He pulled a fast louie and drove down Lower Sloane Street.

I said, "Would someone mind explaining to me what's going on?"

"Tell him, Eddie," the guy in the back seat said.

"Rudy Keen, I want you to meet Gene Vincent."

I whipped around and said, "Gene *Vincent*? Oh, man – I'm a big fan of yours. I love that 'Be-Bop-A-Lula.'"

I stuck out my hand to shake, but his head was tilted up; he was drinking booze out of a flask. When he finished, he wiped his mouth with his sleeve and said, "Thanks."

Eddie looked straight ahead at the road while he talked. Every once in a while he'd turn to me and you could see how frightened he was. "Look, man. I'm not takin' any chances. I don't want the three of us to be in the same place for too long."

"Why?" I said.

"*Why*? Because of the plot! Look what happened when the other three were together."

I said, "Eddie – Preston isn't with Tal Limited anymore. I don't think we have to worry about him."

"Who told you that?" he said, real nervous like.

"The new guy at Tal Limited – Sherman Katz. He was my first publisher, Sal DeGrazzia's old partner. When I told him that we thought Preston was behind Buddy's death, he said he'd do an investigation."

Eddie hit the brakes and we came to a screeching stop. I practically flew out the windshield. "You *told* him?"

"Yeah. What's wrong with that?"

"And Tal Limited knows that we think Allerton caused the crash?"

"Not Tal Limited, just Sherm. Relax. He's a friend of mine."

All the drivers behind us started honking their horns. Eddie hit the gas and shook his head. "You got a brain, Rudy. Why don't ya use it? There's gotta be more than one guy in this. It's too big. Tal

155

Limited is a corporation. How do you know this Sherm of yours ain't in charge of knockin' us off?"

"You're nuts," I said. "I told you, he's a friend of mine."

Gene held the flask in front of my face, offering me a swig. When I told him I didn't want any, he tapped Eddie on the shoulder. "Tell him, Eddie."

Eddie ran his hand back over his hair. "What if Tal Limited got rid of Preston because he botched Buddy's crash so bad?"

"Botched it?"

Gene said, "Go ahead. Tell him."

"Tell me *what*?" I said. "What's he talking about?"

Eddie pulled the car up in front of an antique shop and shut off the engine. It was dark except for a street lamp that sent long shadows up the sides of buildings.

"Buddy's not dead." Eddie looked me right in the eyes when he said it.

I just sat there looking back at him.

"Did you hear what I just told you?"

I said, "Yeah, I heard you."

"So?" Eddie said.

"So I think you've been nipping at Gene's flask one too many times."

Eddie leaned in close toward me. "Lookee here, man. I ain't bullshittin' you. Buddy Holly's alive. They got him at a hospital just up the road. He's covered head to toe in bandages, and they feed him through a fuckin' plastic tube. He was hurt real bad, Rudy." He stopped and moved away, balancing his arms on the steering wheel. "Real bad. Two, maybe three times a day some goons go in and check on him. I seen 'em myself, but I don't know who they are."

Behind me Gene clicked his tongue and whistled. "Crickets spelled backwards, man."

"Is this a joke?" I asked.

Eddie crossed his heart with a finger. "It's the gospel. And I think it's the same people takin' care of him that tried to have him killed."

I said, "If they wanted him dead and the crash didn't do it, then wouldn't they have just killed him some other way? Why would they bother to keep him alive?"

"Money, honey."

"Huh?"

"Only one way to make more money than they did off his death. Bring him back."

I blew some air out of my mouth. Eddie lit a cigarette. We just sat there in the car, and every so often a taxi went by. Funny taxis. They were square.

"How do you know all this?" I said.

Gene leaned over the seat and breathed whiskey breath on me. "Friend of mine. Guitar picker who does session work for me. His wife's a nurse. Burn unit."

"And?" I said.

Gene belched and almost blew me out of the car. "She saw Buddy. Changed his bandages. Said he looked like hamburger."

"Hamburger?"

"Ground sirloin. All cut up. All burned up."

I'll bet I know what you're thinking – that old Jewish proverb: "*Atoyber hot gehert, vi a shtumer hot dertseylt, az a blinder hot gezen, vi a krumer iz gelfn*" – am I right? It means, "A deaf man heard a mute tell how a blindman saw a cripple run." And that's what I thought too, but I could tell they weren't kidding. They really believed every word they'd told me. There was only one thing to do; I had to find out for myself. I asked Gene where the hospital was, and he said it was on Great Ormond Street, not far from Dickens' House.

"Buddy Holly is living down the street from Charles Dickens?"

Gene nodded. "Yeah, man."

"But Dickens is still dead, right?"

"Yeah, man."

"Just checking," I said.

I opened the door and started to get out. Eddie grabbed my arm and said, "Where do you think you're going?"

"I'm gonna find Buddy."

"You can't do that. If they catch you anywhere near him, you're a goner."

"I don't care. If Buddy's really alive, he needs me."

I pulled away from Eddie and slammed the door and went running down the street. I had a feeling he was going to do what he did next. He started up the car and came after me. Boy, I was really tearing. Eddie had the car right behind me, practically put the bumper up my ass – but I got lucky. A cab was coming from the opposite direction, so I flagged it down and jumped in the back seat.

"Hey," I said. "You know of a hospital on Great Ormond

Street?"

"Aye, sir. That would be Children's Hospital."

"Children?"

"Only it's not just for children, sir. That's just the name."

Like everything else in London, it had the wrong name.

"Let's peel some rubber, then," I said.

"Beg pardon?"

Oy. "Leave us journey hence, Jyles."

That he understood. The guy had a lead foot. "Name's McAvory, sir. James McAvory, 'cept all me mates calls me Jimmy."

Swell.

Jimmy and me made some good time. He was a hell of a driver, but he wouldn't shut up. His missis' name was Clara, and they had two children, Kirby and Mona. He had three great passions in life: football, kippers (whatever they are), and Irish whiskey. Only a nip now and then – "when I feel a touch aguish." And talking. He forgot to mention talking. That made *four* great passions. I'd tell you to look him up sometime, but that was thirty-seven years years ago, so if you want to find him, you might try going to a square. He's probably sitting in one right now, sucking his gums.

When we pulled up in front of the hospital I tossed some very colorful money at him and ran up the steps. I heard another car skid behind me, so I looked over my shoulder. Eddie. He shouted, "Don't go in there, Rudy!"

But I did. I walked right in and got lost within seconds. That place was huge. It was pretty late to be visiting somebody, and I had no idea how to find Buddy. I couldn't just go up to a nurse and say, "Excuse me. Could you tell me where they're hiding Buddy Holly?" I walked down a long hallway and noticed people staring at me. The purple pants might've had something to do with it. But it's funny. I realized something – if you want to be left alone in London, you've got to do what everybody in London does: act like you personally own the goddamn city. Hold your head up, stick your chin out, and walk like you know where you're going.

I came to a big wooden desk, and behind the desk was a lady with reading glasses down at the end of her very pointy nose. She was writing in a big book.

"Burn unit?" I said.

She didn't even look up at me. "Second floor, east wing."

"Thank you," I said.

I headed for the stairs, but she called after me. "You can't go there now, you know. Visiting hours are over."

"Oh, I'm not visiting," I said. "My brother's sort of dying and his doctor called me to come and say good-bye before he kicks."

"Poor thing!" she said, and went right back to her writing.

I found the burn unit all right. You couldn't get in there, though. There was another desk and a guy standing behind it, dressed all in white. I didn't know if he was an orderly, a nurse, or a doctor. He gave me a fishy look when he saw me, and I just gave him my I-own-London attitude.

"Yes?" he said.

"I'm here to see the patient."

"Which patient?"

He had me, there. "*You* know which patient."

He lifted his nose at me. I lifted mine back at him. "Visiting hours are until seven-thirty. I'm afraid you'll have to return tomorrow."

I thought for a second. He was about to walk away when I said, "I'm not visiting. I've been sent to check on him."

"On *whom*?"

The English got good grammar. "On the patient whose name I'm not allowed to say."

He looked at my leather jacket. Then at my purple pants. "Did Mr. Krupp send you?"

"Krupp? Yeah. Yeah, that's right. Mr. Krupp sent me."

He opened the little swinging door by the desk, but when I tried to walk through, he stuck his stupid hand in front of my chest. "I'll need verification, of course."

"Verification?" *Shit, what am I going to do now,* I thought.

"Surely you know the procedure," he said.

Think fast, Rudy. "Do you want me to have to go back and tell Mr, Krupp you wouldn't let me see – "

"Mr. Hardin."

"Yeah. Mr. Hardin."

Hardin was Buddy's middle name! The deaf man really *did* hear a mute tell how a blindman saw a cripple run.

"I'm sorry, sir, but at the very least I'll have to ring up Mr. Krupp. I'll just be a moment."

He walked over to a phone and picked it up and started dialing.

"Yeah, you do that. Ring him up on the ..." I didn't want to make a mistake and call the phone a *phone*. I mean, come *on*. If a subway is a tube, the phone could be anything – *toilet*, for instance. So I played it safe and said, "... on the *ringer*."

It's hard to act confident when you're ready to piss down the legs of your pants. Who was Krupp? What was I going to do when Krupp said he hadn't sent me? I watched the guy – the orderly or the altar boy or whatever he was – nonchalantly. He finally hung up.

"He's not in," he said. *Thank God*, I thought. "I'll let you back for a few minutes *this* time, and notify Mr. Krupp later. But I'm afraid in the future I'll have to insist on the standard form of authorization, Mr. – uh – "

"Richardson," I said. "J.P. Richardson."

"Surely you understand. Standard authorization is essential."

"No problem. Next time it'll be standard as hell."

He took me down a hallway, and then another hallway, and started whispering to me. "You can tell Mr. Krupp that there have been no new problems. He's sedated – heavily. When he *is* conscious, he wants to communicate. It's only natural, but it's quite frustrating for him. It's to be 'expected."

"Naturally," I said.

We came to a room at the end of a hallway. The guy took out a key and unlocked the door. It was dark inside – there was just one fluorescent light over a sink in the corner. On the bed there was someone completely wrapped in bandages, layers and layers of them.

"That's *him*?" I said.

"Shhh!" he whispered. "Don't wake him."

"*Wake* him? You mean that guy's *alive*?"

"Oh, certainly. And doing quite well, too – under the circumstances."

I walked over to the side of the bed and looked at him. You couldn't see his mouth or his eyes. He wasn't a person, he was a mummy – one leg in traction, one arm between splints, IV needles stuck into him everywhere. It gave me the holy creeps.

"Can I have a moment alone with him?" I asked.

"Alone? Well, I don't know – "

"He'll be all right. I won't bother him."

"Whatever you do, don't touch him. His tissue is highly sensitive."

"Yeah – I'll watch out for his tissue."

160

The guy looked like he didn't trust me. He kept looking over his shoulder at me as he walked away.

When he was gone, I bent down and whispered near where I figured there might be an ear. "Buddy? Buddy, is that you?"

The head snapped a little, just a little, but it scared my pants off and I nearly jumped out the window. Then I heard low gurgling sounds coming from him, so I crept back next to the bed. "Buddy, do you know who this is? It's Rudy. Rudy Keen."

There was a little groan, but that was the most he could do. I straightened up and started to leave, when I noticed his fingers trying to move. He held out all the fingers on one hand and two on the other. He did it again, but this time he held out three fingers on the second hand. It was like he was trying to tell me something, but what? I watched the fingers slowly stretch out. Five and two. Five and three.

"What does it mean?" I said.

Again – five and two. Five and three. What was he doing, addition? Seven and eight. Seven and eight equals fifteen – so? Seven, eight – *Seventy-eight!* Don't you see? That's what he used to call me, *Seventy-eight.* He knew me. I touched one of his hands, real soft, because you know, the tissue. "Buddy," I said. "It really *is* you." Then he stopped moving his fingers and let his hand just lay in mine. "I'll be back," I told him. "I promise, I'll be back."

8   'Peggy Braun'

"You know, a lotta cats think I'm just a shit-kickin' gee-tar picker who got lucky. They don't know the real Eddie. The real Eddie is a curious guy. I gotta lotta questions about the world. The old mind's always turnin', always turnin'. When I ain't on stage and I ain't makin' records, you know what I'm doin'?"

"Makin' out with fans?" Gene said.

"No, man. I'm readin'. I read everything I can get my hands on, but mostly I like classics. Let me tell you about this old Greek cat, Socrates. He was a real wise daddy-o. He never did write nothin' himself, but this student of his, Plato? Well, old Plato wrote down every cotton-pickin' thing Socrates said that was worth rememberin'. Anyways – Socrates said he had this voice inside his head, and the voice would keep him out of trouble. When things got tough and he didn't know what to do, he'd listen to this voice in his head. You understand?"

"No, " Gene said.

"I'm talkin' to Rudy. You understand, Rudy?"

"Yeah. Socrates heard things. That sounds normal."

"Not things," Eddie said, "just a voice, this one voice." We were driving in Eddie's car to our next date in – where was it? Guildford, I think. The whole week was booked between a bunch of hick bergs. The rest of the band rode in a little van. It was a far cry from The Winter Dance Party Tour. "He called this voice his *oracle*. You know what an oracle is?"

Gene said, "One of them glasses that rich English guys wear in one eye."

"No, man! That's a *monocle*. I'm talkin' *oracle*. An oracle is like a fortuneteller, an advice-giver. When Socrates got in dutch with the law for leadin' the kids astray, he didn't know what to do. He was in deep shit."

"Like Alan Freed," Gene said.

"Right! Right, just like Alan Freed. So he asked his oracle, 'What should I do, man?' Now, I'm not sayin' that I got a voice in my head, necessarily. But I do kinda have somethin' like old Socrates' oracle. Just call it a hunch. And you know what my hunch is tellin' me to do about Buddy?"

"What?" I asked.

"Stay the hell out of it. Just mind my own business."

I'd told them both that I'd seen Buddy, that he was in really lousy shape and couldn't even talk. For the last couple of days we'd been trying to figure out what to do. You just heard Eddie – he wanted to lay low. Me, I wanted to get to the bottom of it. Gene – he said he missed cheeseburgers. Then he asked, "What ever happened to Socrates?"

"Socrates?" Eddie said. "Oh – they killed him."

Gene whistled through his teeth. "Dumb fuckin' oracle."

I said, "We can't stay out of it, Eddie. No matter what we do or where we go, they can find us. Whoever is keeping Buddy alive must have a stake in his career. They probably want to take over the whole record industry, just flat out own the charts. First they get rid of the competition, and then they make a bundle off of legends any way they can. But we know Buddy's alive, and where they're keeping him, and they don't *know* we know that. We can blow the lid off this thing."

"How do we do that?" Eddie said.

"I don't know. I haven't worked out the details yet. If I can get my Uncle Zollie to find out who's at the top of Stek-Circ, though, then we'll at least have someone to blame. We can finally go public – maybe get Sam and Bobby and a bunch of other name acts to stand up with us and tell the press and cops that Buddy Holly's being kept prisoner at that hospital."

"I see a pub," Gene said.

"We ain't stoppin' at no pub," Eddie told him, "We ain't got time."

"Now," I said, "we've got one name – Krupp. When we get back to London we can do some follow-up on who he is. I'll bet you anything he's not the top man, probably just a hired thug. But if we can get a phone number or an address, then we've got a trail. It might just lead us to the boss."

Eddie lit a cigarette and opened his window a little. "Man, I don't know. My hunch keeps sayin', 'Stay out of it. You'll get your ass in a jam.'"

"I haven't got any hunches," I said. "All I know is, I saw Buddy lying there, not able to move anything except his fingers. If you could've seen him, Eddie, then I think you'd be singing a different tune."

"Maybe you're right," Eddie said to me. "When we finish up this week, we'll go back and see what we can find out. But Rudy, not one word to anyone."

"What about Sherm? Sherm might be able to help us,"

"*No.* Especially not anybody connected to Tal Limited. I know he's your friend and you trust him. But all he has to do is say our names to someone else at the agency, and *whamo*. Next thing you know, we wake up in some hospital lookin' like King Tut."

♪ 𝅘𝅥𝅮 ♪

The days went by fast and the shows were pretty good. I'd open, and then Gene would come on, and then Eddie would clean up. Eddie was the biggest star of the three of us, but old Gene was the best guitar player by far. He could play jazzy riffs that would make you dizzy, man. It was too bad about Gene, when I think back on it. He hadn't had a decent hit in years, and I remember his leg was always killing him. He'd hurt it when he was in the army. Even though he tried to act like it didn't bother him during the shows, it did. Hell – sometimes he'd fall over in the middle of a song and he wouldn't be able to get back up; he'd just finish the set on his back. The kids in the audience thought he was doing stunts, but the truth was, he couldn't move. And as if that wasn't bad enough, he had ulcers. I guess I don't have to tell you why. But Gene was good to me, and I liked him. I probably could've shown it more, but I was too concerned about Buddy. He'd been my hero, my best friend, and then he'd died and come back to life as a spool of adhesive tape. Poor bastard.

♪ 𝅘𝅥𝅮 ♪

Ring-ring-ring! *Ring-ring-ring!*

The tour was finished and I'd slept for twenty-four hours straight when the goddamn phone woke me up. British phones –

shpilke city. It was Eddie.

"Guess what I'm doin', man," he said.

"I don't do phone sex, Eddie."

"No – I've got Stek-Circ's London address. I'm gonna look 'em up. Just drop in and say hi."

I was groggy. It was damned hard waking up every morning in the middle of a mystery. "You sure you want to do that?" I said.

"Hey – we're either gonna do this thing or we're not."

"What're you gonna say to them?"

"Just introduce myself, ask 'em how my songs are doin'. They're my publisher. I got a right to be there."

"Listen, Eddie. Try to get some names, I'll run them past my uncle and see if he comes up with anything. Oh – and Eddie?"

"Yeah?"

"Leave a note in your hotel room saying where you went and what time and everything."

"All righty. But why?"

"Just in case."

There was silence. Then he said, "Cripes, you think somethin's gonna happen to me?"

"I didn't say that. I just meant that we can't take any chances."

More silence. "Of course, I *could* always wait till tomorrow or the next day."

"We're either gonna do it or we aren't. You said so."

"Yeah, I know. But all of a sudden my oracle is goin' nuts."

Again with the oracle! "It's not your oracle who's nuts, Eddie."

♪   ♫   ♪

While Eddie was at Stek-Circ, I went to Children's Hospital again to see Buddy. I walked right in and no one paid any attention to me, because this time I knew where I was going. But that guy on the burn unit was still playing watchdog. When I asked to see Mr, Hardin, he said, "I believe I instructed you the last time you were here that you must observe the standard procedure."

"I've got authorization," I said. I whipped out a letter that I'd written myself and handed it to him. It said:

To whom it may concern:

Let this guy in to see Mr. Charles Hardin.
And don't give him a hard time, and let
him stay as long as he wants. And bring
him a Coke, while you're at it, and put a
little *ice* in it.

Respectfully,

Krupp

He read it and then looked over the top of the page at me.
"Very well, then. Have a seat. I'll have someone take you back
shortly."

So I sat down in the waiting room and looked through a bunch
of boring British magazines. Then I picked up a copy of The *Daily
Mail* that was lying around opened to the music section. Look what
I found:

A Not-So-Keen Teen Latrine Scene
Music Review by Randolph Heatherbone

If you are one of those misguided parents who allows
your impressionable teen-age children to attend what are
known as 'rock 'n' roll' dances, this is what your vulnerable
and neglected offspring may have witnessed last night at
the Guildford Hall.

Three garishly clad savages took the stage in
succession and proceeded to writhe and warble in a
shamelessly suggestive fashion. Seldom in key, given to
sudden and inexplicable bursts of falsetto screaming, these
American 'singers' (such an appellation fits them but
loosely) worked their dark magic upon the pimply crowd
in attendance and drove them to ever greater heights of
estrogen and hysteria, not, one presumes, unlike the
followers of Dionysus shortly before they tore his flesh to
shreds.

Gene Vincent, perhaps the most harmless of the trio,

nevertheless served up idiotic droolings and echoey whispers as he performed his hit, 'Be-Bop-a-Lula,' a song about utterly nothing. Mr. Vincent's forté apparently consists of matching breathy delivery to drivel and three guitar chords. If it doesn't rhyme with *bop*, a word stands no chance of finding its way into his lyrics. This reviewer simply held his hands over his ears and yawned until the hoodlum strutted his way to the wings.

Enter Teddy boy number two – Eddie Cochran. If only his talent were as large and cumbersome as his guitar. Someone has done this Yankee a tremendous disservice by deceiving him into thinking that he is a vocalist. He merely screeches at the apex of his severely limited range, serving up fabricated angst about balconies, drive-ins, and hops. Oh, those poor American adolescents! How they suffer in their convertibles in the summertime! One can only wonder for how much longer this sideburn-enveloped *man* can go on convincing his pubescent disciples that his prom occurred just last week.

But they saved the worst for first by allowing the Brooklyn Boob, better known as Rudy Keen, to open the dissonant extravaganza. Keen, in satin pants and studded leather jacket, proved himself to be the most loathsome performer yet to cross the Atlantic and plague our shores in this seemingly ceaseless American Invasion. Crooning songs with such moronic titles as 'Whoa Baby, Whoa' and 'Jelly Baby' in a voice that possessed all the sonority of a lower-east side air hammer, Keen proudly exposed his lyrics for what they are – the epitome of boorish playground obscenity. There is little room for romance or reflection in his paeans. For Keen, life is a series of poorly-timed sexual escapades, characterized by immature erotic play and culminating in ejaculation. What this young New Yorker needs is therapy, or a good spanking – although he might well enjoy the latter all too much, and for the worst reasons imaginable. Keen's set was puerile and unhallowed – in short, P.U..

The nervy bastard! Talk about *chutzpah*! How dare he? Did *he* ever write a rock and roll song? Could *he* make teen-age girls go crazy? Come on – with a name like *Randolph Heatherbone?* It sounds like something you do to yourself in the privacy of your own home.

> "What did you do last night?"
> "Oh, not much. Read a porn magazine
> and randolph heatherboned for a while."

I'll bet he was just jealous of us. Yeah, that must've been it. He was jealous. And what the hell did he mean by that crack about a lower-east side air hammer? If I hadn't been waiting to see Buddy, I would've personally gone down to The *Daily Mail* and punched him in his stuck-up nose. I would've marched right in there and said, "I want to see that bastard Heatherbone. Tell him the Brooklyn Boob is here and wants to punch him in the nose with his *puerile* and *unhallowed* fist, whatever that means." I hate it when writers use those big words that nobody understands. And by the way, my lyrics weren't boorish – they were as exciting as hell.

"Mr. Richardson? Will you follow me, please?"

A different guy dressed in a white uniform held the burn unit door open for me. I threw the stupid newspaper down on a chair and followed him. He walked down the same hall I was in the last time, but instead of going to the door at the end, he stopped in front of one off to the right and knocked three times.

"Hey," I said. "That's the wrong door. He's in the room at the end of the hall."

"Moved him," he said.

The door opened by itself and I thought, *Gee, Buddy must be up and around.* I remember walking in the room – and that's it. The lights went out, *my* lights. When I came to, I was in a car, my hands were tied behind my back, I had a lump the size of a jumbo knish on my head, and I couldn't see, because my eyes were taped shut. Other than that, I was fine.

"Where the hell am I?" I said.

Somebody next to me said to somebody else, "He's conscious."

"Tell heem to shoddop," the other guy said, "or we'll keeck hiz ahs."

One American accent – one German. That was the first thing I noticed.

"Who are you guys? Why'd you knock me over the head? Where are you taking me?"

"Jesus Christ, aren't you a little chatterbox," the guy sitting next to me said. "Didn't you hear what the man said?"

"Yeah, I heard and everything, but why'd you have to hit me so hard on the head? Don't you know you can cause serious brain damage that way? And where the hell are you taking me, anyway? And why are my eyes taped shut?"

The German guy said, "I con't take heez yabbering. Keeck hiz ahs."

"Do you want me to kick your ass?" The guy next to me said.

"No."

"All right, then."

"I just want to know who you are and – "

SMASH! The son of a bitch punched me right in the jaw. My head was starting to feel like a pulverized skirt steak. I'd seen my Uncle Myshkin do that – he pounds holy hell out of a skirt steak with a wooden hammer to make it more tender, and then he ...

Forget it. That's a digression.

I wondered what had gone wrong with that letter I'd written. Then I realized I hadn't left a note at my place saying where I'd gone. I didn't take the very advice I'd given Eddie. Stupid me – I'd *schtuped* myself but good this time.

We drove for about another ten or fifteen minutes and then the car stopped. The guy next to me, the American, he opened the door and pulled me out. "There's a gun next to your ribs, hot shot. One move and your liver's history."

What an imbecile. He had the gun against my *left* rib cage. It wasn't anywhere *near* my liver. But I did what he said, because I was pretty sure there was stuff on that side I needed just as much. They marched me up some steps and I heard a door open. I got pushed inside, thrown on the floor. Hard wood – no carpet. See? A mind for details. If somebody ever kidnaps you, you've got to remember stuff like that, in case they don't kill you. If they don't kill you, at least you can tell the cops later on something about where you were taken. Of course if they *do* kill you, then you've wasted your time memorizing a bunch of crap you'll never be able to tell anybody.

I heard the door slam shut and the two *shmegegges* talked real low, back and forth. The German guy said, "Ah'm gawn to cull Mistah K and tell heem we got de guy."

My mind raced; I was deducing all over the place. We had a guy in the old neighborhood named DeDoose, but he spelled it different. Anyway, I was thinking, *Mr. K must be Krupp; if Krupp works for Stek-Circ, and if Eddie went to Stek-Circ's office like he planned, then he might be in big trouble right now. They'd have both of us for the asking.*

"What'll I do with him?" the American guy said.

"Keeck hiz ahs."

I could've done anything else that afternoon. I could've gone to Picadilly Circus or the Tate Gallery, but not me. I had to go visit Buddy and have the shit kicked out of me. The American guy picked me up as if I was a feather and sat me on a stool. He asked me a million questions, questions like, "Who are you? Who're you workin' for? What business you got with Hardin?" Every time he didn't like an answer I gave him, he punched me and I fell off the stool. Then he picked me up and put me back on it and asked me another question.

I tried to get my hands free of the rope, but it was tied too tight. I didn't want to end up like Sal. I didn't want a hole in my head the size of a quarter. Except I was in London, so when they found my body they'd say, "Look at the hole in his head. It's as big as a shilling." Or a pence. Or a crown. I never figured out the money system over there.

"Doesn't any of this seem the slightest bit redundant to you?" I said.

"Shut up! Who are you?"

"I *told* you who I am. I'm Rudy Keen, teen idol."

WHAM! Back on the floor. When he asked me how I knew where Hardin was, I made up some story about a drunk guy who told me in a bar one night. He wanted to know who the guy was, but I said I had no idea. He finally got it out of me that I knew Hardin was Charles Hardin Holly – *Buddy* Holly. I told him we were friends, *good* friends, but do you think he listened to me? Hell no. He was having too much fun inventing fascinating new bruises on my face.

The German guy walked back in and asked his partner what he'd found out about me.

"Says he's a rock star, a friend of Holly's."

"Boolchit."

"Says his name's Keen," the American said. "Ever hear of him?"

"No."

I said, "Oh, come *on. Rudy* Keen? You gotta be kidding."

The German repeated, "Vroody Keen?"

"Yeah," I said. "Hey – I know. 'Bop-Sha-Bop.'"

"What?" the American said.

"'Bop-Sha-Bop.' You must've heard it. You know – 'Wop, wop, wop.'"

"I tink heez A-talian," the German said.

"No, man. It's a gold record. An international hit. I'll sing it for you. Clap your hands. Come on. That's right. Not so much with the syncopated shit. Just a nice, steady four-four beat. A little faster now. And the piano goes rumble-rumble-rumble, and the lead singer comes in. I was gonna do it myself, but I gave it to the Silvertones – anyway. The lead singer goes, 'Bop-Sha-Bop, Wop, wop, wop, You make me wanna pop, Please don't stop, Bop-Sha-Bop.' And the whole time the background singers are singing, 'Boppa-boppa-boppa, Woppa-woppa-woppa' – you know, double time. And then the guitar goes duh-duh-duh-duh-duh – twang. It's a big hit. I could do it better if I could see, and if my hands weren't tied, and if I wasn't bleeding. You can stop clapping now."

It was quiet for a minute, then the American said, "That's the dumbest thing I've ever heard."

"Oh yeah?" I said. "Well, a million people didn't think so. I can't believe you guys never heard of me – *Rudy Keen?* The Fabulous *Rudy Keen?* Electric Rudy?"

Silence.

More silence.

Lots more silence.

"I'm a phenomenon," I added.

"You're a *nut*," the American said.

"Fine. I'm a nut, You go around taping guys' eyes shut and punching them, but I'm a nut. If you don't want to believe me – call my agency, Tal Limited of New York."

The place went dead quiet again. Pretty soon I heard them whispering to each other. Then the American said, "*You* work for Tal Limited?"

They were sure interested in that.

"Hey man," I said, "they work for *me*. Or you could ask Buddy himself, if you want. He'll tell you. I was on The Winter Dance Party Tour with him. I've even given him ideas for songs. Go ahead, ask him. Go ahead."

The German said, "How con ve do dat? He con't tawk."

"So let him write it down."

"He can't even hold a pen, wise guy." The American.

But I knew Buddy could at least move his fingers, so I told them to get him a typewriter. That way all he had to do was push some keys.

"A *typewriter*," the American said.

"Ya, a *dypewritah*," the German repeated.

We're not talking about a brain trust here. They kept saying *typewriter* the way Marylin Monroe would've said "Relativity." Bottom line – they got Krupp on the horn and told him my idea. About an hour later the German walked back in the room and said, "He vas tellin de troot."

"Good," I said. "So you can let me go now."

"Like vuggin hell. Mistah K vants to meet-chew."

Well, apparently he didn't want to meet me too bad. The son of a bitch made me wait four hours. Four hours of sitting on a stool with my hands tied behind my back, my eyes taped shut, and my face swelling like a beaten blowfish.

♪　♫　♪

"Mr. Keen, I presume." I was half-asleep when he started talking to me in his deep creepy voice. Nearly scared the shit out of me. "Or should I call you Electric Rudy? You certainly have complicated things for us."

He had a British accent, the good kind, like you hear on Regent Street.

"Can't I just say I'm sorry and let it go at that?"

"No, I'm afraid you can't. But we may be able to use your help."

Just what I wanted to do – help the guys who tried to kill Buddy and beat me up.

"What kind of help?"

"That typewriter idea of yours was ingenious. It has allowed us to communicate with Mr. Hardin for the first time since the accident. It seems he's quite fond of you. I dare say he'd be better able to work with you than any other musical therapist we might hire."

"Musical therapist?"

"Yes. There is the problem of security, however. Secrecy. No one was to know of his existence until the proper time."

"Hey," I said. "I'm good at keeping secrets. I won't tell

anybody, I promise."

Krupp laughed. Sounded a little like Vincent Price. "You amuse me, Mr. Keen."

"I do?"

"We don't need your promise. If you talk, I assure you we will seek retribution."

"What – you mean like *sue* me?"

"We can do much better than that. We know where your mother lives."

"My mother? What, you're gonna sue *her*?"

"Third floor walk-up apartment, a brownstone in Brooklyn. Now, I've been informed that you can transcribe musical arrangements and write violin scores. Is that true?"

"Yeah – but what's this stuff about my mother?"

"And you are a skilled musician on a variety of instruments. Correct?"

"Sure – I can play just about anything. But why'd you mention my mother?"

"Arnold – get the violin from my car."

"Who's Arnold?" I said.

"You've chosen a poor time to become inquisitive, Mr. Keen. Arnold assists me. That's all you need to know."

"Oh – *Arnold*. He's the American, right? Yeah, he's been assisting me too. I couldn't knock myself unconscious with my hands tied behind my back, so he did it for me. Great assistant, Arnold."

"And there are times that you *don't* amuse me," Krupp said. "I assume you can play the violin?"

"Uh-huh. But what's this about my mother?"

"Simply a precaution. Silence insurance. I'm protecting my investment. My organization is extremely interested in seeing that Mr. Hardin makes a full recovery and renews his career. There are hospital bills to be paid, production and living expenses to be considered. And you will be compensated for your services as well. But should it leak to the press that Mr. Hardin is alive, it could spoil our opportunity to recoup our losses. Your mother's continued well-being should be enough to encourage you to cooperate."

It was blackmail! He was threatening my mother. I thought, *If only I'd listened to Ma and become a butcher, then her life wouldn't be in danger. So I would've died of boredom, so what? So I never would've been world famous, and I would've had to argue every day with Mrs. Schulstein*

173

about which chicken was the freshest. But then I pictured the old bat inspecting the dead chickens, and I remembered the way she patted the bumpy skin and squawked like a sea gull. *On the other hand,* I figured, *maybe things could be worse.*

Arnold came back and Krupp had him untie my hands. Someone shoved a violin under my chin and stuck a bow in my hand.

"Oh, Christ," I said, "don't make me do this. You don't understand. When I was a kid, I used to get beaten snotless for playing one of these."

"We can relive those days, if you like, Mr. Keen."

So now I was going to get beaten if I *didn't* play the violin. I wonder what it is about that instrument that makes everyone so violent. I think they come from the same root word – vi-o-lence, vi-o-lin. See? All I know is, the world would be a lot more peaceful if the goddamn thing had never been invented.

I complained that I couldn't play with my eyes taped shut. Krupp said in that case, he'd listen from the next room. He sure didn't want me to see him, for some reason. And with no warning – *RIP!* – the tape was pulled from my eyes. *Oy,* God – did it hurt. Right there, stuck on that piece of tape, were my eyebrows. They'd just grown back, and that *yutz* Arnold had pulled them out again! Then I heard a click. When I looked up, I saw Arnold and his German friend (whose name I found out later was Hans) (Hans *Mengele,* I'll bet) pointing guns at my head.

"Play!" Krupp yelled from the other room.

"What do you want to hear?" I said.

"Nothing too difficult. How about 'The Sea And Sinbad's Ship,' from Rimsky Korsakov's *Scheherazade.*"

"Oh, come on! Without a score?" I said.

"Improvise if you have to, but play as though your life depended on it."

I did, too. I gave him eight bars of Korsakov and then slid into "Hound Dog." Afterward Krupp said my talent was greatly overrated. But I couldn't have been that bad, because I'm still alive.

That was essentially the end of my performing career. Krupp owned me from then on. I was glad to do it for Buddy, but I had no idea how long I was going to have to be his nursemaid, parent, therapist, house slave and constant companion. He needed a lot of care. I had to hold the spoon while he ate. I bathed him the best I could (he was still in bandages), and when he sat up in bed, I had to

174

push the rolling typewriter stand over to him so he could tell me what he wanted. For the first couple of weeks after he got out of the hospital, Hans picked me up at my place and drove me to a town house Krupp had got for Buddy on Bow Street in Soho. It was a pretty nice place. There were two pianos, guitars, amplifiers, tape recorders – but I don't know how the idiot expected Buddy to do anything with them in the shape he was in. He couldn't even get out of bed, let alone play or sing. His voice was shot to hell; all he could do was rasp. And he looked so spooky just lying in bed, his face all wrapped up like a dead Egyptian's, those big black glasses over his eyes.

One day after I'd taken the breakfast dishes downstairs to the kitchen, Buddy started pecking out a message on the typewriter: "*I think I have a song idea, Rudy.*"

"Buddy," I said, "your health is more important than any song."

"*But Krupp said last week that I should start writing an album's worth of material.*"

"Krupp-shmupp," I said. "I don't care what he says." Then I saw the look in his big old magnified eyes. He was worried. "Say, Buddy. You're not afraid of this guy, are you?"

"*No.*"

"Because you know what I think? I think if you weren't so hurt, you wouldn't have anything to do with him. He's trying to swindle you."

"*He's been very kind to me since the accident.*"

Accident? I couldn't believe it. He still thought that plane crash was an *accident*.

"Listen to me, Buddy. When you're well enough, I'm gonna sneak you out of here and take you home. It'll be just like the old days. You could hide out for a while and – "

"*Stay out of it, Rudy – *"

When he got irritated with me, he'd keep his face turned to the wall. He wouldn't look at me.

"Tell me this. Why won't you just let me pick up the phone and call a newspaper and tell the world you're alive?"

He sat still as a stone and stared off at nothing. Then he lifted his hand and started typing again.

"*Because of someone I love truely.*"

"There's no *e* in *truly*, Buddy."

"*fuk u. I'll sPill the way i wanT.*"

Whenever he got upset his writing went to hell. "All right, now. Don't get yourself in an uproar. What did you mean about someone you love? Why would that keep you from – "

His fingers hit the keys slowly. I looked at the page and watched the message appear.

"*How diD you fEel when breNDa diSappeared?*"

So *that* was it. They were blackmailing *him*, too, only my publisher won't let me tell you over who – legal considerations. Figure it out yourself. Take a wild guess.

♪ ♫ ♪

Meanwhile, Eddie had been doing his homework. We'd meet sometimes at night in his hotel room and fill each other in on what was going down. I had to be careful going over there; once or twice I'd caught Hans following me, so I'd duck into a tube station and ride the rails for an hour or so. I remember this night I'm telling you about pretty well – it was the night Eddie told me that he'd made friends with a go-fer over at Stek-Circ. The kid was crazy about him, a big fan, and Eddie had pumped him for information.

I said, "I hope you weren't too obvious about it."

"No, man. I was smooth. Bought him a pint and said, 'Tell me everything you know about who owns Stek-Circ.'"

"You call that *smooth*? You might as well have said, 'I know there's a conspiracy and I want to be killed next.'"

Eddie looked hurt. "Now, hold on there. Don't do me that way, Rudy. I got what we were after. The kid says a company called Songfest holds most of their stock."

"Songfest?" I said. "But what about Tal Limited?"

"He didn't say nothin' about them."

We kept getting square pieces to a round puzzle. Nothing fit. I told Eddie I'd run Songfest past my uncle, and then I asked him if he was sure he could trust this kid.

"That li'l ole boy? To him I'm Moses."

"Yeah, well – don't go trying to part the Rock 'n' Roll Sea. Go easy."

Eddie said, "You know our choices – either we do this thing or we don't. How's Buddy gettin' along?"

I shook my head. "Not so good. He lies in bed all day playing his old records over and over. Sometimes he moves his lips to the lyrics, but he can't get a sound out."

Gene was passed-out on the couch, snoring.

"Man, you gotta let me come over and see him one of these days."

"Not yet," I said. "Wait till he's better. He's real self-conscious about the bandages. And if you get caught in there – "

"Don't worry about me," he said. "I'm gettin' pretty good at this spy routine."

He was getting over-confident, too. He was due to go back to the states the next week, and not a moment too soon.

"They're blackmailing Buddy, you know," I said. "He's afraid they'll hurt someone he loves, and we know who that is."

"Don't surprise me at all," Eddie said.

Gene started talking in his sleep. "Hey, baby. Wanna bop? Hm? Ole Buddy's alive, still alive ..."

"You'd better watch him," I told Eddie. "He's gonna get us killed."

"Poor Gene," Eddie said. "What he needs is a hit."

I said, "What he needs is some coffee. About six months' worth."

♪ ♫ ♪

Get this: one day I was at the town house fixing some baby cereal for Buddy (he couldn't chew so good, and he liked Gerber's Oatmeal) when Krupp called and said he wanted me to move in with Buddy full-time. I told him I couldn't, that I had a career, but he said I'd want to think it over before I gave him my final decision. Well, I knew what that meant. It meant I'd better goddamn do it, or else. It wasn't such a bad deal, really. There was a studio there, so I could get some songwriting done. And I could make sure they didn't skip town with Buddy. But the best part was this plan that was developing in the back of my mind. I knew that the better Buddy got, the more being cooped up in the same place would drive him nuts. And when he completely recovered, we'd make a break for it some night when Hans and Arnold weren't around.

But by October *I* was the one losing my mind. Buddy wasn't making much progress and I started worrying about him. The only time I could get any peace was at night when he was asleep and the *Schmuck* Brothers were gone. I used to take midnight walks all by

177

myself around Covent Garden Market. The fog would roll in off the river like a mask the city wore when the sun went down. Hey – that's pretty poetic. *Like a mask the city wore after the sun retired, its golden rays sleepy in the gentle dusk.*

It's a gift. I'm a goddamn poet.

One late night I was making my Covent Garden rounds and I mailed a letter to Uncle Zollie. I gave him Krupp's name and asked him to look up Songfest. I also told him to check in on Ma and make sure she was all right. For the return address I gave him Gene's street and number. Gene had bought a little place in London. Not Eddie, though. Eddie was back in the U.S. and wasn't due to visit for another few months. I was the only one out that night. I sat down on a park bench and wondered what was going to happen to all of us – to me, Buddy, Gene and Eddie. Would we end up in some square in our sixties, reminiscing about our old rock and roll days, and sucking on our gums? Boy, I had no idea what was to come. No idea.

♪   ♫   ♪

"I can't, Sherm. I just can't."

"What do you mean, you can't? It's 'American Bandstand,' Rudy. Did you hear me? '*American Bandstand*.' One appearance and you've got a guaranteed hit."

"I'd like to do it. I really would. But I'm all tied up over here. I can't talk about it."

"What is it, Rudy? Is it drugs?"

"Drugs? Who, *me*?"

"If it's drugs, we'll clean you up."

"If I were any cleaner I'd have to go for sobriety therapy."

"Is it women?"

"*Ahf mir gezogt* – I should be so lucky."

"Then come back for the show. It'll mean three days out of your life."

"Sorry, Sherm. I'll send you some songs. That's the best I can do."

Do you think it was easy turning down that offer? Do you know what that gig would've meant for me? It would've meant albums, first-rate tours, mansions, the gonest sports car collection you can imagine. Babes-a-plenty. And people wouldn't have kept saying "Rudy *who*?" to me all the time. But how could I do it? I had a responsibility to Buddy, and besides, Krupp would've killed me. You may wonder if I'm bitter after all these years. Let me tell you something. I've matured. I've grown up. AND OF COURSE I'M FUCKING BITTER! WOULDN'T YOU BE?

♪ 𝅘𝅥𝅮 ♪

By November the pressure was coming from all sides. Buddy kept bugging me about his plastic surgery, and Krupp wanted a demo of no fewer than five songs. What was I – a genie? It was too soon for an operation, and too soon to expect Buddy to write again. It was out of my hands.

One day me and Buddy were playing gin rummy on his bed, listening over and over to "Peggy Sue" on the record player. I liked that song, but damn – I can't listen to *anything* four hundred times in a row. In the middle of the card game Buddy leaned over and started typing.

"*When are they going to do the surgery on my face?*"

I said, "You heard the doctor last week, Buddy. They have to wait until the tissue is healed enough before they can start work on it."

"*But it's been nine months. Do you think thEir just stalLing me? Do you thinK maybe i'll have to live with tHese scars forever?*"

"No, Buddy. Krupp's hired one of the best plastic surgeons in the world. It takes time. And you spelled *they're* wrong. It's t-h-e-y-apostrophe-r-e."

Then he threw down the cards and pulled the covers over his head. That's what he did for privacy when he was pissed. He couldn't get up and walk out of the room, so he'd pull the covers up over his head. That meant it was time for me to leave.

Gene called up a little later. I told him never to do that, to call the town house, but he said it was important. He had a letter for me from Uncle Zollie. That was what I'd been waiting for, the business dope. I snuck out that night and picked it up.

Dear Rudolph,

So how's the red nose? What's with the year in England – you're never coming home again? You being held prisoner

179

or something? Your mother, she's fit to be tied. All I ever hear is how the two men in her life ran halfway across the world and forgot about her. At least give her a call, already!

Now about the *mishigas* with those foreign companies of yours. I checked the name *Krupp*, and he's not on the board of directors for any registered overseas firm. You sure it's his right name? Sounds like a Nazi, anyway. Songfest – *bupkis*. I wrote to a friend in the old country. He's going to see if maybe Songfest is listed in some other place. I'll let you know when I find out, if I find out, I should live so long.

So Shlomel ain't seen his friend Abey in years and they meet one day on the golf course. Abey says, 'Shlomel! I ain't seen you in years! How's the golf game?' And Shlomel says, 'It's great, Abey. Never been better.' And Abey says, 'And how's the business?' And Shlomel says, 'Business is beauty-ful.' And Abey says, 'And the children – they're all right?' And Shlomel says, 'Couldn't be better. Just great, the children.' And Abey says, 'And how's the wife?' Now Shlomel looks concerned. He shakes his head. 'The wife – I think she's dead.' Abey slaps his own face. 'You *think*? What do you mean, you *think* she's dead?' 'Well,' says Shlomel, 'The sex is the same, but the dishes are piling up.'

Don't be a stranger, Rudolph.

Uncle Zollie

I'd counted on Uncle Zollie so much, but he was getting us nowhere fast. I had to face the truth about him; he was a talker, not a do-er. What a disappointment.

♪   ♬   ♪

Here's how it happened. It was a routine visit to the plastic surgeon's office. I'd dressed Buddy up in a long overcoat and a wide-brimmed hat and shades so people wouldn't stare. Hans and Arnold helped him to the car and later to the professional building. We had to take an elevator – I mean a *lift*, sorry. In England it's a *lift*, which doesn't make sense, because if it's a *lift* on the way up, what the hell is it on the way down? Shouldn't it be a *drop*? Anyway, Buddy had been in the examination room for an hour when the doctor came out to see me. Buddy was all upset because the doctor had told him the skin hadn't healed as well as he'd hoped, and that the bandages would have to stay off.

"No operation?" I said.

"Not yet," the doctor said. "Do see if you can calm him down a touch. He's quite jittery at the moment."

So I went into the examination room and Buddy turned around to look at me. I guess he was expecting the doctor. He just turned around and – OH, CHRIST! HIS FACE! I just wasn't ready for it, is all. The doctor hadn't warned me how bad it was. It's not like he was Frankenstein or anything. You could still see that he looked like Buddy, in a way. The way an egg still looks like an egg if you scramble it. But the layers of skin weren't even, and the mouth wasn't right. It was pretty awful – let's just leave it at that.

He turned away and covered his face with his shirt. He was so ashamed. I felt terrible for him. I walked over and put my arm around his shoulder, but he moved away from me.

"It's gonna be okay, Buddy. The doctor says you have to keep the bandages off, or the skin won't heal right."

"I'm a monster," he rasped. But a bit of his voice had come back; I could hear it. It wasn't quite the *same* voice, but now it had some tone to it.

"You're not a monster. In a few months when you have your first operation – "

"Months? Did you say *months*? What am I gonna do till then? How can I go around looking like *this*?"

It was amazing. He was talking, practically. *Maybe being angry is good for him*, I thought.

"You don't look so bad, Buddy."

He slammed his hand down on the examination table. He shouldn't have done that. His hand wasn't healed yet, either. He grabbed it and winced. "Not so bad? How can you say that, Rudy? I always trusted you to tell me the truth."

Then I remembered my walk through Covent Garden Market

back on that lonely night, and the way the fog rolled in – *a mask the city wore at night*. That was it! I'd get him a mask.

Buddy sat in the back seat of the car with his hat brim pulled down real low and the coat collar up around his face. I had Hans stop at a costume shop in Kennsington, where I bought three masks – a hobo, a grinning clown, and a gorilla head. There wasn't much of a selection.

"Is that all you've got?" I asked the storekeeper.

"Certainly not. Over here we have the ever-popular Fairy Princess. Isn't she beautiful? It's a little more expensive, but worth the price. Feel how soft the hair is. Go on."

"I don't think so."

"Or how about a mean old nasty frightening witch? Isn't she just divine? She has a wart on her nose and magenta eyes – she'll just scare your drawers off."

"I think I'll keep my drawers on, thanks just the same. Just give me these three."

"All right," the guy said. "But I really think you're missing out on the Fairy Princess. The hair is to die for."

I'll bet a hundred guineas he wore the Fairy Princess costume after hours. I'll just bet.

I'd be lying if I told you Buddy was crazy about the mask idea. But it wasn't like he had a lot of choices. He could either let people stare at his scar tissue, or put on a mask. He liked the hobo one the best. In a few weeks, he was up and walking – only needed one crutch. Drinking got to be a problem, especially when he was depressed. When he was depressed, he'd pour himself a couple of tall ones, switch over to the gorilla head, and try to dance to one of his own records. It was like a Fellini movie, only weirder.

Christmas was tough for him. I put up a Christmas tree (can you imagine *that* – *me* putting up a Christmas tree?) and decorated it with dradels, but Buddy wouldn't even look at it. I think it made him homesick. It wasn't exactly a festive atmosphere around that place. What were we going to do – sing carols with Hans and Arnold? Rock around the *tannenbaum*? I kept telling those two guys that we had to get Buddy out of the house more – but they said they had strict orders from Krupp to keep him inside. When I called Krupp to complain about it, he told me to keep my nose out of his business. Then he wanted to know where the songs were.

"He's not ready to write yet. How many times do I have to tell you?" I said.

"He will *have* to be ready. I'm already looking to hire the new Crickets."

"The new Crickets?"

"Yes. I think that's exactly what I'll call them. Instant public identification – a new Buddy, and the New Crickets."

"But you can't do that. I happen to know that Buddy gave the old Crickets the rights to the name."

"Mr. Keen, what say you allow me to handle the legal matters, hm? You get him to write."

He was asking for miracles. That's when I got too curious for my own good. "Hey," I said, "how did you get Buddy to London after the crash, anyway?"

The phone went dead for a few seconds. Then – "You ask entirely too many questions, Mr. Keen."

I'd gone too far. I was going to have to watch my step from then on.

♪   ♫   ♪

I gave Buddy two presents for Christmas. One was a black leather motorcycle jacket. Old Buddy loved motorcycles. When he opened it he got all excited. He said that in the spring we'd buy a couple of Triumphs and race all over England. Like Krupp was going to let *that* happen. But I thought, *Good, let him feel independent. Let him want to spread his wings. And when Krupp tells him no – then maybe he'll be ready to run away.*

The second present was a tape of a song I'd written for him. I called it "Make Believe." It's been a long time, and I don't remember all the words. It went something like, "Make believe you got your face back / That nothing can make you blue / Make believe you're home in Lubbock / With all your friends and family too / Make believe you sold a million / Records in one day." This part I forget. How did it go? "Hm-hm-hm-oh! You probably think that I'm *meshugge* / That I'm off my freakin' nut / But someday you'll be on top again / And everything will be just fine."

Boy, was Buddy crazy about that song. He even started playing the piano again, and the one song he played over and over was that one. He didn't sing – he couldn't. He'd just play the melody on the treble keys with his right hand. Pretty soon we were writing almost every day. By April we had four brand new original songs. If that sounds like slow progress, you've got to keep in mind what a perfectionist Buddy was. He sometimes worked for ten hours straight on the lyrics, changing them until he had just what he wanted.

And was Krupp ever steamed by then. "Where are the songs, Keen?" That's all I heard, day in, day out. One night I sent Arnold over to him with the first four numbers. I hadn't seen Hans in a month and I thought maybe he'd been fired or something, until Arnold told me he was in Hamburg.

"Oh," I said. "Does he live there?"

"No. He's auditioning musicians."

"Musicians? You mean musicians for Buddy? In Germany?"

"Yeah. What's wrong with that?" Arnold asked.

"What's *wrong* with that? Oh. nothing, nothing, That's a great fucking idea. We'll get Buddy an accordion and he can tour with Lawrence Welk. Shoot bubbles all over the stage."

"Look, Keen – "

"He can be the polka king of Texas. Yeah, we'll do Oktoberfest shows. Forget the Crickets. We'll call his band The Fourth Reich."

"I'm tellin' you, you'd better – "

"I can see it now – he can record 'Peggy Sue' in German. We'll call it 'Eva Sue' – or better yet, 'Peggy Braun.' Get me my guitar. See if you like this:

> She's real gone,
> Peggy Braun,
> Buried under Hitler's lawn.
> Oh Peggy, my Peggy Braun.
> Well she's decomposed,
> But I love her, Peggy Braun."

"Hey," Arnold said, pulling his gun out of his belt and pointing it at me. "I think Mr. *K* told you to keep your nose out of the business."

"Fine," I said. "Fine. What do I know? I've only written four big hits. I'm just a major rock and roll act."

"Not anymore, you're not."

And you know what the sad part of it all was? He was right. Nobody remembered me. After a year off the circuit, I'd been forgotten. I was a footnote in music history. A treble clef in the vast staff of rhythm and blues. One lonely groove in the LP of life. A nobody – a has-been at the age of nineteen. Don't get me wrong – I loved Buddy, I really did. I wouldn't have traded my career in for anybody but him. But how much can you ask of a guy? How much? I just hoped he'd get better soon, because the second he did, I'd be the gonest cat in London. I'd hop a silver bird, fly back to the states, make a record, make teen-age girls faint at my concerts, and eat some decent food again.

But for the time being nothing got easier around that joint. The plastic surgeon *still* refused to do the operation, and I had to watch Buddy pace back and forth across the kitchen floor. With a crutch, yet. It sounded like *step-boom, step-boom, step-boom,* till I almost lost my goddamn mind. And dig this – Krupp didn't like the songs I'd sent over. He didn't care for them, said they were "too extreme" – end of quote. So who made him a rock and roll connoisseur? I stuck up for Buddy. I said that Buddy *was* extreme, a step ahead of the crowd. (Actually a *step-boom* ahead of the crowd.)

"We need the old sound," Krupp said.

"Old-shmold," I told him. "The music business isn't supposed to go backwards. You want old, you get Bill Haley. Of course, you'll need two guys to hold him up while he sings."

"Keen, I want five more songs by the end of the week ..."

"Hey, this isn't an assembly line over here."

"... and they'd better sound like the old Buddy. Do you understand?"

But we didn't *have* the old Buddy. We had a guy with a crutch and no face who was single-handedly (literally) writing the newest material anybody had ever heard. I wondered if Edison had to go through the same thing when he came up with the light bulb. "Yeah, so? Where do you put the wick?"

And then I got another phone call. Holy balls, it was Gene. I'd told him a hundred times never to call me there. He was going to get us all killed someday.

"Hello?"

"(Click. Whistle.) Rudy boy. (Click-click. Whistle.)"

"Gene? Are you crazy?" Wrong question. "Whaddaya doing, man? You know better that to call me here."

"Cool down, daddy-o. Why don'tcha do the bop all the way over to my place. Guess who's in town? (Whistle.)"

185

"I don't care if it's the fucking queen – "

"She's always in town. Guess again."

"I can't now. Get off the line. Did you hear me?"

"Eddie's gotta talk to you."

"Shhh! Don't say his name over the phone!"

"He's got some boss information about Stek-Circ spelled backwards."

"Shut up about that!"

"Remember what Stek-Circ spelled backwards is?"

"Yes! For Christ's sake, keep you mouth shut!"

"It's *Crickets*."

"I know what it is, already!"

"He says to tell you and Buddy – "

"DON'T SAY HIS NAME OVER THE PHONE!"

" – that he knows who did it."

"Did what?"

"The plane crash."

"YOU CAN'T TALK ABOUT THAT OVER THE PHONE!"

"But you asked."

"I did not. Asked about what?"

"The plane crash."

"DON'T SAY THAT! DON'T EVER SAY THAT OVER THE –"

"Oh, I get it. You don't want me to talk on the phone about all this."

It had only taken a coronary to get that across to him. "That's right," I said.

"Okay."

"Okay."

"So, Rudy?"

"What?"

Silence. "Then how am I supposed to tell you that Eddie knows who killed Ritchie Valens and The Bopper?"

"SHHHHHH!" And then I hung up. Why didn't he just draw an X on my forehead with a little message next to it – "Insert bullet here."

But if what Gene had told me was true – this was a major breakthrough. I knew that it just might be our ticket out of there, me and Buddy. There'd finally be some justice. Murderers would be put behind bars, maybe even fried in the hot seat. The world would be safe for rock and roll again. It would be the conspiracy trial of the

186

century. We'd all be on TV, on magazine covers, and in newspapers. I could get my career back. Teen-age girls would *finally* throw their bras at me onstage, and back in my dressing room, Hollywood starlets would –

"Where do you think you're goin'?"

It was Arnold. I had one sleeve of my jacket on and I was nearly out the door when he stopped me.

"Huh? Oh. Uh ... I've got to buy an old blues record. Buddy needs it for this song he's writing."

"I'll go get it," Arnold said, pulling me back into the room. "What's it called?"

"Called? It's, uh ... It's called, 'Baby, I'm So Lonely, Got The Back-Porch-In-The-Summertime Blues. By The Bayou. At The Crossroads.' But there are three different versions, and Buddy needs a very rare one. You'd never find it. I'll be right back."

"Yeah, well," the idiot said, "just make sure you are."

I took the Central Line to Oxford Circus. Gene lived around the corner on Margaret Street. (A lot of experts will debate that and say that's not where he lived, but that's because Gene kept it a secret to keep fans away. Who're you going to believe, anyway – experts, or me?) All the way there I thought about the media frenzy we were about to unleash, the Hollywood starlets back in my dressing room, waiting to do all those things that starlets do so well. Movie offers. Vegas. Hefner's mansion and *Playboy* bunnies – thousands of them – with those cute furry tails. I kept looking behind me to see if I was being followed. I was a nervous wreck. An *excited* wreck. I pounded on Gene's door and ducked inside as soon as Eddie opened it.

"Rudy – howsa boy?" Eddie said.

I didn't answer him. I was too busy locking and chaining the door. Eddie was taking hits from a wine bottle, just swigging it down. I could tell he was a little nervous, too.

"Give me the news," I said.

I watched him take another big gulp and then half-close his eyes as he swallowed it down. "Dion's leaving The Belmonts, man."

"*That's* the news? That's why you guys called me over here and made me risk my goddamn life?"

"No, man," Eddie said. "I just thought I'd start out with some business gossip."

"He's gonna have to look for a last name," Gene said. He was sprawled out on his couch with a bottle of Jim Beam.

"Who?" I said.

"Dion. What's he gonna call himself – Dion And The?"

"Don't mind him," Eddie said. "He's as fucked-up as a soup sandwich. Sit down, Rudy. You ain't gonna believe this."

I sat on an ottoman. Eddie lit a cigarette, and for a second I was afraid Gene would go up in flames. The Jim Beam fumes were almost visible. He hunched over and balanced his elbows on his legs as he poured out the story. What a story. Eddie had hired a private detective in Des Moines to gather as many facts about the Dance Party crash as he could. The guy had traced two tickets from New York to Clear Lake, Iowa, purchased by Preston Allerton on the morning of February 2 – a day before the plane went down.

"I got him, man," Eddie said, his eyes wide open, his head bobbing. "I got him linked to the crash. He'll never squirm his way out of this one. Dead-to-rights, baby. I guess he didn't count on having to deal with ole Eddie. Eddie Holmes. Sherlock Cochran."

"But who was the other ticket for?" I asked.

"I got the gum shoe workin' on that right now. I should know in a few days. Then, whamo, man. We go public."

"So it *was* Allerton," I said. "I was right all along. There really *is* a conspiracy, and I'm not just making it all up, and I'm not paranoid or crazy or neurotic."

Eddie said, "At least you're not making it up."

Then Gene sat straight up and stared at the wall with a real gone look in his eyes. At first I thought he was having a seizure.

"What is it, Gene?" I asked him.

"I was just thinkin'."

"Oh," I said. "Well, cut it out."

He clicked his tongue a few times, then: "If Buddy's here in London – who's buried in his grave back in Lubbock?"

Eddie turned his head slowly toward me. "That's a helluva good question."

It sure was. But I could only handle one mystery at a time. I was about to get up and leave when Eddie grabbed me by the arm. "That's not the whole story, junior."

"There's more?" I said.

"Lots more. I found out that Stek-Circ is doin' business with an outfit called Compsong."

"So?"

He told me the goddamnedest story then. He said this

188

Compsong company owned the patent to a newly developed electronic computer that they wanted to lease to publishing houses and record labels. Get this – the computer rearranged the music and lyrics of past hits and turned out *new* hits. The *farshlugenah* thing wrote songs!

"Bullshit," I said.

"Whaddaya mean, *bullshit?*" Eddie said.

"Just bullshit. Who'd believe a thing like that – a machine that writes songs?"

"You think it's any stranger than Buddy Holly being alive?"

He had me. "Well – "

"All right, then. They lease the machine to publishers and give them guaranteed hits. That way the guesswork is over."

"But that way *we're* over," I said. "Rock and roll will die. All that would be left is slick crap for tone-deaf slobs."

"It ain't a pretty picture, is it?" Eddie said. "Now, I'm thinkin' maybe it's no coincidence that the computer comes along right after the plane crash. Couple more murders and the competition is all gone – wiped out. Allerton not only cashes in on collection rights, he makes a fortune on lease rights to the machine and saves the big labels a bundle in royalties. I wouldn't be surprised if in a few years they don't even need musicians anymore, just let computers make the music."

"Wait a minute," I said. "You think Allerton is behind Compsong too?"

"It only figures. We've been blind, Rudy. We've been lookin' at two murders and a couple of attempts. We didn't see the big picture. It's like mass production. Get rid of the workers and put in machines."

I thought, *Could it be? Machines that make music? Applied technology replacing artists?* (Have you heard the top ten recently? There's no one behind the microphone, just a sampler. That's what you get when guys who think like Henry Ford run the record industry – high-tech tin lizzies.)

"Tell me this – " I said. "If it's that big, the plan, why don't they kill Elvis? Why not take out Frankie Avalon? They chart higher than we do."

"They don't *write*, man. They just *sing*. Elvis does, anyway. I'll give you odds they'll both be singing Compsong hits in a few years."

"But the music will go to hell. Their songs will get dumber and dumber the more they get recycled. Do you think Presley and Avalon will put up with that?"

"You want me to sing a few bars of 'Old Shep' and 'Didi Dinah' and then ask me that question again?"

Great balls of fire - he was right. "Eddie," I said, "you're a genius."

"It's not me, man. It's my oracle."

Maybe *genius* wasn't the word I was looking for.

We had it all set. Eddie would call me in a few days and tell me who the other plane ticket was for, then we'd go to Scotland Yard and the media. Just before I left, Gene reached in his pocket and pulled out a wrinkled piece of paper.

"Almost forgot," he said. "Some New York cop called and left a message for you. Says you're supposed to get in touch with him as soon as you can."

"A cop?"

He handed me the paper. Sure as shit - Detective Seymour of the NYPD. What the hell did *he* want?

♪ 🎵 ♪

I had enough to be jumpy about. I didn't need that flatfoot popping up in my life again. I don't know what it is, but sometimes I get a streak of bad luck and it just doesn't stop. Did that ever happen to you - where you go through a whole period of *tsures* and every day there's something new to worry about? I knew this guy once who had a *year* full of terrible things happen to him. First he lost his job. Then his doctor told him he had psoriasis. He was dropping scales all over the place. Then he had a car accident and found out his insurance had expired. He had to go to court for the traffic ticket, and as he was climbing the courthouse steps, scratching his red, scaly psoriasis, he missed a step and broke his hip. While he was in the hospital recovering, the west wing of the hospital caught fire and ...

Forget it. Forget that poor bastard. It's too depressing. The point is - I had my hands full. Buddy was sulkier than ever. He wouldn't eat his baby oatmeal and he always wanted me to play checkers with him. I couldn't get a minute to myself to call Seymour. And as much as I loved Buddy, I hated playing checkers with him. He cheated. Yeah, he did. Sometimes when I wasn't looking, he'd change a king to a square it hadn't been anywhere *near*. I finally got fed up and called him on it.

"You moved your man when I wasn't looking," I said.

"Are you calling me a cheater?" Buddy said.

"Jesus, Buddy. What would *you* call a guy who moved a man when the other guy wasn't looking?"

I can still see it as clear as day. We were sitting at a little table in the den and Buddy was wearing the crazy clown mask. It had this insane grin that stretched from ear-to-ear. It was like playing with Bozo The Psychopath.

The next thing I knew, he threw the checkerboard at the wall and the checkers rolled all over the floor. He grabbed his crutch, and for a moment I was afraid he was going to hit me over the head with it, but he just went off to his room, and a little later I heard the door slam.

I didn't blame him. He was just frustrated by all the songwriting pressure and surgery delays. Besides, it gave me a chance to call Seymour and find out what he wanted.

"Homicide, Seymour."

"It's me – Rudy Keen."

"Well, well, welllll," he said, all stretched out and slow. "Hello, Rudy. Long way from home, aren't ya?"

"Yeah. And I'd appreciate it if you wouldn't bother my friends with messages anymore."

"Now, how else could I have found you, Rudy? You disappeared so suddenly last year. And then I read a review of a concert you performed at, and I found out you'd gone to England, of all places. That was a pretty rotten show you put on, according to the critic."

"It was just hard for him to hear it with his head up his ass. Is that what you wanted – to talk about my review?"

"Sal DeGrazzia, Rudy."

"What about him?"

"He's still dead, and the case is still open."

"So?"

"So I can't forget what a hurry you were in to get him locked up, and the way you punched him out at Brenda Taylor's memorial service. You might not know this, but there was evidence left at the scene of Sal's murder, see?"

"What evidence?"

"I can't tell you that. I don't have to tell you that, unless I decide to charge you."

Oy, vey iz mir, I thought, *not again.* "Look," I said, "talk to my lawyer."

"I can do that, sure. But you know what bothers me, Rudy?"

Yeah, I knew. Having shit for brains. "What?" I said.

"How you ran out of the country the minute the grand jury dropped the investigation. That bothers me, Rudy. Of course, if you don't want to talk, England has very convenient extradition laws."

The son of a bitch was always two steps ahead of me. I couldn't let him pull me out of England *now,* just when I was starting to get to the bottom of the conspiracy.

"Listen, if I tell you something, will you leave me alone? Will you just leave me alone?"

"Maybe. Depends on what you tell me, see?"

"I think I know who killed Sal."

"Go on."

"His name is Preston Allerton. He used to be a big shot at Tal Limited."

"That's very interesting, Rudy."

"Yeah? Why is it so interesting and everything?"

"Because every time you accuse someone of committing murder, that person ends up missing or dead. I happen to be working on a missing person report right now. The fella's name is *Preston Allerton.*"

Jesus! It's against the law in most states, what life was trying to do to me. I said, "You mean *he's* dead *too?*"

"Could be. You probably know more about it than I do."

"No, I don't! What – you think *I* killed him?"

"Did you?"

"Of course not! I've been in England for almost a year!"

"Yeah, I know. Very coincidental."

"That's all it is, coincidence. Hello? Hello?"

Empty air. The bastard hung up on me.

♪   ♫   ♪

Buddy was banging out a song on the piano, wearing his gorilla head, when the phone rang. We were alone, for a change. Hans was still in Hamburg, and I don't know where the hell Arnold was.

Probably out buying some gun cleaner.

"Yeah?" I said.

"It's me, junior." Eddie.

"Well?"

"I got it. You won't believe it. You won't *believe* who the other ticket was for."

"Don't say anything over the phone."

"All right, man. I gotta do a show tonight with Gene. I'll catch you afterwards – say around eleven. Tube station near your place. This is it, daddy-o. We got 'em."

At around ten-thirty that night I told Buddy I was going out for a while. He just ignored me. He was still pissed off that I'd called him a cheater.

I waited at that tube station for close to two hours. No Eddie. He never showed. I went back to the town house figuring that he'd somehow got held up and would be calling me soon.

I found Buddy crashed out on the couch in his pajamas, snoring inside that crazy gorilla head, looking like he was at a Halloween slumber party. The radio in the corner was on full blast, so I lowered the volume and sat down in an easy chair and waited for Eddie to call. Radio Luxembourg was playing "Summertime Blues," one of Eddie's numbers. I didn't think much about it at first. I tapped my foot and put my hand on the phone receiver, ready to pick it up as soon as it rang. Then the station played another of his hits, "Somethin' Else," the one I'd given him the title for – remember? Pretty cool – two Eddie songs in a row. But I thought it was strange when, one after another, Cochran records kept spinning – "Sittin' In The Balcony," "Twenty Flight Rock," "Jeannie, Jeannie, Jeannie."

"What the hell," I said to myself, "is it his birthday or something?" I got up and checked the calendar – April 17. I was pretty sure Eddie's birthday wasn't until October. When "Teen-age Heaven" came on, all of a sudden I got chills along my spine. I knew. I just did. All I could think was, *Oh no, please don't let it be that.*

The announcer broke in, sounding none too cheery, and like I said, I knew before he even said it, because it had been the same way back in Moorhead, Minnesota. "In case you missed the bulletin at the beginning of our tribute, the legendary Eddie Cochran was killed tonight in an automobile accident just outside of London. Friend and fellow performer Gene Vincent was also injured and remains hospitalized. There is no word at present on his condition. All of Europe mourns the loss of one of rock and roll's brightest stars, Eddie Cochran – dead tonight at age twenty-two."

They started playing Eddie's songs over again, but I couldn't listen to them anymore. I thought about picking up the radio and throwing it against the wall, smashing it into a million pieces, but I didn't. I just let go of the telephone, stood up, snapped off the radio, and slumped on the edge of the couch. Everything was still. Everything was quiet, except for Buddy's snoring.

When people ask me where I was and what I was doing when I found out my pal Eddie had been killed, I tell them just what I told you. I tell them, "I'll never forget it for the rest of my life. I was in a town house in London, sitting next to Buddy Holly, who was passed out on a couch, snoring and wearing a gorilla head."

Sometimes they don't believe me.

9   'Hey, Rude'

They took Gene to St. Bartholomew's Hospital – St. *Bart's*, the Bobbies called it when I phoned them. I hopped a tube and had to *schlepp* for blocks in the cold foggy London night. I was all alone in this thing now. I missed Eddie (*alavasholem*). I could still hear his voice in my head, telling me there's no cure for the summertime blues. We'd been *so close* to solving this thing. One more name and we could've cracked the case but good. My only hope was that Eddie had told Gene the name of the guy, and that Gene would live to tell me.

When I was walking down Giltspur Street, my crazy heart started aching and reminded me of all the people I'd lost and how much I missed them. Ritchie, Eddie, (The Bopper) – but most of all, Brenda. I remembered how sweet she was to me, how soft her hand felt on mine. I couldn't figure out why I'd been in such a God-awful hurry to be famous. Why hadn't I jumped off the rock and roll train and spent more time with her when she was – well, you know. When she was *around* and everything. I felt a tear in my eye and wished that I could have traded in all the records and concerts and screaming teenage girls with their tight sweaters and pointy bras and soft flannel skirts with the oversized safety pins in them and their creamy legs and white socks and shiny penny loafers – just to have Brenda back.

I didn't have any trouble getting in to see Gene; I told the doctor that I was his brother, Craddock Vincent. (Craddock was Gene's real last name, but hardly anybody knew that except me.) Before he let me in, though, he warned me that Gene was real doped up. "I'm afraid his mind is cloudy and his speech is slurred," he said.

"Yeah, I know," I said, "but does he have any symptoms?"

He looked at me like I was nuts and told me not to be too long. I hate hospital rooms. They've always got sick people in them.

195

Gene was just lying there – what a mess. One leg was in a cast up to his *pupic* and there were cuts and bruises all over his face. As I got closer I could hear him mumbling. *Maybe he's trying to tell me something,* I thought, *something important.* I leaned over the bed, put my ear next to his mouth, and listened real careful. He was saying –

Do the bop.

I pushed some hair off of his forehead with my hand. He had a hell of a fever. "Gene?" I said.

"Why won'tcha bop?"

"No one's boppin' tonight, Gene. You're in the hospital."

He rolled his head to the left and then to the right. When he opened his eyes they were all glassy. But that was okay, because we're talking about Gene.

"We can do the hospital bop," he said.

"No, we can't."

"Sure, man. We'll just get us some nurses and a crazy beat ..."

"No."

"Why not?"

"Uh – the hospital juke box is broken."

"Oh, man."

"Gene? Listen to me. It's Rudy. You gotta tell me something."

"Rudy?"

"Yeah. I'm here now. It's okay."

"Go get Eddie. Great times, Rudy. We're gonna have great times."

Oh my God, I thought. *He doesn't know about Eddie.*

"Gene, did Eddie tell you – "

"Stek-Circ spelled backwards is Crickets. (Click!) (Whistle!)"

"Shh! That's a secret."

He rolled his eyes. "Eddie's gonna tell us a secret too."

"He is?"

"(Click-click!) Yep. Just as soon as old Rudy gets here."

"He didn't tell you the guy's name?"

"Whose name?"

"The guy who flew to Clear Lake with Allerton?"

"No, man. We gotta pick up Rudy first. Then we're gonna bop, baby. Bop to the beat with Gene."

It was my worst nightmare. The secret had died with Eddie. I was back to square one.

"Get some sleep now, Gene."

His lips kept moving, but I couldn't hear anymore what he was saying. I'm pretty sure it had something to do with the bop, though.

♪　♫　♪

I was stuck in Greenwich, waiting for a late-night tube, a hundred questions storming my brain like it was a fort or something, demanding answers. But who had answers? If Preston Allerton was missing or dead – who killed Eddie? Could Allerton be hiding somewhere, calling the shots? Had a bigger boss taken over? How was Krupp involved? Who would be next? Gene? Me? Buddy again? How much did they know? And who the hell were *they*?

I got home real late, beat and tired and sick about old Eddie, but when I went to put my key in the front door, it was already unlocked. That was funny. I was sure I'd locked it when I left. I walked into the hallway and clicked on the light. After I locked the door I turned around and almost jumped out of my goddamn pink chamois pants. There was a stranger in the house! He was a stubby looking guy wearing a black overcoat. He had a long nose that sort of turned up at the end so you could look right up his nostrils, and big ears with hair growing out of them like old guys sometimes have. His mouth was wide and crooked and hung down on one side, and his skin was kind of yellow – big old acne scars all over it. He was one ugly motherfucker.

"Who are you?" I said. "What're you doing here?" *And what happened to your face?*

"I'll ask the questions, Mr. Keen. How *dare* you leave Mr. Hardin unattended in the middle of the night?"

Holy shit – it was *Krupp*. I'd never seen him before. Every time he was around, they always kept me blindfolded. I used to think it was so I couldn't identify him. But now I knew it was just a courtesy to keep me from puking all over myself.

I told him Eddie had been killed, but he didn't care about that. He said, "There is nothing you could have done for Mr. Cochran, but Mr. Hardin requires your services twenty-four hours a day. It's what I pay you for and it's what I expect. Do you understand?"

Christ, that nose.

"What are you staring at, Mr. Keen?" he said, real angry.

197

"Hm? Oh, nothing. I wasn't staring at your nose at all, I promise." And he didn't even trim his nose hairs!

Man, he read me the news then. He told me that Hans would bring the new band members by in a week and I should rehearse them. We'd start recording two weeks later.

"Buddy won't be ready to record," I said.

He walked toward me slowly until he was about two inches from my face. That's when I noticed he had yellow puss around one eye. I think it was a fake – a glass one. It was sort of crusty. I really thought I was going to eject my dinner.

"Listen to me," he whispered, like Jack Palance, "and listen to me closely. He will *have* to be ready. Is that clear?"

It was the most unbelievable nose I'd ever seen.

"Mr. Keen? I said, is that clear?"

"Huh? Oh, yeah." You could see halfway up to his brain through that thing.

"What *are* you looking at?" he yelled.

"Who, me? Nothing. What's to look at? Say – does Buddy know about Eddie?"

"I haven't the foggiest notion. You are not to discuss it with him."

"But he was Buddy's friend, too."

"We will refer to him as Mr. Hardin, and I don't want him upset. What we need from him are songs."

He didn't care if Buddy had lost a friend. I thought, *To him Buddy is just a songwriting machine.* And that's when a little light bulb went on in my head and I remembered what Eddie had told me about Compsong and the computer that wrote hits. Krupp was connected to Compsong; he had to be. The attitude – treating a human being like a machine that turned out Top 40 tunes. Call it instinct. Call it jumping to conclusions.

♪　♬　♪

The next morning I was in the kitchen making breakfast for Buddy. He liked his eggs sunny-side-up with a bacon strip shaped like a smile underneath them. If you've got kids, you can try that at home for them sometime. Anyway, Buddy sat at the table reading the newspaper, wearing his sad hobo mask. I felt like Emmet Kelly's chef. I asked him did he know about Eddie. All he did was nod. Then I

198

reminded him about the talk we'd had about Stek-Circ, back on the Dance Party tour. Do you know what he said? He said it was an accident, what had happened to Eddie. And I said , "Accident? Are you nuts?" And he said he didn't want to talk about it and then pounded the table so hard he knocked his orange juice glass to the floor. It broke and splattered all over. He grabbed his crutch and hobbled out of the kitchen in his bathrobe, looking like a disabled hobo with a bad case of clinical depression.

I knew why he didn't want to talk about it. It was because of what he'd become, what we'd *both* become – slaves to Krupp. I wanted to fight back, but Buddy was too beaten. Ever since the crash, it was like he'd lost part of himself. I mean more than just his face – his spirit.

♪　♫　♪

"Hello, Sam?"

"Who the fuck is this? Do you have any idea what time – "

"It's me, Rudy." I'd forgotten about the time difference. We were about five hours ahead of New York, so it must've been four in the morning there.

"Oh – Rudy. I was asleep. How are you, man?"

"Not so good, Sam."

"Whatsa matter?"

"It's Eddie."

"What about him?"

"They got him."

He was quiet for a second, like he was trying to understand what I'd just told him. Then he let out a groan and said, "Oh no, man. Oh no."

"They tried to get Gene too. He's in the hospital with a smashed-to-pieces leg."

"That same bad leg he always had?"

"Yeah."

"Oh, shit. Oh man. Oh, shit." That's all he could say for a few minutes. (I cut out a few *oh shits*, just for the sake of decency.) Then he wanted to know if the funeral would be in England or the states.

"I don't know. I don't think we should go, though."

"Why not?"

"You know. Every time two or more of us are together, we kind

199

of end up dead."

"You're right. How're you holding up?"

"It's been rough, Sam. Buddy's driving me *meshugge*."

"Buddy? Buddy who?"

"Buddy Holly."

"Buddy *Holly*?" he said. "Buddy Holly's *dead*."

I completely forgot. I'd never told him what had happened to Buddy. "Oh, geez, Sam. You don't know, do you? I was trying to protect you, I guess, so you wouldn't be a target. Yeah, Buddy's alive. I've been living with him in London for a long time."

Sam went quiet again. All I could hear was static. When he started talking again, he sounded real serious. "Rudy, what's the game, babe? You been drinkin'?"

"Huh? No. It's true. Buddy's in the next room."

"If Buddy's in the next room, put him on the line."

"Well – I can't."

"Why not?"

"Because. He's all pissed off at me."

"Uh – huh. And what's he all pissed-off at you about?"

"It's a long story. See, there's this guy that's keeping us here. Says he'll hurt our families if we don't cooperate. He doesn't actually *say* it. He more like hints at it. I think he's got a songwriting computer and he wants to take over the world and – "

"Rudy?"

"Yeah?"

"Is it drugs, man?"

"No! I'm telling you the truth. Why, just about ten minutes ago Buddy was in the kitchen wearing a hobo mask and he threw a tantrum and broke his orange juice glass. You know how when you get orange juice all over the floor it gets real sticky, and then when you step on it your foot sort of sticks to the floor? Don't you hate that?"

"Rudy – see someone."

"See someone? Who?"

"Someone for your head. I know your career's goin' a little slow right now, but you'll get through it."

He thought I was hallucinating or something, that I was nuts. Can you believe that?

"No, listen, Sam ..."

"I'm going back to sleep now, Rudy."

"Sam, I – "

Click. He hung up on me. I was pretty offended. Hurt, kind of. Sam was my friend. We'd taken *schvitzes* together. I'd seen his hole. You know the one I mean. Don't be vulgar.

♪ 🎵 ♪

Over the next year or so things started to fall apart – and so did I. The doctor kept delaying Buddy's plastic surgery, and Krupp took everything out on me. He was pissed that I rejected all the bands Hans sent me to work with, but cripes, it wasn't *my* fault. Most of them couldn't speak a word of English, and they didn't know what the hell any of my directions meant. Some only played folk songs, and others couldn't play at all.

Let's see now ... how did it happen? I think I was sitting on the living room couch with Buddy. Yeah, I remember now. He was wearing the scary clown mask and he wanted me to give him a Yiddish lesson. Jesus, he couldn't get the hang of it. His accent was all wrong.

"*Kish mir in* toe-kiss," Buddy said.

"No, man," I said. "It's not *toe-kiss*. You sound like a goyim named Zed from Arkansas. It's *tochkes*. Did you hear that? You gotta get that phlegm thing happening in the back of your throat. *Kish mir in tochkes.*"

"*Kish mir in tocccchhhhkkkes.*"

"That's a little better, but now you sound like a Jew with a speech impediment."

And then the doorbell rang. Hans had brought over another band for an audition. I had to real quick get Buddy in his room so they wouldn't see him.

"Why don't I ever get to rehearse with any of them?" Buddy asked.

"You know why, Buddy. What am I supposed to say to them – 'Hi, This scary clown is actually Buddy Holly. He didn't die; he just joined the circus'?"

He slunk off to his bedroom, but before his door slammed he said, "*Kish mir in tochkes.*"

Hans must've been *really* desperate this time. He'd scraped the bottom of the rock and roll barrel. They were *kids*, for Christ's sake. What a menagerie! They wore skin-tight pants and funny pointed

201

shoes, and their hair hadn't been cut in months. They looked like a gang of hoodlum faggots.

"Nice goin', Hans," I said. "What'd you do, kidnap them from a kindergarten detention center?"

Hans said, "Vait teel you heah dem. Dey vill knock you aut."

Somebody should've knocked *him* out. But I figured, hell – they can't be any worse than the last bunch of jokers who played bop versions of Wagner.

Oy, were they from hunger. They giggled and touched the paintings on the wall and tested out the furniture like they'd never seen chairs before. One of them was a real wise-ass who called everything *bourgeois*. He had a British accent – sounded like an English hillbilly. They weren't German at all. Then the wise-assed little bastard walked right up to me, practically stuck his nose in my face, and said, "So are you a Nazi too, then?"

"No. I'm your musical director. My name is Rudy Keen."

"Get out," he said.

"No, really. You know me?"

"You the electric guy from America who plugs himself into sockets?"

Damn. *Everybody* knew that story. "I don't do that anymore," I told him.

"Hey, fellas!" he said to the rest. "You'll never believe who this is – the guy from America who conducts current." Then he turned to me again and said, "Please, sir. Give yerself a little shock for the boys and me. We'll unplug ya if ya start to burn up."

They were the most undisciplined rude little brats I'd ever met. They walked around the place like they owned it and completely ignored me when I told them to go down to the studio and tune up their instruments. I took Hans aside and whispered, "What're you trying to pull here, huh? How the hell am I supposed to work with a bunch of delinquent kids?"

Hans shook his head. "Roody, I svare on my grandmudda's grave. Dey ah unbeleeevable."

They were *impossible*, is what they were, Later on when I was trying to teach them one of Buddy's songs, they kept going off on little riffs, playing "Johnny B. Goode" and numbers like that. I had to scream at them just to get them to stop.

"Knock it off! Knock it off, already! Just play the fucking song like I showed you!"

The rude one, who'd just been standing there with no guitar or anything, said, "So's that your *real* name – Rudy Keen – or is it just a pseudonym-a-nym?"

I told him my real name was Rudolph Kearns, changed from Kearnstein.

"Oh, a Jew, then?"

I said yeah, I was Jewish, what about it?

"You know," he said, "You shouldn't go changing your name, mister. You should be proud of who you are."

"I didn't do it for that. My family changed it at Ellis Island, and– "

"Look at Albert Einstein. He didn't go changing his name, now did he?"

I told him fine, he could call me Rudy Einstein from now on. And the little bastard did, too. He called me Mr. Einstein for the rest of the day, till I got fed up and said, "Where's your instrument, wise guy?"

He mumbled something about pawning it in Hamburg. I saw him eyeing my black Rickenbacker, set up in the corner of the room. "Can I have a bash at that one, Mr. Einstein?"

That was my special custom-made baby – black satin finish, rosewood fingerboard, triple chrome pick-ups, Grover key-winds and dual level pick guards. I hated letting him play it; it was like lending your best girl to a whorehouse, but I needed to hear how they all sounded together.

We ran through the song ten times. They were pretty good, but they needed coaching. The bass player threw in a harmony on top of my vocal and I liked it. It sounded like Buddy when he overdubbed his voice on songs like "Listen To Me."

At the end of the day I was impressed. Hans had been right for once. I told them they'd have to come in for rehearsals twice a week. "I should have a name for you guys by then."

That's when the smart ass spoke up. "We've already got a name."

"Well, you'll have a new one, You'll be backing an established performer when you go in to record, and *he* decides on the name."

"Mr. Einstein," the little *schmuck* said, "either we play under our own name, or we don't play at all."

Attitude city. "Okay, big shot. What do you call yourselves?"

He looked me dead in the eye and said, "The Beetles."

NOW HOLD ON JUST A GODDAMN MINUTE! I KNOW WHAT YOU'RE THINKING! BUT THIS IS TRUE, EVERY SINGLE WORD OF IT! IF I'M LYING I HOPE MY ARM ENDS UP IN A GENTILE CEMETERY! I SWEAR TO GOD THAT BUDDY HOLLY WAS UPSTAIRS IN HIS BEDROOM AND THE BEATLES WERE IN THE BASEMENT WITH ME! WHAT – YOU THINK I'M MAKING THIS UP? WHO COULD MAKE THIS SHIT UP? YOU'D HAVE TO BE A TWISTED BASTARD TO DO SOMETHING LIKE THAT, A REAL WARPED SICK BASTARD!

Let me calm down for a minute. I'm sorry. I'm sorry I flew off the handle like that, but you've got to understand. Over the years, every time I've tried to tell this story to someone, they always give me a fishy look and walk away. Can you imagine how much it pisses me off to know what really happened and then to have other people act like they know better than I do? Other people weren't there. I was. Are you getting an idea of how big this thing was? Huh? It was humongous. Bigger than Watergate. Bigger than James Brown's ... you know. They say it's pretty big.

So the wise guy (who was John Lennon, by the way) told me they wanted to be called the Beetles and I just fell out, laughed my head off. But they didn't think it was funny.

"That's our name," John said, "and we're not changing it, not for you, and not for Mr. Established Performer." Then he narrowed his near-sighted eyes at me and said, "Who *is* this performer, anyway?"

"I'm not allowed to tell you that."

He put my Rickenbacker back on the stand and said, "Well, you'd better be able to tell us next time, or there won't be a next time."

Then they all filed up the stairs and John woke up Hans, who was sleeping on the sofa.

"Hey, Goebbels. Hit-the-road time. The Russian Army's comin' and Berlin's about to fall."

I sat alone in my room the rest of that night, trying to decide what to do about those kids. We'd have to get them haircuts and some decent clothes. Their harmonies were nice – but that was another problem. They didn't sound like The Crickets. They sounded like The Everly Brothers' younger brothers. And *Beetles*, for Christ's sake. Why didn't they just call themselves The Earwigs?

There was a knock on the door. When I looked up, a very

frightening clown face was looking back at me.

"Can I come in?" Buddy asked.

"Sure."

He walked in, sat on the edge of my bed, and turned that ear-to-ear grin at me. He said how did I like them, and I said they were okay but needed direction, and he said he liked their sound.

"They might have a good sound, but that John guy is going to be a problem. He says they won't play unless they can call themselves the *Beetles*."

Buddy just sat there looking like the warm-up act for Ringling Brothers. "Buddy Holly And The Beetles," he said. "That's not bad. You know, we were gonna call ourselves the Beetles when we first started out. But the guys liked the *Crickets*. better. Didja ever hear that track I cut, 'I'm Gonna Love You Too'? At the very end there's a – "

"Yeah, I know. There's a cricket chirping on the fade-out, and that's how you came up with the name." It was a famous story. They'd torn apart the recording studio trying to find the little bastard cricket that had ruined the ending of the song, but they couldn't, so they left the chirping in and became The Crickets. "But Buddy," I said, "I don't think beetles make any noise. And if they did, I don't think anybody would like it. You never hear lovers say, 'Yes, we sat at the edge of the lake listening to the beetles.' They listen to *crickets*, for crying out loud."

But the name didn't bother Buddy. He liked it. All he was really interested in was when he could practice with them.

"I'll have to talk to Krupp, and I can tell you right now he's not going to like the idea."

"Fix it," was all he said.

Sure – I'd fix it. Right after I finished changing water to wine and distributing the goddamn loaves and fish. More *tsures*. That's all I ever got around that place.

Buddy was hot to get some work done. The band had got him excited about a comeback and he wanted to pick out his first single, so we got out the song list and went over it. He wanted to know what I thought of the number we'd rehearsed all day – "P.S. I Love You." Yeah, I know – you thought John and Paul wrote that song, and all the others. They got the credit, but get serious. Kids that age don't come out of nowhere with a bag of hits of that quality – didn't you ever wonder about that? I'm not saying they weren't talented; I guess

205

they were, a little. I mean, not as much as *me* or anything. Nope – they didn't write all those great songs. Buddy and I did. Mostly Buddy, but I helped. Up to that night we'd come up with "P.S. I Love You," "Thank You Girl," "I'll Get You," "Misery," "Ask Me Why," "From Me To You," "There's A Place." "I Saw Her Standing There," and "Not A Second Time." I thought we should go with "Thank You Girl" as the A side and throw "P.S. I Love You" on the flip. Buddy agreed, and so it was set.

I called up Krupp the next day and told him Buddy was happy with the band and wanted to sit in with them. But just like I expected, he said absolutely not, that no one should know he was alive until the record was on the stands. He didn't even want them to *record* together. His plan was to let the kids put down the rhythm track by themselves, and then bring in Buddy on another day to overdub the vocals.

"There's one other problem," I told him.

"What is that?"

"They want to be called the Beetles."

"Please tell me you are joking."

"That's what they want."

"Mr. Keen, I may want to have Rock Hudson's profile, but do you suppose that is possible?"

Not even in an alternate universe. "I'll talk to them," I said.

♪　♫　♪

I had my work cut out for me. Buddy wasn't going to dig that separate overdubbing deal. John wouldn't play unless they could be the Beetles. And Krupp wasn't going to let me live unless I took care of things. The next time the boys showed up, I had a fry-up waiting for them, just to soften them a little. John kept *zeigheiling* at Hans and I had to keep Hans from killing him.

"You leetle Breetish pecka!" Hans yelled. "Ah'll heet yoo zo hod ova da head yoo'll hoff to pool dahn yo undavare to zee vare yoo ah go-eeng!"

"Relax," I told him. "Settle down. I'll make you some sauerkraut."

"Vit da leetle zausages?"

"Yeah, yeah. Zausages. Just leave him alone."

"Und za nooooodles on da zide?"

206

"Don't push it, Hans," I said.

"But Roody, I vant za nooooodles." He took his gun out of his belt and laid it on the kitchen table.

I looked at the gun. The things I had to do to keep from getting killed. "Okay. Noodles."

"Lotza nooooodles?"

"Yes! Oodles of fuckin' noodles! There'll be noodles up to the ceiling! You'll have to swim in 'em just to leave the room! Truckloads of noodles! Shitloads of 'em! They'll be coming out of your goddamn ears! Noodles up the ass, okay?"

Hans said, "Not zat many."

♪ ♫ ♪

It was when we were rehearsing "Thank You Girl," later on; I had to keep stopping the boys because they kept throwing double-layered harmonies on top of my lead vocal.

"It's a *solo* - get it? There aren't supposed to be any harmonies!"

"But it sounds better our way," John said.

"It sounds like the Everyly Beetles."

"We get to keep the name, then, do we?"

Me and my big mouth. "Now listen," I said, "about that name–"

"They can keep it." Buddy was standing in the doorway of the basement studio, a crutch under one arm, the gorilla head covering his face.

"Call the zoo," John said. "Or call Parliament. Ask them if Wilson's escaped."

I took Buddy aside and spoke low. "Are you nuts? Krupp doesn't even want them to *know* about you."

Buddy put an arm around my shoulder and patted my back. "Rudy, I don't really give a goat's dump what Krupp wants. It's time. I'm comin' back, man."

I hadn't seen him show that kind of guts since the old days. It was aces. We were going to be in a hell of a lot of trouble, but all of a sudden I didn't even care. It was Buddy and me against the world again.

Buddy walked over to the piano and hit a C chord. He gave the signal, but no one joined in.

"What's all this?" John said.

"Tell them," Buddy said.

"Are you sure you want me to tell them *everything?*"

John narrowed his eyes. "We don't play with simians, other than Pete."

I walked over to the boys and huddled them around me. I said, "Do you remember when I told you that you'd be backing an established performer? Well, this is the established performer."

"King Kong?" John said. "He hasn't had a hit in years."

"It's Buddy Holly," I told him.

"You mean, Buddy *Hairy.*"

"No, it's really him. I know this might be kind of a surprise, but– "

"You're soft, Keen," John snarled. "Buddy Holly's been dead for years. Come on, fellas. Someone's having a larf on us."

Buddy ripped off the gorilla head, right in front of all of them. Their faces went blank. Poor Buddy. The scar tissue had hardened and was all red and wrinkled in some places, but you could still see the resemblance, especially when he reached into his shirt pocket and put on his big black-framed glasses.

I think John was the most shocked of them all. He got up from the amplifier he'd been sitting on, took a step toward Buddy, reached out – sort of like he was going to touch his mangled face – but then pulled his hand back at the last minute. They all just stared with open mouths. Buddy bravely looked back at them. I think he'd wanted to just be himself in front of someone for a long time. He'd finally accepted what happened to him, and who he was. I stood off to the side watching all this. I don't guess I'll ever see a moment like that again. It was so ... touching, sad ... and really fucking weird.

John was finally able to talk. "But how?"

Buddy looked at him, wearing his old Buddy expression, sort of humble, sort of scared. "They pulled me out of the wreck, or so I'm told. I was pretty much a bag of bones, but I'm gettin' better. Gonna get my face fixed, and my voice. I've waited an awful long time for this. Awful long. I sure would be obliged if you'd play along with me."

John swallowed. His Adam's apple bobbed up and down like one of those weights in a strong man mallet contest. He turned to the others and whispered, "Do you know what this means? We'll be the greatest show on earth."

I don't know if it was the way he said it, or the look in his eye, but down deep I knew it was true, and that I'd be in on it. They really *were* going to be the greatest show on earth.

If you thought it was great to hear the Beetles, you should've heard them with Buddy. Take my word for it – you would've shit. Well, maybe you wouldn't have *shit* exactly, but you would've excreted *something*. They practiced together all afternoon, and when the boys were packing up to go, Buddy said to himself, "Buddy Holly And The Beetles."

John looked a little sorry. "I didn't know," he said. "I didn't know it was *you*. You don't have to keep the name if you don't want."

Buddy smiled. "I like it." Then he turned around to me and asked, "Rudy, what do you think?"

I kept trying to see it on record labels. I closed my eyes. *Buddy Holly And The Beetles*, I thought. "Hey," I said. "What if we change the spelling to B-e-a-t-l-e-s? *Beat*, see? Like in beat music."

"You're fuckin' brilliant," John said.

And I said, "Yeah. That's what it's going to say in my liner notes."

♪　♫　♪

When I look back on the years I spent in London, I think those might've been the best, when the boys stopped by the town house for rehearsals. We all got pretty close, especially John and Buddy. I've still got tapes of our jam sessions. Holly and Lennon duets – can you imagine that? Unreal, baby. The only problem was, after singing one or two songs, Buddy wouldn't be able to talk for days afterward. I began to wonder if he'd *ever* get his old voice back, but I didn't say that to him.

I remember one night when they were leaving, John and the others, and John came over to me and said in my ear, "So Kearnstein, what's the deal with the plane crash?"

"Deal?" I said.

"You know – how did they pull it off, saving him and all? And how come they let everyone believe he was dead?"

I just started cleaning up the room, picking up soda bottles and ashtrays. "Don't ask, John. Just don't ask."

But man, he sure was curious. Every chance he got, he cornered me and asked *how* they saved him, *why* they kept it a secret, and *who* was behind his comeback. I stone-walled him the best I could, but he was sharp as hell and just didn't know how to quit.

Hey – I'll bet you're wondering what happened to Gene. The sad part of the story is, he never did recover much. That leg bothered him every day from the time of that car crash. Sometimes late at night I'd get phone calls from him. It was always the same story. He'd be on his ass, wondering why his records didn't sell in America. Truth was – his songs were kind of old fashioned, and that black leather bit wasn't flying in the U.S. anymore. Everybody had become a pretty boy.

"Look at your songs," I'd tell him. "They're all about the bop."

"*Life's* about the bop," he'd say.

"Well then, get a blazer or two. Wash the Brylcreem out of your hair."

"Gene can't do that."

It used to make *meshugge* when he talked about himself like that, like he was some other guy and not himself. And he did it a lot, even on some of his records.

"No?" I'd say. "And why can't he? I mean – *you.*"

"Eddie told Gene not to."

"But Eddie wouldn't mind. It was different then. When he told you that it was nineteen-sixty."

"No, man. Eddie just told Gene that the other night." Oh, the poor bastard. The poor pathetic bastard. He couldn't get over it – he couldn't accept Eddie's death. I guess it was because they'd been such good friends, and because he'd been with him the night he'd died. Of course, it *might've* had something to do with Jack Daniels.

And the first thing the next morning while I was still in bed all groggy from talking on the goddamn phone to Gene all night – Krupp marched into the town house and demanded to hear the songs we'd picked for the first single.

"Do you *mind?*" I said. "I haven't got any *clothes* on."

"I must hear them now."

So I got out of bed and took him down to the studio in my fucking underpants. I played him the tape of "Thank You Girl" and "P.S. I Love You," and he nearly had a conniption.

"That's *not* Mr. Hardin's voice! That's a nobody!"

"That's me," I corrected him.

"Exactly, Why isn't Hardin's voice on that recording?"

"Why?" I said. "I'll tell you why. Mr. Hardin hasn't *got* a voice."

"It isn't better yet?"

"Why is this news to you? I've been saying it for over a year. Why don't you take him to a specialist?"

"Mr. Keen, I'll have you know that I am already paying a plastic surgeon a thousand dollars a month for facial treatments."

"Which aren't working, by the way."

He picked up an ashtray and threw it on the floor where it blew apart into a hundred pieces and sort of made me think of Buddy's plane, and all my rock and roll dreams. "Are you telling me that I have been financing the comeback of a man with no face and no voice?"

Oy. That sounded pretty bad, didn't it? I tried to think of a better way to put it. "Uh – you mean generally, or specifically?"

"Either!"

"Well, generally, yeah. I'd say you're right."

Then he put his sickening face close to mine and gritted his teeth. "What about *specifically?*"

"Well, specifically that's pretty much it, too."

He stomped upstairs like a storm trooper and yelled at Hans to get the car warmed up; they were going to take Buddy to a doctor for his voice. I stayed the hell out of the way until they were gone. I didn't want to be around Krupp when he got like that. And just when I thought I could finally get some sleep, the doorbell rang. I peeked out the window curtain and saw John. *What's he doing here?* I thought.

I *still* didn't have any clothes on, so I opened the door just a crack and said, "There's no rehearsal today."

He pushed his way in, looking a little pissed. "Look, Keen. Are you playing us for chumps?"

I asked him what he was talking about, and he started complaining that they'd worked for months and hadn't been paid. He said they'd run up all kinds of expenses and so far all they had to show for it was promises.

"Holly or no Holly, we've got to have an advance, or at least signed papers."

I always thought that Krupp or Hans had taken care of them. I said, "Look – I'm only the musical director. I don't handle the business."

"Then who does?" he asked.

"You don't know?"

"If I knew, you think I'd be standing here talking to a has-been

211

in his fucking skivvies?"

You know, maybe I could've gotten dressed if people didn't come barging in every goddamn minute. And let me tell you something – I didn't appreciate being called a *has-been.* John could be like that – he could be very mean. You'd always forgive him after a while because he was so funny, but he'd hit you with whatever he could. Let's say for example you were missing your left hand – he'd call you *lefty.*

So I said, "John, there's an old Yiddish expression."

"I'll wager there is. But where's our money?"

"It goes like this: *Er zol vaksen vi a tsibeleh, mit dem kop in drerd.*"

"Yeah?" he said. "What does it mean?"

"It means you should be patient and let me talk to the man in charge." Which was a sheer lie. It really means, *You should grow like an onion with your head in the ground.*

John poked his finger against my chest with every one of his next words. "You tell the man in charge that he has to deal with me, or there won't be any record."

What I'd like to know is, why was everything always *my* fault? *I* didn't ruin Buddy's voice. I didn't stiff the kids out of their money. Pretty soon they were going to start blaming me for World War II, The Cuban Missile Crisis, and the Profumo scandal. And to make matters worse, when Krupp brought Buddy home, he looked like a guy who'd had a bad day at the races, a guy who'd just watched his favorite horse break a leg around the first turn.

He told me, "The doctor says either the voice will heal on its own, or it won't. He has instructed Mr. Hardin not to sing any wild songs, just soft slow ones, once a day, as therapy."

Some doctor. He'd just turned Buddy Holly into Perry Como.

"That's not your only problem," I said. Then I told him about John. Well, he went ape shit. He broke a flower vase, a crystal wineglass, two lamps, and a little plaster chotchkie of Elvis with his hands folded in prayer.

"That arrogant little prick had the nerve to say *that?*"

I reminded him that the arrogant little prick knew all of Buddy's songs and was one of the best background singers we'd been able to find. Krupp swore. His face turned red. His fake eye dripped puss on the floor, just leaked right out like a glop of tapioca onto the kitchen tile. I thought I was going to ralph. And guess who had to clean it up?

He ordered me to call John and schedule a contract meeting. The *new* plan was to go ahead and record without Buddy. First we'd make the group popular, and then bring Buddy in and amaze the world. He had ideas about press conferences, licensing rights auctions, merchandising schemes.

"Buddy Holly And The Beatles will be on the front page of every major paper and on evening news telecasts. Their licensed products will bring in millions from every country - are you listening, Mr. Keen?"

Yep, I was listening ... to a fucking *nut*. The only thing he didn't get around to saying was, "AND THEN I'LL RULE THE WORLD!"

When Buddy heard that the boys would be recording without him, he went into a nose dive. Oh, Jesus. maybe that's a poor choice of words, in his case. But you know what I mean - he was depressed, all right? He wouldn't talk to me or anybody else. He spent most of his time in the basement studio, doodling on the piano keys. Sometimes he'd play that song I wrote for him, "Make Believe" - only he'd change the words. I heard him sing, "Make believe I died in the plane crash" or "Make believe that I'm still handsome," and I thought, *Still?* It broke my heart to hear him go on like that. I went down to talk to him, but as soon as I saw him sitting there hunched over the piano with that big dumb gorilla head on, I got to feeling so lousy I had to just go back upstairs.

♪   ♫   ♪

"Hey, Rudy. Gene's all alone. Why don'tcha come on by and we can - "

"Bop?" I said.

"Yeah."

It was the day of the business meeting I'd set up between Krupp and the Beatles, but I figured I'd be back in plenty of time for that, so I told Gene I'd stop over for a little while and we could bop. Now hold on - let me explain that. When Gene did *anything*, he called it the bop. If he was eating, he was doing the bop. If he was watching the telly, he was doing the bop. He could be taking a dump, and if you asked him what he was up to, he'd tell you, "The bop." So I took the tube over to his place and we bopped.

"Wanna bop?" he said.

"Sure," I said, with no clue about what I'd just agreed to.

He put on a record (I think it was "Hello Mary Lou") and with his bad leg still all stiff, he started twisting.

"Wait a minute, wait a minute," I said. "What the hell are you doing?"

"Bopping. You said you wanted to bop."

"I don't dance, man."

"Oh, come on, Rudy. You just stand in one place, shake yer hips a little, and yer doin' the bop with Gene."

"No thanks."

"Come on."

"No, really. I'd rather sit this one out."

That might've been the only time I can remember that bop really meant bop when Gene said it.

"Then whadaya wanna do?" he asked, turning off the record player.

"I don't know. Maybe we could bop."

"Okay," he said. He sat down on a chair next to a pile of record albums, picked up a bag, and started filling a pipe. I didn't know he smoked a pipe. I started looking through the albums, turning them over one by one.

"What's with the pipe?" I said.

"It's tea, man."

"Yeah? You smoke tea, for Christ's sake?"

"Oh, yeah. It's good for Gene's voice. Relaxes it and everything."

"You think it would help Buddy's voice?"

"Gene thinks it would help *anybody's* voice." He lit the pipe and then handed it to me. "Go ahead. Take a bop."

"Like this?" I said. I imitated the way he did it – holding it in my lungs a long time and then letting it out in a blast. *Oy*, bloody Jesus! That stuff tasted *awful*. It expanded in your chest and made you feel like you were going to burst. "What the hell kind of tea is this?"

"Home grown."

"Well, haven't you got any Lipton's or anything?"

Gene started giggling. He just sat there and giggled like a little kid. I kept looking through his album collection. He had some pretty gone records. Jackie Wilson, The Platters, Bobby Darin (Bobby was going Vegas and it kind of made me sick), Dion, Clyde McPhatter. Pretty soon I started feeling funny, like I'd been sitting there on the floor for about a hundred years.

"Hey – " I said, "how long have I been here?"

"You mean like *right here*, or like on the planet?"

That was the heaviest thing I'd ever heard – *on the planet*. It sounded so ... spiritual, I guess. *How long have I been on the planet? And where was I before that? And how long was I in the place I didn't know before I was on the planet wondering how long I was on the planet?* "Wow," I said.

Gene gave me the pipe and I smoked some more tea and practically coughed my head off. Then I looked at the Bobby Darin album again. It was all silver, except for Bobby standing in the center with his arms out, like he was Jesus being crucified, and he was holding an untied bow tie in his hand. I thought, *It's the bow tie that's the message. There it is, untied in his hand, and he's holding it out to show us, to show us that it's ... It's – a BOW TIE. Heavy!*

And then it happened. I turned the next album over and I nearly had a mystical shit fit. The picture on the cover was Lonesome Hank, the guy who'd given me the guitar strings and the picks back in Milwaukee in that creepy little emporium.

"I know this guy!" I said to Gene.

Gene's eyes were half-closed little slits by then. He looked at the album and said, "We all know him, man."

The album cover said *HANK WILLIAMS' GREATEST HITS*. How could that be? That son of a bitch died in West Virginia in 1953! What the hell had he been doing in Milwaukee in 1959?

"Gene? Did you hear me? I met this guy just a few years ago in a little store in Milwaukee."

Gene was filling the pipe again and talked without looking at me. "A little place called Lonesome Hank's Music Emporium?"

Hair stood up on the back of my neck. I was freaked-fucking out. "Yeah!"

"With a Gibson guitar in the window?"

This was incredible. "Yeah!"

"And nothin' else in the whole store except a few picks that kinda glowed?"

"Yeah, yeah, yeah! This is too much, I tell ya. I've been there once!"

Gene lit a match on the side of his jeans and said, "Oh hell, man, You only been there *once?*"

Do you remember that? Do you remember I told you the last

thing old Lonesome Hank said was, "Say hi to Buddy for me," just before that goddamn shop disappeared in the snowstorm? If you don't, go back and look it up. It was about a hundred pages ago. And hold on to your hat – then Gene told me he'd been visited by a *lot* of dead rock and country stars, including Eddie. He said he'd run into Eddie twice since he'd died, once at Lonesome Hank's shop, in L.A., of all places, and once in a public men's room – I didn't think I wanted to hear about that, though. Anyway, it all made sense at the time (probably because I was stoned out of my fucking head), but it doesn't anymore. I asked Gene about it a few weeks later and he didn't know what I was talking about. He just changed the subject to the bop.

Do I have an answer? Can I come up with one logical explanation for having met Hank Williams in Milwaukee in 1959? Well, no. Not really. But I've got a call in to Robert Stack at "Unsolved Mysteries." So far he hasn't called back – but he's a busy guy, Stack is. Hair dying alone must take up most of his day. When he gets back to me, I'll let you know what he says. Maybe you'll see me on the show, re-enacting how I got lost in a blizzard and went through a worm hole. They could get Gary Busey to play Buddy's part, and maybe some unknown redneck to play Gene later on when I find the Hank Williams album in his living room. I'll bet they'll leave the part about smoking dope out, though. Prime time, you know. During prime time they like to pretend the world is a nice place, a Brady Bunch barbecue, so they'll probably show me and Gene sitting around wearing Dockers and eating *cookies*, or roasting marshmallows in the fireplace. You can't do realism on TV ...

... which is why if you happen to be a movie producer and you're reading this right now, you ought to get your people on the horn to my people right away so you can snap up the rights to my story. Just *think* about the possibilities – Holly and the Beatles together on the big screen, with *me*! We're talking Academy Award – oh yeah. And box office? 100 million the first weekend, guaranteed. The casting is a no-brainer – Brad Pitt or Tom Cruise. And get some good actors to play the other guys, too.

What was I saying? I lost my goddamn place again. I got stoned, had a mystical shit fit, and then ... I think I went back to the town house. I was on my ass, real sleepy. When I opened the door I wasn't ready for what I found. The boys and Buddy had turned the joint upside down and were running all over, having a squirt gun fight. Chairs were broken and magazines were thrown on the floor, and they ran past me laughing like hyenas while they soaked each other with little pistols. John stole Buddy's crutch and hid it, so Buddy had to crawl around on all fours, and then John attacked him from behind and got his gorilla head and pants all wet. Just as Buddy crawled to a table and pulled himself up, son of a bitch, wouldn't you know it? Krupp walked in.

Everybody froze. It looked like a mannequin convention. Krupp stared at the mess, at each of the boys, at Buddy, and then me. It was the first time in years that Buddy'd had fun, and I hated to see it get ruined.

"I can explain this – " I said.

Krupp's head turned real slow, like it was attached to an electric motor. "Is *this* what I pay thousands of pounds a month for? So that you can neglect your duties and allow roughians to destroy a choice piece of real estate?"

Buddy in his gorilla head was stranded over at an end table, holding on to it so he wouldn't fall over. John slid his crutch out from under a couch and handed it to him. The rest of the guys started cleaning up the place while Krupp chewed me out. He called me incompetent. Lazy. Irresponsible. He said he should've known better than to leave such an important project in the hands of a one-hit wonder.

That's when John got into it. "Are you going to stand there and *take* that from him?"

I swallowed hard. "You can't call me that."

John said, "Atta boy, Einstein."

"No?" Krupp said. "And precisely why not, Mr. Keen?"

"Because," I said. "Because I had two hits. You forgot to count 'Bop-Sha-Bop.'"

"Yeah," John said. "He's a *two*-hit wonder."

I knew it was going to happen the minute John opened his mouth. Krupp turned his ugly mug to him and demanded, "And who are *you?*"

John puffed up his chest and stuck out his chin, looking down his nose at Krupp. "I'm John *Winston* Lennon. But you can call me Harvey."

"He's the leader," I added.

Krupp told me to shut up and fix some tea. I hated the bastard. I would've killed him if I wasn't a pacifist. He led John over to a table

217

and said that since he was the leader, he needed his signature on the contract. It cracked me up because he kept calling John *Harvey*.

"Now Harvey, if you will just scan these documents I am certain you will find everything in order."

When I came back into the room with a tea tray, John was wearing black-rimmed glasses and holding the contract up close to his face.

"Is this *it*?" John said, throwing down the papers. "Two fucking pence a side?" He whipped off his glasses and jumped up from his place at the table. "I wouldn't put me Hancock on that even if you didn't have a hideous gob."

Krupp turned red and his hands made shaky fists. "You'll bloody sign it, and you'll like it!"

"Get yerself another boy, mister. C'mon fellas."

And with that they all fell in behind him, walked out of the town house, and slammed the door. The sound of that door slamming hung in the air like a bullet next to a song title in the pages of *Billboard*. (How's that for writing, huh? Who says Rudy Keen can't turn a phrase? I mean other than all those music critics.)

Then Krupp turned on me again. It was all my fault, he said. I didn't follow orders. I should never have let those uncivilized Teddy boys meet Buddy. And then he told me that the fate of Buddy's career rested on my shoulders. Yadda-yadda-yadda. I'd heard it all before. He opened the front door like he meant to take it off its hinges and snarled, "I wouldn't want to be in your shoes, Mr. Keen."

So I was like – What does he mean? Does he mean he's going to kill me? Is he going to hurt my mother? What does he mean? I was going to crack; I just knew I was. I couldn't take the pressure anymore. The truth was, I *was* a one-hit wonder. No use denying it. Sometimes you just have to face the music and pay the piper and grab the cow's udder and milk the son of a bitch, and then not cry over it if it spills. I knew what I was, all right. I just didn't need anybody *reminding* me all the time.

I went to my room and locked the door and stayed there the rest of the night. Buddy knocked a few times and tried to get me to come out, but I wouldn't. "Rude?" he said. "You wanna talk?" I didn't even answer him.

A little later I heard piano notes floating up from the basement studio. Buddy had a new song. God, it sounded pretty. I opened the door to hear it better. His voice was carrying the melody, but he was singing low, like the doctor had told him to. I crept down the stairs until I could make out the title verse—"Hey Rude." Sound familiar? It ought to. You probably heard that song for the first time in 1968, with a slightly different title – but that's another story I'll get to later. Wait till you hear *that* one.

I walked into the studio and stood next to him. He was humming now; he didn't have all the words down yet. When he finished, he turned his shaggy gorilla head to me and said, "It's for you, Seventy-eight."

He got up from the bench, grabbed his crutch, and thumped upstairs. I picked up the lead sheet from the piano. "Hey Rude," it said, "by Charles Hardin Holly." It was beautiful, man. For a second I thought I was going to start bawling. I folded up the sheet and put it in my pocket. I've still got it. It's framed in my den, next to my purple satin pants.

♪   ♫   ♪

I sat around my room like a *shmulky* for the next couple of days, wondering what to do about the Beatles. Just when I'd given up hope of anything ever going right in my life – guess what? John called. He apologized for walking out the other night and said he wanted to make that record after all. Could I arrange a meeting with Krupp, he wanted to know. *Could* I? It was too good to be true!

But wait – it really *was* too good to be true. John never apologized to anyone. Something was up. I didn't find out what till the night of the meeting.

Krupp showed up early, antsy as hell. He kept calling the Beatles *northern hicks*, and wanted to know why he should be at their beck and call. But he knew why. They were his only chance for a Holly comeback. He paced and fidgeted till he just about made me goofy.

When the doorbell rang Krupp's fake eye started spinning around in its socket till it nearly went into fucking orbit. What a nutty bastard. I opened the door and got the first of two big surprises – they had a *new* guy with them.

"Who's he?" I asked. "Where's the drummer?"

"We drummed him out," John said.

That did it. "Look, John. What're you trying to pull here? We'll have to start rehearsals from scratch. Your other drummer knew all the arrangements, and he at least *looked* like a rock and roller. He was kind of like James Dean."

"Well, this is Ritchie, and he's kind of like somebody, too. We just don't know who, yet."

Neither did I. And fancy-shmantzy, all of a sudden they had a roadie. They called him Mal. And right behind him was a handsome, well-dressed gentleman who carried a leather briefcase. He introduced himself as Mr. Brian Epstein, their manager.

I glanced at Krupp just in time to see him shoot from the couch to his feet. He hadn't counted on anything like this. For a second I thought his glass eye was going to pop out and fly across the room, possibly kill somebody.

John walked toward the basement door and said, "Give us a holler when it's settled, Eppy." The others followed him downstairs.

Christ, what a scene. Krupp started screaming at Epstein, every swear word you've ever heard. I never realized he had such a fucking dirty mouth. I ducked down to the studio just to get away from him. John picked up my Rickenbacker and started playing a song I hadn't heard, and the band joined in with him. The song – "Love Me Do."

"What do you think of *that*, Keen?" John asked me when they'd finished.

"I don't know. Nothing special. Needs some work on the middle eight."

"It bloody doesn't, you know," he said. "That's our first single. It's going to be number one."

I said, "What?"

Then Krupp yelled at me from the kitchen. "Mr. Keen? May I see you a moment?"

I ran up the stairs and when I got to the top, Krupp yanked me by the arm and pushed me against the refrigerator. The son of a bitch was one giant nerve. His slanted mouth twitched and his phony eye tried to hypnotize me. Around and around it went.

"What did you think of that song of theirs?" he hissed.

"It's a nice little tune, but it just misses."

"Can you shape it up a bit, turn it into a hit?"

"Hey," I said, "hold on. You're not giving in to them, are you?"

"It's called a *concession*, Mr. Keen. If it saves a few percentage points and my autonomy, it is *not* giving in."

Which meant he'd already given in. For a guy who talked big, he sure caved in like a house of cards. Buddy's "Thank You Girl" was ten times the song "Love Me Do" was. The whole idea had been to launch Buddy again, not the Beatles. You can quote me on this – the deal they struck that night did Buddy in. They agreed "Love Me Do" would be the first single with "P.S. I Love You" on the slip side. Eighty percent of future releases would be Buddy's songs, but they'd be credited to John & Paul until he was able to perform in public. Till then, Buddy Holly was a ghostwriter.

You want the *emmes*? I thought the whole thing stunk. Or I did until Brian Epstein sat me down on the couch next to him later on and explained it all over tea. He said a group image was very important to Buddy's comeback. The guy was so goddamn charming, it started to make sense to me. He knew all my songs, too. He even recited the lyrics of "Radda-Radda-Ready," called it a "sparkling gem." Boy, he really knew his music, and his gems. But what really impressed him was how many stars I knew personally. He kept saying, "Honestly – you know so-and-so?" And I'd say, "Oh, yeah. We're thick as thieves. Two peas in a rock and roll pod. Birds of a goddamn feather."

Then Sam Cooke's name came up, and he was just blown away. "Sam?" I said. "Oh, hell, yeah. We've taken *shvitzes* together. Sam's got the greatest hands in the world. Gives a massage like nobody else."

Old Epstein was sure interested in that part about the massage. He wanted me to describe it to him. In detail.

"Well, you know how when there's a sore spot on your lower spine, and it gets touched in just the right way – not too hard and not too soft, but just perfect? You know what I mean?"

"Oh, yes," he said. "Yes, I do." And then he invited me to spend the next weekend at his home outside of Liverpool. He told me he had a whirlpool bath and that we could both use it. I remember thinking he was a very generous guy, a very classy guy, the kind of guy I should've been hanging around with. He complimented me on my great build, too. He felt my calf and asked me if I'd run track in school.

"Hey," I said, "I hate to brag, but I got a letter for the two-twenty low hurdles."

"I suspected as much," he said, smiling.

Man, I couldn't wait to get away from that damn town house for a whole weekend.

But later in the evening he got a little stubborn and refused to sign the papers unless he got to meet Buddy. Krupp said he didn't want Buddy disturbed, and Brian said maybe he wasn't really alive. Krupp gave in again, and as I led Brian upstairs. John popped up from the basement and said, "You sure you want him so close behind you, Kearnstein?"

What the hell is he talking about now? I wondered.

It wasn't a world-stopper, the Holly-Epstein meeting. Buddy came out of his room in his scary clown mask, and after they said a few words to each other, I took Brian back down to sign the contracts. On page after page he scribbled his name next to Krupp's, and that's when John poked me in the ribs with his elbow.

"Ow," I said. "Cut it out."

"Made a new friend, did you?" John whispered.

Then he did it again, he poked me in the ribs.

"Knock it off," I said.

"You like him?"

"Yeah."

"How come?" he wanted to know.

"Well, for one thing, he's a big music fan. He's classy. He's real professional."

"He's fucking queer," John said, and then started snickering.

Oy, g'vald! And I had a date with him the next weekend!

Krupp and Epstein shook hands, and the boys all toasted each other with scotch and Cokes. Me, I perspired a lot. Brian kept looking over at me and winking, but I just turned away. On the way out he called to me, "See you next Saturday, Rudy."

And just before the door closed I said, "Oops, sorry! I forgot I've got an appointment."

Out on the sidewalk I could hear John laughing like a maniac. Not funny.

Krupp held the contract in his shaking hands and said sort of to himself, "They're going to be very sorry about this someday. They're going to live to regret it."

♪   ♫   ♪

Months later (just picture one of those calendars like in the old movies that get their pages blown off) Buddy and I were watching the BBC Evening News together. He was pretty well toasted; he'd been kind of down and had boozed it up all afternoon. The announcer, a starchy guy with white hair and really bad English looking gums, said that a commission was being set up to investigate the assassination of President Kennedy. Man, that really got to me, when they blew away old JFK. I'll never forget where I was and what I was doing when I found out he'd been offed. I was just coming out of ... no, that's not it. I remember it like it was yesterday. I was sitting in a – I wasn't sitting at all. I think I was standing at a ... huh. Where the hell was I? I haven't got a clue. I'll bet I'm the only person in the world who can't remember where he was when Kennedy got killed.

Anyway, it really pulled my chain that if you were a president and you bought the farm, they set up a commission. But if you were a rock and roller, nobody cared. Think about it. Did you ever hear of *The Commission To Investigate The Death Of Ritchie Valens*? (*Alavasholem.*) Hell no. Radio stations just play "La Bamba" once a year on February 3rd. That pissed me off.

But then the news flashed to The Beatles' arrival in America. Buddy sat up like a pointer dog and moved closer to the TV screen, as if he'd just spotted a duck. Jesus, you should've seen it. You probably did. La Guardia was going mega-*meshugge*. Teen-age girls by the thousands, all screaming and losing their goddamn minds. Buddy and I had both seen a lot of crowd reaction in our day, and we were pretty used to teen-age girls pulling on their silky hair, exposing their tender necks, crying tears down their soft, pubescent cheeks, and shaking their cute little rounded hips, bouncing up and down and jiggling their ample –

Okay, okay. That's a digression. But it's a hell of a good one.

The point is, we'd never seen *anything* like this. Those babes were going to be on the room service menu. The television station overdubbed "I Want To Hold Your Hand" on the news footage, and even though Buddy had written that song, all he had to show for it was an advance from the publisher. I could tell it bugged him a lot that he didn't get any recognition for his work.

He tossed back some more of his highball and said, "They don't need me."

"How can you say that?" I said. "By writing those songs you've made the greatest comeback in history. You're a genius, for Christ's sake!"

And you know what he said then? He said, "John's already as good as I am."

"No he's not!" I really didn't think he was.

"Oh, yeah. He's at least as good as me. You haven't heard some of the stuff he's doing. He's got a new song he calls 'I Feel Fine.' It's hotter than cow spit."

"Wait till you appear on stage with them. You'll see."

Buddy poured another drink – three fingers at least. "What would they do with me?" he said. "I'm just a no-faced dead man."

It was sad, hearing him say that, seeing what he'd become. He scratched under his clown mask, got up, tripped over a lamp cord with his bad leg, and then limped off to bed.

10 'A Long Hard Schlepp'

Can you even imagine what we were thinking while the Beatles conquered the world? Could anybody have dreamed it? Let me change that – we didn't have *time* to think. Krupp turned Buddy and me into Top 40 slaves. He came to me one day and said, "The boys are making a movie for United Artists. They need a soundtrack."

Just like that! Like we could pull a soundtrack out of our pockets and say, "Here, *schlemiel*, here's your goddamn soundtrack. What's next?"

So I asked how many songs that meant, and he said thirteen. I socked my head with my own fist and said, "*Thirteen*? Oh, sure. Fine. Would you like to enjoy them here, or do you want them to go?"

He said he actually only needed eleven, that John and Paul had written two songs already. He played an acetate demo for me and said, "See if you can build around those."

"Now you want them *custom*?"

Krupp was a businessman. He had no idea what it took to turn out creative work. To him all you did was call the factory and order a bigger shipment. So after I hit myself in the head again, I asked him what the name of the movie was.

"You can come up with that, too."

"What – we gotta *name* the movie? What's it about?"

"It's about the Beatles on the road."

"So call it *The Beatles On The Road*," I told him.

He didn't like that. Said it was too generic.

I asked him, "What are they going to be doing on the road?"

And Krupp said, "They want it to be an honest representation of their lives in the middle of Beatlemania."

"So we should call it, *Schtupping Teen-agers In The Dressing Room And Getting Drunk*. How's that?"

He said I was annoyingly sarcastic. I told him I was sorry and would work on being endearingly sarcastic. The *schmuck*.

Buddy and I got on it right away. We sat down and listened to the acetates again – "Any Time At All" and "And I Love Her."

"What do you think?" I said.

He balanced his chin on his hand and thought. His masks had begun to wear out, and the only replacement Hans had been able to find was the Fairy Princess, the one the costume shop owner had tried to sell me a few years before. I wasn't used to Buddy as a blond. It was like collaborating with Sleeping Beauty. "Oh, hell, Seventy-eight. I don't know. They're okay, I guess. Not much to hold up a movie, though. How're we supposed to come up with the name of a movie from those?"

"Maybe we could put the words of the two song titles together and get something."

Buddy wrote the titles down and stared at them. I said, "How about, *I Love Her Any Time At All*."

"Waall, that's fine if the movie's about a hooker with an open schedule."

I thought that was a pretty good plot. I would've bought a ticket to see it, but it wasn't what Krupp wanted. We gave up on trying to name the movie and concentrated on writing songs instead. By mid-afternoon Buddy had knocked out "I Should Have Known Better" and "Tell Me Why." The guy was incredible. We finished the rest of the songs in two weeks. You can hear Buddy's rock-a-billy roots on "I'll Cry Instead," and my Brooklyn bop shtick on "Can't Buy Me Love" (I was still thinking about hookers). But we still had no theme song, no lead-off for the movie title. Buddy wanted to go on working, but I was dead tired and needed to get some sleep.

"Oh, come on, Buddy," I said. "I can't work anymore. It's been a long hard *schlepp*."

Buddy's pretty little Fairy Princess head lifted up when I said that, and he banged his hands down hard on the piano keys and just let the chord ring out for about three seconds. Then he started singing, "It's been a long, hard schlepp ..."

"That's it!" I shouted. It had theme song written all over it. But Buddy didn't like *schlepp* in the title. He changed it to "Long Hard Day," but still wasn't happy with it. I moved the words around and came up with "Hard All Day Long."

Buddy turned his princess face to me, and for a second I thought, *Why can't I meet a qirl who looks like that?* "Rudy," he said, "maybe you're right. You *do* need some sleep."

"Why? What's wrong with it?"

"Sing the first verse using that title."

So I pounded the piano keys and sang, "I've been hard all day long – " and then stopped. "Oh, geez. I see what you mean."

The censors would never let that go by. They'd think it was something dirty again, in their dirty little sick twisted pervert minds. We decided to call it a night and went up to our rooms, but just before Buddy opened his door, I said, "You gonna wear that to bed?" I was talking about the mask.

"Of course not."

I didn't quite know how to say it. "Would it be okay ... you suppose it would be all right if I – "

Buddy looked at me through the face of that Fairy Princess with her golden hair and pink cheeks and pouty lips, and said, "You get kinda lonely being stuck in here all the time, don't you?"

"Well, I don't know if I'd call it *lonely* exactly – "

He pulled off the mask and handed it to me. "Sweet dreams," he said.

He was right, though. I did get pretty lonely, among other things. Sometimes a guy just needs female company, you know?

A few seconds later there was a rap at my door, and Buddy said, "Remember, it's just a mask, and I've got to wear it again."

"All right," I said. "I'll *wash* it, okay?"

♪ 🎵 ♪

I guess by now everybody knows the story about Ringo coming up with the title, *A Hard Day's Night*. But they don't know how it really happened. He supposedly said it after a long filming session. That's just a myth. Jesus, I hope you don't believe that old *bobbeh meisseh*. What *really* happened was, early the next morning, after club-hopping in London all night, the boys crashed at the town house. John was looking for a place to sleep and thought maybe I was up by then. He came barging into my room saying, "Hey, Rudy – you mind if I just –" I sat up in bed, half-asleep, and saw him staring at me, and at the Fairy Princess mask on the pillow next to mine. He blinked, rubbed his eyes, and said, "I'm sorry. I thought you were alone. It's been a hard day's night."

All of a sudden Buddy came running into my room in just his

hobo mask and boxer shorts, "Rudy!" he yelled. "Did you hear what he said? That's the title we've been lookin' for— 'A Hard Day's Night!'"

I had them *both* in there now, looking at me lying next to the Fairy Princess.

"Can't anyone have a little goddamn privacy around here?" I said, shoving the mask under the covers. Cripes, you'd think they'd never seen anyone in bed with a mask before. But that's the *emmes*, that story. You can take it to the bank.

♪　♫　♪

Buddy had been right about me being cooped up too long in that joint. The boys were going out on the town again that night, and when they asked me to come along, I jumped at the chance. Freedom. Chicks. Music. More chicks. It was risky because Krupp always had a shit fit when I went AWOL, but to hell with Krupp. *Let* him pop his eye out, I figured. Besides, Buddy said he'd cover for me.

We hit a bunch of clubs in Mayfair and South Kensington. The minute John and the others walked in, they got swarmed and dragged off by celebrities. Me, I got stuck by myself at the bar. Same scene at every club we went. The last place we stopped at was no bigger than a can of King Oscar's. People were dancing all pushed up against each other; there wasn't enough room to breathe, for crying out loud, and the music was too damn loud. I almost lost an eardrum. Some guy tapped me on the shoulder and said, "'Scuse me, but aren't you Rudy Keen?"

Who the hell do you think it was? Huh? Go ahead, take a guess. Go on. Go *on*. All right, I'll tell you. It was BRIAN JONES, of the Stones. What a great guy; we hit it off right away. He told me that I was a rock and roll legend, one of his heroes. Me! He said I was a "... progenitor of the early primitively pure music," and I said, "I am?"

I wished they'd turn down the volume of the sound system. He had to practically scream into my ear. "Rudy, I used to sit in my fuckin' room and listen to 'Whoa Baby, Whoa' till I wore out the fuckin' grooves. It's very fuckin' tribal." Brian swore like a sailor when he was loaded, and he was pretty loaded just then.

"Yeah," I said, "it *is* kind of tribal, isn't it? What was it you called me a minute ago?"

"A progenitor."

"That's me, all right. Sometimes I can't stop progenitoring."

After a few more drinks than he needed, he was hanging on to the side of the bar to keep from falling on his face. That's when he started talking about a songwriting computer – the one Eddie (*alavasholem*) had told me about. Compsong, remember? I held him steady – he was swaying like a bad suspension bridge – and I told him I'd heard a rumor about the computer.

"Oh, Rude – it's no fuckin' rumor; it's fuckin' *true*. They've already started using the fuckin' thing."

"*Who* has?"

He tilted his glass up and drained it. He went to set it down, but accidentally threw it across the bar and almost nailed a good looking babe with it. "Mostly fuckin' American acts. But every fuckin' top ten hit on the fuckin' charts came out of the fuckin' thing, 'cept for ours and the fuckin' Beatles."

I looked at the far end of the room, at John, who was chain smoking and had two girls with him in a corner. Lennon always got the chicks. I don't know how he did it.

"How come you guys and the Beatles don't have to get your songs from the computer?" I asked him.

Brian tried to light a cigarette, but he held the lighter about a mile away from the tip and kept missing it. "It's in our fuckin' contracts, 'cause we've proved our fuckin' worth. It doesn't fuckin' pay for them to make us use it right now. See – where the fuck are you?"

"I'm right here next to you."

"Oh. There you are. See, with the other fuckin' acts, they give 'em a fuckin' computer song and make up phony fuckin' composer names. No fuckin' royalties to pay out. They charge the record companies *half* the royalty rate, and pocket the other fuckin' half for them-fuckin'-selves. Fuckers."

"But at least you don't have to put up with that," I said.

He clicked the lighter a few more times. Missed again. "But our fuckin' contracts are up in nineteen-seventy."

"Yeah? What happens then?"

He slid a finger across his throat, like he was cutting it with a knife. "'Tsall fuckin' over, then."

Okay, he was pretty lit up, but Brian was on the inside of the British record industry, and I had a feeling he knew what he was talking about – kind of. What would happen to The Beatles after 1970? Or Buddy? Or me?

I finally grabbed the lighter and lit his cigarette myself. He was making me nuts missing it all the time. He took a few drags, pinched the cigarette between two fingers, and whisked it out of his mouth as he exhaled, covering me in a cloud of smoke. I went into a coughing spasm.

"Sorry, mate. Rude? Where are you?"

I waved the smoke away and almost brought up a lung. "I'm here."

"Oh, you're back. You know, I've been hearing a few fuckin' rumors myself – about a fifth fuckin' Beatle."

"Nix," I said.

"'Bout a fuckin' guy who ain't supposed to be fuckin' walkin' around any-fuckin'-more."

"You got to keep quiet about that."

He smiled, looked around for his drink, and grabbed one that belonged to the guy sitting next to him. "It's fuckin' *true*, then."

I didn't answer him. It was getting late. They were starting to close the place up. "Tell me what I am again," I said.

He motioned for me to come closer. I leaned in toward him and he whispered, "You're a bloody fuckin' rock 'n' roll genius mother-ass progenerating generator, is what you are."

I just liked hearing it.

♪　♫　♪

Hans drove us all home at four in the morning. The boys had their own limo now, and while Hans was saying, "Eetz ownly po-lite to sha-ah de vomen vit de drivah – " John closed the little window behind him so he couldn't hear us.

"I wouldn't share a case of the pox with him, the bloody Nazi. Hey, George – got any prellys? I'll have to use toothpicks to keep me eyes open."

But George didn't have any. (Prellys were speed. I took one once by accident, thinking it was an English aspirin. I stayed up for five days, vibrating like an electric dildo.)

"You know," I said, "I was talking to Jones tonight."

John said, "Jones? Brian Jones?"

"Uh-huh. He told me I was a real – what did he call it? – a real *procreator*. But he's heard about Buddy. You guys are gonna have to keep your mouths shut about him."

John squinted at me. "Hold on, Einstein. Before you go

swearing us to secrecy, maybe you wouldn't mind telling us once and for all how it is that Holly got pulled out of a wrecked plane and shipped to Krupp in England."

He just wasn't going to let that alone. "I told you not to ask."

"I know. I'm asking anyway."

All their eyes were on me. I couldn't put them off this time. "I admit, it's fishy, okay? I don't know how the hell he ended up here. I don't even think the crash was an – "

"Go on," John said.

"Nothing."

"You don't even think the crash was an ... an *accident?* Is *that* what you were going to say?"

Oy, my head – it was pounding. Why couldn't he just be fab and shut up? "I don't know," I said.

John leaned back and threw his hands up. "I *told* you, didn't I?" he said to the others. "Didn't I tell you it was too suspicious, Holly turning up alive?"

"Hey, you've got to keep quiet," I warned him, "at least until I can prove who was behind it. That's what I tried to tell Eddie, but he got mouthy. Look what happened to him."

"Eddie?" John said. "Eddie *Cochran?* You think he was murdered?"

"I *know* he was murdered."

John started counting on his fingers. "Eddie, Ritchie, The Bopper – that makes three of them, all murdered."

"You can't really count The Bopper, so it's only two. Quit exaggerating. But if we go around blabbin', Buddy and I might be next, or maybe – "

John's face froze. "Or maybe what? Maybe *us?*"

"Better you shouldn't get paranoid."

He pounded his fist on his knee. "Fuckin' A, I knew it!"

"Just give me some time to get to the bottom of it. Besides, even if I'm all wet and there isn't any plot, you've still got to shut up about Buddy or it'll ruin the surprise for everybody when he joins you."

"When he – ?" He looked at the guys and then back at me. "Oh, yeah – when he *joins* us."

I didn't like the way he said that. I didn't like it at all. It was a pretty silent ride the rest of the way, and I could tell they didn't have any plans to let Buddy into the group. Not anymore. Not when they were the greatest show on earth.

♪   ♫   ♪

I almost had a baby when I heard that John had gone on vacation to Spain – *with Brian Epstein.* Yeah! After all the shit he'd given me about going to Liverpool with a queer, he turned around and went to *Spain* with him the minute the movie was wrapped up. Go figure. Now he could learn Spanish and tell all the locals, "*El Beatle tiene un grande homo.*" Hey – it was his business; I didn't give a damn.

What I gave a damn about was Buddy. He already knew they didn't need him, but it was going to kill him to hear them say it, especially after all the time he'd spent with John. After Dylan turned the boys on to grass in America, John came back and got Buddy stoned and told him what an artist he was, how rock and roll owed everything to him. He was just trying to help him get some confidence back, but he over-did it. Imagine – getting buzzed and having John Lennon tell you you're a rock God. Maybe that doesn't sound like a big deal to you – but one day while John was in Spain, Buddy and I were changing guitar strings and had a little conversation. He must've been high as a goddamn kite. He put all the treble strings on the top of his Fender and the bass ones on the bottom. And Christ, did he ramble. Listen to what he told me:

"You know, Rudy, sometimes I wonder why the good Lord saw fit to give me so much for a while – success, money, fame – and then take it all away. But I realize now he chose me. He chose me 'cause he had big plans for me. Yass, yass. I remember Mason City, Rudy. I remember it. You look at the photos of that there plane. No one shoulda walked away from it."

"But you didn't *walk* away, Buddy."

"Waalll, you know what I mean. They were all taken, all killed – Ritchie, J.P., the pilot. Ask yourself why, Rudy. Why me?"

"It just happened that way, I guess," I said.

But Buddy shook his head while he fastened the G string where the A string should've been. "That's where you're wrong. I was *chosen.*"

Oh, boy. "Chosen for what?"

Buddy just smiled and nodded. "I'm the one."

"Which one?"

"*The* one."

I'd had enough. "Well," I said, "that's just great. That's just fine. I'll call up my rabbi and tell him the waiting's over. The messiah's here – and he's from *Texas.*"

"You can joke about it if you want," Buddy said.

"Oh, for Christ's sake, Buddy. You're not *God.*"

And then he gave me this smile, this very knowing, peaceful-as-hell goddamn smile, and stood up and went to his room. I had to re-string his guitar for him all by myself.

Not only was I sharing a town house with The Promised One, I had to find more clues, just when I'd pretty much stopped caring about solving any mysteries. Really, I was at the point where I figured, *To hell with all of them*, and then one morning after I'd made breakfast for Hans and Arnold, I found Hans's pay stub on the counter. I couldn't fucking believe it – the son of a bitch was drawing a salary almost double mine. For what? For *schlepping* us around in a car? But then I accidentally dropped it, the stub, and had to crawl under the table to get it. Shock? Horror? Those aren't even the *words* for it. The labels on the bottoms of the kitchen chairs said HOGARTH INTERIORS. And what company logo do you think I found on that pay stub? STEK-CIRC. This whole operation was being run by the very bastards who'd tried to kill Buddy in the first place, and now I had the missing puzzle piece in my pocket.

♪ ♫ ♪

"Uncle Zollie?"

"Huh? Rudolph? You still playin' private detective in England?"

"I'm not playing. You gotta help me."

"All right, already. So I'll help. Vot you vant I should do?"

"Find out all you can about a company called Compsong. Check the international registries again."

"You got time for a joke?"

"No! My life's in danger and you want to *joke*?"

"It's just a leetle vun, for cripessakes, Mr. My-Life's-In-Danger. All I ever hear from you is, 'My life's in danger.' I got news for you, sonny boy, all our lives are in danger. Ve're all gonna die. So vot's the harm in enjoying a leetle?"

"I haven't got *time* for jokes. I got the messiah here waiting for dinner. I'll call you next week." I slammed the phone down good and hard and thought to myself, *I need Ephraim Zimballist Jr., and instead I get Buddy Hacket.* If they ever make a movie of my life, I won't go see it. The supporting cast will make me nuts.

So get this. I called Uncle Zollie back a few days later – and Jackpot City, baby.

"Rudolph? I got the dope for ya."

"What – you're a junkie now?"

"Look who's making vit the jokes. I bust my hump chasing down your Compsong, and all of a sudden you're a funny man."

"What did you get? Tell me."

"I don't know I should tell you. I go out of my vay, I slave over a hot phone all day, and then you tell jokes, but you got no time for mine."

"I'll listen to your jokes."

"My feelings, they're hurt."

"I'm sorry. Will you please tell me what you found out?"

"You'll let me tell vun eentsy-beentsy joke?"

"After you tell me the news."

"I got your vord?"

"YES! Now *please.*"

"All right. You remember the last time I checked, there vas no listing for your *farshlugenah* Stek-Circ or Songfest? Vell – in Belgium there *is*, only they're listed by the company that owns Songfest – Compsong. Bingo. Compsong is the parent company, and Songfest is the subsidiary, only *it's* registered in Amsterdam. Still, I got no connection to Stek-Circ."

Oh my God – *that's* how they did it. "Yes, you do," I said.

"Yes I do vot?"

"You've got the connection."

"Vare I got a connection?"

"The last thing my friend Eddie (*alavasholem*) found out before he was killed was that Songfest owned most of Stek-Circ's stock. They're all related. Do you know what that means?"

Uncle Zollie said, "Incest?"

"Yes, incest! *Corporate* incest."

"Then they should be registered in the Ozarks. Now, Mr. My-Life's-In-Danger, you got time for a joke?"

I was too busy piecing together the subsidiary puzzle in my head to pay much attention to him. "Sure," I said, tracing Compsong to Songfest to Stek-Circ, and trying to see how that led to Hogarth

Interiors and Tal Ltd..

"So Boiny runs into his old friend Ira, who he hasn't seen in ages. *Ages.* A blue moon. It's been so long – "

"I get the idea," I said. "It's been a long time."

"A long time? I just told ya – *a blue moon.* So Boiny says to Ira, 'Jesus Christ, Ira? Is that *you?*' And Ira says, 'Yeah, vot's left of me. Is that *you,* Boiny?' And Boiny says, 'Yeah it's me. How long has it been?' And Ira, he shakes his head. 'Ages, Boiny.'"

I said, "Okay – it's been a long goddamn time. We've already established that."

Uncle Zollie said, "Don't interrupt. Now, Boiny says to Ira, 'You still joggin'?' And Ira, he says, 'Are you kiddin'? At my age, I couldn't jog a memory.' And Boiny – "

"I've heard it," I said.

Uncle Zollie almost went ballistic. "NO, YOU HAVEN'T HOID IT!"

"Yes I have."

"Did you hear me, Mr. I-Know-Every-Joke-In-The-Voild? You haven't hoid it!"

"Okay. I haven't heard it." Jesus. What a grouch.

"So Boiny winks at Ira and says real confidential-like, 'You gettin' any on the side?' And Ira, he looks surprised. 'On the side?' he says. 'It's been so long since I got any – '"

"'I didn't know they'd moved it,'" I finished for him.

I could feel the phone receiver getting hot in my hand. Uncle Zollie must've been boiling on the other end.

"You told me you hadn't hoid it!"

I said, "But you *told* me to say that."

"And you said it!"

"Yeah, but I – "

"So if you say it, you should mean it!"

"How could I mean it?"

"By TRYING, Rudolph! By TRYING! You never even TRY to mean vot you say!"

"I'm sorry."

"Again, a good joke ruined."

You see how he made me nuts? There was no winning with him unless I told him exactly what he wanted to hear – and *still* I couldn't win. "You know what?" I said. "You're right."

"I am?"

"Yeah. I should mean what I say."

"No more vill I tell you jokes."

I should live so long. "Well," I said, "if that's the way you want it."

"Of course, maybe I'm being hasty. I'll have to a leetle vile *think* about it."

After everything I've been through, I'm surprised I'm still sane. When Uncle Zollie wasn't making me *meshugge*, Buddy was, or John was, or Krupp was. Or fans – yeah. Gene forwarded a letter to me from a fan who wrote –

Dear Rudy,

I have to see you. I need to tell you something face-to-face. It's very personal. *Very* personal. Please tell me how we can get together.

And it was signed, "Calvin Ray-Bob Stoges," some horny weirdo redneck from Iowa. I could still remember when fan mail used to come from girls.

But even all of that couldn't keep my mind off Stek-Circ. Eddie had given up his life trying to stop it, and what had I done? Nothing. I was ashamed of myself. There was only one thing to do, and I did it. I broke into Stek-Circ's offices to get the proof I needed.

I just made that sound a lot easier than it actually was. Me – what kind of goddamn cat burglar was I? I'll never forget it, my night as Bond, Rudy Bond. It was November of 1964, a cold and damp night – so unusual for London. I'd never broken into a building before, and this one was right out in the open on Theobalds Road. I might as well have had a spotlight on me. I tried all of the typical spy gimmicks – paper clips in the door lock, credit cards in the doorjamb. I went through seven paper clips and three credit cards, and the damn thing wouldn't budge. I stood there looking at the door handle, wondering what to do. Some spy. What – did I think the lock would open because I was staring at it? Who was I – Uri Geller? I ended up putting my old fire escape climbing skills to work and broke into a second story window.

Stek-Circ's offices were on the third floor, and wouldn't you know it? The door was locked. I worked on it for about fifteen minutes with my last paper clip, and then I ran out of patience and busted it open. Almost broke my shoulder doing it.

It gave me the creeps being alone in there with the lights out. There were wall-to-wall file cabinets, and I didn't know where the hell to start. I pulled the joint apart and found sheet music to a bunch of songs, including some of mine. I looked through a few, just for old time's sake. There was "Jelly Baby," one of my big hits. I held a desk lamp over it, just digging the poetry, when I noticed something that made me shit bricks. Instead of saying, "Jelly bop and Jelly stroll / Jelly pop me in your roll," the last line was changed to "Jelly dances oh-so-bold." What kind of crap was that? They'd *censored* me! And do I have to point out that *stroll* and *bold* don't rhyme? It was like letting a cartoonist touch up the *Mona Lisa*. But as important as artistic integrity was, making sure my ass didn't get blown away by an international syndicate was more important. I'd come for proof.

And I found it. Oh my God – I couldn't believe it, even though it was right there in my hands. The back office had just one desk, and inside that desk was a black leather binder with no label or anything. I opened the cover. On the first page it said, "PROJECT DESTINY." I thought, *Destiny? They've got a crystal ball?* There was a list of collection rights profits that showed how much they saved on royalty pay-outs. On the next page was the name COMPSONG, and under it some legal stuff about "song leasing" and more royalty scales. Page three was an agreement between Stek-Circ and the Beatles' publisher – Northern Songs. It gave Stek-Circ secret licensing rights for foreign markets, and at the bottom of the agreement it said, "Termination date: April, 1970."

It was just like Brian Jones had told me – in five more years, the Beatles were finished. What a find I had! But wait – there's more. When I got to page four, I almost dropped the goddamn book. It was a rock and roll all-star roster – and nearly everybody on it was dead. A hit list! I slid my finger down the page.

1958	~~Sam Cooke~~	[Sniper attack]
	~~Eddie Cochran~~	[Run over on desert highway]
1959	Buddy Holly	[Plane crash]
	Ritchie Valens	
	What's-his-name, the fat guy	
1960	Eddie Cochran	[Motor crash]

237

| 1961 . . . . . . | ~~Sam Cooke~~ | [Bludgeon in steam bath] |
| 1964 . . . . . . | Sam Cooke | [Lure into motel with woman – justifiable homicide with handgun] |

Holy shit! Yeah – they had Sam's name listed, and the first two attempts were crossed off because they hadn't been able to do the job. That explained his hole. His bullet hole. Right away I thought, *I've got to warn him.*

Between you and me, I was a little offended that I'd been left out. I always got left out. Even today in music history books, you hardly ever see my name next to Eddie's, or Buddy's, or Sam's. I sat there on the floor of the office wondering how come I wasn't good enough to get murdered, when all of a sudden I caught myself and thought, *What are you thinking? Are you nuts? Be glad! Thank God you're not on that list!*

I was still a little hurt, though.

Page five – unthinkable. It read like something out of a science fiction movie. The heading said, "THE ELIMINATION OF SURF MUSIC." It was a scheme to destroy a well-known beach music singer's genius with drugs. You know who I mean – that surf boy. They called it a "... gradual process by which he will be rendered profoundly stupid," or something like that. I don't remember all the details, just that they were going to sell him a lot of dope.

So you're probably wondering, "You mean you didn't take the black book?" Yes, I took it. What – you think I'm an idiot? Of *course* I took it. But there's a problem. Just hold on and let me get to it.

I read that page over three or four times. It was so *sneaky* to do a thing like that, to render a guy profoundly stupid. They had to be stopped. I slammed the book shut and got up and straightened the office up. Then I had to go back down to the second floor, climb out the window, and shimmy down the edge of the building, which was like a kind of crisscross brickwork that tore at my groin as I slipped lower and lower. It was the only time in my life that I almost wished I didn't have genitals. (I said *almost*.) When I was safe on the ground, I took out the little book from my pants waist and read some more. *Oy!* I should've read page six while I was still up there. Handwritten across the page in blue ink was this:

What to do about R.K.?

238

R.K.? Unless they meant Robert Kennedy (and as far as I know he didn't have any hit records), that was *me* – Rudy Keen. If they found the book missing and suspected me at all, they'd kill me in a snap. What else could I do? I had to climb all the way back up there and break into the building again and put the book back in the desk. So I haven't got it. I'd show it to you if I did, honest. And let me tell you something – after the second time down that building, I could've sung opera in Italy.

♪　♫　♪

"Uhh ... [groan, mumble]. Hello?"

"Sam? It's me. Rudy."

"Rudy?"

"Yeah. Rudy Keen. You all right?"

"I would be if some bastard in England didn't keep calling and waking me up. Don't you own a goddamn clock? Do you know what time it is?"

"Yeah, it's – oops. Forgot again. It's the middle of the night there, isn't it?"

"[Sigh.] What's the matter, Rudy, having another tiff with Buddy Holly?"

"No. He's sleeping."

"Oh, man. You didn't get help, did you?"

"Listen, Sam. This is important. You gotta do what I tell you, and don't ask any questions. *Stay the hell out of motels.*"

"And what am I supposed to do when I'm on the road – sleep on the streets?"

"Oh – and Sam, I don't want you with any women."

"Say *what?*"

"You heard me. Stay away from women. I don't want to hear that you've been seeing any."

"Look, man. I know we're close, but I don't have those kinds of feelings for you. Now let me get some fuckin' sleep."

Click.

"Sam? Sam?"

Well, I'll be a boweevil in a rayon patch. (That's one of Buddy's old expressions.) He hung up on me again. How could I protect him if he wouldn't let me? There was only one way – I had to call that Detective Seymour bastard, and I hated calling bastards like him.

And wouldn't you know it? All he wanted to talk about was Sal DeGrazzia's murder and Allerton's disappearance. I told him for the thousandth time I didn't have anything to do with those cases, that I was just interested in him looking out for Sam Cooke. Of course the nosy bastard asked me why, and I told him in case something happened to him, and he said what, for instance.

"Well, I don't know. In case he gets ... shot, or something."

"Excuse me. The line is bad. Did you say *shot?*"

"Or something."

He sounded suspicious as hell. He asked me if I was threatening Sam's life, and I told him to quit being a *putz*, that I was trying to *save* Sam's life, not threaten it. And then he wanted to know from who, and I told him it was *whom*, not *who*, and I didn't know from *whom*. I just wanted to make sure he wasn't seeing any women.

"Ohhhh, I see," Seymour said. "I didn't know it was like that with you and Sam."

"It's not!" I said. Didn't he know how macho I was? Wasn't he aware of my raw masculine image? Some cop. No wonder New York had such a crime problem.

"Forget it," I said. "Forget I even called."

"No," he said. "No, I won't forget you called, see? You'd better pray that nothing happens to Cooke, Keen, because you'll be the first person I'll arrest."

And then *he* hung up on me *too*. I wished to Christ everybody would stop doing that. I was getting damn sick of it.

♪　♫　♪

"Your name was there, Buddy. Right near the top of the list. They *wanted* you to die in that plane. Buddy? Did you hear what I said?"

I was trying to explain to Buddy about the black book I'd found at Stek-Circ's offices, but he was busy working on a song. I'd cracked the case, and all he could do was tinker around on the goddamn piano.

"Listen to me," I said, "they had Eddie (*alavasholem*) listed too. It even said 'car crash' next to his name. And Sam's next. He's going into a motel with some woman, but he won't come out. Not alive, anyway. What more proof do you need?"

He stopped playing and slouched on the bench. "Look here,

Seventy-eight. Who's the greatest songwriter of all time?"

"*You* are, but – "

"How much money has Stek-Circ made for me in the past three years?"

"I don't know. Millions, I guess."

"And who came back from the dead?"

Oh, friggin hell. It was his God rap again. "*Lazarus*, that's who, for Christ's sake! You've got yourself mixed up with a guy who woke up in a tomb a couple thousand years ago!"

Do you think he'd listen? Forget it. He just kept playing and singing that song of his. He'd been singing for weeks. It didn't even bother his vocal cords anymore. And here's the funny thing about it – he sounded a hell of a lot like John. I didn't know if he was imitating him, or if his voice just healed that way. But sometimes I'd hear him belting out a number and I'd swear that Lennon was in the next room.

He stopped in the middle of the song. "When am I going to get my Fairy Princess mask back?"

"You gave it to me," I said.

"I *lent* it to you."

"Look, Buddy. We've gotta get away from here."

"But I haven't had my facial surgery yet. I haven't made my comeback."

"People's lives are at stake."

"Where's my mask?"

"They're going to make a very famous beach music singer, that surf boy (you know who I mean) *stupid.*"

"Don't be silly. That's like trying to make a rainy day wet. I want the mask."

"All right, already! Enough with the mask! I'll go get it right now, if that's all you can think about."

He started playing his song again, something about a ticket to ride, and I went up to my room for the mask. I spent close to a half-hour upstairs because I wanted to say good-bye to her – I mean *it*. I was sure going to miss those pretty blond curls and rosy cheeks. Long eyelashes. Pouty mouth.

I know. It was just a mask. But it was a hell of a *sexy* mask.

♪   ♫   ♪

241

One night Krupp barged in without even ringing the doorbell first. He went around closing all the shades and made a lot of phone calls. I pretended to be busy in the studio; I was afraid my face might give away what I knew about Stek-Circ and Project Destiny. But he came looking for me and said he wanted Buddy at work on a new album, immediately.

"But he just gave you 'Ticket To Ride' and 'It's Only Love.' Why don't you take it easy on him?"

He gave me a bunch of shit about staying on top in the music business. Then he asked me something really strange.

"Do you still have a telly in here?"

"Yeah. We'd go nuts without a TV. Why?"

"I want you to break it."

"Break it?"

"Must you repeat everything I say, Mr. Keen? It's a sign of imbecility."

"Yeah, but why do I have to break it?"

"Simply do it, and make sure Mr. Hardin is not disturbed while he's composing. I want that troublemaker Lennon kept away from him."

I tried not to look into his eyes, but he reached out and grabbed my chin and *forced* me to look at him.

"Is something wrong, Mr. Keen? Hm?" he said out of his crooked mouth. His bad eye rolled over once.

"Wrong? No. Wrong? Hell, no."

He stared at me like he could see right through to my brain. I kept waiting for the eye to roll over again, but it just sat there.

"Just one final instruction, Mr. Keen. No newspaper is to come into this house under any circumstances. Do I make myself clear?"

No TV, no newspaper – he was trying to keep something from us, but I wasn't going to stick around much longer to find out what.

♪　♫　♪

December 12, 1964 – some dates just stay with you. I hadn't had a decent night's sleep in weeks. Buddy was always banging on the piano and getting me out of bed to play guitar or work the tape recorder so he could dub demos. For what? Where was this getting him? If the world only knew! The genius behind the Beatles' songs was living across the hall from me, wearing a latex mask and reading the "Bhagavad Gita." Incense and candles burned twenty-four hours a day while he played with slot cars and wrote lyrics in the margins of old copies of *Billboard*. I had to get out, even if it was just for a walk. I was sick and tired of being locked up all day with a megalomaniac who thought he was realted to Jesus. (Give me a half-pound order of reality – he wasn't even Jewish.) I sure missed the old Buddy, the way he was before he became a messiah without a face, or a clue.

"Rudy? What in tarnation is wrong with the TV?" he yelled up the staircase. He didn't want to hear about a worldwide conspiracy to kill rock and rollers, but he was worried about the goddamn TV. "The confounded TV is on the blink!"

I was going to have to find a woman, too. It had been two weeks since I'd given the Fairy Princess mask back to him, and I found myself sometimes thinking about sneaking into his room to have a few minutes alone with her. But if he would've caught us, I mean caught *me* with *it* ... never mind.

I put on my jacket and decided to take a walk down to the neighborhood drug store so I could pick up some magazines. Now that our newspaper delivery was canceled, I needed something to read. I came walking down the stairs to find Buddy waiting for me, his hands on his hips like he was disgusted.

"Fix the damn set, Seventy-eight."

"I can't," I said, "I just got through breaking it."

He tapped his foot. He scratched his head. "You broke it? Why in Sam Hill would you do a thing like that?"

"Orders. Ask Krupp, if you want to know."

"Waaalll, what the hell am I supposed to do about the TV in the meantime?"

I opened the front door and looked back at him over my shoulder. "You're the chosen one. You'll think of something. Maybe you could turn some bread and wine into a Motorola."

At the drug store – no, the *apothecary* – I picked out six or seven of my favorite magazines (never mind which ones; that's none of your business) and then got in line to pay for them. That's when the fecal matter hit the turbine. I saw a newspaper stand over by the check-out clerk, The *Evening Standard*. At first I just thought, *Boy, I sure miss my Evening Standard* – until I got close enough to read the headline.

AMERICAN SINGER SHOT DEAD
EVENTS OF SLAYING SHROUDED IN MYSTERY

Please, God, I thought, *please let it be Robert Goulet*.

But oh man, oh shit, oh man – right under the headline there was a picture of Sam Cooke. "Dispute in motel room," it said. "Shot by woman," it went on. Didn't I tell him? Isn't that exactly what I'd said? Well, okay – not exactly. I'd told him to stay away from women, but it was *practically* exactly what I'd told him.

I went loose in my boots, man. The magazines fell out of my hand and opened (tits and ass all over the floor – but it's none of your goddamn business) as I walked up to the stand and just stared at the awful news.

"Sir?" the check-out clerk said. "I'm afraid you'll have to wait your turn in the queue."

For what? I didn't want that newspaper. I didn't want to stand in any queue. (In London, lines are queues, but why should that surprise you? They pee in *water closets*.)

It was a long walk back home. *Sam*, I thought, *why didn't you listen to me? You'd still be alive, and maybe they would've shot Robert Goulet instead, just for target practice*. I remembered him then, my friend Sam, and all the times we'd spent together. I saw him showing me that bullet wound, and I thought of PROJECT DESTINY, with Sam's name crossed out twice. And then this: *What to do about R.K.?*

I was next. I took slow steps as the London fog blew in. I knew. Yes, I knew – right that minute there could be an assassin up in some second-story window, his rifle aimed at me, pulling back the hammer as he fixed me in his sights. Any time it could happen ... now, a second from now ...

BLAM!

I hit the sidewalk. A little Triumph sports car swooshed past me and disappeared around a corner. It had backfired, that's all. Some people on the street pointed at me and laughed. I stood up and kept walking. *So laugh, you idiots*, I thought, *laugh*. They didn't know that half the songs they hummed along to were written by a man who was supposed to be dead, and the other half were programmed by a computer. Sure, they could laugh. They didn't know what it was like to be hunted, all alone in a rock-and-roll jungle while no one believed you.

How could I have been so stupid? I was walking up our block

when it came to me why Krupp had canceled the newspaper delivery and had me wreck the TV. It was so we wouldn't get wind of Sam's murder. It was so obvious! I couldn't go on like this – that much I knew. Maybe I could write a letter to somebody and ask for help. But who? The Lord Mayor? The Queen? Yeah – maybe the Queen. What would I say?

Dear Your Majesty,

My name is Rudy Keen. You've probably heard of me. I used to be a teen heart-throb from Brooklyn, until an evil world-wide conspiracy to kill rock stars sabotaged Buddy Holly's plane in Clear Lake, Iowa. But Buddy didn't die (like everybody thinks), so the conspiracy guys flew him to London and hired me to fix his eggs with a bacon smile and record his new songs. They want to shock the world with his comeback, but he hasn't got a face, so instead he and I have written most of the Beatles' hits. But now Lennon has got Buddy convinced he's the messiah, and it's miserable to live with him. And he took back the Fairy Princess mask from me.

You look like an intelligent babe, so I thought I could trust you. Will you please help me? If you don't, they're going to kill me, and then all the music you hear will come out of a computer, and a very famous beach music singer, that surf boy (you know who I mean) won't be able to write any songs because he'll be too stupid. You wouldn't want that, would you? I mean, even though you people in England don't surf, you still like the music, right?

Your temporary immigrant,
Rudy Keen

I didn't know what it was, but something about that letter I'd written in my head didn't sound believable. I *did* lay it on a little thick, that bit about her looking intelligent and everything. Maybe I could change *intelligent babe* to *royal chick*. I don't like to exaggerate.

I could see the town house then, and I didn't want to go back in there. It was a prison. I slowed down. I had to escape, but where

245

would I go? Wouldn't they find me in Brooklyn? I thought about visiting my father on the *kibbutz* – for about one second I thought that. Forget it. He hadn't been there for me when I needed him. And I didn't think I could hack that work-in-the-fields routine. I needed music, not fertilizer. Maybe Tahiti. Naw – too much sun. I get a rash. New Zealand? What the hell is in New Zealand, pygmies? That could've been cool. At five-five I would've been the tallest guy on the island.

All I did was open the goddamn door, that's all. A split-second later two guys had me spread-eagle on the floor with a gun to my head. One of them flashed a badge in front of my face, but it was too close and I couldn't read it.

"You are under arrest by the authority of the New York Police Department, with complete cooperation of the British government, in connection with the shooting death of Sam Cooke."

"Who the hell are you?" I said.

"I just showed you my badge."

"I know, but I couldn't see it. Ow! Quit bending my arms like that. They're not made of rubber, you know!"

They clapped some cuffs on me and yanked me to my feet. I'd never seen these two before in my life. And wasn't that Seymour something? Instead of protecting Sam when I told him to, he waits for him to get killed and sends his goons to arrest me. *Schmendryk!*

"What're you doin' to my legs?" I asked.

One cop held the gun on me while the other one snapped chains on my ankles.

"Leg irons," he said. "Standard procedure in a high-flight risk."

"What flight? I can't even walk!"

"Just shuffle."

"Shuffle?"

"Yeah," he said, "first you shuffle to the left, then you shuffle to the right."

"And then I do the hokey-pokey with all my might? What are you – a dance instructor? It'll take me a *week* to get out the door that way."

"No, it won't," he said, and they both lifted me off my feet and carried me.

"Wait! Wait! Wait!" I shouted.

They put me down. The guy with the gun said, "What is it?"

"I didn't kill Sam. I've been in London for five years."

"You can tell that to the detective."

246

"No, I can't, 'cause he won't believe me."

"Tough luck," he said, and started to pick me up again.

"Wait! Wait! Wait!" I shouted again.

"What is it now?"

"I've got a very important letter I have to write to the Queen."

"So send her a telegram from New York."

Just then Buddy walked down the stairway, wearing the Fairy Princess mask. "Ask him!" I said. "He'll tell you I couldn't have killed anyone – he knows I've been in England all this time."

"Him?" the cop said. "That's a *man*?"

"Yeah! Don't let the rouged cheeks and pouty mouth and long golden hair fool you."

"What've you guys got goin' on here?" the other cop said.

"Nothin'! That's *Buddy Holly*."

The two dicks looked at each other, and the one with the gun said, "Sure it is. And I'm Elvis Presley."

"Show 'em, Buddy! Go ahead! Sing 'That'll Be The Day.' C'mon! Sing, why don't you?"

"Let's go, pal." They lifted me up again and carried me to the door.

"Just one goddamn song, Buddy! Sing 'Peggy Sue' or 'Ollie Vee!' Sing 'The Sound of Music' for all I care, only *sing* already!"

But Buddy just stared at me out of those two pretty Princess eyes and waved good-bye.

♪   ♫   ♪

I'm not saying it wasn't good to see the old USA again. I just wished I didn't have to come back that way, all tied up between two flatfoot dicks like a common criminal. A squad car picked us up at the Arrival ramp at La Guardia, and people gawked while they loaded me into the back seat.

"Hey," I said to the guy who sat next to me. "I just remembered I didn't bring any clothes. We'll have to go back."

"Relax, Keen," He said. "We got nice uniforms for guys like you. You like stripes?"

Wise ass. "On zebras I like stripes. On me I like satin and leather."

"Oooh, you'll make lots of friends in the penitentiary if you dress like that."

"Penitentiary?"

"Maybe you can get your bunk mate to wear a cute little mask like your Buddy Holly friend."

"Bunk mate? Whadaya mean? Huh?"

They just laughed like a couple of *shmegegges*, but I was starting to worry. I can't sleep in the same room with anybody else. I've got this sinus condition, and I drain at night.

It was like one of those bad dreams that you have over and over again. The Midtown North 18th precinct station hadn't changed much since the last time I was questioned – doughnut crumbs on the floor, boogers on the wall. Lieutenant Seymour had me booked and taken down to the lie detector room again, only this time I told him I wasn't answering any questions without my lawyer present. So they kept me hooked up to about a gazillion electrodes for two hours before Uncle Zollie showed up. He was all jumpy and full of questions. The minute he walked in the room he said, "Vot you did this time, Rudolph – kill another manager?"

"He's kidding," I told Seymour.

"He'd better be. Some lawyer. You sure you want him to represent you?"

"Vot," Uncle Zollie said, "I'm not *good* enough for youz? I can defend a moida suspect as vell as the next lawyer."

Seymour said, "We haven't said he was suspected of murder, see?"

"And vagrants and nuts I do pretty vell vit, too. Hey, officer. Have you hoid the one about the priest and the rabbi who go to the hooker?"

"Not *now*, Uncle Zollie!" I said. Jesus. Talk about no sense of priorities.

And then those stupid questions – I knew them all by heart. *What's your name? When was Dinah Shore buried in Grant's tomb?*

"Now, see. I want you to take it from the top, Keen," Seymour said. "Tell me everything that happened since Sal DeGrazzia was shot in the head, leaving a hole the size of – "

" – a quarter, I know," I said. "Christ, you want to know *everything*?"

"Everything."

"You got five years?"

"I've got as long as it takes."

Did *he* ever need to get a life. But I figured, *He wants to hear*

everything? Fine. I'll tell him everything. I started way back at the Winter
Dance Party tour and told him how I ran into Hank Williams in a
snowstorm, and how Buddy didn't die in the plane crash, but instead
got flown to England where the two of us discovered the Beatles and
wrote all their hits.

"And I found a little black book in Stek-Circ's offices that lists
all the stars they've murdered, and all the ones they're *gonna* murder.
That's how I knew they were gonna kill Sam. They're gonna get me,
too. And they're gonna make a very famous beach music singer, that
surf boy (you know who I mean), profoundly stupid through drugs,
and Buddy Holly is gonna make a comeback as soon as he gets
plastic surgery, only there won't be much time left for him as a
songwriter because there's a computer that writes all the top ten
songs. Now, can I please send a telegram to the Queen?"

Seymour looked at Uncle Zollie, and Uncle Zollie shook his
head and shrugged and looked at the floor. The lie detector guy said,
"According to the machine, he's telling the truth, or what he *thinks*
is the truth."

Then they all stared at me as if I was a side-order of bacon at
a Passover Seder, all except Uncle Zollie, who was still looking at the
floor and mumbling, "I don't understand it. He used to be almost
normal."

Detective Seymour asked Uncle Zollie if they could speak alone
for a few minutes.

"Hey," I said. "One of the guys who arrested me said I'd get to
send a telegram to the Queen when I got here."

"It's all right, Rudy," Seymour told me. "You just write it out
on a piece of paper, see, and we'll send it for you."

So I picked up a piece of paper as Seymour and Uncle Zollie
left the room, and I started the telegram.

"Can I take these damn electrodes off?" I asked the lie detector
guy. The wires got all tangled every time I tried to write.

"Sure, kid. Just pull 'em. They pop right off. Can I get you
anything?"

Get me anything? Why were they suddenly being so nice to me?

"You know what I'd really like?" I said.

"What?"

"A hoagie sandwich. I haven't had one in years. You know what
they put on pizza in England? *Corn.* I kid you not. Can you believe
that?"

249

"I believe you, kid. Honest."

"And they pee in closets over there."

"Imagine that."

"Yeah! They're all crazy. Sometimes I felt like I was the only sane person in the whole country."

"I know what you mean."

When Seymour and Uncle Zollie came back they looked real serious.

"Well?" I said. Did I pass the audition?"

Seymour scratched his head and started pacing. "We're dropping the charges, Keen."

"Good. I can't wait till Ma hears all this. She'll think I'm out of my mind. Just you watch."

Uncle Zollie sure was down. His arms hung at his sides and his chin was so low it hit his chest. "She'll vait, Rudolph."

"Wait? Wait for what? I'm going straight home, just as soon as I get my hoagie and they send this telegram to the Queen. She'll help me, boy. She's got clout. Did you ever see that crown she wears? Looks like Tiffany's-gone-nuts." Then I looked at Seymour. He was motioning the lie detector guy with his head, sort of tilting it. "You guys gonna drive me home?"

The lie detector guy got up and left the room.

"Hey! He forgot my telegram."

"Just stay calm, Keen. We're going to make a little stop before we take you home."

"A stop? Where? I don't want to go anywhere but home."

"It's a place where you'll be able to relax for a while. Get some rest. Talk to some people who can help you."

"But I don't want to rest. I want to go home."

"Now, don't make this more difficult that it has to be," Seymour said, twisting an arm behind my back. Two cops came running into the room with a white jacket and wrestled me to the floor.

"Whadaya doin'? Huh? I told you the truth! Ask the lie detector guy! He said so!"

Son of a bitch. They put me in a strait jacket, and Uncle Zollie just stood there, watching.

"Don't hoit him," Uncle Zollie said. "He's my sistah's kid. She'll have a conniption."

"Sister-shmister, Uncle Zollie! Get me the hell out of this

goddamn thing! What kind of lawyer *are* you, anyway?"

They loaded me into a paddy wagon. Ever ride in the back of a paddy wagon? They're urinals on wheels. I never got my hoagie sandwich, and I'm willing to bet they never sent that telegram to the Queen. I spent the next ten months in Bellevue, for *observation*, they said. What observation? I wondered. *I* was the one doing all the observing. I observed morons screaming and talking to walls. I observed guys in white uniforms hosing down lunatics. I observed cockroaches in my room. And I observed one guy who ate his own shit, like it was a delicacy or something. I got observation, all right. It's a miracle I'm not permanently disturbed, is all I can say.

But when you're in a joint like that, you learn that no matter what, you shouldn't tell the truth. My psych doctor, Dr. Shmeck, asked me to tell him the conspiracy theory every day. For seven months I went over and over the same story, and when I'd finish he'd say, "Now, that didn't *really* happen, did it, Rudy?" And I'd swear to God and Moses that it did, and then I'd tell him he should call himself Dr. *Schmuck*, not Dr. Shmeck.

And then one day, one day I was so tired of trying to convince him, that when he said, "Now, that didn't *really* happen, did it, Rudy?" I said, "Hell, no. I made it all up."

Before you knew it, I had visiting privileges and the run of the place. The more I said I made it up, the more freedom he gave me. And after another three months of telling him what a stupid liar I'd been, he let me out. I've still got the diagnosis. My problem was I'd never been breast-fed as a baby, and I was resentful. Also I had a complex Oedipus something-or-other and secretly wanted to kill my father and run off to the Catskills with my mother. Really – that's what Dr. Shmeck said. And he called *me* crazy.

Now, maybe it takes me a long time to catch on. I'll admit it. But after ten months of sitting around in a loony bin and after meeting seven guys who all thought they were Jesus (and one wasn't even circumcised) (when I pointed that out to him he performed an instant *briss* on himself with a can opener) (you wouldn't have wanted to see it, believe me), I began to get a taste of reality. It started when I called up Sherm at Tal Ltd..

"Who is this?" Sherm asked.

"It's me, Rudy."

"Rudy? Rudy *Keen*?"

"You know a lot of Rudys? Why do you sound so surprised?"

"You mean, other than the fact that you haven't *called* in four years?"

"I've been a little busy. Look, Sherm. What ever happened with that investigation?"

"Investigation?"

"Yeah. You know – the one you were doing about Stek-Circ and all the rock and roll guys that they killed."

Sherm coughed and covered the mouthpiece for a second. "Oh – that investigation."

"Yeah. So what did you find out?"

"Nothing. There was no plot. I conducted a very thorough – "

"No *plot*? Are you kidding? Don't you remember I told you what Sam Cooke and Eddie Cochran said – about somebody trying to get them?"

"Yes. I recall that, Rudy. But – "

"And now they're both dead. You call that not a plot?"

Sherm sighed. "Listen, Rudy. I don't want to ask you anything too personal, but the word's out that you've been committed to Bellevue."

"Yeah – that's where I'm calling from. They're letting me out of here as soon as the paperwork is done."

"You're cured, then?"

"Sherm – have a little faith, will ya? I was never crazy."

"I didn't mean to suggest that you were. It's just that you *are* in Bellevue, and people are saying you think Buddy Holly is alive."

"So?"

Sherm dropped the phone and then picked it up again. "So, you don't see a problem with that?"

"What problem? Buddy *is* alive,"

Sherm groaned and said, "You're not going to tell anybody else that, I hope."

"Of course I am. I've got an appointment with a reporter from The *New York Times* as soon as I get out of here."

"The *Times*, for Chrissake?"

"Hey, people have a right to know, you know. *You* might not have found anything out about the plot, but I did. Stek-Circ's behind it all. They call it PROJECT DESTINY."

"Project *what*?"

"Long story. I can't stay on much longer. There's a guy here with a rubber hose and he keeps looking at me. So can you get me any gigs?"

"Gigs? Oh, geez, Rudy. I don't know. Have you even been playing much?"

"Sure! Every day, practically, till I got here."

"With who?"

"You mean *whom*. *With* is a preposition, and so you need to follow it with an objective – "

"*Whom* have you been playing with?"

"Now it's *who*. You forgot to use the preposition."

"Goddamn it, Rudy – will you stop with the grammar and tell me who or whom the fuck you've been playing with?"

"With Buddy."

"Oh, Christ. I'm sorry I asked."

"Sometimes with the Beatles – mostly John. So what do you think, are you going to call Dick Clark for me?"

"And tell him what? That I've got a client in Bellevue who's been playing rock and roll with a dead musician from Texas and one of the Beatles?"

"Well, you might want to phrase it a little different. But get me on 'Bandstand,' man."

"You haven't even got a record out."

"So I'll make one."

"The business has changed, Rudy."

"Naw. It's still all bullshit. What kind of gigs do you think you can get me?"

"God, Rudy. You're asking a lot. Maybe some summer carnivals or something."

"Carnivals? Carnivals? I don't *do* carnivals."

"No one remembers you, Rudy."

"What – are you saying I'm a has-been? A one-hit wonder? A *shmer'l*?"

"Well ... what's a *shmer'l*?"

"Please don't tell me you think I'm a *shmer'l*!"

"How can I tell you if I don't know what it is?"

Jesus. *Goyim* in New York spoke more Yiddish than Sherm. How could you be someone named *Sherman Katz* and not know what a *shmer'l* is? "A *shmer'l* is a *shmer'l*. A nobody. A nothing."

"Oh."

"So?"

"So what?"

"So do you think I'm a *shmer'l*?"

(Pause.)

(Another long pause.)

"Sherm?"

"Maybe I can get you a Knights Of Columbus dance, but I can't make any promises. Call me tomorrow."

I knew it was all over for me then. I was finished. My own agent thought I was a *shmer'l*. I'd been away too long. I looked in the metal mirror on my hospital room wall and ran my hand through what was left of my pompadour. It was getting pretty thin, man. I drew on some eyebrows, but that didn't help much. I was over the hill. I'd probably end up giving violin lessons to little kids who'd grow up to hate their parents. I'd go door-to-door, *schlepping* my violin around Brooklyn, and have to listen to *yentas* call their kids downstairs. "Ira, come down. The violin *shmer'l* is here." Things might've been different if I hadn't fallen for those rock dreams. If I hadn't got the star bug so bad. If Brenda were still alive.

When I had my stuff all packed and they let me off the locked unit, I was taken down an elevator to the lobby. I could've left right then and there, but today was Thursday, and Thursday meant chili in the cafeteria. Say what you want about Bellevue, but their kitchen staff made a kick-ass killer chili. I went in and had two bowls. Unbelievable. Hot, tangy, make-your-throat-smoke chili. Um! Then I belched, picked up my bag, and went back out to the lobby.

I knew I was crazy for thinking this, but I was going to miss the place. The white walls, the padded cells. All those guys named Jesus. I asked the receptionist to call me a cab, but she said I didn't need one.

"What," I said, "that's part of the therapy? I got to *walk* home?"

"No, sir. There's a limousine waiting for you out front."

"A limousine? For me? You must have the wrong guy. I'm Keen."

"That's what the driver told me. He's supposed to pick up a Rudy Keen."

That was funny. I said, "Huh. I wonder who ordered me a limousine?"

"I don't know, sir," the receptionist said.

"I'll bet it was Ma, right?"

"I really don't – "

"Go on. You can tell me."

254

"But I have no idea who ordered it."

"She wanted it to be a surprise, right? I get it. This is her way of saying she's sorry I was never breast-fed, and that she's finally proud of her son. I was in Europe for five years, you know."

"Is that right?"

"Oh, sure. I'm a famous musician. I helped start the Beatles."

She chewed her gum kind of slow when I said that. "Uh-huh," she said.

"If you don't believe me, you can ask a guy on the fifth floor. A guy named Jesus. And if you think *my* story is hard to believe, wait till you hear *his*."

She started sliding her chair backwards, away from me. "Isn't that nice, the Beatles." she said. "Make sure you say hello to Ringo for me."

"Okay. I don't know when I'll see him again, but okay. Who should I say said hello? What's your name?"

"Just tell him the receptionist at Bellevue said hello."

"Okay. Hey – be honest. Don't you think the rings on every finger is a bit much? I told him from the start it was kind of gaudy."

"Have a nice day, sir," she said.

What the hell. I guess she liked the rings. Me – I thought he was over-doing it.

I picked up my bag and walked out that big door into the free world for the first time in nearly a year. Can you imagine how good it would've felt to have fresh air and sanity again? Me too. But I was in New York.

The limousine was waiting right out front – a Lincoln Continental stretch job. Midnight blue. Sleek, elegant. The driver opened the door for me and I climbed in. When he was behind the wheel, he said, "Good day, Mr. Keen."

Star treatment, baby. I felt like I was on top again.

"Yeah, good day," I said. "Listen, what did Ma pay for this? You should give her a deal, 'cause she's on a fixed income."

"The arrangements are complimentary, Mr. Keen."

"Really? I'll be damned. I thought everybody in New York had forgotten me by now. Must be some big record company trying to wine and dine me. Say – before you take me home, could we stop by The *New York Times*? I've got an appointment with a reporter."

"Certainly, sir. Are you sure you wouldn't rather go home and rest up first?"

"Oh, yeah. I'm sure. I've been resting for ten months. If I get any more rest I'll be exhausted."

We pulled into traffic and you would've thought I was visiting royalty the way I drew stares, just like the old days. I sat back and snapped on the radio. John Lennon was singing "Nowhere Man." It was the first time I'd heard that song, but I knew in a second it was one of Buddy's. His signature was all over it. *Poor Buddy*, I thought. *Krupp's probably still promising him a comeback.*

"Mr. Keen?" the driver said.

"Yeah, I know. You want an autograph."

"No, sir. It's just that I notice we're low on gas. Would you mind very much if we stopped at a service station?"

"Hey, you gotta have gas right?"

"Yes, sir."

"What about the autograph?"

"No. thank you."

Christ. I couldn't *give* them away.

We pulled into a station and he got out of the car, saying he'd only be a moment. I thought at first he'd gone to get an attendant, but he just walked away down the sidewalk and out of view. I figured maybe he had to make a phone call or something.

I slid my hand over the leather interior. Nice. I could get used to this. But you know me and road trips – pretty soon I had to go. I mean, I *really* had to go. I was a walking methane plant – almost asphyxiated myself in the back seat. I opened the door and got out and I was on my way to ask the station manager for the washroom key, when *kaboom*! The goddamn car blew up and knocked me twenty feet across the concrete drive. I opened my eyes and saw all kinds of debris and crap falling from the sky, and what was left of the limo was burning fast. You should've seen it – black clouds of smoke swirling up about a hundred feet in the air, people screaming and running for cover, broken windows everywhere. It was just like a barbecue Uncle Myshkin gave once when he thought he could light the coals faster if he used kerosene.

The driver never came back.

There I was, lying on the ground, my hands all scraped and bloody, glass splinters in my ass. I looked back at the smoky wreck, and the first thing I thought was, *Jesus, what the hell did they put in that chili?*

11   'Surfin' Lobotomy'

"Who'd vant to keel you vit a bomb?"

"I'm tellin' ya, Uncle Zollie, the same guys who tried to kill Buddy Holly."

"Now yer talkin' that crazy shit again. They were supposed to turn you into a normal decent person at the asylum."

"I *am* a normal decent person."

"You vant I should get a second opinion?"

"I don't *need* a second opinion."

"How do you know it vas a bomb?"

"How do I know? It blew the whole limousine up! What else could do that?"

"I dunno. Did you eat the chili?"

"Yes, I ate the goddamn chili!"

"Vell, then – "

"What's so hard to believe – that there's a world-wide conspiracy that tried to kill Buddy Holly?"

"Not so much."

"That the conspiracy used Buddy to write songs for the Beatles?"

"Vell, it's a stretch."

"That they're trying to take over the music publishing industry with a secret computer?"

"Hey – it could happen."

"And that they want to kill me because I'm a songwriting genius and I know too much?"

"You shoulda quit vile you ver ahead."

♪   ♫   ♪

After the bomb incident I'd moved in with Uncle Zollie, for a couple of reasons. First, I didn't want Ma to get hurt. And second, ever since I'd got out of Bellevue I was being followed. I didn't know who the hell he was, but for weeks every time I turned around, this guy, this very *zhlubby* guy, was behind me, sometimes pretending to read a newspaper, sometimes just standing there in a crowd on the street, but always watching me. And what a fashion plate. Royal blue suit with pants above the ankles, one of those stupid hats – what do you call them? *Porkpie.* Giorgio Armani's retarded brother. I figured he was the hired assassin, the one who planted the bomb and rented the limo. Whenever I spotted him, I'd run. But goddamn it, the next day he'd pop up all over again. He was like a Jack-in-the-box. Wind him up and he dresses bad and then kills you. I'd told Uncle Zollie about him, but of course he thought I was seeing things, hallucinating. The first thing he'd ask me when he got home from the office was, "Vell, did you see your little man today?" And when I'd tell him I had, he'd say, "And anybody else, did *they* see the little man?" And I'd say I didn't know, that it didn't matter if anybody else saw him, because he was after *me.* Then Uncle Zollie would say, "Uh-huh. And the little man, did he have a bomb?" He talked to me like I was a nut! "Vell, Rudolph – is he in the apartment vit us now? Do you see him now? Is he sitting on the sofa?" It just about drove me out of my skull. Sometimes I'd play along with him. I'd tell him, yeah, he was right there in the apartment, "And vot's he doin' in the apartment right now?"

"Having a Philly cheese steak on one of your kosher plates."

I could drive *him* nuts, too,

One morning after pacing around the apartment and peeking out the blinds like a paranoid *schlepper*, I wondered if this was what the rest of my life was going to be like – waiting for the Knights Of Columbus to call and for the assassin to show up and blow my brains out. I filled in newspaper crossword puzzles, watched soap operas, dusted the furniture, and looked forward to greeting the milkman. I was twenty-four years old and I'd turned into my mother.

One night the phone rang and Uncle Zollie answered it. He said, "Hel-*lo*? Huh? No, he ain't here. I don't care. I told ya, he ain't here. Who is this? *Who*? Yer kiddin'. Vot? Yer kiddin'. No, you ain't. No, you ain't. Yer fulla shit." And then he banged the receiver down and went back to watching "I Dream Of Jeannie."

"Well?" I said. "Who was it?"

"Shh," Uncle Zollie said. "Jeannie's gonna toin Major Nelson into a monkey."

"But who was on the phone?"

"Someone for you."

"Who? Nobody's supposed to know I'm here."

"Jack Lemmon."

"Jack Lemmon? Really? What – did he want me to play at a Hollywood bash or something?"

"Rudolph, the son of a bitch vas an impostah. Believe me. Look! Look at Major Nelson!"

"But how do you know he was an imposter?"

"I know, believe me. Ha! He's gonna eat a banana!"

"But how do you know?"

"'Cause he's tryin' to peel it vit his little monkey hands!"

"No – I mean, how do you know it was an imposter?"

"How do I know? Vill you keep quiet and let me vach the show if I tell you?"

"Yes!"

"All right, Mr. Can't-Shut-Up-During-A-TV-Show. It's eazy. The minute he opened his mouth, he had a English accent. Does Jack Lemmon have a English accent?"

"No."

"Like I told ya."

Then I thought for a second. "Are you sure he said Jack *Lemmon*? Did he maybe say, John *Lennon*?"

"Oh, yeah. That vas it. Who the hell is John Lennon?"

Oy! For twelve months I'd been locked up in either a crazy house or Uncle Zollie's apartment (big difference) and I'd seen nobody and done nothing, and now John Lennon called and the *shmegegge* hung up on him.

"You just hung up on a *Beatle*, Uncle Zollie!"

"I did? Jack Lemmon's a Beedle?"

"No! John *Lennon* is a Beatle."

"Eh, so vot. Beedle-shmeedle. They all look the same."

Luckily, Lennon called back. Somebody up there looks out for me. Well, *sometimes* He looks out for me, and other times He plays mahjong and lets my life go to hell. Guess what Lennon wanted. He wanted me to come live with him. That's right. I'm not making this shit up, you know. What would be the point of that – just to make a couple hundred thousand dollars on a book and even more on movie rights (which are still available, by the way)? No, this really happened. I kept asking him why he wanted me to move in with him, but he sounded depressed and said he didn't want to talk about it over the wire. He called the phone the *wire*. I thought he'd gone crazy, because the next thing he told me – the Beatles were going to hang up their rock-and-roll shoes. No more touring. He said he wanted to fly me to San Francisco for their last show, and then on to London to live in his house in Weybridge, in Surrey.

"Oh, Christ – I can't," I said.

"Look," John said, "you've got to. I can't talk about it now, over the wire, but I'll pay you well."

"I really can't, John. How well would you pay me?"

"Name yer price."

"No – forget it. I can't."

"Give me one good reason," he said. When he wanted something, he wouldn't take *no* for an answer.

"One reason? Okay – warm Cokes."

"Oh, bloody hell, Kearnstein! That isn't a reason!"

"People saying *bloody* all the time."

"Five hundred pounds a week."

Hey – that wasn't bad money. It wasn't a million bucks, but it wasn't bad money. "Nope," I said. "Can't do it."

"A thousand pounds a week."

"Out of the question."

"Kearnstein, don't be a spastic!" Everyone was all the time a *spastic* to John. "I'll give ya fifteen hundred pounds a week, and wall-to-wall women."

We flew first class on a BOAC 707 from San Francisco to London. (I know what you're thinking. You're thinking that with my life up for grabs, limos blowing up and assassins hunting me down, then I must've been one horny bastard to take a chance flying overseas just for wall-to-wall women. Well, so what if I was?) John was *shikker* the entire way, tossing down scotches, chain-smoking, and mumbling deatils about what was going on behind the scenes in London.

"Krupp, the bloody bastard. He's putting the squeeze on us to take Buddy into the group. He bloody well knows his contract expires in six months, and he's getting desperate. I told Eppy, forget it. We don't want Holly." Just then John reached into his blazer pocket and pulled out the biggest, fattest joint I'd ever seen and lit it. He held the smoke in for about a half-hour and then almost fainted when he blew it all out. "So Eppy told him to sod off, and you know what the fucker did?"

"Hey," I said. "Where are those women you told me about?"

"Don't worry about them. So Eppy says sod off, and Krupp says why don't you replace Lennon with Holly. The bastard. Eppy refuses and the next thing you know, he gets picked up in some swanky pub outside of London by some big son of a bitch who gives him a blow job and then beats the mother shit out of him. Want a hit?"

"No, thanks. Those women, though. Any of them blonds?"

"Yeah. So where was I? So Eppy gets the crap beat out of him and Krupp calls him the next day to find out if anything had happened to make him change his mind. Christ, he had two broken ribs and a ruined bridge. But he still tells him to stuff it. This whole time Holly's in the hospital having mega-fucking plastic surgery – about thirty operations a day or something. Krupp calls back and says he'll be ready to play live with us in four or five weeks. Eppy says no, hangs up on him, and the next night he gets picked up in another pub by a sailor who does him and then beats the shit out of him *again*. And this time the bastard writes a message in Magic Marker across Eppy's chest, saying – *Negotiations are over.*"

"Yeah, that's too bad. So these blonds, what do they look like?"

"Will you bloody listen to me?" He took another huge hit off the joint and washed it down with four fingers of scotch. "Ahhhhh. So by now Eppy's shittin' bricks. *Stonework*. He could be a Jewish mason, for Christ's sake. He's afraid to go out, he's afraid to pick anybody up, and he even asked me would it be so bad to let Buddy play a few gigs with us. And I said, 'Eppy, have you lost your freakin' mind? We're the *Beatles*, not the goddamn Crickets. No fuckin' way!' With Eppy caving in and the heat still on, *I* decided to take over the decision making. I thought, Well, Krupp wants Holly to play concerts with us? Fine. We'll stop playing concerts – for good. And then I went a step further and started telling the press exactly what Krupp doesn't want them to know yet. I can play rough too, ya know. I don't suffer fools gladly. Look here. Get a load of this – "

He reached below his seat and took out a rock and roll magazine from Mersey, folded to an interview.

LENNON SALUTES A LEGEND;
SAYS BUDDY HOLLY IS STILL ALIVE

Int.: One can't help but admire your loyalty to an early influence, John. But surely when you speak about Buddy Holly being alive, you mean it in a figurative sense, as in the vein of being alive in the spirit of the music you make.

Lennon: Yer bloody ass!

Int.: But I meant that everyone knows Holly is buried in Lubbock, so certainly your comment is intended as a form of hyperbole, the greatest sort of homage that can be paid to an artist.

Lennon: Yer bloody ass!

Int.: Perhaps we are not understanding one another. To be 'alive' has connotational implications that are symbolic as well as literal. I am simply suggesting that in the case of Buddy Holly, you are communicating in a more symbolic manner.

Lennon: I don't know what you're talking about, all that intellectual crap coming out of your gob. I meant what I fuckin' said – that Buddy Holly is *alive*. He has a manager who's pressuring us to take him into the group, and we think it's not right, it's not fair. Buddy is a great rock 'n' roll artist, but he's Buddy and we're the Beatles, and never Mark Twain shall eat meat.

Int.: Interesting the way you utilize stream of-consciousness and a sense of absurdity to mix reality with fiction. Do you feel that you perhaps have borrowed such technique from James Joyce?

Lennon: Yer bloody ass!

I put the magazine down on my lap when I finished reading. John swirled the ice cubes around and around in his plastic cup.
"Well?" he said. "What do you think of that?"
"You know," I told him, "I'm not real picky. There's something to be said for brunettes, too."

262

That was a pretty brave interview to give, but you could tell the interviewer didn't believe him. Isn't that something – there it was in black and white, John telling the world that Buddy Holly was alive, and no one listened. And with all the crap going down between Krupp and Buddy and the Beatles, why fly me, of all people, to England? What could *I* do about it? And where the hell were my women?

[EDITOR'S WARNING: EXTENDED DIGRESSION AHEAD.]

It is *not* a digression! Why would the bastard put that there? I'm sitting here reading the galleys, which I just got from the publisher, and I'm pretty pissed about that digression *chozzerai*. I'm just going to cross that warning out with a blue pencil, and it better not make it to the final page, or I'll sue. All I was going to say, and I'm not digressing or anything, was that by the time we got to London it was already tomorrow there. It's real gone, real bitchin' the way that happens, the way you can just fly into the future a couple of hours. If you kept doing that, you could cheat yourself out of half your life. You'd never get to live today, because you'd keep going into tomorrow. Isn't that heavy? Don't try to think about it too much or you'll fry your circuits. Digression my ass. You know, it's not too late to cancel this contract and sell the book to Doubleday.

[EDITOR'S NOTE: DIGRESSION COMPLETED.]

And we'll just cross that little son of a bitch out too. I'd better not see that in the trade edition, or heads are going to roll.

Now, where was I? Lennon got stoned, we flew into tomorrow ... oh yeah! We landed at Heathrow and there was a limousine waiting there to take us to Surrey. It was a nice place, John's place, what I could see of it in the dark. The boys dropped us off first and then went on ahead in the limo. I watched the red taillights float down the drive and disappear. We spent the next half hour locked out on the front porch because his wife and son were away at his mother-in-law's, and John didn't have any keys. I couldn't get over that, how he didn't carry keys to his own house. We had to lean on the doorbell and throw pebbles at second-story windows until the housekeeper woke up and let us in. The two of them mumbled and grumbled insults at each other.

"Ruffian. Coming in at all hours of the night like a stray cat."

"Fat cow," John said, winking at me.

In the hallway he kept talking to someone named Sidney, even though the housekeeper had gone back to bed and there was only the two of us. I thought maybe he was tripping, until he took off his coat and flung it at a suit of armor.

"Hold that a minute, will you, Sid?"

Sidney was the armor. It was a hell of a thing to keep at your front door.

I was hoping we'd order food in and call some of those women over. You always heard stories back then about the wild Beatle lifestyle and Swinging London, but it must've been a load of crap, because John couldn't wait to hit the sack.

"But I'm not sleepy yet," I said. "Let's have a party."

"Yer daft," John told me. "Don't you get jet-lag?"

"Uh-uh. I get *shpilkes*."

"Well, just don't get them on the carpet. Just had it cleaned." Then he cackled like a madman, called me a hyperspaz, and climbed the stairs doing an impression of a hunchback. Me, I stayed up with Sidney and told him the story of my life.

I don't know what the hell time it was, but the next day I woke up on the hallway floor. The doorbell kept ringing and Beatles kept walking in, all upset and excited about something. The whole house was flooded with sunlight and it nearly blinded me. *Oy*, what a back ache I had.

"I've had three so far today," one of them said.

"You have, have you?" That was John. "Well, I've had two, and if I never have another one, it'll be fine by me."

I sat up quick. "I haven't had *any* yet! It's my turn!"

They were all there, all four of them, pacing around, trading a joint between them.

"What do you know," John said, "Kearnstein's resurrected."

"You promised," I told him. "You said there'd be wall-to-wall women, and now you've had two, and I'm batting zero."

John said, "Right, then. George, wake the housekeeper for Rudy."

"Women?" one of the others said, but I can't remember which one. "I thought we were talking about death threats."

I said, "Death threats? Oh. That's different. None for me, thanks."

John took three or four steps and then spun around. "The bastard phone rang not more than an hour ago, and when I picked it up, a guy who sounded like Peter Lorre told me I was a dead man." He fished in his pocket and pulled out a piece of paper. "And look at this letter I got this morning."

The letter said:

Rest in peace, Johnny.

"Looks like Lorre's writing, too," one of the others said.

"It's Krupp," I said.

John leaned over and peered at me nearsightedly. "Of course it's Krupp, you wretched nit. We know who it is. We just don't know what to do about it. Why do you think you're here?"

"Women," I said.

"You help us get rid of Krupp, and we'll buy you the bloody Rockettes."

"Me? You want *me* to get rid of Krupp?"

How do you like that? They'd bribed me and lied to me just to get me back to England to take care of their dirty work. I couldn't even take care of my *own* dirty work.

Then John said he'd be damned if he was going to be intimidated into taking Holly into the group. "And what *about* Holly?" he yelled at me. "Do you think he's in on this? Do you suppose he knows what Krupp is doing to us?"

"I don't think so. He pretty much leaves the business to Krupp. He's too busy rehearsing to be the messiah. I *told* you not to get him started on that ego jag. He's probably got the stigmata by now."

John picked up the phone and called NEMS, their agency, and asked how many security guards they could send over. In less than forty minutes the house was surrounded by five men in suits. Every once in a while the boys would peek at them through a curtain and then close it real fast. John took the phone off the hook so no more threats could get through.

Then everyone got the munchies. I hadn't had any dope, so I wasn't as hungry as the rest of them, but I was a *little* hungry. That is, I was, until I saw what they had to eat. *Warm eggs* - they don't keep them in the fridge. They irradiate them. *Blood pudding. Kidney pie.* I couldn't stand to look at that *drek*, let alone eat it. But I got lucky and found a fancy jar of pickled snacks on a shelf over the sink. No label, just a jar of pickled snacks. There were only two left, but they were good. Really tasty.

"Hey, Kearnstein," John said to me, "have some kidney pie, why don't you."

"No, thank you."

"The blood pudding's good. Try it."

Right. Just what I wanted in my pudding – blood. "Thanks, anyway."

"My Lord, boy," the housekeeper said. "Don't you want to eat *anything?*"

"Yeah," I said. "Do you have any more of those pickled mushrooms?"

The housekeeper said, "Pickled mushrooms? We don't have pickled mushrooms."

"Yeah, you do," I said. "or you did. There were two in this jar here." I held it up to her.

John dropped his fork and narrowed his eyes. "Where did you get that jar?"

"Up there, on the shelf."

His mouth fell open and he slid his chair back from the table. "MY GOD! THOSE WERE A GIFT, YOU NINNY!"

"They were just pickled mushrooms," I said.

"THEY WERE RINGO'S TONSILS!"

I waited for him to smile, hoping it was a joke. But it was no joke. *I'd swallowed human anatomy!*

I cupped my hand over my mouth and ran for the bathroom. But when I took the corner I slipped and crashed into Sidney, who came toppling over on me in about a thousand pieces just as I projectile vomited and painted the wall a new shade of green. I wretched and gagged for about five minutes, pushing away Sidney's shield and visor. This was worse than getting a tattoo. Now my *stomach* would have to be buried in a gentile cemetery. I'm telling you, by the time I go, they're going to have to take me apart and shovel me in *piecemeal*. And wouldn't you know it? While my digestive tract was trying to work its way out of my mouth, the goddamn doorbell rang.

John came around the corner, saw me in the middle of the mess, and said, "Look what you've done! It wasn't bad enough you'd eaten Ringo's tonsils – you had to kill Sidney, too!"

You'd expect a little sympathy. And insult upon injury, he told *me* to answer the door while he cowered behind a love seat. The doorbell kept ringing and ringing, and some of them said to answer it, and some of them said *not* to answer it. I picked myself off the floor, stumbled to the front steps, and turned the knob.

In walked Brian Jones, straightening his clothes. "Christ!" he said. "Do you have any idea what's going on out – " Then he saw who I was. "Rudy! When did you arrive? Oh, I *say*," he said, looking at the floor. "Sidney's puked himself to pieces, hasn't he? Do you know, five men just finished frisking me? One of them tried to have babies with my cashmere blazer. Where are the boys?"

Beatle heads popped up from behind chairs and end tables.

"We thought you were going to kill us," John said, standing up.

"Well, I just might, if you try to do to me what you've done to poor Sidney. Is your phone off the hook? Epstein called me. Says he's been trying to get through to you all day. Something about an emergency."

As soon as John put the receiver back on the phone, it rang. He answered it, covered the mouthpiece, and said to us, "It's Eppy." Then the rest of the conversation sounded like this: "Um-hm? Again, eh? You did? He did? But you like it rough, don't you? No. Absolutely not! I don't care, no Holly! Look, did you ever consider celibacy? Well, it's not that bad. Would you rather die? You *would*?" He covered the phone again. "Eppy's been bashed, for a change." Then back to Brian: "Keen's here, from America."

The housekeeper heard that as she was wiping up my vomit. "American, it figures."

"Just a minute," John said. "Rudy, he wants a word with you."

I took the phone. "Hello?"

"Rudy," Brian said, "sweetheart! Have you ever seen Spain this time of year?"

"Uh ... no."

"Well you really ought to. It's magnificent. I'm leaving for Madrid next week, and I just happen to have an extra ticket – "

I told him I couldn't, that I was allergic to Spanish food. He kept insisting, in that charming way he had, and I almost gave in. Hey, I'd never been to Spain, okay? Let's see how fast *you'd* turn down a free trip. But then John started poking me and whispering, "Tell him to *do* something about this!" So I asked him how come he didn't go to the police and get Krupp locked up.

"Sweetheart, it's our word against his. And if we tell the authorities about Buddy Holly, Krupp won't rest until we're all dead. Besides, I'm afraid I've been a bit of a silly goose by funding some of Compsong's operation, however inadvertently, which is a violation of trade laws, so we must keep this quiet. Not only that, but if it gets out that someone is threatening the boys, imagine the copy-cat attempts they'll have to suffer. No – the police are out. Do you like bullfights?"

By the time I got off the phone, two things were pretty obvious: #1) Brian couldn't do anything to stop Krupp, other than to refuse to extend Buddy's contract; and #2) he was even hornier than I was.

John was *mega*-pissed after that conversation with Brian. "Eppy's useless!" he shouted, kicking a chair and throwing sofa pillows around. Then he stood perfectly still for a moment. He had an idea – and that's when he pointed at me. "You!" he said.

"Me, *what*?" I said.

"You're going to Holly."

"Oh, no I'm not."

"Yes, you are. You're going to tell him what Krupp's up to and get him to take the pressure off. Holly's our only chance."

"But what if Hans and Arnold see me?"

"Just case the joint before you go in. And while you're doing that, I'll be giving an interview to The *London Times*." He picked up the phone, dialed, and then held the receiver against his shoulder. "I'll get some lucky journalist over here in twenty minutes and make his career for him. Tomorrow everyone will know about Compsong."

"You can't do that," I told him.

"I can't, huh? I'm doing it, though. Ritchie, find me a bottle of acid. I need a trip."

He wouldn't listen to me when I said it was a bad idea, taking LSD before an interview. You couldn't stop John once he got started. A security guard from NEMS drove me into Chelsea, and as much as I didn't want to get near that old town house, I was relieved as hell to be out of Weybridge. With all four Beatles there, John's living room was the most dangerous rock and roll scene since Holly climbed into that Beachcraft Bonanza with Valens.

Oh – sorry. And the Bopper.

The driver left me off two blocks away. I put on my shades. Cool. I was very cool. What I thought I'd do was, I'd ring the doorbell and then run down the steps, so if either Hans or Arnold answered, at least I'd have a head start. I climbed up the steps slow-like, looked both ways, touched the doorbell, and then beat it back down to the sidewalk. I was ready to blast, man. But when the door opened, a pretty young lady holding a baby was standing there.

"Yes?" she said, in a British accent.

268

I walked up the steps and – Jesus Irving Christ – she was breast-feeding the baby. Right out in the open like that. In Europe they do that stuff. I think it's fine, you know? (Even though I never got to do it.) But it made me feel like I was crashing a dinner party.

"Excuse me," I said. "I didn't mean to catch you at a bad moment or anything – "

"It's quite all right. I can manage. Are you a solicitor?"

The kid had quite an appetite. "Solicitor? No, not me. That's against the law, isn't it? Listen, if you want, I can come back in a few minutes when you're not so – *attached*."

"Hold on," she said. "Time for the switch." She closed one side of her dress and opened the other, letting her breast fall out. It was big and round. "What was it you wanted?" she asked me.

Hell if I knew.

"Sir?" she said. "You wanted something?"

"Huh? Oh, yeah. I used to know a guy who lived here, and I wondered if you knew where I could find him."

"Oh, you mean the former tenant, Mr. Hardin."

"Uh-huh. That's him. Hardon. I mean Har*din*. Former? Did you say *former* tenant?"

"Yes. He moved out well over three months ago. I'm afraid he didn't leave a forwarding address."

"Oh," I said. "No phone number or anything?"

"I'm terribly sorry, but no."

There went one plan down in flames. "That's all right. I'm sorry I bothered you."

"No bother. Is there anything else, then?"

I started to shake my head, when all of a sudden I thought of something. "Yeah – could you tell me how you know when it's time to change?"

"Change what?"

"Uh ..." I tilted my head toward her. "You know."

"Oh, you mean when it's time to switch him from one nipple to the other?"

"Yeah."

"It's easy. You can just tell. Instinct."

"Oh. Instinct, huh?"

"Yes. G'dday, " she said.

Hey, I've got no hang-ups about it. None at all. I think it's natural. I like nature. I like it a lot. Anyway, I knew what I had to do.

I had to get back to Weybridge with the news. But before I called a cab, I stopped by this one restaurant I used to eat at. It looked pretty much the same as it did before. New tablecloths, maybe. The waitress gave me a menu, but I wasn't too hungry. When she came back and asked me what I wanted, I got a sudden craving.

"Milk," I said.

"In a glass?"

"If that's the best you can do."

♪ ♫ ♪

When I got back to John's house it was completely dark. At first I thought he'd gone out someplace, but then I heard voices in the den, and when I went to check it out, I found John and a reporter sitting on the floor. Between them was a black box with flashing lights and a Lava Lamp. This *yutz* of a reporter kept asking stupid questions like, "Could you tell the fans, is the mustache going to stay?" And if you think the questions were bad, you should've heard John's answers. He was totally swacked on acid. Real gone, man.

"It's coz of the UFOs and the Bermuda Triangle, is what. They predicted them in The Book Of Revelations. *There's* a story for you. You oughta look into it. And look into the computer as well."

"Computer?" the reporter said. "*What* computer?"

"The songwriting computer, the one that's going to put us out of business. It's mentioned in the *Tibetan Book Of The Dead.*"

"I thought you said it was in Revelations?"

"I did? Well, it's in there, too. First they killed Buddy Holly, Valens, The Bopper, then Cochran and Cooke, and then Holly came back to life, and now they're coming after us."

"*Who* is coming after you?"

"The people with the computer – open yer bloody ears! It's a computer that writes songs, a Univac, or a Unisex or something. Fuckin' computer – I *hate* it!"

Get the picture? *Sgt. Pepper's Lonely Lunatic Asylum.* The reporter went into a British mumbling routine and said that John must've been mistaken, that there couldn't be any such computer, it wasn't real. And John said, "Oh, it's real. It's as real as that disgusting giant green insect crawling up yer arm."

The reporter jumped about a mile and started brushing his

arm off like a crazy guy, till he saw there was nothing on it. It was all in John's head. And the idiot – instead of realizing that John wasn't going to tell him anything he could publish, he went back to the same dumb kind of questions.

"Tell us what your relationship with your parents was like."

Oh, boy. When John heard that, he looked like someone had just slapped him across the face. His eyes got cold, like little ice cubes, and for a second I was afraid he was going to kill the reporter. But instead, he started screaming, just blood curdling screams.

"AAAAAAAGGGGGGGGHHHHHHHHH-*MUMMY*! AAAAAAAAAAGGGGGG-HHHHHHHHLLLLL – *DADDY*!"

Hysterics? Are you kidding? You've never *heard* such hysterics. He was throwing a primal right in front of us. Yeah, yeah – I know. You're going to say that John didn't do that primal scream thing until years later when he went through therapy. Are you ever wrong. In the first place, John never went *through* that therapy. And in the second, John had screaming fits as long as I knew him. Jesus Christ, could that guy scream. Nearly scared me to death every time he did it.

I yanked the reporter up by the arm and said, "I think you'd better go now."

And John was going, "AAAAAAAAAAGGGGGGGHHHHH HLLLLLLLLLLLLL LLLL – MUMMY-DADDY!"

"But my interview – " the reporter said.

"Interview?" I hustled him to the front door, found his hat, and slapped it on his head. "You give a Beatle a nervous breakdown and you call it an *interview*?"

"AAAAAAAAAGHGHGHGHGHGHGHLLLLLLLLLLLLLAAAAA AAAGGGGGGGGHHHHHHHHHHHHLLLLLLLLLLLLLLLLLLLLIL LLLLLLAAAAAAAAAAAGHHGHGHGHGH!"

Oy, vey iz mir. John was up and tearing ass through the house, pulling his hair out and knocking over lamps. I pushed the *schmuck* reporter down the front steps and slammed the door. I was just leaning back against the wall, running my hands over my hair, when John walked into the hall, as cool as could be, as if nothing had happened.

"I just got rid of him," I said.

He looked confused. "Rid of who?"

"The reporter."

"What reporter?"

My God, he didn't even remember. I said, "Are you all right?"

"I'm fine. I was just talking to Mary."

"Mary? Who's Mary?"

"The *Virgin* Mary. You know, Jesus's mum."

"Oh ... that's nice. On the phone?"

"On the *phone*? Are you daft? No, she's in the next room. Wants to know if we have any Popsicles."

Um-hm. The Virgin Mary just happened to be in Surrey and thought she'd drop in and have a Popsicle with John Lennon. Why should I be surprised? "I'll check the freezer," I said.

"She wants banana flavor."

"I'll see what we have."

Jesus Christ. What a night. What a place. I got more peace in Bellevue.

♪   ♬   ♪

"I can't live there anymore. Those guys are giving Beatlemania a whole new meaning. It's making me insane, I tell ya. Look at my hand – look! See how it's shaking? And look – I got a rash. I get a rash when I'm nervous."

I was talking to Brian Jones in a pub over a warm, flat Coke.

"Fuckin' relax, will you?" he said.

And I said, "Relax? *Relax*? How the hell am I supposed to relax when I'm having an apocalypse? And my hair's falling out. See how thin it's getting? Christ, I'm gonna be bald. I'm gonna be a bald singer with a rash. *Look* at me!"

"Oh fuckin' my – it *is* fuckin' falling out, isn't it? The fuckin' pomp's all gone out of your fuckin' pompadour."

Then, get this – he told me he'd just bought this farm in Sussex where Winnie The Pooh used to live – not *Winnie*, for cripes sake, but the guy who invented him. Cotchford Farm, it was called, and there was a spare room over the garage. He said I could move in if I wanted. If I *wanted*? I almost kissed him, I was so relieved. (I wouldn't really have *done* it, I mean I wouldn't have kissed him or anything. Brian was a *guy*. Although his hair *was* a little like the hair on the Fairy Princess mask, real blond and straight, very soft ... never mind.)

The Beatles went into the studio and begged me to come with them to keep a lookout while they worked, but I'd had enough. I took an offer from Gene Vincent to open for him on his comeback tour. Some comeback. Poor Gene. When I saw him I couldn't believe it. The guy was a mess; he could barely stand up. I felt so bad for him, forgetting all his lyrics, falling on his ass every time he tried to jump around. He was constantly smashed – it was humiliating. I tried to get him off the stuff, but it was no good. "Gene," I'd tell him, "look what's happened to you." And he'd take a swig of Jack Daniels, smile like a goofy fat kid, and say, "Gene can't bop no more." And I'd say, "Bop? You can't even fuckin' walk."

Sad? Let me tell you, it damn near broke my heart. It took me and two roadies to pick him up off the stage and load him in the car between shows. It shouldn't have been allowed to happen. There should've been a home for hopelessly bloated rock-and-roll has-beens. Come to think of it, there was. *Graceland.*

Gene brought his Burn-Out Tour to America, but I bailed out. I didn't much appreciate the audience yelling, "Hey, Baldie!" at me while I tried to sing my greatest hits, and I couldn't go on watching Gene fall over every night. Before I left, though, he handed over a bag full of letters addressed to me in his care.

"Fan mail!" I said. "I'm still getting fan mail!" I was pretty excited, until I sat down later on and opened them up. Every one of those goddamn letters was from Calvin Ray-Bob Stoges, that crazy hick back in Iowa. "I need to see you, Rudy." "I've got to talk to you. Please." My luck. I get an obsessed fan, and it's a guy.

♪　♫　♪

Cotchford Farm was nice, but there was nothing to do there, so on weekends I took the train into London and gave the Beatles a break by working on *Sgt. Pepper* with them. Now, I'm not saying I played on all the tracks on that album, but once when I was on break from being the lookout, I made a very valuable contribution. You put that record on and listen to side two, right between "Good Morning Good Morning" and the reprise version of "Sgt. Pepper's Lonely Hearts Club Band," and you'll hear me. You know that part where a chicken clucks and screams and then turns into a distorted guitar note? I was the chicken. Yeah. George played the guitar, but big deal. *I* did the chicken. I learned how to sound like one back at Uncle Myshkin's butcher shop when I was a kid. He needed somebody to kill the chickens before he hung them upside down, all bumpy and naked in the window, and so he taught me how to wring their necks. I got pretty good at it. In fact, he used to call me the little chicken choker. "Rudolph, you chokin' the chee-ken?" That's all I ever heard from him. Anyway, that chicken scream on the album, that's *exactly* the sound a chicken makes when you choke him. I don't do it anymore, though. I quit choking chickens years ago.

Even after *Pepper* was finished, the death threats were still coming in hot and heavy, so John and the boys decided to go visit this Maharishi guy who was suddenly all the rage. They wanted me to go too – but I said nothing doing. John was convinced they'd be safer if they went to live with him.

"He has a protective aura," John told me.

"Aura my ass," I told him back. "He's got bad sandals and needs a taylor and a hair stylist."

Even Jonesy was going with them. He kept after me about joining up, right till the last day.

"It'll be spiritual, Rudy."

"It'll be stupid, Brian," I said.

I thought they'd all gone nuts. What was to stop Krupp from killing them while they were in Bangor? Somebody takes a pot shot at you while you're sitting next to the Maharini, and what – the bullet has a transcendental moment and decides it won't tear your head open? Please. It was reality testing time, and as far as I was concerned, they'd all flunked the test.

Then one night while I was watching TV, they showed a clip of John in this ridiculous paisley thing that looked like a muumuu. I'd never seen him so scared. He kept turning his head, real nervous-like, like he was trying to spot a sniper, and this press guy said, "How do you feel about the death of Brian Epstein?"

I almost fell off my chair. They'd killed Brian! Buddy's contract was up, Epstein didn't re-sign, Epstein was dead. The conspiracy guys had waited till the perfect opportunity came up – the Beatles were out of town and Brian was all alone. This time instead of bullets or bombs, they'd got wise and overdosed him, those sons of bitches. And there was John, trying to keep his bladder under control, because he damned well knew they were all next. He said they all missed Brian, but that the Mahaloony assured them that he was with a higher power or something. Right! The higher power was the coroner, and Brian was with him somewhere on a table in half a dozen pieces.

I knew it was all over for them then. And do you think Krupp *wasn't* after them to sign with him? He always wanted total control of the group, and with Epstein out of the way, now was his chance. It was no coincidence that all four of them disappeared for months after he died. Remember that trip to India? Don't tell me you fell for that. What – are you that gullible? They weren't in India. They were *hiding*. Jonesy and I found that out through the NEMS grapevine.

And here's something else that only a few people know about, even today. When it came time for a Stones' record or a Beatle record to be released, one of the boys would always ring up Jonesy to work out a schedule so the discs wouldn't come out on the same day. Why split the kugel when you can both *nosh* all of it? Well, now the Stones had a new record due out, but Brian couldn't get in touch with any of the boys.

"Just put it out, already, and screw 'em if they're going to ignore you."

"I would, you know. Normally. But I'm scared to."

"Scared?" I said. "Of what?"

What else was there to be scared of? It was Krupp. Brian hadn't told me while it was going on, but he spilled it all just then. For months Krupp had put the squeeze on the Stones to take Buddy into the group. "You don't need Mick and his silly arse twitching when you can have Buddy," was what Krupp had said. But Jones got mouthy with him – told him, "Buddy *this*, mate. We don't even do his kind of music."

Krupp was sharp, though. He said hell yes they *did* do Buddy's kind of music, that their first single, "Not Fade Away" had been a Holly tune. Then he said, "You've got two choices. Either take Holly, or take a fall."

Brian tried to act tough. He told him where to shove his choices, and ever since then he'd been getting the same kinds of death threats the boys used to get. One of them really shook him up. I was there at Cotchford Farm when he opened the letter. In it was a snapshot of a real tombstone. Engraved on it was this:

Brian Jones
1941- 1968
He's Gathering Moss

He went pale when he saw it, and for him that was quite a trick.

275

A *whiter* shade of pale. And then he ups and faints. Hell – I didn't know what to do with a fainted guy. I slapped him around a while and held an open bottle of brandy under his nose until he came to. The first thing he said was, "That was my tombstone!"

"I know," I said.

His jaw dropped and his eyes, his crazy eyes, they sort of went back up into his head.

"Hey," I said, "can you see your brain when you do that?"

"My own tombstone," he mumbled. "It's hideous ... vile ... obscene."

I picked up the picture and looked at it closer. "It's nice marble, though."

And then he fainted *again*. He kept leaving me to do all the work. He wouldn't wake up this time when I slapped his face, so I hauled off and whacked him good until my hand stung, but he was out cold. So I left him on the floor and sat there staring at the photo. I wondered what it would say on my tombstone.

The Fabulous Rudy Keen
He'll Be Right Back After A Brief Intermission

It'd been a hell of a long time since any of us in the inner circle had seen Buddy, and more than a year since Krupp told Epstein that the plastic surgery was scheduled. If the operation had been a success, where was Buddy? Wouldn't Krupp have tried to jump-start his career by now? Wouldn't there have been records and shows? But there was nothing. Brian and I figured the worst had happened – Buddy came out of surgery looking like an anchovy pizza and Krupp had him rubbed out. And here's a coincidence – I don't care how much the public saw of the Beatles on TV and in the papers, none of us had seen *them* either. Not up close and personal, anyway. What was going on?

I remember I was washing Brian's car for him one day in August of 1968. I had the radio booming, hoping to hear a new song I'd written and sent to Lennon. I thought maybe he'd have Apple release it and surprise me with a contract. It was my first surf song, one I dedicated to the memory of that very famous beach music singer's brain. The surf boy. You know who I mean. I called it "Surfin' Lobotomy." It was about a surfer guy who loses his mind and forgets which direction to point his surfboard, and he ends up out in the middle of the Pacific hanging eight, because he can't count to ten anymore. It was quite tragically beautiful.

Anyway, Jonesy was in London quitting the Stones. Oh sure, you think the Stones were fed up with him and kicked him out. That's what he *wanted* you to think. But the *emmes* was, he was too scared to stay in the goddamn group. The way he saw it, let Mick and Keith take the heat. He was *Gonesville*. So I was scrubbing the wire wheels of Jonesy's car, when Paul's voice came blasting out of the speaker – it was "Hey Jude." For everybody else, that was a new song, but I'd known it for years, ever since Buddy had written it to cheer me up. Don't you remember I told you about it? This is a *mystery*, for Christ's sake – you've got to start connecting the dots. I can't do everything for you. It's back in chapter 9, I think. Go check it out. It was supposed to be called "Hey Rude," not "Hey Jude." Who the hell was *Jude*? They'd changed the title and the lyrics, but it was Buddy's song, which meant *Buddy was still alive*. It meant more than that – it meant Buddy and the Beatles were working together again. And it probably meant Krupp owned them all.

I'm not the kind of guy that sits around and waits till he figures out what to do. You know me by now. Action, baby. I hopped in Jonesy's car and drove to London. Never mind I couldn't drive. So what, the steering wheel was on the wrong side and everyone in England drove in the left lane? And forget the minor inconvenience that I couldn't get the goddamn gearshift out of second gear – I *went!* Yep. I went straight to Apple headquarters. I wanted to see with my own eyes if Buddy was still alive. And I wanted to give him a piece of my mind for selling that song. That was *my* song. He wrote it for *me*. If anyone should've recorded it, *I* should've.

By the time I pulled on to Savile Row, the transmission was smoking so bad I could hardly see where I was going. Hot damn, my luck was holding out; Lennon was inside. I knew he was because his Rolls Royce, the psychedelic one, was parked right out front. I told him when he had that damn car painted what a waste of money it was, but do you think he listened to me? Christ, was it ugly. It looked like it was being eaten by giant botulism cells. I parked Jonesy's car (still smoking) right ahead of the Rolls and marched up the steps into Apple.

When the cute little receptionist asked me, "Can I help you?" I looked her right in the breasts and said, "Yeah. You can tell Lennon to get down here on the double, and I want to see Buddy

Holly, too."

I'd been around the block a few times. I knew the ropes. You go in sounding determined if you expect to get anywhere.

About two seconds later I was escorted back down the front steps and thrown on the sidewalk by two gorillas with arms like fat *kishkes*. They tore holes in the knees of my puce satin pants – brand new from Harrods' bargain basement.

"And stay out, mate," one of the bouncers said.

What I *could've* done is, I could've gone back in there and told them who I was – but if they'd forgotten me, it would've depressed me too bad. I would've said something like, "Do you know who I am?" And they might've said, "Yeah, you're the little *putz* with the torn puce pants." And I would've said, "I'm *Keen*." And they would've said, "Not hardly. You're not even groovy." And then I would've been even *more* depressed, so instead I got back in the car and sat there till I got a little dignity back.

Calm down, Rudy, I told myself. I put on the radio to relax a little, but goddamn it, they were playing "Hey Jude" again.

"It's *Rude*, not *Jude*," I said, denting the speaker with my fist. The bastards. First they make me *schlepp* all the way to England, *then* they steal the song Buddy wrote for me, and then they have me thrown out of their offices. I was so pissed that I started the car and threw the gearshift into first. I *thought* it was first, anyway. But it wasn't – it was reverse. How can you tell? They're so close together – first, reverse. Why do they make them like that? When I hit the gas the car shot backwards and – WHAM! Glass sprinkled and metal parts flew into the street. *I'd smashed the shit out of Lennon's psychopathic Rolls*! I just about tore off the whole front end. If you think I wanted to stick around for those two troglodytes to wipe up Savile Row with me, you ought to have your head examined. I gunned the engine again, but the cars were welded together, I tried jamming the gearshift into first, but the goddamn thing came off in my hand. *Now what?* I thought.

I opened the door and got out, but a crowd had started gathering around me. When I tried to walk away, a British guy in a suit grabbed my arm and said, "Just where do you think you're going, son?"

"Huh? Me? Uh – it's all part of the movie."

"Movie?"

"Yeah. We're filming the Beatles' new movie. It's ... uh – *A*

Hard Day's Magical Mystery Car Wreck ... Tour, or something. Hey, you want to be in it?"

"Well, I – "

"You're perfect for the part. Just look directly into the camera – up there in the second floor window."

He looked up at an Apple office and straightened his tie. "By Jove, an actual motion picture. Do I have a speaking part?"

"Speaking part? Sure, sure. Just yell, 'I did it; come and get me!'"

He cleared his throat and gave it a shot. "I say!" He was ad-libbing already. "I bloody did it! Come and get me!"

"Louder," I said. "And take this." I handed him the gearshift. "Just keep waving it in the air while you say your lines."

"I BLOODY DID IT, YOU BUGGERS! COME AND GET ME!"

He was quite a ham. I wish you could've seen him holding up that gearshift and screaming that he did it in the middle of that crowd. I slipped away, and when I got to the other side of the street, I looked back and watched as the bouncers nailed him and put him in a full nelson. He made the front page of The *Evening Standard* that night. His name was Reginald Hollingsworth, III. There was a picture of him with his suit all ruffled, and underneath, the caption said, "'But I'm in the Beatles' new movie, I tell you.'"

The only way back to the Pooh farm was by train, so I hopped a tube to Marylebone Station, which is where they filmed part of *A Hard Day's Night*, in case you don't know. It was my idea to shoot the opening scenes there, but do you think I got credit for it? Do I ever get credit for *anything*?

I was kind of a mess after having been thrown on the sidewalk and then wrecking the car, so I went into a men's room to clean up. I filled a sink with water and washed my face. Felt good. I reached for a paper towel to dry off, but when I opened my eyes and looked in the mirror, I saw him standing right behind me – *the assassin from America*! The son of a bitch had followed me to England.

"Waall, Keen. So I finally found you."

I flew out of the men's room, still dripping, and ran like hell through the station lobby. He was right on my tail.

"I know it's you, Keen! Ya'll stop runnin'!"

Ya'll? What the hell part of New York was *he* from? And can you believe it? He was still wearing that *shmaty* hat and the same royal blue suit with the cuffs that were too short. He must've been an assassin on a budget. I pushed my way past people and took off toward the train platforms, but I couldn't shake him. That guy was like living flypaper. My only chance to escape was to climb down on the tracks and hide underneath a train. I *know*! It was insane – you can get killed doing that, and I had a very healthy fear of death, which is why I was running away from an assassin in the first place, but that's what I had to do. I stretched out between the rails, very still. (Do it yourself sometime; you'll never need a laxative again.) I heard the assassin as he ran past me. "Keen?" he called out. "Keen? Where in dad-blazes are ya?"

His footsteps got fainter and fainter, and I knew I'd lost him. I thanked God about a hundred times and was just about to get up, when the train I was under blew its whistle and started rolling – *right over me*! Those big wheels turned past my ears, and you could hear the crunchy sound of metal-on-metal. *Thumpa-thumpa, thumpa-thumpa.* I didn't move a muscle in my body. I didn't even *breathe*. All I could see were the bottoms of the cars going faster and faster, and then the light, a bright, bright light. *Oh shit!* I thought. *It's the light they always tell you about, the one you see when you're dead!* But this light had pigeons sitting on it. *Pigeons? Heaven's got pigeons?*

It wasn't heaven. It was just the glass ceiling of Marylebone Station. The train was gone. I sat up and thought about how lucky I was – lucky to be alive, and lucky that I wasn't the guy who had to clean that glass ceiling.

12 'Back In The U.S.S.R.'

"Are you sure it was the same song?" Brian asked me. I was back at Cotchford Farm, and I'd just told him about "Hey Jude."

"My teeth should fall out if I'm wrong." Then I thought I'd better be more careful about saying stuff like that, because I was already losing my hair.

"Then Buddy's still alive and with the Beatles again."

"Yeah – and I'll bet Krupp's running the whole show. I went to see them at Apple and they had me thrown out."

"They wouldn't even talk to you?"

"No! I got treated like some nobody *shmendel*. And you haven't heard the worst yet. You know that assassin? I saw him in a men's room."

"The one who tried to kill you in America?"

"Same guy. He chased me all through Marylebone Station. It's a miracle I'm alive."

"Where's my car?"

Uh-oh. "Did you hear that part about it being a miracle I'm alive?"

"Rudy, where's my car?"

"You mean *some* of it, or all of it?"

Old Jonesy went ape-shit when he heard about the accident. Here I'd almost got killed and all he could worry about was his goddamn car. It was supposed to be a big deal, the car – an Astin-Martin or something. I'd never even *heard* of an Astin-Martin. I figured, how much could a no-name heap like that be worth? A couple grand? Three, maybe? When he told me what he'd paid for it, I almost passed a kidney.

So I did the only reasonable thing I could – I told him John had rear-ended me with his Rolls. Served him right, too, because you know what he did to me? Remember that surf song I'd sent to him and the other Beatles? They *stole* it. Flat-out ripped me off. They took

281

a beautiful tribute song to that beach music singer's brain, turned it into "Back In The U.S.S.R.," and put it on the *White Album*. Did I get one red cent for it? Do Hasidim get communion? Don't be ridiculous. And hey , dude – surf boy, if someone's reading this to you, I just want you to know I'll be glad to stop in at your beach house sometime and personally play the original version for you, and explain the lyrics if I have to. I swear it.

And while we're talking about loons – that John! Was *he* a case. One day he's a regular old Beatle, and the next, he's got hair down to his *pupic* and a beard and he starts hanging around with this artist and crawling inside of bags! Jesus. He walked out on his marriage, pissed off the Queen by sending back his M.B.E., and acted like he thought he was God. It was kind of like the way Buddy acted before I was arrested and got my ass pulled out of London. He didn't *look* like himself anymore. He didn't even sound quite the same. New look, new voice – what the hell was happening to him? And get a load of that photo on *Two Virgins*. Would you mind telling me, what is that? It looks like a mohel's worst nightmare. Why didn't he just call the goddamn album *Beatle Schwanze?*

And let me tell you what a drag Cotchford Farm got to be. Brian was broke – had to borrow money from me to pay for his booze. You should've seen him, man. He was turning into a blimp, a junior dirigible. All day long all he'd do was eat, drink, and make lists of musicians he wanted to get for his new "super group" – people like Clapton and Ginger Baker and McCartney, like there was a chance in hell any of them would join. Meanwhile the death threats doubled. I had to screen the mail before I could show it to him, throw out the "You're dead, Tubby" letters so he wouldn't freak out and go running for the woods.

One morning while I was watching him pour cabernet sauvegnon on his Cheerios, I came right out and told him I wanted to split, to go home to Brooklyn. He'd just pulled the free surprise from the cereal box, a whistle or something, and he started begging me not to go. He said he'd pay me, and I said with what? He didn't have any money. He told me once his new group took off, he'd have millions of pounds. (If he would've said he'd *weigh* millions of pounds, I might've believed him.) But in the end I promised to stay. How can you say no to a fat guy with a whistle?

For the next few months when he wasn't driving rock stars nuts with phone calls, pleading with them to join his band, I read Pooh stories to him out on the patio under a statue of Christopher Robin. When the weather got warmer we used his pool, even though neither of us could swim. If I waded out of the shallow end, I sank like a rock, and all Brian could do was float around like a big white cork. It was on one of those days that he mentioned he'd been hearing stories from inside sources – stories that McCartney was dead. We were both pretty worried because of all the stars Stek-Circ had killed. But why Paul, I wondered.

"I just saw Paul on TV yesterday," I said.

"They say it's a double, a stand-in."

Soon the rumors leaked to the media and then *everybody* was talking about them. People thought that the reason the Beatles were keeping Paul's death quiet was so the money wouldn't stop rolling in, but the truth was, just like the rest of us, they were scared, afraid they'd be next. It was all part of the conspiracy. They couldn't go public, but that didn't stop them from sending secret messages to their fans. Disc jockeys started finding clues in their songs. At the end of "Strawberry Fields," John says, "I buried Paul." If you played "Revolution #9" backwards, you could hear a guy saying, "Turn me on, dead man." (I didn't get that one. Why the hell would anyone want a dead man to turn him on? Isn't that necrophobia? Or maybe it's necromancy. It's one of those necro things.) Brian and me, we spent a whole day playing all of their records backwards, looking for more messages. Between cuts on the white album we found one that really pissed me off. Play it backwards and you can hear John saying clear as day, "Rudy Keen is an asshole." Yeah! Boy, that really frosted my ass. Go get that record right now and play it backwards. Do it before you read another sentence. We can listen together. And I know why he did it. It's because he was mad that I'd ruined his car. I thought about suing him, but Brian said we had to find out first if Paul was really dead so we could finally nail Krupp. He wanted to get him in the worst way. The picture of the tombstone was still eating him.

How can I ever forget the next day? How? It was July 2, 1969. Brian had gone into London to pick up his Astin-Martin at the body shop. It had taken them close to nine months to rebuild the damn thing. When he drove up past the front gate, he left the motor running.

"Rudy," he called me from outside, "get out here!"

I practically killed myself running down the stairs. "What's the matter?" I said. I thought maybe he'd seen the assassin.

"Put the car away and come right back in. I've got something to show you."

I wondered what the hell it was. I jumped in the car and found the body shop bill on the passenger seat – £10,000. I hoped he didn't expect *me* to pay for it. My earnings had dipped a little, a little below nothing.

All I remember doing is putting the gearshift in first. That's it – that's all I remember. The next thing I knew, the goddamn car smashed back against the stone gate support. *I* didn't do it. The son of a bitch car did it to itself. I'm not kidding – it tried to commit auto-suicide. I got out and looked at the back end. It wasn't that bad – just a few scratches. But I didn't want Brian to have a coronary, so I picked up the muffler and the hubcaps and the struts and the bumper and the taillight fragments and the chrome trim and the trunk lid and threw them all in the bushes and pushed the car into the garage. Hey – if he asked what had happened, I was going to tell him John did it again. I didn't much appreciate that asshole remark on the song.

Brian was in the kitchen hunched over a big glossy photograph on the table. He had a magnifying glass in his hand.

"What's that?" I said.

"A record exec friend of mine gave it to me. It's a print of the Beatles' next album cover."

"That's a pretty dumb looking cover – four guys crossing a street. What's it called – *Four Guys Crossing A Street?*"

"*Abbey Road.* Won't be released for months. Start looking. There's got to be a clue here somewhere."

You've seen that cover a hundred times. You probably even know some of the bullshit clues people found, like the license plate that says 28 IF – like Paul would have been 28, *IF* he'd lived. But that's all bullshit. The important thing is the Beatles themselves.

"That's a pretty good stand-in for Paul," I said. "He looks just like him."

"It *is* him," Brian said.

"How do you know?"

"His feet."

You remember – Paul isn't wearing any shoes in that picture. I said, "His feet?"

"Yeah. I know his feet. Those are his feet."

"You *know* his *feet?*"

"I'm pretty sure that's why he's got his shoes off – so people will know it's no double. What this cover says is, 'Paul's alive.'"

"It *does?*"

"Certainly. What do *you* think it says?"

"I think it says, 'Hurry up and cross the goddamn street, 'cause there's traffic coming.'"

He ignored me. "Look at the way they're dressed. It's reminiscent of a funeral scene. Maybe George is supposed to be the gravedigger."

"You know his *feet?*"

"And Ringo would be the undertaker. Look at John – he's all in white. That would make him – " and then he stopped short. "Oh, Jesus Christ."

"That makes him Jesus Christ?"

"No." Brian dropped the magnifying glass and turned to me. "It's John. John's the one who's dead. *He's* the one who's been mouthing off to the press about Compsong, not Paul. And his is the only face that's hidden – it's hidden behind his hair. John would never let a cover like this go out. He loves his face more than the fans do. That's not John."

I picked up the magnifying glass and had a look. I could see a part of his nose, maybe. That was it. But then I looked to the upper left of John's head. "*Oy, g'vald!*"

"What?" Brian asked me.

"That guy! That guy watching them from across the street – that's *Krupp!*"

Brian grabbed the glass back. "Bloody hell, you're right. It *is* him. No one else on earth looks like that. Good God, what a face. Can't he have something done about it?"

"You think it's true, then? You think John's the one who's dead?"

Brian straightened up and folded his arms in front of his chest like he'd just trounced me in gin rummy. "I'll know tomorrow. I'm going to try to see Paul. I'm going to ask him to join my new super group – "

Vey iz mir. There he went with that super group shit again.

" – and I'll know if it's him or not."

"Just ask him to take his shoes off. You'll know in a second."

"If it's *not* him, or if it is and he admits that John is dead, then my next stop will be Scotland Yard."

But Brian never made it to Scotland Yard. I'd been out for a hike in the country most of the next day, July 3, 1969. A lot of people don't know it, but I'm a big nature lover, something of a bird expert, a gynethologist. That day I saw a lot of birds, and I could identify them pretty well. There was a brown one and a little gray and black one, and a blue one – anyway, I got lost. I must've walked all over Sussex trying to find my way back. And it didn't get any easier when it got dark out. Finally, after about eight hours of walking and screaming, "Hello? Does anybody know where the hell I am?" I got back to Cotchford Farm. The lights were all on and there were people inside. I thought Brian must've been having a party. I knew I was going to hate to see the liquor bill. I went out back and sat by the pool, because I didn't like his friends much. They were talking and laughing inside, and it made me lonely. I looked out into the English night and thought about those times out on the road with Buddy, back when I was a kid, and I thought about home, the busy New York City streets, and I thought about Brenda. We might've been happy together. We might've gotten married and had kids and lived in a little house somewhere. Maybe we would've taken walks outside next to a little swing set and a garden, and had picnics and grown old with each other, if she hadn't gone and got savagely killed by savages.

Glup.

What the hell was that?

Glup.

It sounded like bubbles or something, like when you fart under water, and it was coming from the pool. I grabbed the long pool net, because I was pretty sure I was going to find one Jesus of a big frog, and I was petrified of frogs. Slimy sons of bitches. Big eyes. Weird tongues. But when I looked in the pool I saw Brian lying on the bottom. He wasn't moving. Quick as I could, I took off my shoes – they were brand new and had cost me a fortune, real imported cordovan leather, with specially built lifts that made me two inches taller. And then I remembered about the chlorine, so I unbuttoned my Carnaby Street silk shirt (tailor-made) and took it off. Then I dove in without thinking twice. If I'd thought twice, I might've remembered I couldn't swim. *Plunk* – right to the bottom, just like a rock, like I told you. I grabbed Brian and tried to push him to the surface, but no dice. Once I'm on the bottom, that's pretty much where I stay. I had to walk under water, pulling him to the shallow end, and then I sat him up on the steps. He was barely breathing,

"Brian? Come on, Brian! You're scaring the shit out of me!" I slapped his face like I did all the time whenever he fainted, and his lips started moving. "What?" I said. "I can't hear you!"

I put my ear down to his mouth. He was whispering real faint-like. "Paul ... [Gulp!] ... alive."

"He's alive? Paul's alive? You recognized his feet?"

But now his eyes closed again and the breathing stopped.

"Brian? Who did this to you? Was it Krupp? Huh?"

He nodded just a little, but his eyes were still shut. "John ..." he whispered.

"Oh, forget John. Did I tell you what he did to your car again, by the way?"

"John ..."

"I'm telling you, forget him, already. He's got insurance – let them fork over the cash. We'll put in a big claim. And I still think we should've sued him over what he said about me on the white album. The nerve of that guy. But I know what he'll say. He'll say it's just a coincidence that when you play the record backwards – "

"John ... Buddy."

"What?"

"I ... need ... air."

"Yeah, I know. But what was that bit about John and Buddy?"

"Air ..."

"Yeah, yeah, yeah. But what about John and Buddy?"

Christ, I should've known artificial respiration, or better yet, *genuine* respiration, because he needed the real thing. You should always know that stuff, in case someone tries to murder one of your friends in a pool. I pumped his arms, but that didn't do any good. I tried to get him out of the pool to lie him down flat – I thought maybe I could jump up and down on his chest to get him breathing again – but I couldn't budge him. And then I knew he was gone. I'd found him too late. I sat down on the side of the pool next to him, put my face in my hands, and cried. I bawled like a baby. All he'd wanted was a second chance, a comeback. That's all. Was that too much to ask? He never hurt anybody. He didn't deserve to die.

But then my survival instinct clicked on. I couldn't be found there with him, or they'd think *I* killed him. I started thinking that maybe the people in his house *weren't* his friends. It could've been the assassin again – or a whole *houseful* of assassins. Maybe they were waiting for me to come home so they could give *me* the big final swim. I got dressed even before I was dry (ruined my goddamn shirt, too, goddamn it), dumped old Brian back in the pool, and ran the hell away, ran for miles before I stopped.

The next day it was in all the papers. They called it "accidental drowning." Accidental my rock-and-roll ass. It was stone-cold murder. Brian wouldn't have drowned accidentally – he floated real good. He would've just floated around that pool all night, even if he fell asleep. I've seen him do it. Besides, he nodded when I asked him if Krupp was the one who'd done it to him. He as much as said so. What I couldn't figure out was what he'd tried to say about John and Buddy. Damn it.

I got a room at an inn for a few days and then went back to Cotchford Farm to get my stuff, but somebody had beat me to it, cleaned the place out. They took everything Brian owned, and my guitar and suitcase (which had three new Givenchy shirts in it). What if I'd had gold records? They would've taken those too. But I didn't. Have any gold records, that is. I *should've* had, but that's another story.

I couldn't go to the funeral. No thanks. I don't like seeing guys in caskets with their eyes closed, looking all waxy. Can't handle it. There'd be a bunch of miserable fake bastards hanging around looking sad, acting like they were going to miss the hell out of him, after they wouldn't have anything to do with him when he was alive and pulling whistles out of Cheerios boxes.

But I *did* go to the church and stand outside for a while, just to send him off, you know. I stopped by a stone wall and folded my hands and prayed. "Say hi to all the guys for me, and make some good music up there, Jonesy. You finally got your super-group."

"Well, goll-darn it, Keen. It's about time."

I spun around. There was the assassin. He was standing no more than six feet away, wearing that *farshlugenah* hat and the royal blue suit that looked like it came directly from an ORT outlet in Waco. He had beady little eyes and a shit-kicker grin.

He said, "I've been after you for nine years. Been hot on your trail, but you always slipped away like a weasel through a fence slat." He reached into his suit, and I knew what was coming next.

"So shoot me, already!" I dropped to my knees and closed my eyes, "But just do it fast. Get it over with!"

288

I waited and waited and waited, but no shot. The bastard was torturing me. I thought, *He'll probably just wait for me to open my eyes and THEN blow my head off, so the last thing I'll see is my brain splattering on the sidewalk.*

"Shoot y'all? Why in Sam Hill would I wanna do a thing like that for?" When his hand came out of his suit, it was holding a 45 RPM record, not a gun.

"You're not going to kill me?" I said, standing up.

"Heck, no."

"Not even beat the crap out of me?"

"Tarnation, no. Where do you get fool notions like that? Here–" He handed me the record. It was "Whoa Baby, Whoa," my old hit. " – I was hoping you could put your John Henry on that. That there's the first song me and my wife danced to back in Des Moines, at the Roll-And-Bowl."

"An autograph? You've been chasing me all this time for a friggin' *autograph*?"

"Just make it to Calvin Ray-Bob and Denise."

"*You're* Calvin Ray-Bob Stoges?"

"I've been sending you letters, but I never got no response." The assassin was just a hick fan? It didn't make any sense. (That's probably what you're thinking, too, that it doesn't make any sense, but just hold on. I know what I'm doing. And who's writing this goddamn book anyway – you or me?) I signed the record and handed it back to him. "I was sorry to hear about your friend," he said, "that Jones fella. I knew you'd be here. It's a terrible thing."

"It's a *broch*," I said.

"A *what*?"

"Forget it. So is that it? You'll leave me alone now?"

"That's just something Denise asked me to do. I got business with you that goes way back, but every time I found you, you hightailed it. You are the jumpiest man I ever saw. You got grasshoppers in your drawers?"

"What kind of business?"

"You suppose we could go have us a drink and talk about it?"

"What kind of business?" I said again. "Look – if it's got to do with some girl I met on the road, I didn't know she was yours."

"Nothin' like that." That was a relief. "If you'da messed with Denise, I just woulda broke your knees with a crowbar." Premature relief. "Whaddaya say – time for a drink?"

Are you ready for a trip to "The Outer Limits" featuring Calvin Ray-Bob Stoges – in a pub, in Sussex?

"... and the detective business wasn't doin' so hot in Des Moines. Mostly adultery cases, like Jim Happs. Jim's wife wanted me to follow him to see if he was wooin' Mable Hobert when he said he was goin' to pick up chicken feed over in Peosta. He was, too. He was wooin' Mable Hobert. So was everybody else in town. So it was that, mainly. That and a runaway pig, sometimes. Till one day, one day when I get a phone call from a famous entertainer, friend of yours, I believe."

This story wasn't kosher. There was a pig in it. "Yeah?" I said. "Who?"

"Mr. Eddie Cochran."

"*Alavasholem!*"

"Well, maybe he was Eddie Alavasholem at first, but he changed his name to Cochran. Say, I didn't know he was Jewish."

"No, no," I said. But do you think I wanted to try to explain it to him? "Never mind. Just tell me about Eddie."

"He didn't even look Jewish. Anyways, I get this call from Cochran, and he wants me to see if I can't trace down an airline ticket. I did, and I gave him the name of Preston Allerton, and then he said could I maybe find out who flew with him out of New York to Clear Lake, Iowa, on the day of Feb-u-ary second, nineteen fifty-nine. I remember this clear as a bell, 'cause it wasn't long after the crash of the little plane that killed Buddy Holly and Ritchie Valens."

"And The Big Bopper," I said.

"Well, heck yes. I'd clean forgot about him."

"So has everybody else. Go ahead."

"So I got back to work on the case. It took me down a bunch of blind alleys and this time the airline was no help – didn't want to fork over the name. But I had a friend in ticket sales over in Dubuque, so I called him up and asked for a favor. Couple weeks later he came through for me, but by then Eddie was deader 'an a doornail. I didn't know what to do with the information till I talked to a Mr. Vincent here in England. He said I should give it to you."

"You told Gene you had information?"

"I couldn't talk to him so good. He was kinda stuck on somethin' he called the *bop*. Anyway, he gave me your name." He sipped his drink and put it down slow. "Say, would you mind tellin' me what this was all about?"

"You *know* who was with Preston Allerton on that flight?"

"Didn't I just say so? But what's this all about? It's been drivin' me crazy with wonderin' for almost ten years."

I said, "Who was it?"

"Well, all right. You don't have to tell me if you don't want to. The other passenger was a guy called Sherman Katz – that's with a *K*, not a *C*. Katz. Helluva funny name. Once knew a guy named Wilber Doggs, and that was a funny name, too. Say, are you all right?"

I'd choked on my warm Coke when he'd said Sherman Katz. *Not Sherm*, I thought. *He couldn't be mixed up in this.*

"Are you *sure* that's who the ticket was made out to?"

"Surer than rain in September. You all right?"

All along, it was Sherm. Oh, God – everything was falling into place. Sherm was Sal's partner when Stek-Circ put them out of business. Sal's girl dies (she knows too much), Sal dies, and Sherm heads up Tal Ltd., which just *happens* to be affiliated with Stek-Circ. Then Buddy, Ritchie, and what's-his-name go down in a plane. Eddie, Sam, Epstein – Stek-Circ had an interest in all of them. Jones discovers something about the *Abbey Road* cover he wasn't supposed to, and they make a tea bag out of him in his own pool. All my friends, gone – and the whole time I'd been feeding Sherm everything he needed to know about their private lives, their whereabouts, their schedules. And Sherm was the last guy I talked to before that mystery limousine picked me up and blew sky high. *It was Sherm.*

Calvin Ray-Bob Stoges put his hand on my arm. "Is there some trifle I can do for you? You look more troubled than a hound in a porcupine nest."

"Calvin," I said, "you don't know the half of it. I'm more troubled than a Brooklyn Jew at a Selma Klan rally." And then I just let it all out. I told him the whole conspiracy story – about Buddy, the Beatles, Stek-Circ, the black book, the whole *shpiel*, but not before I ordered a Guinness and poured it down. You're right; I shouldn't drink. But it was the only way I could get through it all. I was numb in about ten seconds, *shikker* out of my mind after two minutes.

Calvin tossed back a shot of whiskey and ordered another. "You mean to tell me that there's a *true* story?"

"Yer goddamn right I do, ol' Calvin. Ol' buddy-boy, ol' Des

291

Moines private dick-a-roonie."

"And that Brian Jones you were livin' with, his drownin' was murder, not a accident?"

"'Course it was no accident. Ol' Brian was a world-class floater, ol' boy. Ol' boy-o-boy. Ol' Calvin. Ol' thing."

The barmaid brought him his next shot and Calvin sat there twirling it. "Well, I'll be. That's stranger than flyin' pigs at a toad rodeo."

"You betcher sweet country ass it is, baby. It's stranger than Sephardic goyim on Rosh Hasha-nah-nah. Ol' Calvin Ray Bob-A-Louie."

He stood up. "Well?" he said.

"Well what?"

"Ain't ya gonna have Sherman Katz arrested?"

I looked at all three Calvins standing in front of me. He was multiplying. "How? I can prove that ol' Sherm was in Clear Lake with Preston *Putz*-head, but how do I prove it was a conspirsity?"

"Ya'll mean *conspiracy*."

"Easy for you to say."

Calvin thought for a second. "What about that black book you was tellin' me about?"

"What about it?"

"Let's go get it.

I wiggled my finger, like he should come closer. "Calvin?" I said.

"Yeah?"

"Fuck you."

"Well, dad-blaze it! You want to stop the killin', don'tcha? You want to put those bad guys away, right?"

"Sure. Sure I do. I've been trying for ten years."

"Well, then, we're breakin' into Stek-Circ and gettin' us that black book."

"Shit, I'm not gonna do that. Hell, no. Not this boy. Go screw yourself. Nuh-uh. I'd rather have shingles. You can wait for hell to sprout icicles before I get near *that* goddamn place."

♪　　♬　　♪

"Is that it? The building with them monster heads on the top corners?"

We were in Calvin's rental car, across the street from Stek-Circ. "Those are *gargoyles*, not monster heads." He was a nice guy, but Jesus, talk about your Yahoos. "Stek-Circ is on the third floor. But I'm not going in there, I tell ya. Not for love or money or all the real estate in Shaker Heights. Why, I wouldn't go in there even if Marianne Faithful decided not to be faithful anymore and was waiting for me on a water bed with a can of whipped cream and a sign that said, *'I'm tired of Mick; take me, Rudy – I'm yours.'*"

♪   ♫   ♪

"You got hold of it?"

I was nearly two stories up, grasping at the brickwork that had been so easy to climb years before. There was a lot more gravity this time.

"I can't do this," I said. "I'm drunk and stuck on the ledge of a building."

"Ya'll'd better do it, or you'll be drunk and dead on the sidewalk. Keep goin'. Don't stop."

Inch by lousy inch I pulled and kicked my way up. I stopped for just a moment to look down, way down where Calvin was standing below me. I git dizzy and almost fell.

"You sure this door can't be broke into?" he said, rattling the doorknob. I watched as he pulled a little leather case out of his suit pocket. Inside was a thin piece of metal that he slipped into the lock. The door swung open.

"You son of a bitch," I yelled. "Why didn't you *tell* me you could do that?"

A few minutes later the third floor window above me opened and Calvin leaned out. "Give me your hand."

"If I give you my hand, I'll slip and fall, goddamn it."

"No, you won't."

"Yes, I will."

"No, you won't."

So I held my hand out and slipped. Why the hell did I listen to him? He was from Iowa, where they've got toads and porcupines and pigs. He grabbed my arm just in time and hoisted me up and through the window. I collapsed on the floor, panting and sweating like a bastard. He stood there looking cool and unruffled. I hated him.

293

"There's more 'an one way to grease a pig," he said.

"Shut up," I said.

It was pretty dark inside, but I could see well enough to realize that Stek-Circ had expanded. The office took up half the floor now, and everything was different – new desks, furniture, filing cabinets.

"Where's the danged book?" Calvin asked me.

"I don't know," I said. "They've changed the whole joint. You look through those desks and I'll check out that room over there."

Calvin didn't waste any time. He was a very skilled ransacker. He just tore the desks apart and dumped everything on the floor. I walked into the other room. That was funny; there were rows and rows of flashing colored lights. I found a light switch and clicked it on.

"Jesus-Rhythm-And-Blues-Christ," I said.

Calvin came running in. "Whadja find?" Then he saw it. "What the – "

It was the Compsong computer – a huge gray box with spinning spools of magnetic tape and buttons all over it.

"That's it, Calvin. That's the future of music. From now on every song you hear on the radio or a juke box will come from this."

"Look," he said. "It's printing something."

I walked over to a stack of cards that the machine had spit out. I picked one up and read it.

"What's it say?" Calvin asked.

"I get it. Each one of these cards is a custom-programed song, complete with words and music. Here's once called 'I'll Be There,' and it says it's for The Jackson Five. And this one, 'One Bad Apple,' is for The Osmonds." I flipped the cards over. "These are the dumbest lyrics I've ever read."

"Wait till you read *this* one, then," Calvin said. "It's called 'Hunk Of Burnin' Love,' and oh-my-Lord! It's for the king!"

"Don't be silly. The Windsors don't make records."

"I meant Elvis."

"Christ, they've even got Elvis." Not that it mattered after all those stupid movies he'd made. "We've got to wreck this thing before it pumps out any more crap. It could ruin music for a whole generation."

And that's what we did. We took that monster apart. We threw chairs at it, pulled the tape from the reels, kicked in circuit boards, until all the lights went out and the cards flew all over the floor.

Calvin said, "What should we do with all them cards?"

"Rip 'em up. Rip 'em up good."

I personally ripped up "You Picked A Fine Time To Leave Me Lucille" and "Mandy," thinking I'd done the world a favor, but they must've had duplicates somewhere. All I can say is, I tried. I tried to save the music business, not to mention your ears.

Then we went through every file, every desk drawer, but we couldn't find the black book.

I said, "They must've destroyed it."

"Not necessarily. There's more than one way to – "

"Yeah, yeah. I know – grease a pig. Why the hell would anyone want to grease a pig, anyway?"

"Oh, they're great fun, greased pigs. You get yourself a whole buncha boys tryin' to grab 'em, and they slip and they slide – "

"It gets pretty boring in Des Moines, doesn't it, Calvin?"

"It's hell sometimes, Rudy."

I noticed that for the last minute or so he'd been staring at an oil painting on the wall. He got up, walked over to it, lifted it off the hook, and can you dig this? There was a wall safe behind it.

"What – you got x-ray vision?"

"I just get hunches."

He put his ear up against the wall and started turning the dial.

"I suppose you want me to think you can open that thing, huh? Cut the crap, Calvin. Do you know what the odds are against finding the right combination? You could be here for months and not come up with it. Even Mike Hammer couldn't – "

The tumblers clicked and the door swung open.

"I'm sorry," Calvin said. "Were you sayin' somethin'?"

I wasn't even going to tell you that part of the story. I was afraid you'd think I was going too far and making stuff up. But so help me God, it happened. I was speechless. You can keep James Bond. Give me a hayseed in a bad suit any day.

He reached inside and pulled out the black book. It was a little worn and ragged around the edges, but it was the same one.

"Look familiar?" Calvin asked.

We put it down on a desk and started turning the pages. There were the parts about Eddie, Sam, the plane crash, and "What to do about R.K.?" – but they'd added a lot more. Right after the plans to turn that very famous beach music singer into a surfing vegetable was a section about the computer:

20 Year Obsolescence Plan

Disco
Punk
Rap
New Aqe
Alternative

Calvin leaned closer to me. His suit smelled like corn husks. "What's it mean, Rudy?"

"I don't know. Turn the page."

Sometimes I wish we hadn't looked any further, that I'd never found out. As big a pain in the ass as John could sometimes be, he didn't deserve this. Take a look for yourself.

1969 – John Lennon confirmed dead in Japan, Poisoned by tainted sushi.

"Holy foreign cuisine," I said. "Jones was right."

"What's sushi?" Calvin asked.

"It's *John* who's dead, not Paul."

"But what's sushi?"

"Sushi? Think of it as raw, far-eastern muskie."

Calvin whistled through his teeth. "What a terrible way to go."

But if John was killed in Japan, who was that on the cover of *Abbey Road?* Who was the guy wiggling around in a bag? And whose Rolls Royce had I trashed?

I must've shoved the black book accidentally, because a handful of Polaroid photos fell out. I picked them up off the desk and shuffled through them. Calvin looked over my shoulder and said, "Ugh! Who's that, and what happened to his face?"

"That's Buddy Holly. That's what the plane crash did to him." At least, the first picture was of Holly. In the next ones you couldn't tell who it was; the features were different. In shot after shot, his face changed right in front of our eyes. The last photo was of John.

I lined the snapshots in order across the desk, beginning with Holly on the left, and ending with John on the right. I knew what I was seeing, but my brain wouldn't accept it. I didn't want to believe it was true.

Calvin scratched his head. "What does it mean, Rudy?"

"What does it *mean?*" I said. "You can see safes behind paintings, you can open them without knowing the combination, but then you look at this and you don't know what it means? Go to the next page of the book."

Calvin reached out and slowly turned the page, his hand trembling. And here it is, world. This is what you've been waiting for – the best kept secret in music history. And remember who you're hearing it from, Rudy Keen – rock legend. I want a little recognition this time. That's KEEN and it rhymes with TEEN and it stands for BRILLIANT. Not only have I proven to you that the 1959 plane crash was no accident, and that Buddy Holly survived, and all those other stars *including* John Lennon were murdered by a sinister worldwide conspiracy, but look at what Calvin and I found on page 57 of the black book:

OPERATION DEAD-RINGER

After years of delay, and now with Lennon safely out of the way, intensive plastic surgery procedures have been implemented. Since it is no longer viable to introduce Holly as himself, surgeons have successfully altered his facial structure to resemble John's. He is a near perfect duplicate. Recordinq is still a problem, but vocals can be touched-up by utilizing modern studio wizardry and P.M.'s talent for imitation. Holly's mental condition is at times unstable; he is given to periods of grandiose delusions durinq which he believes he is God, particularly after LSD use. Electric shock therapy still an option, although our recent acquisition of the Rockettes seems to have had a calming effect upon him.

My legs gave out and I had to sink down onto one of the secretary chairs. I looked at the photos of Buddy's face and then at the black book. When I felt like I could talk at last, I said, "This is what Jones tried to tell me with his dying breath. He said, 'John – Buddy,' but I didn't know what the hell he meant. He'd found out the truth about Lennon, and that's why he was drowned."

Calvin said, "You mean to tell me that Buddy Holly is John Lennon?"

297

"You're catching on, Calvin."

"But what was that about the Rockettes?"

"He owns them."

Calvin's eyes grew big. "*All* of them?"

"Yeah, and I'm just sick about it. They were supposed to be mine."

"But at least you've got your proof, Rudy."

"Finally. Hey, what're you doing?"

He was back at the safe, rummaging around inside. "Seein' what else I can find." He pulled out an old yellow newspaper and brought it over to the desk. He spread it out, flattened it with his hands, and said, "I can't read it. That there's not English, is it?"

I was surprised he could even read English. The paper was German, from 1943. I could pick out a few words here and there.

"What's it say?" Calvin asked.

"I don't know. Something about a musical director for the *fuhrer*, the dirty bastard. I can't make out the rest."

But I didn't have to make out the rest – the picture next to the story said it all, a young lean-faced S.S. officer. It was Sherman Katz. The caption identified him as Captain Sherman Katzenmueller, and went on to say that he had arranged the music for a concert to be given privately to Adolf Hitler.

"No wonder his Yiddish was so bad," I said. "He's not a Jew – he's just passing."

"Rudy, remember them hunches I was tellin' you about?"

"The son of a bitch is a closet Nazi!"

"I'm havin' another hunch."

"Not now, with the hunches. Look at this *shtarker* wearing an S.S. cap and a swastika armband – an Aryan poster boy! He's the mastermind, Calvin. Krupp just takes orders from him. Quick, get Nuremberg on the line. We've got ourselves an escaped Nazi criminal!"

I heard a click behind me. I turned around and out of the shadows of the office stepped none other than Sherman Katz – make that *Katzenmueller* – with a gun pointed at us.

"So, the exploding limousine failed, and you've come back for your proof, have you, Rudy?"

Calvin whispered to me, "*That was the hunch I had.*"

I scooped up the Polaroids, stuck them in the book, and held it behind my back.

"Put the book down, Rudy."

I stood up and backed away from him. "Why, Sherm?"

"Why what, Rudy? Why build the world's largest musical entertainment network? Why succeed wildly where others enjoy only scattered success? Or do you perhaps mean, why are you so stupid that you have to ask why?"

Even though he was a Nazi, it hurt to hear him say that. I used to look up to him. I lowered my head and said, "You were like a father to me."

"Please, don't insult me."

"You believed in me. You told me so – you called me your little songwriting genius."

"Genius? Ha-ha-ha-ha-ha!" Hey, it wasn't *that* funny. "Sal called you that, not me. The only thing you were ever a genius at was ruining your own career. You were useful to us when we needed Holly to recover. That's all. After his recovery was assured, who needed *you*, a pathetic nobody?"

"Oh yeah? What about the Third Reich, huh? What happened to *that*, if you're so goddamn superior, Sherm? Or should I say, *Captain Katzenmueller?*"

Calvin slapped my arm. "Why'd you go and tell him you knew that for?"

"Ahhh," Sherm said, "I see you've been doing your homework, little Rudy."

"Yeah. I know everything. *And don't call me little!*"

"So short, and so sensitive."

"You're a Nazi," I told him. "You used to play for the fuhrer."

Sherm raised his nose in the air, like he was going to blow storm trooper snot at me. "Yes, I did, and I'm proud of it. Oh, those were glorious days. The stirring, uplifting strains of Wagner, balm for the soul. Those enrapturing summer nights along the Rhine, pure German music wafting through the free wind of the Fatherland. Adolf nodding and beating time with his horse swatch, the debonair little mustache twitching in approval. A higher purpose I have never served – much preferable to the loathsome drivel your American youth clamor for, those unwashed pimply dregs of a decadent society."

I would've given it to him good, boy, but I didn't know what a pimply dreg was. I think there was an insult hidden in there, somewhere. And also he had the gun – don't forget that.

"What'd you say?"

"I *said*, I detest the very vinyl that rock and roll is pressed upon, like your 'Bop-Sha-Bop,' that moronic paean to autoeroticism." Moronic peon? Who did he think he was calling a moronic peon? And what did autos have to do with it? "But cornering the publishing market of popular music has made me richer than I ever thought possible in my wildest dreams. And there is the additional bonus of weakening the moral fiber of your country's already debased youth. Success is sweet, Rudy. Too bad you never tasted it yourself."

"You didn't succeed," I said.

Calvin said, "Sshhh!" and motioned to me with his eyes, but I didn't pay any attention to him. I was too pissed at Sherm.

"Why, of course I succeeded. Look where you are standing – inside the world's foremost publishing firm. Look who has the gun trained upon you."

"Everything you got, you got by killing and stealing, starting with Sal, your own partner."

"Sal was a swine."

"*Oy* – was he a swine. But you didn't have to kill him. You destroyed music's most talented stars (with one obvious exception). You call that success? Look what you did to a very famous beach music singer, that surf boy, you know who I mean – making him profoundly stupid through drugs. You ought to be ashamed of yourself. And what about Valens, Cochran, Cooke, Epstein, Jones, and Lennon? And what about The Big Bopper?"

"The Big who?"

"The Big Bopper – you know. J.P. Richardson. Remember?" And then I started singing, "'Chantilly lace has a pretty face, and a ponytail, hangin' down – '"

"Oh, yes. I completely forgot about him."

Poor J.P.. Even the guy who *killed* him forgot about him.

"Yeah, all those guys. Guys the world loved. Guys who had their whole lives in front of them. Success is about making things better, not destroying people. But the worst crime you ever committed, the most horrible, the one I'll never forgive you for, was killing the girl I loved."

Sherm looked confused. "Girl you loved? *I* killed the girl you loved?"

I nodded and almost started crying, just thinking about it. "Yeah," I said.

"Are you trying to tell me you're *straight?*"

"What's *that* supposed to mean, huh? You bet I'm straight. I'm as straight as a banana." I get all excited and confused when I'm mad and arguing with someone. That was a bad comparison, the banana. I meant *arrow*, straight as an arrow, not a banana. "You killed Brenda Taylor. All that was left of her was her sweater and her shoes."

"Taylor? Wasn't she Sal DeGrazzia's girl?"

"Well, for a while," I said. "For a while she was, okay? But she loved me. Or she would've, if you hadn't gone and killed her, maybe. There was a chance. It wasn't out of the question or anything."

Calvin kept saying, "Pssst!" to me out of the side of his mouth, but I was still too upset to listen to what he was trying to tell me. Sherm shook his head and let the gun lower a little. "I'm afraid you're mistaken there, little Rudy. I never killed the Taylor girl."

"Sure. Sure you didn't kill her, the sweetest, most wonderful girl I ever knew. And Hitler wasn't a murderer. He was just a poor, misunderstood sensitive bastard. And you and the other S.S. boys never hurt anyone either, did you? And I suppose you guys weren't giving it to each other every night, in those cozy tents, taking the buddy system a step further, huh?"

The hammer of Sherm's gun clicked back, and Calvin went "Pssst!" again.

But I couldn't stop. "All you Nazis are sadistic faggots. It's well known. It's in the history books. You all took it in the *tushy*. That's why you were always doing the goosestep."

The gun was shaking in his crazy shaking Nazi hand. "SHUT UP! SHUT UP, SHUT UP, SHUT UP! I'LL KILL YOU!"

I saw the movement at my side, just a blur. Calvin rushed Sherm, the gun went off, and Calvin collapsed in a heap on the floor. It was over in a second. I looked at him lying there. A red trickle stained the carpet. He was hurt bad, and bloodstains are the absolute worst to try and get out.

"Now," Sherm said, calmer, as he walked toward me. "You don't want to end up like your hillbilly friend, do you, Rudy?"

I stared down the barrel of his pistol. If I didn't hand the book over, he'd shoot me and take it. And even if I *did* give it to him, he'd shoot me anyway, the bastard Nazi, and I'd be half of a matched set of bookends on the floor next to poor Calvin, who was busy at the moment bleeding to death.

That's when I heard Uncle Zollie's voice in my head. I

remembered what he'd told me once when he had a rough legal case and his client wanted him to do something illegal. "If they make you do vot you know is wrong, you pretend to do it, and then you do vot you know is right anyvay. Remember that, little *shmendel.*"

Real slow, like freeze-frame film, I pulled the hand holding the book from behind my back. I held it out to him, and just as he went to snatch it, I put it out the window.

"I'll drop it – I swear I will. Put down the gun or it's gone."

Sherm stopped in his tracks. "You little *dummkopf.* Give me that or I'll blow you to pieces!"

I looked back and forth between him and the book. I was cornered. He jumped at me, and since I didn't know what else to do, I threw the book out the window as hard and as far as I could. Sherm leaned out toward it, but he leaned too far and lost his balance. I saw the desperate look in his eye as he reached for me, like I should try and help him. I pretended to offer him my hand, and when he went for it, I yanked it away and stuck my thumb out as if I was hitchhiking. I watched as he tumbled through the air and landed on the street below with a *splat*, like a fascist water balloon. It was pretty cool. It *wouldn't* have been cool if he was just an ordinary guy. But a Nazi? A Nazi falling out a window is *tres* cool. Still, it made me throw up. I've got a very weak stomach, even for exploding Nazis. The cleaning staff was in for a surprise the next time they showed up. And if you like irony, you'll like this. The black book was lying on the street next to Katzenmueller, just a few inches from his hand, like he was still trying to grab it. It would've made a great cover for a mystery. In fact, I tried to get my publisher to use it for this book, but they wouldn't do it. They said it was too graphic and not representative of the overall theme. I don't know what the hell they were talking about.

I went to check on Calvin, but it was too late. He was gone. Dead City. Another victim of the Stek-Circ connection. Pigs would run loose back in Des Moines and Jim Happs would probably keep wooing Mable Hobert, and Jim's wife wouldn't have anyone to follow them. And Denise would dance alone at the Roll-And-Bowl. Good old Calvin. *Alavasholem.*

There was only one thing left to do, and that was to get the book. I ran out of the office and down the stairs to the front entrance, when I heard a car come tearing around the corner. It stopped right next to Katzenmueller's body, not too far from where his appendix was lying on the pavement. (I think it was his appendix. I'm better with giblets, actually.) A door opened and someone leaned out and picked up the black book. I can't say for sure who it was – all I could see was a dark sleeve and a gloved hand – but I can give you a damn good guess. The door slammed shut and the car sped off into the night, leaving me standing alone in the street, empty-handed.

13 'True Love Ways'

The plane's engines whistled as we sailed out over the Atlantic.
I was glad as hell that it was all over and that I was going home again.
I tried to open the little complimentary bag of peanuts they give you,
but it was stuck shut. On the front page of The *London Times* folded
on my lap was a photo of John Lennon planting an acorn for peace,
but behind the metal-rimmed glasses the eyes of Buddy Holly looked
up at me. I squeezed the peanut bag and thought about what a long
haul it had been from "That'll Be The Day" to "Cold Turkey," from
a recording studio in Clovis, New Mexico to a new mansion in
Tittenhurst. What a story. It sounded more like a cheap trick
dreamed up by a desperate writer than it did reality. But if there's
one thing I learned, it's that most of life is like a cheap trick, and the
rest – I guess that's what they call truth.

I bit the plastic bag but it wouldn't give, and then I wondered
about a lot of things. I wondered why Buddy had left all the people
from his old life behind, and how he could live with himself, and why
there was no mention in The *Times* of Sherm biting the pavement,
and why the customs dogs always picked me, *me* – out of a whole line
of passengers – to attack and try to hump my leg off, and what the
hell acorns had to do with peace. By now I was banging the bag of
peanuts against my armrest when it dawned on me that maybe
Buddy knew exactly what he was doing. Maybe it *was* better to let the
people who loved him believe he was dead, to let them keep their
memories of him the way he used to be. And maybe Krupp and Stek-
Circ were so powerful they could hush up Sherm's death. As far as
I knew, they could've come back and picked up his body and
appendix themselves. They'd made Allerton disappear, hadn't they?
No one ever found a trace of him. And maybe I just naturally
aroused dogs. It could be hormonal or something. It used to work
with teen-age girls. But the acorn bit – I still don't get it.

I gave the bag one more good *swack* against the armrest and almost blinded a lady across the aisle.

"My eye!" she screamed.

I slumped down in my seat and rang for the stewardess.

"Oh, my eye! I can't see!"

The stewardess came running. "Ma'am? Are you all right?"

"Something shot in my eye and I can't see!"

"Hey," I said, "when you get a chance, could I have some more peanuts over here?"

But she wouldn't give me any more. She said they were all out, but I think she was lying.

When I knocked on the door of our apartment in Brooklyn, I didn't know what I'd say to Ma after so long. I was kind of nervous. Would we know each other? Would she disown me? The reason I wondered if she'd disown me is because of something I haven't told you about. One night when I got drunk with Eddie and Gene, we all ended up in a tattoo parlor, and I got my ass tattooed. Yeah. It was a picture of a 45 RPM record, and on the label it said, "Electric Rudy." I don't suppose I have to tell you how I worried about the problem that was going to cause at the cemetery after I croaked. If I didn't get it removed, they were going to have to take my *tochkes* off before I'd get buried. Then you'd have to visit me in two places, and one of the markers would read, HERE LIES RUDY KEEN'S ASS. THE REST OF HIM IS IN HALLOWED GROUND.

The door swung open. There she was, hair a little whiter than I remembered it, face a little thinner, more wrinkles.

"Yesssss?" she said, looking at me like I was a stranger. "Can I help you?"

"Ma," I said. "It's me, Rudy. Your son."

"My son? Don't make vit the jokes. My son is a een-ternational musician, not a bald-headed *schlepper*."

She was about to close the door on me, but I stuck my foot inside the entrance. "It's me, Ma."

"Who're you callin' *Ma*? You're not my son. My son don't got a pot belly," she said, poking her finger in my stomach.

"Would you cut it out? You're no spring chicken yourself, you know."

She came a little closer and touched my head with her hand like I was contagious or something. "Rudolph? Can it really be *you*?"

"Yeah. Invite me in, why don't you?"

"Not so fast. I seem to recall someone sayin' he vas gonna become a famous stah."

"Ma – "

"You famous?"

Two minutes. I'd been home two minutes out of the last eleven years and already I wanted to leave again. "Not exactly," I said.

"Huh. You said you vas gonna be. You rich?"

She was going for the whole nine yards – my mother, the *yenta* quarterback. "No, Ma. I'm not rich."

"Vell, I'll be. You still viggle yer heeps?"

"Only when I try to fit into my pants. Now let me in. I'm home for good this time."

"Oh, no, you ain't." And with that she slapped an envelope in my hand. It was from The United States Government, and it was torn along the top. I pulled the letter out and read it. It began, "Greetings!"

I'd been drafted. My mental health exemption had expired. I dropped my suitcase and wiped my forehead and thought about all the GIs in the barracks who'd point and stare at the tattoo on my ass.

"For seven years you run off vit the Peedles, and ven you come home for vun day, yer off vit the Ah-my. You vant I should talk to Uncle Zollie and get you out?"

I just kept reading the notice over and over. "Greetings!"

"No," I said. "It's cool. If Elvis did it, I can do it."

"Sure, sure. So you can come home vit a twelve-year-old *shiksa*, like that Elvis Pretzle."

"*Presley*," I said. "Elvis *Presley* – and the shiksa was fourteen, not twelve. Don't exaggerate."

"Presley, Pretzle – who cares? Go in the next room and say hello to yer faddah."

I dropped the letter. It sailed back and forth like a deflated kite and landed on the floor.

"What?"

"You hoid me. Yer faddah – he's home too, from his *mission* in life. The two of you, honest to God. You should get togetha and you can staht another new country for show-biz nothings."

I hadn't seen my old man since I was twelve. "Forget it," I said. "I'm not saying anything to him."

My mother pulled my ear and dragged me into the dining room. "He's yer *faddah*. Have some respect. You sprang from his loins, already."

"What kind of talk is that?" I said. "Springing from loins."

"Get in there and say hello or you'll spring out the dooah."

It was the last thing I wanted, a reunion with my father, the guy who missed all my track meets, the same guy who was never there to tuck me in at night. I would've rather taken swimming lessons from Krupp's thugs in Brian Jones' pool than be in the same room with him.

I walked into the dining room and stood about seven feet from the table. He was sitting there behind a newspaper that he held out like a blanket. I didn't say anything. What do you say? *Hello, where have you been for the last sixteen years?* I shifted my weight. I cleared my throat.

The paper came down slowly. He stared at me. He cocked his head and stood up.

"Rudolph? Rudolph, my son?"

"Oh," I said. "You remembered, then."

He walked over to me with his arms out in front of him like he was walking a tightrope strung along the dining room table.

"Remember? Remember? Of *course* I remember. You're my own flesh and blood vot sprang from my loins!"

At least I knew where Ma got that loin crap from. It's weird hearing your parents talk dirty. Does any son need to hear that?

I said, "It's a little late for all that. Or maybe it's just slipped your mind that you went out for the *Jewish Star* sixteen years ago and never came home."

"Slipped my mind? Never for one minute, Rudolph. Never one minute did I forget my little boy whose hair I used to stroke vile he lay in bed till he fell asleep. Vot happened to your hair, by the way?"

"I'm not your little boy anymore."

"You'll *always* be my little boy," he said, and then he wrapped his arms around me in a big hug. I just stood there, my hands down at my sides.

"I got a tattoo on my ass," I said.

"Congratulations."

"Aren't you going to disown me?"

"Disown you? Hell, no. Vy vould I do that?"

"I just told you. I got a tattoo on my ass."

"So vot? Get one on your *shmecky*, for all I care."

"But they won't let me be buried in a Jewish cemetery."

307

"Vot – you ready to be buried? That's just a *bobbeh meisseh*. You've been listening to your mother, I see."

"You mean it's not true? They won't take my ass off?"

The old man cracked up. Laughed till he was blue. When he was through, and after he'd blown his nose into his handkerchief with a terrific *honk!* – he grabbed my arm and led me into his bedroom. I mean, *Ma's* bedroom. I pulled my arm away from him and stopped before following him in all the way. He pulled a big book from one of the suitcases that were lined up aginst the wall.

"I vant you should see somethin'," he said to me. He sat down on the bed and put the book on his lap.

"No, thanks," I said. "I don't want to see it."

He looked up at me like a wounded Ashkenazi Teddy bear. "Don't vant to see it? But Rudolph – it's all about *you*."

"What is?"

"The scrapbook. See? I got every newspaper clipping about you from the beginning. Look at this – 'On Tour In England Vit Eddie Cockle.'"

"That's *Cochran*."

"Yeah. And here ve got 'Teen Keen Questioned At DeGrazzia Murder Scene' – vich I hope you had nothin' to do vit."

"No."

"And I got all your records, even the ones you didn't sing on, but just wrote."

Of all the goddamn things. He wasn't kidding; he had them all. I sat down on the bed next to him as he turned the scrapbook pages, and my career passed before my eyes. It was sensational. It only filled three pages, but they were three sensational pages.

"Rudolph," he said, when he got to the end, "it vould be a great honor for me if you should put your John Hancock on the record that started it all – 'Bop-Sha-Bop.'"

"This is too much – you know my music?"

"Don't make vit the visecracks. Of *course* I know your music. Vot kinda faddah vould miss a chance to brag to his friends about his famous son? Listen to this." He went, "A-hem," and then started to sing: "'Bop-Sha-Bop, I'm gonna pop all over the place.' Vot you think?"

"Close enough."

"Yeah. I got tired of them folk songs they made us sing every night at the kibbutz. Jesus Christ, 'Hava Nagila' up the tushy. So I'd put on some of your hot rock and roll and boogie." He handed me the record and a pen. "Please," he said, "sign. For me."

I took the pen and noticed his hands were all worn and had calluses. I felt – I don't know – *proud*, kind of. Something special was happening between us. It was about fathers and sons, and loins. I guessed that having a kid was a real gone thing. I couldn't say for sure back then, because even though my loins kept springing and springing, I didn't have any children.

I was about to sign the record when he stopped me. "Tell me somethin'. That time in Massachusetts ven you electrocuted yourself – I never could figure out. Vas that for real, or just a shrewd publicity stunt?"

I almost told him the truth, but he thought I was such a big deal, I just couldn't. "Publicity stunt," I said.

"That's vot I thought. That's vot I told everybody. 'My son, he's no *shmegegge*. He knows how to plug in a ax.' That's vot they call a guitar, right? A ax?"

"Yeah, sometimes."

"That's vot I thought. Hmph! You sure stole the show from Darin that night."

"Yeah, man. I was on fire." Literally.

"I got just one more question," he said, rubbing the gray stubble on his chin.

"What is it, Dad?"

"Dad. You called me Dad. Did you hear vot you said?"

"I heard. What's the question?"

"Not just a question – the most *important* question."

"Oh," I said. "I know, I know. You're going to ask me if I've been a *mensch*, like you always told me to be."

"Not really."

"No? Well, then you probably want to know if I've kept the Torah in my heart."

"That's important, but it's not vot I had in mind."

"What, then?"

He looked toward the door to make sure Ma wasn't around anywhere listening, and then he leaned in close to me. "*Did you nail Shelly Fabares?*"

For Christ's sake. "Hey, give me some credit."

"I am!"

"I'm a former teen throb."

"The throbbest!"

"So you mean, How many *times* did I nail her, right?"

"Ahhh – that's my boy!"

No – that was probably Elvis, the lucky bastard. But what the hell. Let an old man have his dream. Let me have *mine*, for that matter. I'm telling you, every time I see an old "Donna Reed Show" episode, I still get excited.

♪ 🎵 ♪

In September of 1969 I took a train to Fort Briggs where they gave me a crew cut, some bad clothes and an M 16 A-1 rifle. I was in the Army. It was a valuable experience. I learned to salute, spit, and shit in the woods. I even picked up a slight southern accent. *Oy, vey iz mir, ya'll.* Nine months, two weeks and three days later, I was a civilian again. I had clout, man. And it's a good thing, too, because I was going nuts by then. The uniforms had no tailoring qualities at all – thick scratchy wool, no lines whatsoever. And my M 16 kept misfiring and blowing up in my face. They can call me up to finish my stint when they perfect the goddamn things.

Soon after that I lived my worst nightmare – I became the violin *shmer'l* I was always afraid I'd end up being. I listened to ten year olds hack away at Beethoven and was constantly pulling their bubble gum off the seat of my pants. I was in hell.

Till one day, one bright November day when I got a call from the offices of *Playboy*. They wanted to do an interview with me. *Finally*, I thought, *finally I'm going to get the kind of recognition I deserve.* The public had started to rediscover the hot rock and roll acts from the Fifties – Buddy, Gene, Eddie, and me. It took them that long to catch up to us. We were American myths by then. Only after the interview started did I find out the article wouldn't be just about me. It was one of those nostalgia pieces – "Where Are They Now?" – and included conversations with Pinky Lee, Spanky from Our Gang, Dale Evans, and me.

I met the interviewer at a coffee shop and poured on the charm. It's in issue #975. Don't bother looking it up. I'll give it to you here.

PB: You were a seminal influence on the musicians who were part of the 1950's rock scene, weren't you?

Keen: Seminal? Naw, I never got personal with those guys.

PB: But everyone knows that you played with Buddy Holly.

Keen: Hey, we were two consenting adults.

PB: No, I meant that you were his opening act.

Keen: Oh, sure. I'd get the crowd all warmed up for him with my driving –

PB: But then you dropped from public view. What happened?

Keen: To me? I went to England. I wrote most of the Beatles' early songs with Buddy.

PB: Buddy who?

Keen: Buddy *Holly*. What – you forgot about him already?

PB: But Holly was dead by then.

Keen: No, he wasn't. They flew him to London to recover from the crash. *Oy*, he looked like sheer hell, too.

PB: Uh – perhaps we should move on.

Keen: That crash was all part of a conspiracy, you know.

PB: Then there was the Army.

Keen: Did you know that Brian Epstein had a crush on me?

PB: About your time in the Army – according to your service record, you were given a dishonorable discharge.

311

Keen: Hey, I don't want to talk about this.

PB: Something about a shower incident at Fort Briggs.

Keen: I told ya, I don't want to talk about it! Don't you want to hear about what *really* happened to Buddy Holly?

And then, right in the middle of my interview, it switches straight to Pinky Lee. They just left me hanging there and the next thing you know, they're asking Pinky about his stupid hound's-tooth suit. Like anybody gave a rat's ass about that *farshlugenah* suit! What about my satin pants, huh? What about my leather jacket? *That's* what they should've been interested in. And the picture of me they ran, it was a candid taken while I was sitting in the coffee shop booth, my hands up in front of my face at the point when they asked about the shower incident. And listen, it never happened, that shower bit. That was just a bunch of shit, that's all. You can't believe everything you read, you know. Some of the stuff you read is pure bullshit. Can you believe they pay guys big bucks just to make up bullshit? It's a crime, is what it is.

After that interview ran, my life was pretty much in the toilet. My big break was gone and I had no future. That's when I started thinking about suicide. How much worse than teaching brats to play scales could blowing your brain out be? I remember one day Bobby Marrovitz's mother canceled his lesson, so I took the train into Manhattan and walked around Central Park. It was one of those early spring days when the New York sky was light blue and the trees hadn't gotten their leaves yet, but it was just a matter of time. I was on a walkway right across from Columbus Circle and I could see the Essex House up ahead, real tall, like it was standing at attention. I was depressed as hell, thinking about when I was young and hot on the trail of success, shopping my songs to the *shnorrers* on Tin Pan Alley. I stepped in some mushy yellow grass and ruined my new suede shoes, and I figured, *That's it. Now there's nothing left to live for. Even my shoes are a fucking mess.*

Just then I heard a car radio blaring, and when I looked up I saw a cab speeding toward me down a park concourse. What I was going to do, I was going to wait till it got real close and then jump in front of it, just end it all on the grille of a Checker. But what did I hear coming from that cabbie's radio? Of all the songs ever written, which one was playing at top volume at that very moment? It was "Make Believe" – the one I'd written for Buddy when he was down and out about his face and his career. And who was singing it? *Buddy.* Buddy pretending to be John, that is. He'd changed the title to "Imagine." My song – that was *my song.*

You've got to keep in mind, this all happened in a split second – the cab speeding closer and closer, the radio blasting, me ready to jump. But when I heard that haunting piano refrain, I kept my feet planted on that sidewalk and I froze like a statue. It was like a message, a message that I shouldn't do it. I could only think of two things – first, how much I loved and missed my old friend Buddy, and second, all those royalties I was being screwed out of. The cab sped right on by. I was still alive. And then a bird shit on my head. I already told you, I was like a statue. But there again, I figured it was another message, like a sign from God, because I became unfrozen when the bird shit on me. It was as if God was telling me, "Some days your shoes get ruined and birds shit on you, but it's no reason to throw yourself in front of a cab and get flattened like a latke. Take the good with the bad." And so I thanked God for letting me hear my song at that moment, and for sending the bird to shit on me.

I know what you're thinking. Yes I do. Yes I do – shut up! Quit thinking I don't. You're thinking, "Listen, Keen. How many coincidences do you expect me to believe?" All I can say to you is, "Why? How many are you *willing* to believe?" And if you don't believe them, what can I do? Am I supposed to lie just because you might get fed up with the *emmes*? Hell no; I can't do that. I've got a moral obligation to tell this story, a responsibility to the memory of Buddy Holly, and a hell of a big publishing advance.

I wandered through the park, thinking about Buddy being John. The song *proved* he was John, as if I needed any more proof. He'd recently moved to New York, and John would've never done that. He was as English as they come, a middle class boy from Menlowe Avenue in Liverpool. But *Buddy* would've moved there. That's where he'd lived before The Winter Dance Party Tour, right in the Village. And where's the first place he goes when he gets back to New York? The Village. It all fell into place. And then I started wondering if that lady he was married to (you know who I mean) (you do, don't you?) knew he was really Buddy, or if he went around putting on an act for her too, with that phony English accent.

So there I was, walking around like a dazed nut, not even

paying attention to where I was going, until I ran right into a chick who was wearing a beret and pushing a baby carriage, and I accidentally knocked her flat on her ass. The carriage went rolling down a hill all by itself, and the chick screamed, "The baby, you moron!"

I guess it took that to snap me out of my daze. The next thing you know, I went running after the carriage. I wasn't in the best of shape, and the carriage, well, it had a pretty good head start on me. And, oh, Christ, there was a big fallen branch further down the hill, right in the path of the runaway baby. I ran and I ran and huffed and puffed and nearly broke my neck chasing the thing, but I could see what was going to happen. The carriage was going to hit the goddamn branch and go flying – which is just what it did. It went back on two wheels, and when that baby got thrown in the air, I swear, seconds turned into minutes and I felt like I was running in slow motion. Up, up he went, flipping over once, over twice. I dove underneath him, reached out as far as I could, stretched every muscle – can you picture this? Now we're both in the air and I've got my arms out like I'm Superman or something, and the next second is going to determine whether I go to jail for the rest of my life, or if I end up a hero, and the baby's coming down fast now, with this expression on his face like he's thinking, *What the hell is going on here?* Just imagine the Gerber baby gone berserk, okay? So the kid's all freaked out and I'm diving under him, straining for that extra inch, when I hit the ground, get the wind knocked out of me, think I'm going to die, close my eyes ... and the baby falls right into my hands like an NFL pigskin.

"Touchdown!" I yelled.

Is that an incredible story or what? Huh? I should've sent it in to *Reader's Digest*. Well, the chick who was on her ass didn't think it was funny at all when I yelled "Touchdown!" And the baby was bawling and bawling. I'd caught him, right? But that didn't seem to matter to them. When I knelt down next to the chick (still on her ass), she snatched the kid away from me like I *didn't* just save his life.

"Your kid's fine," I said. "Honest. Just a little shaken, is all. Right, kid?"

And he bawled and bawled.

I tried to lighten them up a little. "You ought to put him in the Olympics, boy. He can really – "

And then the world stopped. The birds fell silent, the

skyscrapers threatened to fall, my heart jumped into my throat, and a host of violins rose in crescendo. I knew then, I *knew* I was either dreaming or I'd died and gone to heaven. Another possibility was that I'd finally gone completely insane – but no. I looked in her eyes and –

"You should *really* be more *careful*, walking around without even *looking* where you're *going*," she said.

It isn't possible, I thought.

"It's bad enough having to put up with muggers and transients and – excuse me, sir, but why are you looking at me like that?"

It can't be, I thought. *But it is. No, it's impossible. But it isn't impossible. MY GOD! MY GOD! IT'S ... IT'S ...*

"Brenda!" I said, and then I fainted.

When I came to, there she was; the most beautiful woman in the world (she'd put on a few pounds, but hey, who hadn't?) was fanning my face with her beret. I looked into her gorgeous eyes again, the same eyes I remembered (except they were older, crow's-feet and everything, but I'm not criticizing) and then I fainted again.

Is this not even more unbelievable than the runaway baby story? It just blows me away how fate or destiny or carriages conspire behind our backs to make life turn out the way it does. And speaking of blowing, what a beautiful mouth she had. I mean, she was like blowing on my face to revive me. I hope you haven't got a dirty mind, because I would never –

Anyway, when I woke up again she was blowing me, I mean *on* me, and I said her name again. "Brenda!"

She looked confused, and the baby was still bawling, and I thought, *Will someone please shut the damn kid up!*

"I'm afraid you've made some mistake, sir," she said.

My heart, my poor heart, it was breaking. "Don't you remember me?" I said.

She shook her head. "Nuh-uh."

"It's me. It's *me*!"

"Me *who*?"

"Me Rudy. Rudy Keen."

She mouthed my name a few times and wrinkled her forehead.

"'Bop-Sha-Bop? Wop, wop, wop. You make me wanna – '"

"Rudy? You mean little Rudy Keen, the kid who wanted to be a songwriter?"

"You remembered!" I said, and then I hugged her. I hugged

her so hard she had to pound my back to make me let go so she could breathe, but I kept my arms around her.

"Oh, Rudy, I didn't even recognize you! How long has it been?"

"It's been a long time. It's been – hey. You're supposed to be dead. How come you're not dead?"

"You don't know, then?" she said. "You still thought I was dead?"

"I was there when they buried your sweater."

"I'm so sorry I put you through that."

"And your shoes. They threw them in, too."

"Sal made me do it. He made me fake my own death so they'd leave me alone. He was so afraid they'd come after me to get to him – it was the only way. Poor Sal. They finally got him. Poor, sweet Sal."

Can you believe it? She *still* didn't know what a bastard he was.

I kissed her cheek and said, "Oh, Brenda, couldn't you have told me?"

"I tried."

"When?"

"That night I was going to meet you."

"But you never showed up." I hugged her again.

"Yes, I did, but I had to leave. (Don't touch me there, please, Rudy.) I was being followed. (Please don't touch me there.)"

"Sorry."

"They were following me, so I had to get away from them, lose them somehow. Oh, Rudy, it's so good to see you after – what's that on your head?"

"Huh? Oh. Bird shit. A bird shit on me, but it's okay 'cause I think it was a sign."

She set the kid down next to her, pulled a Kleenex from her purse, and wiped the bird shit off my head. "I tried to get in touch with you over the years, but I never knew where to reach you."

"Didn't know where to reach me? You must've followed my career."

"What career?"

"Whadaya mean, what career? My music career – all those records."

"You made records?"

For Christ's sake. How could she have missed my entire career? It filled a scrapbook, that career. Okay, so *part* of a scrapbook.

316

"You never heard 'Jelly Baby'?"

"No."

"How about 'Angel On The Highway'?"

"Car wreck song?"

"Yeah! You know it?"

"Uh-uh. Lucky guess. The title – "

"Oh, yeah."

Then I looked at the baby. He was quiet now, the little guy. And it dawned on me – *She must have a husband*. Oh! Talk about heartbreak! First God gives me what I wanted most in the world, and then He takes it away. I felt like Job. I was Job, Job Keen. The next thing you know, I'd lose my camels.

"So," I said, a little cooler now, "who did you marry?"

She smiled. "Oh, I'm not married."

Four of the most beautiful words ever! I was the luckiest man in the world for the second time that day!

"You're not?"

"I guess I never met the right man."

"The kid's a bastard, then?"

"Rudy!"

She was horrified, "I mean *illegitimate*, that kind of bastard, not like he's a son of a bitch or anything."

"Rudy!"

Jesus. Everything you said you had to be careful of. "I didn't mean anything by it. So when did you have the kid?"

"I'm his nanny. He's the son of_____." (I had to leave out the guy's name, because the publisher tells me we've got enough lawsuits already. He's a real famous guy, though. Take my word for it. You've probably heard all the rumors about him. Personally, I don't believe them. I don't think you can make gerbils do that.)

"So he's not your kid?"

"No, silly."

"And you're not married?"

"No, I told you."

I hugged her again. "Brenda, I've missed you so much. You'll never know how many times I've thought about you. You'll never know – "

"Rudy, stop it. I told you not to touch me – "

"I'm sorry. My hand slipped. Anyway, I was saying – over the years I thought about you every minute. There wasn't a night that went by that you weren't in my dreams."

"You're sweet."

"I even wrote a song about you."

"You did? You wrote a song about – cut it out, Rudy. I'm not kidding. You don't want to ruin this moment by doing that."

The hell I didn't. Hey – I've got no excuse. I guess all guys are ass-grabbing swine when it comes right to it.

I asked her how she'd managed to disappear for so long, and she said she'd been living under an assumed name. "Ever since – well, ever since that night when I was followed, I've been afraid."

"You had *reason* to be, believe me. Wait till you hear what happened to *me*."

Was I in luck – Brenda had the whole weekend off. After we dropped the kid off at the apartment of the star whose name I can't mention or I'll get sued into the next century, she brought me home to her little place in Queens. We lit candles and had herbal tea, and all night long she sat next to me on her bed while I told her my story. When I finished at dawn, I had to sort of nudge her awake.

"Hey," I said. "You missed the ending."

"Oh God, there's *more*?"

"Of course there's more – it's the best part. So after Sherm exploded on the street and blew his appendix out – I *think* it was his appendix; it could've been his spleen or his gallbladder – a car came out of nowhere, sped right up to him, and somebody leaned out and snatched up the black book."

Brenda rubbed her eyes. "Uh-huh. And then?"

"And then I came home. That's it."

She yawned a couple of times and then said, "Rudy?"

"Yeah?"

"Have you ever considered therapy?" I told her I didn't need therapy, and she said, "Oh, Rudy, yes, you do."

She meant after everything I'd been through, that's all.

The sun came up, turned the sky all rosy, and the birds outside started chirping their goddamn little beaks off. Brenda wanted to go to sleep, but that wasn't about to happen. I ain't bragging, but I've been known to be a bit of a love god in my time. She had no choice. And that's when all my dreams came true. We made beautiful, passionate, soulful, exotic, heart-stopping, breathtaking, absolutely filthy love. It was a Roman feast, a romantic symphony, a bedroom demolition derby. She wouldn't call me Thor like I wanted her to, but it was the wildest minute of my life.

♪　♫　♪

On June 1, 1976, I made Brenda the happiest woman in the world. I had a vasectomy. We'd been married for a few years and had two boys, who we named Eddie Cochran Keen and Gene Vincent Keen. That was right around the time I inherited Uncle Myshkin's butcher shop. I wish you could've been there for the reading of the will; it was quite touching, especially the part where the lawyer read, "... and to my nephew the chicken-choker, I leave the business, and my oldest customer, Mrs. Schulstein, who, at a hundred and four, should drop dead tomorrow."

Brenda and I renovated that old shop. Now it's *Rudy Keen's Rock And Roll Deli Scene*. Looks like a diner from the Fifties, a real gas. I put my music memorabilia on the walls – my leather jacket, the patch cord that electrocuted me, one of my old posters, and a bra that belonged to a girl named Irene who said she didn't want it back after I autographed it. And I had a juke box installed, one with all the great singles of the era, mostly mine. Shopping for gefilte fish didn't have to be a drag anymore; now customers could rock around the Manischewitz bottles while they listened to me.

I think those were the happiest days of my life, back when little Eddie and Gene scooted through the deli, throwing bagels at each other and messing around in the chicken schmaltz. They weren't all happy days, though. I'd lost the few friends I had left. Gene passed away on October 12, 1971, and Bobby went soon after – December 20, 1973. Oh yeah, I had sleepless nights, wondering if Stek-Circ was involved. But let's spread a little reality on the matzo – Gene didn't need any help dying. He'd done a pretty good job of killing himself as long as I'd known him. And Darin – the old ticker had been in rough shape for years. Besides, those guys weren't ever going to hit the charts again. Bobby would've sold more records if he'd really *been* a carpenter. No, what concerned me was the whole new wave of rockers, guys like Janis Joplin, Mama Cass (what – you thought they were *women*?), Hendrix, and Morrison. They were the real threat to the Compsong computer. And how devious – the drug overdoses, slipping Cass a dry sandwich. Now, I can't say for sure that they were all murdered; I didn't hang with that generation. But I did think it was awfully unusual that Morrison died three months after Gene (especially since they'd become drinking buddies and were working on projects together), and *two years to the day* after Brian Jones – July 3, 1971. It's almost like someone was sending a message. If you say *coincidence* again I'm going to have to slap you. And when is Robert Stack going to call me back? Enough with the UFO's already, Robert! Get yourself a *real* unsolved mystery.

It's practically folklore now, that December night in 1980 when Lennon (Holly) got out of the limo at the entrance of the Dakota Building and shots rang out. I read this somewhere – a few minutes later, while he was lying on the back seat of a squad car, the cop turned around and said, "Do you know who you are?"

Yes, *he* knew who he was, but nobody else did, including the cop.

Do you know who you are, Buddy? I should have a nickel for every time the question goes through my mind. Now that I think about it, maybe even Buddy didn't know who he was anymore. And just when you suspect you can't stack another ounce of irony on a story, the world went ahead and mourned the wrong guy.

All I can tell you is, it was no accident, no chance assassination by a wacked-out *meshugennah*, like the newspapers want you to believe. Do you think for one minute that Mark David Chapman wasn't working for the conspiracy? Was it just *another* coinicidence that Buddy got hit two months after his first record release in five years? And how about the *chutzpah* of that Chapman *schmuck*, sitting down in front of the Dakota, reading *The Catcher In The Rye*, and blaming the whole thing on J.D. Salinger? That's what he said! He said if you want to know why he killed Lennon (Holly), you should read *The Catcher In The Rye*. So I did, and I got news for you; there's no place in the book where Holden Caulfield says, "I think you ought to go kill John Lennon." The bastard. He shot my first hero, my mentor, my best friend.

I've got more questions for you. I'm just one big question mark. Do you know *why* he blamed J.D. Salinger? Huh? Did you ever wonder why Salinger hasn't published since 1965, and why he lives all alone in a remote place I'm not allowed to mention? What – you think Compsong hasn't branched out into book publishing? Oh, yeah, man. The computer isn't just writing songs; now it's writing novels, too. It was bound to happen. Get rid of the famous writers, save a bundle on advances. Have you read any fiction lately? Are you going to tell me that stuff isn't programed? Because if you are, I've got a copy of *The Bridges Of Madison County* I think you should read. That book ought to come with a label from the Surgeon General, **WARNING: READING THIS CRAP MAY SEVERELY LOWER YOUR I.Q. AND CAUSE WRETCHING, GAGGING AND POSSIBLY DIARRHEA.**

But my story doesn't end there. It ends about five months before the Dakota incident. I think it was July, a real nice summer day. I'd got up early to make blintzes, and I was just putting a tray of them in the display counter, when the little bell over the door jingled and I looked up to see who'd come in, hoping like hell it wasn't Mrs. Schulstein, who was a hundred and nine by then. I did a double-take – couldn't believe my eyes. *You* would've said it was John Lennon, but I knew better. I dropped the blintz tray and walked out from behind the counter, wiping my hands on my apron. You've seen pictures of him from that period. He was thin, real thin, and his cheeks were drawn and kind of sunken. His clothes were black, all black, and he looked like he could use a good meal. He'd come to the right place, because my blintzes are to die for. We were standing inches apart from each other, *inches*, and what does he say to me?

"I'm looking for Rudy Keen."

And I said, "Well, you can stop looking."

It was pretty goddamn weird. There I was looking at John Lennon, but I was talking to Buddy Holly. It was like they'd become one. He kept glancing over his shoulder at a car out front, a green Mercedes. I got this feeling he was ready to run back out the door any second. "He's here, then?" he said.

"Cut it out, Buddy."

"Buddy?" he said. "I'm afraid you have me confused with someone – "

"Don't you *know* me, Buddy?" I said.

He squinted, "Rudy? Is that *you?*"

"It ain't Frankie Lymon." (Remind me to tell you sometime what happened to *him*.)

"But you can't be Rudy. Rudy isn't fat and bald."

I wasn't going to put that part in. Nobody needs to know he said *that*. But I'm going for accuracy, and as long as I am, let me point out that I'd put on a couple of extra pounds, maybe, and I was a little thin on top, but I wasn't fat and bald. I was just plump and scarce.

So I said, "Well, you didn't always look like a relief ad for

Biafra, either."

"Waaalll," he said, "I'll be a guppy in a sand trap. It *is* you." He reached out and shook my hand, and I got some blintz jelly on his sport coat sleeve. "But how'd you know? How'd you know it was me, and not John?"

"How did I know? Are you kidding? I've known for *years*. Have you forgotten that I'm an intuitive genius?"

He didn't say anything.

"Don't you remember what a shrewd sense of perception I possess?"

Again, nothing.

"Buddy – did you hear me?"

He cleared his throat. "I just thought maybe Brian Jones might've tipped you off before he drowned."

"Tipped me off? Well, yeah. Yeah, he did, but I would've figured it – "

"Or that maybe you went back to Stek-Circ and found that little black book you'd told me about a long time ago."

"There was that, too, but let's not forget what a genius I am. And what does it matter how I found out? What I want to know is, why are you coming here now?"

He couldn't keep still. His head was always turning from side to side, like he was afraid to be in public. "Because," he told me. "Because I ... I owe you, Seventy-eight."

"You mean royalties? Royalties from 'Imagine' and 'Back In The U.S.S.R.'?"

"Tarnation, no. I owe you for sticking by me all those years in London, and for takin' care of me."

I brushed it off. "Forget it. I did it 'cause you were my friend. What about those royalties?"

He chuckled a Texas chuckle. "You always were such a kidder."

Who was kidding? But I hadn't seen him in so long, and before you knew it he was talking about his family and I was talking about mine. I told him all about my kids and about finding Brenda alive in Central Park. You know what he said? He said it was the strangest story he'd ever heard. I thought that he must have an awful funny way to measure a strange story after everything *he'd* been through.

We were leaning up against the juke box, shooting the shit, when all of a sudden I couldn't do the small talk routine anymore. What was the point? I blurted out, "Why'd you do it, Buddy? Why did you pretend to be John after they killed him with tainted sushi?"

"Rudy," he said, "I swear to you, man, on my grandma's Bible, all I ever wanted was to make a comeback as *me*. I didn't know what Krupp had planned, or what he'd done to John. After the operations when they took off the bandages – why, I just about died all over again. They'd given me another mask, only this one was permanent. Every morning I'd wake up and look in the mirror, and there was John. I might as well have been the Fairy Princess."

"I wish you were."

"What?"

"Nothing," I said. "Nothing. Go on."

He took out a handkerchief and dabbed his forehead. It was hard for him to talk about it. "The boys didn't like the idea, and I sure as shootin' didn't like it, so after an album or two the group fell apart. Krupp made me a solo circus act. He had strings on me, I tell ya, forcin' me into crazy stunts all over the world. It just about drove me over the brink, till that night."

"What night?"

"The night he was walking me out to an airliner on a runway in Majorca. I was coming back from holiday, and I was walking right behind Krupp when he tripped, lost his balance, and fell right into a running jet engine. We'll call it an accident, all right? We'll just say I accidentally bumped him from behind."

"You mean – ?"

"Yep. *He was sucked to death.* Not a pretty way to go, but then again, he wasn't pretty."

"Then it's all over, the conspiracy?"

"Oh, no, Rudy. I never said that. It's bigger than ever. It's industry-wide. Of course, Stek-Circ doesn't exist anymore – been bought up by super corporations. But you can't get a record out 'less it comes from the computer – most artists can't, anyway."

"Except you and Paul, right?"

"I didn't say anything about Paul. Haven't you heard 'Silly Love Songs'?"

"Ohhhh, so *that* explains all those albums. I should've known."

Just then one of my sons ran in from the back room and squirted Buddy in the crotch with a water pistol. I can't explain why, but I got all shivery when it happened, seeing that gun pointed at Buddy. Buddy picked him up and said, "Waall, now. Which one are you – Eddie or Gene?"

My boy said, "Wanna bop?"

Buddy lowered him down again. "I guess that answers it, all right."

Gene scooted out again, and then Buddy acted awkward, like he didn't know what to say or do next. "That's all I came for, Seventy-eight. Just to tell you I appreciate everything you done for me, and that I owe you."

I shook my head. "You don't owe *me*, Buddy. You owe them."

He scratched his head. "I'm afraid I ain't readin' you."

"You owe the fans. The *fans*, not me. You let them down. You stopped making music."

He went into this song and dance about being a parent, about baking bread.

"Oh, come on," I said. "I've done all that too, but there's still enough time in the day to pick up your guitar – which is mine, by the way. I never got my Rickenbacker back."

Buddy grunted. "I *do* pick up the guitar – but why should I make more records? For what?" He tapped the front of the juke box. "Just a bunch of plastic circles goin' 'round and 'round. Look where it got *them* – they're all dead. They'll never make music again."

"That's where you're wrong, Buddy. That's exactly where you're wrong. They still make music. They make music every day, and always will. Listen." I found a quarter in my pocket and dropped it in the juke box and hit P-38. "Be-Bop-A-Lula" rang out, Gene's voice echoing all through the deli. "Hear that? Old Gene's still rocking."

Buddy frowned and pushed his glasses back up his nose with one finger. "You're wackier than a cow chewin' funny weed. That's not Gene. That's just vinyl spinnin' under a needle."

"That's all any of us ever were. That's all we still are. We're the music – don't you get it? We're the music, Buddy, and the music lasts forever. Why, over here I've got Eddie any time I need him. If I'm kind of down, I spin a little "Somethin' Else,' and there's Eddie, clear as a bell, telling me that anything's possible. And over here I've got John on B-15. Push a button and he'll sing 'I Feel Fine,' and then *I* feel fine, too. That's all any of us were meant to do, to leave the dreams, man. Dreams on plastic. Let me show you. Wanna hear 'Bop-Sha-Bop'?"

"No, that's okay."

"Really, let me play a little 'Bop-Sha-Bop'."

"I'd rather not, if you don't mind."

"It's no trouble."

"All the same – "

"Remember that groovy chorus?"

"I remember."

"Wasn't it bitchin'?"

"It was a real bitch, all right."

"Sometimes that song will stick in your head all day once you've heard it."

"That's what I'm afraid of. I mean, I've been writing my own songs lately, and I've got to keep my head clear so I can finish them."

"You have?" I said. "You've been writing again? That's great! So it's not all about baking bread, is it? Every once in a while you've got to rock and roll, because it's your real love, and it makes you feel free as a bird."

He took a little note pad and a pen from his blazer pocket. "How's that again?"

"I said, it's your *real love*. Makes you feel *free as a bird*."

He jotted something down, and I don't suppose I have to tell you what. He did it to me again! He used my phrases for the titles of the songs that Lennon supposedly left behind. I'm telling you, I ought to copyright everything that comes out of my mouth.

For the next ten minutes or so I tried to convince him to record again. At first he hemmed and hawed and said he couldn't, he just couldn't, but I wouldn't give up.

"It's what you were put here for. You'll never be yourself, not completely, until you start spinning out the dreams again."

He rubbed the stubbles on his chin. "You really think so?"

"Oh, yeah! You're like the Picaso of songwriting."

"True."

"But there's one more thing, Buddy."

"What's that?"

"You've got to come clean. You've got to tell everybody."

"Tell them?"

"Yeah. Tell them who you really are."

I might as well have lit a stick of dynamite in his pants, the way he carried on. He said the media would have a field day, that he'd have to live through the circus all over again, and there was no way he wanted to do that.

"So you turn your back on the circus," I said. "You can hide out. Go up to Dingleton Hill in Cornish, New Hampshire, where J.D. Salinger lives. No one will ever find you."

(Oh, shit. I wasn't supposed to let that out, where Salinger lives. Boy, is he ever going to be pissed at me. Forget it. Forget I ever said anything. You can keep a secret, can't you?)

Buddy said, "And wouldn't Mother love to hear that I'm Buddy Holly, after she's been married to John Lennon for the last eleven years."

"*Oy!* You mean she still thinks – "

"Yep."

"Well – that could be inconvenient, I guess."

Little Gene came running around the corner again, yelling, "Daddy! Daddy! Daddy!"

"What is it?" I said.

"I just bopped in my pants!"

"Go and tell Mommy, sweetheart. Daddy's busy."

He ran out to the back room, this time yelling, "Mommy! Mommy! Mommy!"

"I'd better be hittin' the trail," Buddy said.

"But at least think about what I told you."

"I will. I promise. In the meantime, you enjoy your family. You must be tickled, havin' Brenda back and all."

"I am! You know how she was always my fantasy? I'll tell you something – finding her and marrying her was like a *double* fantasy."

Out came the little note pad and pen, like two old friends. "A *double* fantasy, huh? That's a nice way to put it."

I know! That's what he called his last album, *Double Fantasy*. Once, just *once* I wish somebody would ask my permission first. Or give me a credit, an acknowledgement – *anything*. What would it have hurt to put on the back of the record sleeve, "Inspiration by Rudy Keen"? They could've used microscopic print, or braille, yet, and I wouldn't have complained. Braille's nice – it's embossed, it's got texture, it's finger-friendly.

Before he turned to leave, he patted my shoulder, and I said, "Buddy? Be careful. You know what I mean. Just be careful."

And that's when Brenda walked in from the back room, just in time to hear him say, "I will, Seventy-eight. Don't worry." The little bell tinkled as he closed the door behind him, and he walked out of my life forever.

Brenda's eyes bulged. For a minute I was afraid she'd eaten

some bad kugel and gone into dietary shock or something.

"It's *him!*" she cried.

"It sure is."

"He called you Seventy-eight!"

"That's what he called me, all right."

"Why would John Lennon call you by Buddy Holly's pet name for you?"

"Because he's Buddy Holly, not John Lennon."

"Oh, my God! You mean that crazy story – it was the truth?"

"Well, it depends on what you mean by the truth," I said.

"I mean *truth*. You know what truth is, don't you?"

"Does anybody really know what truth is?"

"Rudy, truth is truth."

"No. 'Truth is beauty, beauty, truth.' That's Keats."

"I saw him with my own eyes."

"Who, Keats?"

"NO! John Lennon!"

"You mean Buddy Holly."

Brenda slumped over the pumpernickel shelf and said, "I don't know *what* I mean anymore."

Poor kid. She needed to relax. I walked back to the juke box, fed it a quarter, and hit D-27. "True Love Ways" – one of *the* great make-out songs of all time – poured out of the speakers like rock-and-roll honey. I lowered the front shades and then strutted my fine stuff back to my wife, my first love, the mother of my children, who, and I'm not kidding about this, looked like she was about to lose control of one of her bodily functions. (Of course, I was a teen idol once, and I've done that to countless women. It could've been a spontaneous orgasm, but I didn't ask her. It wouldn't have been the first time.)

"Dance?" I said.

"What?"

"Dance with me."

I put my arm around her and swept her off her feet. It was like one of those old spotlight dances on "Bandstand," the two of us all alone in the deli. Buddy's voice melted all around us as we tripped the light fantastic.

Just you know why,
Why you and I,
Will by and by,
Know true love ways.

Sometimes we'll 'sigh,
Sometimes we'll cry,
And we'll know why,
Just you and I,
Know true love ways.

Brenda whispered, "I just can't *believe* it. All this time, you've been telling the truth."

"Shh. You're gonna ruin the mood," I said, as we glided past the gefilte fish and swayed down the chicken liver aisle.

Throughout the days,
Our true love ways,
Will bring us joys to share,
With those who really care.

"You understand now, don't you?" I said. "The danger I've faced, and what I've had to keep to myself."

"Yes, but it's all just so incredibly – "

"And the history I've shaped."

"To think that you shaped history!"

"Yeah. Say, do you feel romantic?" I asked.

"Yes, yes! I never thought it could be so – take your hand out of there, Rudy. Right *now*."

"Don't forget the mood," I said.

"Mood-shmood. CUT IT OUT!"

"Brenda, let's do it. C'mon. Whadaya say?"

"Here? Right *here*, in broad daylight? No! Absolutely not! Have you lost your – "

Sometimes we'll sigh,
Sometimes we'll cry,
And we'll know why,
Just you and I,
Know true love ways.

It may have been seventeen years ago, but some things are indelible, burned right into the old memory banks. Like Brenda's clothes tossed over the kosher rye bread, the mad scramble of passion, Mrs. Schulstein walking in on us. I'd forgot to lock the door. But she'd had a nice long life. Hell, one hundred and nine years – some people would settle. It was a little embarrassing explaining to the paramedics what had happened. They kept saying, "Right on the counter, for Chrissake?" And I said, "Yeah, like you've never done it in the back of your ambulance." We didn't kill her on purpose. She was just shopping for chicken in all the wrong places.

That was the same year Buddy was taken from us. The Winter Dance Party Murders had come full circle. He'd been killed, reincarnated as John, and now he was gone again, gone for good. But there *is* a silver lining. Nine months after our afternoon of deli love, little Sam Cooke Keen was born. My vasectomy had been a failure! I've always felt somehow that he was given to me in place of Buddy, to help me through the loneliness of losing my oldest and dearest friend. Sam's a great kid. He's got a lot of soul.

And I don't want you to go away thinking that Buddy died in vain. He did something pretty heroic that not too many people know about. He scheduled a news conference for December 9, 1980, one he never had a chance to attend. One that the sinister forces behind Compsong didn't *want* him to attend. But I know what he would've said, and I know why he would've said it. He was going to reveal his true identity. Why? To blow the whistle on the conspiracy. To stop the senseless slaughter of innocent rock stars. And to make his album go quadruple platinum. Hey – it's a business. That's why they gave the order to silence him.

But you and I know that Buddy can never be silenced. He's still rocking. He'll rock today, tomorrow, a hundred years from now. It's like I told him – the music lasts forever. As long as there's someone listening, he'll always be alive.

And so will I, if you send right now for my collection of hits, *The Fabulous Teen, Rudy Keen!* Thrill to my biggest hits – "Whoa Baby, Whoa" and "Jelly Baby." Sing along with holiday favorites, like "Away In a Groovy Manger" and "Hark the Herald Angels Bop." ($19.95 for cassette tape, $23.95 for compact disc.) Mail orders to:

I'm Hot For Rudy
P.O. Box 6969
Bay Ridge Station
New York, NY

It'll excite you and your friends and alarm your neighbors! This is a one-time offer, not available in stores, none that you've ever heard of, anyway. HURRY! ORDER NOW!

And the next time you're in the neighborhood, stop by Rudy Keen's Rock-And-Roll Deli Scene. We'll spin a few sides, relive the old days, and you can nosh one of the house specials. Unless the shades are drawn and you can hear "True Love Ways" on the juke box. In that case, take a hike. I don't get lucky often enough as it is, and you don't want to wind up like old lady Schulstein, do you?

Photo by Dick Fowler

About the Author

Greg Herriges is the author of three novels, including this, his latest, THE WINTER DANCE PARTY MURDERS. His articles and short fiction have appeared in THE CHICAGO TRIBUNE MAGAZINE, SOCIAL ISSUES RESOURCES, OUI, CAVALIER, and YO FRANKIE.

His landmark meeting with J.D. Salinger in 1978 prompted him to turn to writing professionally, and is the subject of his current book-length work-in-progress.

Herriges is an English professor at William Rainey Harper College, in Palatine, Illinois. He lives with his wife and son in a suburb of Chicago. Check out his website at: http://members.aol.com/RudyKeen

WORDCRAFT SPECULATIVE WRITERS SERIES

Prayers of Steel, **Misha**, ISBN: 1-877655-00-7, $5

The Magic Deer, **Conger Beasley, Jr.**, ISBN: 1-877655-01-5, $5

Lifting, **Mark Rich**, ISBN: 1-877655-03-1, $7.95

The Liquid Retreats, **Todd Mecklem & Jonathan Falk**, ISBN: 1-877655-01-3, $6.95

Oceans of Glass and Fire, **Rob Hollis Miller**, ISBN: 1-877655-04-X, $7.95

The Seventh Day and After, stories, **Don Webb**, ISBN: 1-877655-05-8, $7.95 *

Pangaea, stories by **Denise Dumars**, ISBN: 1-877655-08-2, $7.95

Scherzi, I Believe, stories by **Lance Olsen**, ISBN: 1-877655-11-2, $9.95 *

Ke-Qua-Hawk-As, **Misha**, ISBN: 1-877655-13-9, $9.95*

The Raw Brunettes, **Lorraine Schein**, ISBN: 1-877655-12-0, $6.00 *

The Eleventh Jagaurundi . . ., stories, **Jessica Amanda Salmonson**, ISBN: 1-877655-14-7, $9.95

The Blood of Dead Poets, **Conger Beasley, Jr.**, ISBN: 1-877655-15-5, $9.95*

Unreal City, **Thomas E. Kennedy**, ISBN: 1-877655-17-1, $11.95
(made possible with a Literary Arts, Inc., publishing fellowship)

Burnt, a novel by **Lance Olsen**, ISBN: 1-877655-20-1, $11.95
(made possible with a Literary Arts, Inc., publishing fellowship)

The Book of Angels, a novel by **Thomas E. Kennedy**, ISBN: 1-877655-23-6, $12.95

The Din of Celestial Birds, stories, **Brian Evenson**, ISBN: 1-877655-24-4, $10.95

The Explanation and Other Good Advice, stories, **Don Webb**, ISBN: 1-877655-25-2, $9.95

* signed and numbered limited editions

Wordcraft of Oregon books are available through Bookpeople, Small Press Distribution, Mark Ziesing Books, Chris Drumm Books, Amazon.com, BBR Distribution (England). Check with your local bookstore or request a catalog from Wordcraft of Oregon, PO Box 3235, La Grande, OR 97850. Send email inquiries to: wordcraft@oregontrail.net